AMBER CASSIDY

First Sight

First edition

ISBN: 979-8-9890036-0-0

This book was professionally typeset on Reedsy.
Find out more at reedsy.com

Contents

Preface   vi
Acknowledgement   vii
Prologue   1
Chapter One   5
Chapter Two   14
Chapter Three   20
Chapter Four   29
Chapter Five   34
Chapter Six   39
Chapter Seven   43
Chapter Eight   48
Chapter Nine   53
Chapter Ten   60
Chapter Eleven   65
Chapter Twelve   71
Chapter Thirteen   77
Chapter Fourteen   82
Chapter Fifteen   88
Chapter Sixteen   93
Chapter Seventeen   99
Chapter Eighteen   105
Chapter Nineteen   114
Chapter Twenty   121
Chapter Twenty-One   129

Chapter Twenty-Two	136
Chapter Twenty-Three	142
Chapter Twenty-Four	147
Chapter Twenty-Five	156
Chapter Twenty-Six	162
Chapter Twenty-Seven	168
Chapter Twenty-Eight	176
Chapter Twenty-Nine	183
Chapter Thirty	190
Chapter Thirty-One	197
Chapter Thirty-Two	204
Chapter Thirty-Three	210
Chapter Thirty-Four	217
Chapter Thirty-Five	223
Chapter Thirty-Six	230
Chapter Thirty-Seven	236
Chapter Thirty-Eight	243
Chapter Thirty-Nine	249
Chapter Forty	255
Chapter Forty-One	262
Chapter Forty-Two	269
Chapter Forty-Three	275
Chapter Forty-Four	281
Chapter Forty-Five	287
Chapter Forty-Six	292
Chapter Forty-Seven	298
Chapter Forty-Eight	305
Chapter Forty-Nine	310
Chapter Fifty	320
Chapter Fifty-One	330
Chapter Fifty-Two	336

Chapter Fifty-Three	342
Epilogue	348
The End	353
About the Author	354
Also by Amber Cassidy	355

Preface

Like many others, I grew up watching the fairy tales we all know and love. My passion for stories grew from childhood animations to chapter books, TV shows, and movies, but the premise always remained. I love, love. Romance novels are my escape and a beloved serotonin boost.

I started writing for myself. Getting the stories out of my head and onto paper has helped ease my ever-racing mind. I can only hope that others might enjoy them as I have.

While my writing centers around the love story, there are also depictions of darker themes and explicit sexual content. Please be advised, this novel is intended for adults only.

Enjoy!

Acknowledgement

I don't know if I would have had the chance to fulfill my dream of writing a book if it weren't for my family's incredible support. The opportunity to be home with my daughter has been a dream within itself and has allowed me the mental clarity to focus on writing in my spare time.

So, thank you to my husband for showing me what true love looks like every single day and to my baby girl for sticking to her nap schedule <3

Prologue

Nathan

My head tips side to side against the cold metal interior of the cargo plane. The rattling from all of our equipment pierces a spot in my brain, making my head pound. I keep my eyes closed, trying to drown out the noise around me, hoping for a small moment of peace.

Unfortunately, it's not long before I hear the grunt of someone plopping down in the seat beside me, and more so sense their stare. I crack one eye open, questioning whether I should play dead or not.

Seeing that it's Sergeant Thompson, our second in command and one of the veterans on the team, I hardly contain my sigh. He's a good guy, and a great leader, but tends to play big brother even when nobody asks.

"Why so quiet, Nate man?" He asks, slapping my knee. The nickname makes me roll my eyes. He's the only one who would dare call me that.

"Didn't sleep much last night." My answer is short, my tone clipped. Nothing unusual for me, I'm not much of a talker. Everyone on the team knows that. Except, Thompson refuses to ever leave me alone, and my best friend on the team, Jesse, ignores my attempts to cut conversations short, accustomed to my budding personality since we were in Special Ops training together.

"Too busy with your girlfriend?" He laughs, not taking the hint that I don't want to chat.

"No, I broke up with Sierra a couple of weeks ago." I shrug. "She got mad when we got called out for the last mission. Told me to pick her or the team... You can guess how that went."

Thompson laughs, understanding exactly what I mean. He's married, been married for a long time to a great girl. He's made sure we all know it, but he knows how turbulent military relationships can be. He's tried to play couples counselor to plenty of the other guys on the team over the years.

"Well, then what's keepin' you up at night?" He probes, not letting me steer away from the conversation. I consider lying, making up some bullshit excuse, but there's no point. He'd know I was lying, and then I'd feel like shit anyway. He's a good guy to have in your corner, and I consider him a friend even though I'm far from friendly most of the time.

"Old ghosts," I tell him reluctantly, not wanting to share more. He looks like he wants to ask more, but he doesn't need to. He's lived this life long enough to know exactly how the darkness lingers. How each mission could potentially end your career or your life. How every close call slowly chips away at your resolve.

Jesse and I joined this team right after Thompson's buddy died on one of their classified operations in Afghanistan. From the pieces I've gathered, political tension is so high between the countries that his friend's dead body had to be flown back to the States discreetly, without proper honors or protocol. The rest of the team didn't return in time for the funeral, so the last glimpse he had of his friend was with half his head blown off in the field. Thompson mentioned that they were still in a hot zone, enemy territory. He had to drag his lifeless body 100 yards and leave it until it was safe enough to come back for extraction.

He told me that part after witnessing one of my nightmares for the first time. I woke up in a cold sweat one night when we were all piled into a studio apartment in some run-down city in the Middle East. I barely made it to the bathroom before I hurled.

"It takes time to fight your demons but they'll eventually go away." He offered me some whiskey when I finally stopped hugging the toilet.

I saw the vacant look in his eyes that night, and I should've known he was trying to convince himself as much as he wanted to convince me. I wasn't brave enough then to tell him what triggered my nightmare, or how close to home his story hit me. I'm not sure I'm brave enough now either.

Before I can further consider telling him which ghost was keeping me up last night, the intercom goes off over our heads, signaling we're making the descent for landing.

He gives me one final hard look, like he's staring straight into the darkest part of my soul, before slapping me on the shoulder, his way of telling me he's here for me. We busy ourselves gathering our gear, silently trying our best to mentally prepare for whatever is waiting on us once we step off this plane.

I didn't know that would be the last real conversation I'd ever have with Thompson. He was killed in action the next

3

day. A road bomb blew up a truck right next to us while out on patrol. The momentum of the blast forced his body through the air, only stopping once it met the resisting force of the closest mud brick building. My ears were ringing from the explosion, but that doesn't stop my nightmares from replaying the sickening crunch of his bones breaking from the impact.

We took him home in a wooden box with an American flag draped over it. Something I've long become accustomed to. His widow met us on the tarmac, her rounded belly a brutal reminder of how devastating this job can be.

Sometimes, I can still hear her gut-wrenching sobs when I close my eyes at night, another one of those moments I wish I could erase. Instead, I'm stuck tucking it into the dark recess of my mind, along with the other things that haunt me.

I'm not sure how long I have before the darkest parts are too much to repress. Until I'm consumed by the memories that have turned me cold and detached, just so I can survive.

Chapter One

Callie

Commercial... Commercial... Static... Jingle Bells... Ick. I am in no mood for Christmas music, especially since Halloween was just last week. Ugh. At least this overcast weather fits my sour mood. Maybe if these mountains weren't cutting off all of my phone service, I could listen to something other than the car radio.

I hit the power button with a little too much aggression, silencing the holiday cheer that was pouring out of the speakers. There is nothing to occupy my mind, no music, no cars, just me alone on this empty, winding highway. At least the view is nice. I've always enjoyed driving through this part of the state, being surrounded by thick forest only to catch a quick peek at the mountain tops when you round a bend, or the thick fog lingering in the valleys.

It's not enough to keep my thoughts totally at bay though. I keep circling back to the mess that my life has become. This road trip is an advanced version of the walk of shame. With my tail tucked between my legs, my car is loaded with all my stuff and I'm heading back home to my parents. I only left a few months ago, hardly enough time to pretend it wasn't all a big mistake on my part. Broke the lease to my apartment and everything, just to move to a new state with a boyfriend I hardly even liked.

Mark was nice, at least at the beginning. We were friends, and we had some things in common, but we were both ready to move away from our hometowns. He got a job offer, so I followed. Offered to split his rent and everything. I thought it would be safe. Moving in with someone you know so you don't have to jump feet first all alone seems like a smart idea. How naïve of me.

It started with a few fights about little stuff, splitting household chores, and bills. Basics every couple who moves in together goes through. Then he started accusing me of cheating on him while he was at work, never mind the fact that I was working full-time.

As an online data analyst for a travel agency, I handle my entire job remotely. So even though I'm home, I'm working. He continuously accused me of having people over during the day, no matter how many times I denied it. I was in a completely new state. He was the only person I knew or even spoke to. I hadn't even attempted to make any friends yet.

It was worse when he drank. After a month of us living together in our apartment, he came home drunk from a night out with his new coworkers. He got mad when I refused to have sex with him, so he tore the apartment apart. I'm surprised our neighbors didn't call the cops, but it was a busy city, and they're probably used to tuning out domestic disturbances. I was lucky he didn't hurt me. He only upturned furniture and broke a few dishes.

He apologized the next morning and swore it would never happen again. I didn't believe him, but I wasn't ready to admit my failure, that I shouldn't have moved away from home in the first place. From that point on we acted as roommates and nothing more, only communicating when necessary. It felt like a good solution for about a month, but the entire time I was walking on eggshells.

Unfortunately, after a few more unnecessary fights, instigated by him, I'd seen enough red flags. I knew I was done, but I felt stuck. I needed time to get my things in order to make a clean break and leave. It took a few weeks to get my affairs back in order.

Slowly, I packed my things so it wasn't obvious, and made sure I acted as normal as possible to avoid any awkwardness or hostility. I cleared out all of my mail and personal documents, making sure I would be leaving no trace of myself once I was ready to go. All the while I made dinner for him, and sat on the couch with him in the evenings when he did come home, never mentioning my plan to leave. His erratic moods left me feeling too unsafe. I don't know how I couldn't have seen that side of him from the start of our relationship. Gone was the friendly boy I watched Star Trek movies with. In his place was a possessive, angry man.

Last night was the final straw. He came home drunk again, immediately getting in my face demanding I have sex with him. Of course, I didn't want to. I hadn't been intimate with him at all since the first drunken incident. Deep down, I think he knew I was planning to leave even though I hadn't said anything. This time, his tantrum was worse. I genuinely feared for my life, and I thought for sure he was going to hit me. Instead, he left multiple fist-sized holes in the drywall right next to my head.

He didn't touch me, yet I was terrorized. Something on my

face must've made him realize he fucked up. As soon as his eyes focused on my tears, or maybe he saw the fear on my face, he turned and bolted from the apartment. That was the last I saw him. I ran around gathering the bags I had packed and left. It was late, and I was exhausted, so I drove to the first Walmart I saw and slept in my car in the parking lot.

Slept is putting it generously. I spent most of the night overanalyzing every decision I've ever made in my life, hyper-vigilant of my surroundings since I was alone in my car in an unfamiliar area. It felt like payback for all the times I berated myself for not being more adventurous, and always playing things too safe. Being out of my comfort zone would be putting it mildly, and look where it's gotten me.

I was so ready to move away from home, to "see the world" and all that crap, always seeing the latest travel trends and feeling like I was missing out. However, I don't think I've ever craved a home base more than I do now. Unfortunately, even when I get back to my parents' house, I know it won't quite feel like home anymore. It's a familiar place, but I've outgrown it. I have no next step, no plan. I'm perpetually one step away from reaching my final destination. That's how I've always felt.

It terrifies me because my whole life has been about following the master plan. From the moment my fifth-grade teacher suggested I take advanced math classes, I started worrying about my grade point average. My GPA would get me into a good college, but I needed extra-curricular activities if I wanted scholarships. From student counsel to track and field, I worked my ass off, just to stay on the right path.

When college rolled around, I did everything by the book.

Earned every credit as efficiently as possible to graduate as fast as possible to get a good job. Then I did exactly that. I landed a job that utilized all my strengths, and let me excel at all the things I had put so much time and effort into. After working remotely for two years in an apartment I paid for all on my own, I felt stagnant. Even though it was everything I had ever wanted, I wasn't happy.

It seems unfair. I followed all the rules, and only led myself by logic, yet I couldn't figure out what I was supposed to be doing next. So, I jumped headfirst into a relationship. The one time I forced myself to throw caution to the wind, and it backfired completely.

I'm ready to go back to my boring, cut-and-dry life, but is that all there is for me?

I've been driving for four hours now and I still don't have my answer. With two more to go until I'm "home," I'm hoping for an epiphany.

I called my mom this morning and told her what happened. She didn't tell me "I told you so" even though I deserved it, but she did scold me for not calling her sooner.

"Callie Anne, your dad would have come and got you. Day or night. We would have come to help you."

"I know, Mom. I just needed to do it on my own. I'm sorry."

"I'm just glad you're okay, sweetie."

"Me too, Mom. I love you guys. I'll be home soon."

Deep breaths. I try to distract myself again from my thoughts, not needing the fresh wave of tears to escape my eyes like they want to. I try the radio again, but only get static and old man talk shows.

The highway is still empty. I've only seen a few cars here and there, and the road is starting to straighten out. I'm afraid without all the curves and bends to pay attention to I'll start zoning out. Maybe I'll stop at the next exit, and get some more caffeine and some lunch to get through the rest of my drive.

POP! THUMP! Thump, thump, thump... My wheel jerks to the right.

No... Please don't let this happen, I do not want to deal with a flat tire right now. Slowly, I maneuver my car to the shoulder, and from the jerky way it's handling, something is severely wrong.

I check my phone, and of course, there still isn't any service. I'm still two hours from home too. Who would I even call? UGH.

Dammit, if I don't have the tools or skill to fix my flat I will be stuck walking. I don't even remember the last gas station I passed, or any signs indicating one up ahead. Shit.

As I get out of my car to check the damage, the pit of anxiety in my stomach makes me slightly nauseous. Yep. Really freaking flat. Fuck my life.

I'm surprised it's not raining, that would put the icing on the cake for this shitty day. I'm sure my ex would be laughing in my face right now, telling me that I deserve it. Although, as bad as a flat tire in the middle of nowhere is, I have no regrets about getting away from him.

As I wallow in self-pity, I pop my trunk and brace myself for the task at hand. I'm lucky enough to have a father who forced me to change a tire before I ever even had my license. Lifting the cover off of the spare, I thank God that there is a jack and tire iron right next to it. I've had this car for a few years but have never thought to check. The spare is heavy but manageable, I make quick work of lifting it out and rolling it over to where the flat is.

The rumble of an engine approaching draws my attention as I pull all of the tools out. It's the first car that has come by since I've been pulled over on this deserted freeway.

I look over my shoulder toward the sound and see a beat-up gray work van slowing down. My stomach coils tightly. Alarm bells start going off in my head. I've never been more nervous about being alone than I am right now, and there's probably no one around for miles.

Maybe I'm just being judgemental. Maybe it's a nice old man who is dying to help a damsel in distress. My optimism fades as the vehicle rolls to a stop about 10 feet from the back of the car, the brakes loudly protesting, making me cringe.

Two men start climbing out of the van before I can wave them off, both in their mid-thirties if I had to guess. Greasy hair and patchy facial hair, along with worn out, ripped clothing. My unease has me white-knuckling the tire iron in my hand.

"What seems to be the problem, baby doll?" The driver of the vehicle asks with a smug look on his face. He's skinny, too skinny, making him look sickly. His skin looks discolored from a lack of bathing.

"Just a flat tire, but I have it covered. Thanks, guys," I state, matter-of-factly, trying not to show them my fear.

"You don't even have the old tire off yet, it'd be an awfully tough job for a *woman*," the passenger slurs in my direction, but immediately looks to the driver, seeking validation. This one is shorter, and a lot rounder, the dark patches of facial hair stand out oddly against the paleness of his face.

The way he said "woman" has my hackles rising. These are not good men. This is not a good situation, but I don't have any weapons. My phone is useless. The universe really fucking hates me.

"I've done this before, I'll be fine," I force through my teeth.

"Nah, I'd like to see this, wouldn't you, Bub?" The driver says to the passenger, and I guess his brother, clearly egging each other on.

"We don't have anywhere to be, Tony. Let's see how she does," the one called Bub snickers.

"I'd rather you guys left," I speak calmly, even though my heart is beating through my chest. I'm surprised by how steady my voice comes out.

"HA! She doesn't want us here, Bub. We just try to be helpful and this lady has to go on being a *bitch*." Tony's enunciated slur makes me flinch. He slowly starts circling the car, cutting me off from the driver's side. My eyes bounce back and forth, not able to watch them both at the same time.

Bub starts creeping towards me like it's a game of cat and mouse. Except it's two mangey, feral cats versus me, the mouse. I raise the tire iron like I'm preparing to swing an ax, "Get the fuck away from me, both of you!" I yell, the panic in my voice clear now.

At the same time, like it's been rehearsed, they lunge at me from either side. I swing the tire iron, knocking Bub in the side of the head, causing him to stumble off to the side clutching his temple. Tony grabs me by my hair suddenly, pulling my ponytail so tightly I'm afraid my hair will be ripped out by the root. The pain is there but it's still nothing compared to the terror I feel.

This is what every woman fears. It's the worst-case scenario that we all whisper about. No one wants to be at the mercy of any man who wants to do you harm, let alone two. How can I fight back when I'm outnumbered? Out strengthened?

"You hurt my brother, you dumb *bitch*." He throws me to the ground about five feet from my car, into the gravel and weeds on the side of the road. I swear I feel each individual rock scrape across my skin as my momentum carries me across the rough shoulder.

Finally coming to a stop, I gasp trying to catch my breath after having the wind knocked out of me. I'm struggling to regain my bearings, but in my peripheral vision, I see the woods about 100 yards from me. If I can make it there, maybe I can outrun them, and lose them in the trees. It's my only chance.

"Bub stop whining. You got hit by a woman, you're being a pussy!" Tony yells at his brother, not paying me any attention. I take the opportunity and jump up, but as soon as I take a step toward the trees, I get yanked down by my ponytail, again. I land hard on my back, my lungs temporarily deflating once again from the impact. I wheeze, attempting to suck in more oxygen, but it feels like I'm suffocating.

"Dumb bitch!" Tony yells, slamming his boot into the side of my head, hard. Everything goes black...

Chapter Two

Nathan

S itting on the ground deep in the Blue Ridge Mountains, my back aching from leaning against a boulder, I am utterly alone. The rock digs into my spine, but I ignore the dull pain, too lost in thought.

Two months since leaving the Army. A decision that proved difficult, but after serving 13 years I was done with the orders. I was done with the deployments, and I was done being forced to associate with commanders who got high on belittling those under them. I'd have to put in seven more years before retirement, but after spending my entire adult life in the service already, I couldn't stand the idea of wasting away anymore. I needed a break.

Enlisting in the Army was for my father, a dream he had while I was growing up to follow in his footsteps, and a dying wish he bestowed upon me before losing a battle with cancer my junior year of high school.

At the time, I felt like I was doing something important, making my family proud, but a commitment like that at 18 years old isn't fathomable. The first couple of years flew by, enlisting, starting boot camp, finishing boot camp, and being stationed. Being surrounded by a bunch of like-minded guys my age, drinking too much when we weren't on duty, and chasing girls in bars. It seems like a fever dream now.

Not long into my second year, my best friend and roommate, Chester, was killed right outside our local hangout. It was a shitty bar with cheap beer and free pool tables. It was 2 a.m. We were paying our tabs when Chester slung an arm around my shoulder and our other buddy, Robby. He told us he was leaving with the only chick left in the bar and that he was for sure getting laid. We all laughed at him as he left towards the parking lot with her, then took bets that she just wanted a ride home.

Looking back now, it kills me that he didn't wait for us to follow him. Two gunshots and tires squealing, while Robby and I stared at each other. Standing at the bar, we were frozen for what felt like minutes but were mere seconds. Not processing what we heard.

By the time we ran outside, Chester was dead on the pavement next to his car, blood pooling underneath him. The girl was gone, and the car was long gone. I had nightmares for months, the "*POW! POW!*" of gunshots then running in slow motion trying to make it to him before he bled out.

The coroner told his mother that the second shot was the one that killed him, but that it killed him instantly, and there was nothing we could have done to save him. He swore to her that her son felt no pain, and probably had no idea what hit him. I wanted to believe him, but the memory I have of Chester's face as he lay dead on the pavement will haunt me forever. His eyes were wide open like he had seen a ghost. His face showed the fear he must've felt.

The bar didn't have cameras. The police collected evidence

but admitted that there wasn't much they could do without names or video of it occurring. The bartender swore it was a gang initiation, but she was a known gossip, so no one took what she had to say to heart.

Still, Chester's face haunts me. I dread closing my eyes at night, knowing what I'll see in that dark corner of my mind. It was the first time I had ever held a lifeless body, but it wasn't the last.

His death was a pivotal point in my career. After that night, I needed purpose, something to put my energy into so I didn't think about the questions I had that would always go unanswered. Chester always wanted to be Special Forces. From the moment I met him, he said that was what he joined the Army to do. The other guys and I would rag on him, tell him he was a wimp and that he'd never make it, but I hope he knew I didn't mean it. I admired him for having a goal, a purpose. I was lost in this life that was hand-picked for me by my father. I never would have joined up if it weren't for him, and once I was in it, I didn't have a plan.

I applied for Special Forces a month after Chester died. I decided to live my life for him since he didn't get to achieve his dreams. Every time I wanted to quit, every time I was yelled at, spit on, or degraded, I kept my eyes forward. Eyes towards the goal. Eventually, Chester's goal turned into my goal. My life became consumed by my new role in Special Forces. I wanted to be a part of the best units, the best teams. I wanted to do cool shit. Shit that other people could never dream of.

I wanted to save all of the people like I couldn't save Chester. I threw myself in front of bullets, took the lead busting down doors, and ran down streets riddled with IEDs.

I wanted to make a difference, but years of training turned into years of missions, teammates killed, and innocent casualties. The dark corners of my brain were getting deeper and darker, multiplying. After a decade, I realized the job was all I had. I had just returned from an overseas mission, and when I powered my phone on there were two voicemails left three days prior. One from my mom and the other from my sister, both excitedly telling me Happy Birthday. I hadn't even remembered my own birthday...

That was my 30th birthday, and like the day Chester died, my perspective on my life changed drastically. I realized that I had lived my life for my family, then I lived my life for Chester, then the job, but I needed to start living life for myself.

I started planning for life as a civilian, but it still took me another year to finally get out. I loved being a soldier but I knew that continuing down that path would lead me to an even darker place, and I didn't want to lose myself entirely.

With that in mind, I had a cabin built up in the mountains, in the western point of North Carolina. A cabin surrounded by nothing but forest for miles. The sanctuary I needed to find myself again after so many years of living for other people.

That's where I've been the last two months, my dream home. I had plenty of money saved up from years of nothing to spend it on. The contractors had it built within a year, so all I had left to do once my military contract ended was to officially move in.

Unfortunately, it didn't take long for the restlessness to creep in. Even though it was a cabin in the woods, it was far from desolate. I was lucky enough to have all the amenities I needed to live normally, so chopping wood for the fireplace occupied my time for a while, but I only needed so much. The fireplace is just for extra heat, for show. My HVAC system runs on propane.

Down the mountain is Whitewater, a small town with precisely one grocery store, and one restaurant, which is actually just a diner. Small means no crowds, no hustle, no bustle, just the way I like it. I go into town about once a week, maybe every two weeks, so I always have plenty of food stocked up. It has the smallest population in Rollins County, which in itself is what most would refer to as a very rural county.

I decided to start hunting, as a hobby -not out of necessity, but because I'm bored. It felt good to carry my rifle again. Ghosting through the trees gave me a sense of comfort I hadn't had since my last mission. Even saying that in my head makes me feel inhuman. Stalking prey gives me comfort?

What kind of sociopath have I become?

There is an undeniable adrenaline rush that comes with pulling a trigger. An adrenaline rush that I welcomed after two months of stale boredom.

That's where my thoughts keep going as I sit on the top of a ridge, ass in the dirt, back leaned against this giant rock. The butt of my rifle is propped on my thigh, the barrel balanced on a branch in front of me, aiming towards the grass clearing about 50 yards below me. The brush in front of me obscures me from any game that might wander into the field below.

This was supposed to be my trial for a new life and I am already getting the tightness in my chest, that feeling that I might have made a bad decision. I miss my brothers, my teammates, but more than that, I miss having a purpose. Apparently, I'm not cut out for retired life. I planned on taking time to figure out my next move, figuring out a job to do as a civilian, a job that makes sense for a man who has been in the worst parts of the world and has seen the evil that lives there.

Then lies my next problem. Most civilian jobs require a certain level of social prowess, something I am severely lacking, something I never cared to master. All I've needed these last 13 years is my orders and my unit. Even these last few months, other than a couple of phone calls to my mom and my buddy Jesse from my team, I haven't spoken to anyone. Maybe a hello or have a nice day to the cashier at the grocery store, but I don't tend to draw conversations when I am out in public. I've been told I don't have an approachable demeanor. Hell, that's always been fine by me.

When you've seen what I've seen, there isn't much to talk about. I'm not interested in small talk, and I don't want to talk about shit that doesn't matter. I don't think people really want to hear what I have to say either. The normal person wants good light-hearted conversation, they ask how you are and they don't expect a real answer. They want you to say all is well and move on with their day. It's a waste of time and I've never had the patience for fake niceties. Another reason people tend to steer clear.

That's just the version of me that was created after my best friend died. The version that kept hardening after every mission, every kill shot and every teammate lost. It was naïve of me to think leaving the Army would fix anything for me. All I know is to kill or be killed.

I have no purpose now. Maybe this is where I belong, in these God-forsaken woods.

Chapter Three

I wish this boat would stop rocking, my head is pounding... But, why am I on a boat? No, that doesn't make sense...

My brain is full of sludge, I am trying to think but nothing is processing. Slowly my consciousness comes back into focus, but my head is still throbbing. I can feel my pulse battering the inside of my skull.

My fingertips brush across cool metal clearing some of my confusion, bringing me back to reality. The swaying that I thought was a boat is actually the rhythmic bouncing of a car, the tires crunching across gravel is deafening from my position against the floor. My thoughts are foggy but I try to backtrack. What happened to me? And why am I here?...

My subconscious starts retracing my steps, but I have to grasp my recent memories.

I was driving.

I was driving in my car through the mountains. Then I heard a pop and my wheel jerked. I blew a tire, so I pulled onto the shoulder...

My memory sweeps back in like a tidal wave, making me

cognizant of everything that happened.

I realize the two men sitting in the front seats about two feet from me are Tony and Bub, incredibly too close for comfort. My cheek is pressed against the bare aluminum floor of the van, so I try to stay still. I don't want them to know I'm awake.

I do a mental inventory, besides my pounding head, I seem to be okay physically. My hands are clasped in front of me, tied at the wrists with a zip tie. My legs aren't bound though, so I'll consider that to be good news.

The van rocks and hits bump after bump. "Damn, Tony, couldn't we have gone a different way?" Bub asks, whining.

"What did you want me to do, dumb ass, take the main roads when we have a fucking woman in the back?" Tony shouts back at him, startling me.

The sudden intrusion of his anger is like a whip, and no matter how hard I try not to burst into tears, I can't help it. The water pools in my eyes and I silently sob as the gravity of my situation sinks in. I watch true crime documentaries, not participate in them. I have no idea how I'm supposed to survive this.

They continue driving for what feels like an hour, but my perception of time could be way off. My head is still throbbing. It bounces off the floor of the van with every bump in the road. My attempt to stay silent and unnoticed has worked. They haven't so much as glanced in my direction. I could be dead for all they probably care.

I know I should try to break the zip tie at my wrists, but I am too afraid to move. All of my muscles are tense like every fiber of my being is terrified. My self-preservation is begging me to escape, but I'm frozen. I know I can't fight two grown men off, so my only hope is to run and hide if I get the chance.

If I hide long enough that they give up looking for me, then I can find help. I have no idea where or how I'll get help, but that's not my main focus right now, I just need to escape from these lunatics.

Suddenly, the van stops, lurching my body forward so hard I almost roll completely over. "Now what are we supposed to do?" Bub asks the leader of their duo, seeming to always look to Tony for guidance. A younger brother seeking reassurance from his older brother, maybe?

"Get in the back, grab a hand saw, and start sawing." Tony grumbles, "Fucking, idiot," as Bub gets out of the van and walks towards the back. Their relationship seems hostile, not surprisingly since they were willing to attack and kidnap a stranger off the side of the road like maniacs.

The handles on the back door creak as the door is opened, so I close my eyes and lay as motionless as possible. I do my best to slow my breathing, but I feel like I am going to hyperventilate at any moment. I hear him tinkering around, moving tools, looking for their saw presumably. I swear I feel his eyes linger on me for a few seconds and I don't even breathe, praying my acting skills are up to par.

The door slams closed and I have to stop myself from exhaling all the air in my lungs in relief. He didn't notice I was awake, but I was afraid that I might pass out again from holding my breath steady and my body taut for so long. My head is swimming from the exertion. I can hear my blood rushing in my ears.

Tony starts shouting out his window from the front, "Don't start there, start down at the bottom! What the fuck are you doing? URG!"

He kills the ignition, gets out of the car, and slams his door.

I wait ten seconds... Then, slowly lift my head to look towards the front. Both of them are out of the van. I can't hear them anymore but I can hear the faint sound of sawing. I use my bound hands to raise myself up, even though I'm shaking and I'd rather stay curled up in a fetal position on the floor, I have to see where they are.

I barely raise my head up between the front seats to peek out the windshield, and I see both men standing just ahead. There is a tree blocking the roadway, the road being an abandoned-looking gravel lane, which explains the bumpy drive.

Bub is sawing at the tree with a flimsy hand saw, while Tony is standing next to him shaking his head like a disappointed supervisor. Both of them have their backs facing me. This is my chance, but what's my fucking plan? I could lock the doors, turn the van around, and speed back the way we came. That is if the way we came was a straight shot. I don't remember any turns, but I was blacked out for some of the drive and I don't know for how long.

I steal a glance at the ignition, then the console, then the dashboard. Of course, the keys aren't in here. Dammit, that would have been too easy. I would've taken my chances and tried to make it back out to civilization.

Glancing behind me, the back of the van is filled with tools, paint cans, and a couple of small ladders. I check again to make sure my kidnappers are distracted, then I grab the sharpest tool I see without having to dig around and make any noise. A Phillips head screwdriver. Not great, but better than nothing.

As I slowly move closer to the back doors, wedged between two paint cans is a box cutter. Yes, that's better. I pick it up, not wanting to waste time with the zip tie now, in case they decide to return to check on me. I'll try to create some distance between us first. I tuck the screwdriver in the flat, side pocket of my leggings, grip the knife in my left hand, and grab the handle of the back door with my right. It's a little awkward, but I manage to slowly pop the handle without making any noise. I let out a breath. Okay, here goes nothing.

I push the back door open, trying to ease it open so it doesn't alert them, but it's no use, the hinges squeak– *loudly*. I freeze for just a second and chance a glance back. Both Tony and Bub are looking right at me through the front windshield. Oh no.

Before I can second-guess myself, I jump out of the van and take off. I am so thankful I decided to wear tennis shoes today, but I am still a little wobbly on my feet after being knocked out and lying on the floor of the van for so long.

"Get back here, you dumb bitch!" Tony yells. I can hear them gaining on me, so I veer to the left, straight into the trees. I start zig-zagging through the overgrowth, hoping they will lose sight of me and not be able to catch up. The branches snag at my clothes and pull at my hair, but I keep running, ignoring the lashes of pain.

"Shoot her, Tony, shoot her!" Bub yells, making me panic even more when I realize how close his voice sounds.

Oh God, and I didn't even know they had a gun. The fear pushes me forward even faster, cutting left and right through the thicket, I keep my head ducked, waiting for a bullet that never comes.

Finally, after running for a couple minutes I realize I can't hear any footsteps behind me and I might have lost them. The crunchy autumn leaves that litter the ground are my only hope to not be snuck up on, so I stop running and hide behind a tree that's twice as wide as my body. I don't dare sit down. I know my legs will give out if I let them rest for too long.

I try listening to the forest around me for any signs of the two men, but my heart is beating too fast and too loud. My throat and lungs are burning from running for so long, it hurts to breathe.

I'm not overly athletic. I work out every day but nothing that would prepare me for this. My adrenaline is the only thing keeping me from collapsing, but my legs are shaking and my hands are going numb. I have to try to cut the zip tie.

There isn't a great way to hold the box cutter with both of my hands bound together. I clench the handle of the knife between my knees and slowly try to slice the plastic of the zip tie. But it's not enough leverage and the blade isn't sharp enough, it would take me an hour to get through it this way. My wrists are already raw from the incessant rubbing.

I try a technique I saw in a movie once, swiftly pulling my hands apart as hard as I can, hoping the thick plastic will just give out. Unfortunately, all I accomplish is immense pain. I bite my lip to keep from crying out, but a soft whimper still escapes.

I maneuver the knife around in my hands, tucking the blade just inside the zip tie at my wrists. I try to slice at the plastic this way, from the inside out, my fingers only providing the smallest bit of leverage, but it starts to work. Relief pours through me at the thought of actually getting my hands free, of getting through this. I sniffle back the tears I feel burning in my eyes, needing to focus on the task at hand.

I get about a quarter of the way through the plastic before I hear, "Ay Tony, she's over here!" Making my blood run cold.

So focused on my wrists, I didn't hear the sound of anyone

approaching me. I look up to see Bub standing about 10 feet from me. He gives me a creepy smile before lunging in my direction, but I bolt on instinct despite my fatigue, barely escaping his arms grasping me.

I make it just through another patch of brush when I get tackled from behind. I hit the ground hard, the air knocked from my lungs as I'm crushed from above by this smelly brute. My jaw hits the ground so hard, I swear my teeth crack.

My arms are pinned underneath me and I'm unable to move from under his weight. He sits up suddenly, straddling the backs of my thighs, and my stomach sinks.

"I'm gonna teach you a lesson 'bout running from us, girl," he slurs in my ear from behind me, making me buck harder against him. I try to escape but all I manage to do is thrash my face into the dirt.

"No, no, no!" I scream out, attempting to wiggle out of his grasp. I claw my fingers into the leaves and dirt underneath me, trying to crawl out from under him. I don't want him to touch me, I won't let him.

I feel a sharp stinging between my wrists, reminding me of the knife still tucked between the heels of my hands.

Bub grabs the elastic waistband of my pants and starts yanking them down my hips as I'm still fighting to free my arms. If I can just get the knife out and face outward again, maybe I can fend him off. I struggle for a little more room, but he's too heavy. He feels like dead weight on top of me.

"What's this?" He asks as he pulls the screwdriver out of my pocket, "A weapon? Naughty, naughty. Tony's going to be very angry about you stealing from us." He chuckles to himself menacingly.

Bub grabs both of my bare butt cheeks in his hands

squeezing painfully hard, grunting in appreciation. I think I'm going to vomit. I can't let him rape me, the way he's touching me is violating enough.

"Tony isn't as nice as me, he'd probably shove this handle right in your ass," he laughs while I whimper at his cross words.

"But I'm nice, aren't I nice?" He asks. "I just want a little piece of ya for myself."

He grabs my thong, but before he can pull it down, I use all of my strength to twist my torso in a last-ditch effort, slashing the box cutter across his face.

"Ahhhgg," he yelps, falling to the ground beside me, flinging his body around in the dirt.

I crawl away from him, struggling to pull my pants back up with my wrists still bound. God dammit, I still needed to get my hands free, but the knife went flying out of my hands with the momentum of striking his face. He took the screwdriver, so I have no more weapons, I'm on my own.

I get up, steadying myself on a tree next to me, my legs feeling like gelatine. I don't know how much longer I can make it, but I have to keep going.

The tree next to me explodes. Bark sprays all over my face, just as I hear the loud "*POW!*" of a gunshot.

"Don't fucking move, bitch, I won't miss the next time!" Tony yells from about 15 feet away.

"She cut me, Tony, she fuckin' cut me, kill her!!" Bub yells, still on the ground where he fell.

"Oh, I'm gonna do a lot worse than kill her, brother," Tony slurs in my direction, making his intentions clear.

He told me not to move, but I think I'd rather risk dying than be caught by these evil men. Ducking my head, I dodge and sprint away as fast as my legs will take me, I just hope I'm fast enough.

Chapter Four

Nathan

S till lost in my thoughts, I glance periodically down into the valley below me. I haven't seen any sign of deer or anything else this whole time, but at least there's a great view. The trees line the field along the right side, the leaves varying shades of orange, red, or yellow. The browning grass is tall, probably knee-high, and it's riddled with wildflowers, though a couple of nights of frost have been too much for the blooms to survive.

The crisp fall weather, with its changing leaves, is the perfect way to experience the mountains, but I'm curious about how harsh the winter will be. The air up here is thin and bitterly cold already. I imagine snow flurries will come any week now.

The entire valley below me spans less than a quarter mile across. A shallow river runs parallel to the trees along the left side. I can tell it's shallow because of how light the color of the water is, and the way the sun shines on it almost makes it sparkle. The banks of the river on either side are rocky, and the side closest to the field of grass is a steep embankment. The 12-foot incline of eroded rock means the river most likely floods in the spring, once the snow melts up in the mountains. On the farther side of the river away from me, there are more trees, the thick forest going on for miles.

The sun is high in the sky, it's only about midday, but I left my cabin early this morning before sunrise. I've spent hours already stuck inside my head, the clarity I've been seeking with a hunt is no use today. After one final sweep of the area, I decide to head home. I'll get back to my cabin, make dinner, wake up tomorrow, and repeat. I need something else to occupy my time, I am not ready for this unemployed shit.

Standing up from my perch, I sling my rifle over my shoulder and knock the dirt off my camouflage pants. I'm getting used to wearing hunting camo now, and not the digital camo I lived in for so long in the army. I also don't mind not needing to be clean-shaven every day. My five o'clock shadow has turned into a few days of stubble. My usual high and tight crew cut has also grown out, the dark hair on my head is starting to look unruly per my usual standards.

As I turn to head down from the top of the ridge, I hear a gunshot echo through the trees and it makes me pause. It normally wouldn't concern me since I'm on public land, but that shot sounded close by, it also didn't sound like a hunting rifle. Still, it's none of my business. I'm about 8 miles from my cabin and there are access roads all throughout these woods. It could be one of the "neighbors" that live on this mountain or any Joe schmoe from town.

I keep heading down the hill, not quite shaking the feeling that I should be on the alert right now. That's ridiculous, I'm not in the Middle East, I'm not in enemy territory, I'm no longer in the United States Army.

Yet, halfway down the hill my feet stay rooted in their spot.

A prickling feeling on the back of my neck forces me to kneel and pull my rifle back off my shoulder. I brace my elbow on my knee for support and aim my rifle back into the field before me. I'm at a slightly lower vantage point now but I'm still able to see most of the area through my scope. I scan the field, left to right, right to left. Nothing. The field is empty, with no signs of life.

I look up from my scope. The prickling is still pulling at the back of my neck, but there's nothing there. My brain is so fucking bored that it's playing games with me. Even as I tell myself that it's a waste of time, I continue monitoring the area. Slowly, back and forth.

Screw it, I'm getting out of here. As I start to stand up to leave, I catch a glimpse of something in my peripheral vision. So far to the left of me I almost can't see it, something is coming out of the tree line. I watch as it immediately drops a few feet to the river bank. The embankment on that side isn't as steep as the side that is closest to me, and it's not as rocky. The dirt spans about 20 feet before reaching the river's edge.

My eyes are definitely playing tricks on me, or my brain is even more fucked up than I thought, but it looks like a person lying there. I raise my scope to eye level so I can get a better look and sure as shit, there is a woman laying face down on the dirt and rocks, "What the fuck?"

She's lying face down, but I watch as she slowly lifts her head, her eyes trained on the river. Then she whips her head to the side to look back over her shoulder. I follow her line of sight through my scope. Standing right behind her, on the edge of the tree line, is a man with a revolver pointed right at her. What the hell is going on?

With no time to ask questions, I don't hesitate, aiming and

31

firing my weapon before he can fire his.

POW!

It's a long shot, and I didn't have time to assess how the distance would mess with the trajectory. Regardless, I hit my mark on his right shoulder, not center mass, but it will do.

Keeping him in my line of sight, I watch as he drops the gun and stumbles back in between the trees. I can't see him anymore, but I know the gun's still lying on the ground. I glance back toward the woman, but she's not lying in the same spot. I look up from my scope and see that she's wading through the river, her hands raised above the water, bound together by something. "Come on lady, just get across the river and over that ridge before the bastard goes for his gun again," I mumble to myself.

If she makes it up and over the rocky incline to get to the tall grass she'll be hidden enough and it will give me a chance to help her. I scan the tree line, waiting to see if the man who had the gun has given up or not. A couple yards away from where the gun is laying I see a shorter man stumble out through the trees, blood covering his face. I don't see him holding any weapons, but it directs my attention away from the first guy for two seconds too long. The initial guy retrieved the gun and took cover back behind a tree. Dammit!

Initially, I'm not sure if the second man is a victim or not, but then he starts picking up rocks and chucking them into the river at the woman. That's enough indication for me to aim in his direction and fire another shot, *POW!*

Not waiting to see if it was a kill shot, I pivot back to check the first guy's location. A faint screech is carried through the air so I'm guessing guy number two is at least injured. I pop my left eye open to gauge how far the woman has made it across the river.

She's climbing the rocks now. I only have to hold these guys off for ten more seconds to give her a chance. Once she crests the hill, I'll have time to run to her before the men can cross the river after her. They won't have a shot since they'll have the low ground.

Everything happens at warp speed. The first guy raises his gun from the tree line, the gun being the only thing visible, and he fires it at her. I aim exactly where I think he is standing and blindly shoot into the trees, hoping I hit some part of him.

Almost all at once it's the "*POP!*" of his shot, then "*POW!*" of mine, right before the woman's scream echoes through the valley.

Looking up from my scope, I can barely see her body because of the grass, but she is lying face down at the top of the ridge. She doesn't move, but I do. I don't know if the gunman hit her or not, but I'm not waiting to find out. I have to make it to her before they do.

Chapter Five

Callie

I can't move. My head is telling me to get up and run, but my body isn't listening. I'm shivering from head to toe. My thoughts are jumbled and I'm struggling to register what just happened. I was shot at multiple times, ran through freezing cold water, and somehow managed to use the last bit of energy in my body to face plant into this tall grass. One shot was so close to hitting me, that I swear I felt the bullet zip past my head.

Breathe, just breathe, I think to myself. I need to move, I need to keep going. I'm not safe, I'm not safe. The mantra in my head isn't helping, my limbs won't respond, and my adrenaline's been depleted. All I can manage to do is lay here and play dead. Except it might not be an act for long, minutes pass and I still can't make my body move. These might be my final moments, and nothing of great importance seems to be crossing my mind. All I can focus on is the earthy smell of the grass on my face, and the coolness of the ground against my cheek.

Faintly, my ears pick up a noise past the sound of my own ragged breathing. I hear the weight of something -no, someone- landing heavily in the grass beside me with a *thump*!

This is it, they've caught me. They're going to take turns raping me if they don't kill me first. I hardly have the nerve, but I flop my head to the side, needing to see what's in store for me, preparing myself to come face to face with a gun. Instead, I look into the face of a man I've never seen before. His cool, gray eyes stare at me intently, but I'm too exhausted to even act startled. All I can register is that he's not one of them. Not Tony, not Bub.

It takes me a second to realize his mouth is moving, that he's saying something. "Are you okay? Were you shot?" He stops focusing on my face momentarily, his eyes bouncing back and forth between me and the river below us.

"I don't know," is all I can manage as a mumbled response.

Wait, was I shot? I remember the blast of bullets, one ricocheting too close to me as I ran, but no pain. I mean, I'm definitely in pain, but not how I would be if I was shot.

However, I don't say anything else to him, I don't know this man and he could be just as dangerous as the other two. Again, my brain is telling me to flee, but I'm in total muscle failure.

"Can you move? We need to get away from the edge of the river bank. It's not safe," he says to me, eyeing me cautiously, like he's trying to figure me out too.

Duh, obviously it's not safe, but I don't say that. He seems like he is trying to help. For the time being, I decide to go along with it, not that I have any other choice.

"I don't think I can run anymore," I admit with a croak in my voice. "I'm so tired."

"That's okay, I don't need you to run, I need you to stay low and crawl over behind that fallen tree." I barely shift my attention as he points at a tree that's lying on its side about 10 yards ahead of me, too focused on how calm his gravelly voice is.

I nod my head in acknowledgment, not trusting my voice, and try to raise my chest off the ground with shaky arms. My movements are stunted by my bound wrists and I collapse back to the ground.

"Wait," he says, and I look back over at him to see a knife in his hands. I cringe away seeing the blade so close to me. Maybe I read this guy all wrong.

He instantly notices my startled expression, raising his hands in a way that indicates he doesn't intend to hurt me. "I can cut your wrists free so it's easier to crawl."

I don't want to be anywhere near another man with weapons, but I'm desperate to have my hands free. At this moment I have to make a choice, either trust a stranger and hope he doesn't hurt me, or try to figure out how to make it on my own even though I'm exhausted and scared to death. I don't have time to analyze my recent track record for making the wrong choices in my life, all I know is I'm desperate for this man to be nothing like the other two who attacked me.

Hesitantly, I shift my arms so I'm closer and he can reach me better, but keeping the rest of my body as far from him as physically possible. He slips the knife between my wrists and with one swift tug it slices through the zip tie. Just like that, I'm free.

I stare at my raw wrists, flooded with relief. I didn't know if I was going to make it through this day alive, but having my hands back after being bound for hours gives me just an ounce of hope that everything will be okay. I use that feeling of hope to spur myself forward. On shaky arms, and barely moving legs, I inch through the tall grass toward the tree. I glance back at this new mystery man, expecting him to be following me but he's still in the same spot.

"I'm right behind you, but I need to make sure they don't try to cross the river and sneak up on us. Keep going." His commanding voice is steady and sure, giving me the assurance I need to propel forward.

I keep my eyes forward, barely able to make out the bark on the trunk of the tree through the tall grass, but my new wave of determination refuses to let me quit. At what feels like a snail's pace, I crawl to the backside of the tree trunk and collapse. Breathing heavily, I barely have a chance to catch my breath when a large body crashes down next to me, again. It startles me, but it's short-lived.

He easily covered the distance from the river bank in seconds versus what took me minutes. This new man is still a stranger, but so far his company is much preferred over the other two. I'll take what help I can get at this point. At least until my lungs stop burning, or my legs feel a little less gel-like.

"They never came out of the tree line or attempted to cross the river, so they might have given up," he tells me, "but they could've just needed time to regroup." He doesn't look at me as he talks, still facing the river, anticipating any threats.

"You going to tell me what the fuck is going on?" He calmly asks me after a couple of minutes of silence. His voice is low and rough, but not at all harsh, as if he isn't the slightest bit disturbed by what's happening.

I glance up into his face, as he kneels next to me using the log to prop up his gun. Caught off guard when I meet his eyes, not expecting to see such obvious concern, but also the deepness in his gray eyes is unlike anything I've ever seen. Like, dark storm clouds before it rains. My eyes linger on them while I formulate my answer, still trying to process the events of today myself. I decide the best I can do is vocalize some of the questions that are racing through my head.

"I wish I could tell you anything that makes sense, but those guys kidnapped me off the side of the road. I don't know why, I don't know where we were when I got away, I don't know where they were taking me, I don't know where I am now. They were pissed when I ran, they were even angrier when I fought back, but I was not going to die today, I was not going to make it easy on them," I ramble, choking back a sob. Tears started pouring out of my eyes at some point and I have to wipe them from my cheeks. "I don't know who you are, and I don't know why you are helping me or if I can even trust you, I just know that I'll try to kill you if I have to." I end my blubbering speech, looking directly into his stormy eyes, so he knows how serious I am. I'm too pissed off and exhausted to care anymore.

After a few seconds of studying me intently, he finally responds, "You're safe with me, I promise."

That's all he says, he doesn't reply to any other part of my rambling. He doesn't act offended at all by my threat to kill him if I need to. If anything, he seems pleased by it.

Maybe, it's the fatigue of the last few hours, or my brain isn't firing on all cylinders, but my intuition is telling me that he's being honest. I think I'm safe with him.

At that realization, I let my head fall back against the trunk of this rotting tree and shut my eyes against the tears continuing to spill down my cheeks. I think I'm going to be okay.

Chapter Six

Nathan

There will never be anything more admirable to me than a survivor. And that's what this woman is. She has been through hell, emotionally and physically. Her face and hands are covered in dirt, she has blood coming out of wounds on her wrists, a split in her bottom lip, and what looks to be a dark purple bruise forming right above her temple on her forehead. She is soaking wet from the waist down from crossing the river, and I can see her body shivering uncontrollably.

Her sweatshirt is torn in a few places, and strands of her hair are falling loose from her hair tie, pieces of twigs and leaves stuck in various places, the evidence of running through the thick brush and branches in these woods I'm sure.

Her head rests against the tree, tears rolling down from beneath her closed eyelids. Even with the path of wetness that the tears are leaving on her cheeks, she doesn't seem distressed, but more so trying to collect herself.

Her breathing is evening out, and aside from the trembling, whether it be from the cold water she was in or her adrenaline crashing, her muscles aren't tensed as if she is prepared to run.

She hasn't said as much, but I'm hoping her body language is an indication that she trusts me. Or, at least believes that I'm not going to hurt her. Trust can come later. She doesn't know me or my work history. All she knows is that I'm a strange man, and men are usually a woman's biggest threat in life. I understand if she might be hesitant around me for a while.

As much as I don't want to do this to her, we have to keep moving. Even behind the cover of this fallen tree, we are sitting ducks. I need her to push herself farther, at least until we are in the coverage of the forest. It's another 30 yards to the tree line, then a mile to where I parked my 4-wheeler.

I give her another minute, letting her compose herself. I am keeping a close watch on the ridge. I haven't seen any sign of the two men from the river bank. I'm positive I at least wounded both of them, maybe if I'm really lucky they're bleeding out in the woods where they'll be picked apart by scavengers.

All the things I did, and was ordered to do in the army, I sometimes wondered if I was just as bad as enemies we fought. Witnessing a situation like this reaffirms the real evil that lurks in this world. If it weren't for the risk of exposure while crossing that river, I would've run after those guys in an instant and put a bullet between their eyes. I'd make sure they saw it coming.

I push my anger aside. I need to focus on getting her safe, that's the priority.

"We've got to keep moving." I pause, waiting for her reaction. She peeks her eyes open, staring off towards the cloud-covered sky with fluttering eyelashes. The look of serenity on her face, despite her current situation distracts me for a moment. Her eyes and cheeks are red from crying, and the bruise on her forehead is getting darker by the minute, yet she's one of the most beautiful women I've ever seen.

"Okay," she says quietly, wiping the remaining tears from her cheeks, and looking at me finally. Her voice draws my attention to her lips and the cut there. It doesn't look too deep, but it's probably uncomfortable. It will heal up in a few days, but it pisses me off that two grown men had the nerve to hurt her.

My eyes linger on her mouth a second too long and when I shift my focus back up her face, I'm met with hazel eyes. A mix of blue and green that looks bright in contrast to the redness rimming her eyelids. She's looking at me, waiting for instruction, but I'm stuck. It takes me longer than needed to formulate my next sentence. I clear my throat, blaming it on the chaos of this situation, or maybe because this is the most I've spoken to anyone in months.

"How are your feet?" I ask, knowing her shoes are still soaked from wading through the water.

"Uhh, I'm not sure, they feel pretty numb." She moves her feet back and forth as if to wiggle her toes, testing her movements.

"Do you think you can walk to that tree line?" I gesture over my shoulder to the woods that she is facing. "Once we get out of this clearing we should be alright. Even if they try to follow us they won't be able to track us, it's too overgrown."

"Okay," she states simply. Even through her exhaustion, I can tell she's not a quitter. She is determined to get through this, and I'm going to do everything in my power to help her.

"Okay," I confirm, "walk in a straight line, I'm going to follow right behind you, keeping a lookout. If I tell you to drop, you drop to the grass and flatten yourself like a pancake.

Got it?"

"Got it," she doesn't hesitate.

"If I tell you to run, take off as fast as you can, and do not look back, do not slow down. Run until your legs give out, or until you find the access road. It's straight ahead. If you follow it to the right, it'll take you to a main road eventually and you can flag down a car for help. Got it?" I ask again.

"But, what about you?" She counters, instead of agreeing.

"Don't worry about me, you're the one that matters." Her eyebrows pinch together like she isn't quite sure how to interpret what I'm saying.

"I've trained for things like this. I know you don't know me, but my goal is to make sure you are safe. If we get separated, I'll find you. If you get out of these woods and I don't, my name is Nathan Wolfe." I pause, clarifying, "So, you can look up my obituary online."

Her mouth drops open, dumbfounded by what I just said. It seems harsh to a civilian but I've accepted the risk of death a long time ago. I've had my affairs in order since I was 18 years old. I'd rather risk my life to save someone than anyone being forced to give up their life due to circumstances they didn't ask for.

She didn't ask for any of this to happen to her, the choice was forced onto her. I made my choice by helping her. As soon as I saw her laying on the river bank with a gun pointed to her head, the decision was made and I immediately shifted into active defense mode. I was ready to be who she needed at that moment- a sworn soldier, a protector, a defender. Whatever it takes to save an innocent life.

Chapter Seven

Callie

I cannot comprehend the selflessness of this man, Nathan, he said his name is Nathan. In contrast to how my day started, it doesn't seem real that this stranger would be willing to give his life to save mine. I feel like I have emotional whiplash. I am not cut out for such an adventurous life, the high and lows in such a short span of time is making my head spin.

"Can you do that? Can you run if I tell you to?" He asks again, not an inkling of worry in his voice.

"Yeah," I mumble, "I will." If I was a child I'd have my fingers crossed behind my back. As worn out as I am and as ready as I am to be out of these woods, no part of me could live with myself if I left him behind.

"Okay, go ahead and start walking, I've got your back," he tells me, confidently, making me believe that he truly does have my back. I don't have the words to explain how grateful I am that he's here with me. So, with one more deep breath, I brace my arms on the log, using it to push my body up. I'm not sure that I would have been able to stand up on my own.

Every part of me aches. My legs are shaking so badly that I

think my knees are going to buckle. My shoes feel like they're filled with concrete. My feet are miserably wet and cold. I take a second to stabilize myself, but Nathan follows my lead, standing up behind me, still facing the river bank.

"When you're ready," he encourages, his deep voice steadying me.

I start walking, and even though my joints feel like they need to be greased, I try to keep a steady pace. The soft crunch of the dry grass is the only indication that Nathan's walking behind me, matching me step for step. He's right there but I still can't help feeling exposed walking through this open field. I wrap my arms around myself trying to fake some sense of security.

"Almost there," I whisper more to myself than to him. A couple more steps and I'm enveloped into the trees. I exhale deeply, not realizing I had been holding my breath. I brace both of my hands on a tree and hang my head, trying to regulate my breathing.

"Still no sign of them, I think we're in the clear," Nathan says from the edge of the tree line. He slings his rifle over his shoulder and turns to look at me. We make eye contact but neither of us says anything at first, letting everything that has happened sink in. I finally notice that he's wearing head-to-toe camouflage. That paired with the rifle makes me realize he's a hunter. A random hunter in the middle of nowhere saved my life.

I'm overwhelmed with emotion, the day taking its toll on me. I have to squeeze my eyes shut to keep myself from crying, again. "Thank you, I don't think I could've made it out of that field alive if it weren't for you," I manage to say through trembling lips.

"Nah you didn't need me, you would have made it. I just couldn't let you have all the fun." He responds, smirking at me almost nervously, finally breaking his hard facade.

I am about to crumble and this man is attempting to make a joke. I can't help it, I start to laugh. The kind of laugh that has me doubled over bracing my hands on my knees. This is ridiculous, this whole day. I can't decide if I'm the unluckiest person alive for being taken in the first place, or the luckiest person alive for running into Nathan when I did.

"I'm Callie by the way," I say after I finish laughing, immediately feeling depleted of all my energy again.

"It's nice to meet you, Callie." He scrunches his forehead after he says it, probably realizing how that sounds after meeting under these circumstances. He rubs his hand through his short dark hair, contemplating. "You know what I mean," he says with a shrug. This conversation is clearly not easy for him.

I stand there, not knowing what to do next. I should be more assertive, taking control of my destiny and all that, but I think I'm okay with Nathan taking the lead. At least until I'm not so exhausted. Whenever that will be.

"My 4-wheeler is about a mile out, we can take that back to my cabin and get you dry. Then I can get you in touch with the authorities in town, they need to know what happened." He watches me, trying to gauge my reaction. To which part I'm not sure, but I am mostly stuck on the fact that I have to walk another mile.

"I... I don't know if I can..." I don't finish my thought.

"Listen, I know you don't know me but I promise I'm not going to let anything happen to you. You're safe with me."

I realize that he thinks my hesitation is about going back

45

to his cabin with him, which makes sense, but I've already resigned that he means me any harm. I know that logically it is stupid for me to trust him after knowing him for all of two seconds, but his actions have driven home that he is a good person. A bad person wouldn't have done all that he has done for me. He risked a lot if he only planned to hurt me in the end. Then again, maybe he has nothing to lose.

"I stand by my earlier statement, that I'll kill you if you try to hurt me. But against my better judgment, I trust you. I just don't know if I can make it another mile," I hide my face in my hands, ashamed of my weakness and not able to watch him scrutinize me.

Before I can register his movements, my legs are swept out from under me and I'm cradled in his arms. A small squeak escapes me.

"I'm sorry if this is too much for you, but you've done enough and I meant what I said about getting you to safety. We can't stay here, we've got to keep moving in case they decide to cross the river." There is no question in his voice, he intends to carry me for a mile.

"You can't do this, I'm too heavy and it's too far. I can't ask you to do this," I insist.

"You didn't ask, I've carried men twice as heavy as you farther distances, and I'm not giving you a choice," he states bluntly. Leaving no room for argument. He seems to be much more comfortable giving orders than partaking in small talk.

I'm not sure how I feel, but I'm too tired to fight it. My weight doesn't seem to be bothering him as he moves effortlessly through the overgrown trees. I'm 5'6" and have meat on my bones, but he is hardly breathing heavy and his footsteps are light, he's not struggling at all. I let myself relax, and try not to worry so much.

Unfortunately, my brain doesn't know how to completely shut off. I can't believe this happened to me. I'm mad at those disgusting men, I'm mad that they took me so easily. I'm mad that I didn't kill them for what they did. What if they go back out to the highway and find another girl to attack? What if they go back to my car and find my wallet, get my information, and come after me?

I squeeze my eyes shut, my head is still throbbing. At some point though, my head ends up resting on Nathan's shoulder. My nose is pressed against the collar of his shirt. He smells good, not like a fragrance, just masculine. My ex always smelled like whatever cheap cologne his mom gave him for Christmas, I hated it. When I tried to gift him a scent that I preferred, he never even took it out of the box. Jerk.

I mentally shake off those thoughts, especially the ones about Nathan's scent. I am losing my mind. I realize I still have my eyes closed, and peek out from between my lashes. His jawline is sharp, chiseled down to his chin. A dark dusting of stubble where a beard would be stands out against his light skin. I'm too nervous to look into his eyes, afraid the closeness of our faces would make my examination incredibly awkward. Instead, my eyes trail down his throat, the stubble almost reaches his Adam's apple.

I can't ever remember a time that I've felt this comfortable being carried by someone. I've always felt like I'm too big, that it's too awkward because of my height, but I don't feel like that at all right now. After the terrible day I've had, I let myself enjoy being held by strong, capable arms.

Chapter Eight

Nathan

I was being honest when I told her that carrying her wouldn't be a problem. The only difficulty has been not being able to see the obstructions at my feet with her in my arms. Luckily, I've made quick work of any obstacles and haven't stumbled. I don't think she would take kindly to me accidentally dropping her.

After a few minutes of walking, I feel her relax in my arms, even laying her head against my shoulder making me think she might have fallen asleep. I knew she was exhausted, and I had a feeling she wasn't going to let me carry her unless I insisted. I took a risk by swooping her up into my arms without permission. I could've earned a slap in the face for it. My gut keeps telling me to take care of this girl, and I learned a long time ago to trust my intuition in hairy situations. Sometimes it's been the only thing to keep me alive.

I am hyper aware of how her body feels in my arms, she's still shivering, or trembling, I can't tell which. I tuck her tightly against my chest as I step over a fallen sapling laying across my path, her head nestling in under my chin. I don't loosen my grip on her even after I clear the obstacle, convincing myself that sharing my body heat will ease her tremors. She either doesn't notice or doesn't care.

I glance down at the top of her head, making sure she isn't looking up in the direction of my face. I use this opportunity to examine some of her features more closely. Her hair tickles my jaw at this angle, and the fresh scent of her shampoo lingers on my senses. A splatter of freckles across her nose draws my attention, they'd be hard to see if I wasn't so close to her, making me aware of how unusual this proximity is for two strangers. She's biting her lip, like she's deep in thought, or worrying. My eyes are drawn to where her teeth drag across the pink skin.

"Are you okay?" I ask her softly, not trying to startle her since both of us have been silent for so long. A soft sigh escapes her, making me wonder if that's the only response I'll receive, but after a few seconds, she continues.

"Just wondering why this happened to me," she whispers. It's so faint, I can hardly hear her.

"Can I ask how it happened?" I don't want to push her, but I am curious about the details.

"I got a flat tire. I pulled over to try to put on a spare when they pulled up behind me. I knew they were bad news right away, but they cornered me and knocked me out. The next thing I knew I was in the back of their shitty van. I've concluded that I've done something to piss the universe off." Her whole body shudders, so I give her a reassuring squeeze where my hands cradle her leg and upper arm, not sure how to comfort someone in a situation like this.

"Do you remember the road you were on when you got your flat?" I asked, trying to figure out how far from her origin point they took her.

"I was on I-83, I'm not sure exactly where but there was no cell service and I hadn't seen a gas station or any signs for miles," she exhales.

"That's probably an hour from here, less once you get on the main road, but cutting through the mountain on the access roads is risky. They must be familiar with the area." I imagine they wanted to stay off the radar, but who knows where they were taking her.

"I wasn't sure how long I was unconscious, I was terrified when I woke up. I just really hope I can get back to my car. I had all my stuff in it, my phone, wallet, and my laptop for work. What if they took my information? Try to track me down?" She buries her face further into my collar like she's subconsciously trying to hide. The tip of her nose brushes against my neck sending a jolt down my spine. What the fuck was that?

"I won't let that happen," I state matter of factly, without a doubt in my mind that I'm going to see this through to the end. I'm not going to let her get hurt. I'm involved now and I don't intend on abandoning her. She wipes her cheek across the collar of my jacket, and sniffles.

"Sorry," she says softly. "It's been a rough day."

God damn, this woman is going to make me set fire to this whole fucking mountain to make sure those bastards suffer. I try to reign in my anger again, not needing her to interpret my aggression in the wrong way, but I want to put my fist through one of these tree trunks. In the same breath, I have to stop myself from leaning my forehead against hers to comfort her in some small way. A gesture way too intimate and not at all appropriate in this situation.

Not sure how my day ended up here, but I don't mind that

50

I was in the right place at the right time to help Callie. Who knows what would have happened to her out here, there is no one for miles. If I had packed up and left my hunting spot 10 minutes sooner than I did, I wouldn't have had any clue that she was out there, I wouldn't have been able to help her, and I surely wouldn't be holding her right now.

We stay silent the remainder of the walk, both of us lost in our thoughts. I see my four-wheeler up ahead and close the remaining distance before setting Callie down on the back of it.

"The good news is there is no more walking, bad news is that we have to ride a couple of miles to get back to my house and it's going to be cold, especially since your clothes are wet," I say apologetically, shrugging off my jacket to offer her.

"Let's just get this over with." She swings her leg over the other side to straddle the seat, pulling on my camo. Her arms cross over her stomach, trying to keep herself warm, while I attach my rifle to the 4-wheeler and climb on the seat in front of her.

"You're going to have to hold on to me. The ride is rough and I don't want you falling." I unzip the pockets of my base layer, glad I had it on under my jacket even though it wasn't that cold today. "Put your hands in here," I motion to my sides, "it might help a little to keep them warm." I turn the ignition and the engine fires up, at the same time her hands slide into my pockets. I can feel them through the fleece lining, and I'm painfully aware of how low they rest on my abdomen.

"Hold on tight!" I project over the noise of the engine. Her fingers flex and her palms flatten against me, holding on tighter. Releasing the clutch, I start towards home going as fast as I can with her on the back. If I was alone I'd be pushing

51

the throttle but it's hard for a passenger to anticipate the movement the quad makes across the terrain. She's weak already, one sharp turn could throw her off the back.

I cut across an access road and continue on trails that lead back to my cabin. I can feel her head tucked between my shoulder blades, blocking her face from the sharp wind. Her nails are digging into my stomach and her legs are squeezing the outsides of mine, holding onto me. This is probably taking a toll on her but the sooner we get back the better.

It takes about 15 minutes, but we finally arrive at the bottom of my property, and the steep driveway leading to my cabin. I reach behind my back and wrap my arm around her torso as we ascend my driveway, making sure she doesn't lose to gravity and fall backward. It also makes me aware of how much I like having my arm around her.

The driveway levels out bringing us to the clearing that my home sits on. A large yard surrounds my custom post and beam cabin, all of it surrounded by the thick woods that cover this mountain. It's a small home, meant for a loner like me. A wrap-around porch sits on three sides, a stone chimney taking up the fourth.

The small pole barn in the back is normally where I park the four-wheeler, but I can feel how tense she is under my arm. I need to get her inside now, so I pull right up to the front steps.

I cut the ignition, finally letting go of her, but I still feel the vibration of the engine against my back. Except, it's not the engine, it's Callie clinging to me, trembling from head to toe.

Shit.

Chapter Nine

Callie

I can't stop shaking. Every muscle in my body is locked up and I can't move. I don't know if it's because of my wet clothes or straining to hold onto Nathan for so long, but I can't let go of him. I can't move my limbs. I don't even feel him stop or turn off the engine. He's patting my hands that are still stuffed inside his pockets. I faintly realize that I am clawing into his stomach but I can't uncurl my fingers.

I feel him carefully pull one hand out at a time, loosening my grip by gently rubbing the pads of my palms. He climbs off his seat and carefully lifts me in his arms, cradling me against his chest as he had before. I am not aware enough of my surroundings to take in the details of his cabin, but I feel him bound up a couple of steps and maneuver me just enough to get his front door open. The only thing I notice is the warmth against my cheeks as we enter.

I lose the feeling of his arms as he sets me down on the ground in front of a fireplace. I've never had tunnel vision but I imagine this is what it looks like, the edges of my vision are blurry and I can't make out any details around me. All I can focus on is the faint glow in front of me getting brighter and warmer. My body is still shivering so hard that my teeth are chattering, and my eyelids are becoming painful to keep open.

I start drifting in and out of sleep, fighting to stay awake but losing. I'm dizzy from trying to stay conscious, my head feels like it's swimming. I can't tell if what's in front of me is real or if I'm dreaming. My fatigue is playing tricks on me.

I've never been this affected by exhaustion before, it's worse than being drunk. At least after drinking too much, you can blame yourself for being careless. You lay in bed with the insufferable spins, cursing that last shot of tequila your friend ordered. You swear you'll never do it again, you'll stop drinking so much, but a week later those thoughts are long forgotten.

This feeling is more akin to death. If someone told me this is what it feels like to drift to sleep for the final time, only to wake up next in whatever your version of heaven or hell is, I'd believe them. My brain no longer feels connected to my body. My consciousness is floating above me, looking down on me instead of from within.

I'm jostled slightly, pulling me from the depths of my fatigue. I recognize the jerky movements, the unmistakable tugging of my pants being pulled from my body. What's happening? Why are my pants being pulled off?

"No, NO, no no…" I mumble or yell, I can't tell. It's like déjà vu, Bub's attacking me and all I can do is cry out, feeling helpless to stop what's happening to me. My breaths come out in gasps as if I'm suffocating, face down in the dirt again.

"I'm sorry, Callie, I'm sorry but I have to get the wet clothes off or you'll keep shivering. Fuck, I'm sorry," Nathan apologizes, over and over. His words are distant at first, fuzzy, but slowly become clearer and clearer as he continues apologizing, and continues talking me through what he's doing.

I sob in relief once the fog clears and I realize it's Nathan here with me, not Bub or Tony. In my haze I forgot where I was, I forgot I was safe. I let the tears fall, not caring to wipe them away. I don't care that I am naked from the waist down. I don't care that I am a trembling mess, I'm safe. I'm safe.

As quickly as my shoes, socks, and pants leave my body, I'm wrapped in a giant blanket. I relax as he slowly tucks the entirety of the blanket around me, cocooned from my neck to my feet, enveloped in the warmth my body desperately needed.

I can already feel the shivers easing, my body melting into a pile of goo on the floor. I turn my head away from the fire for the first time since laying here and watch as Nathan continues tucking the blanket under my legs. He seems to be deeply concentrated like he's afraid one gap of cold air will send me into hypothermic shock. His face is hard, his mouth downturned at the corners, worry lines creasing his forehead. He briefly flashes his eyes in the direction of my face, stalling his movements when he realizes I am looking back at him.

"Callie, I..." He stops like he isn't sure what to say, another apology forming on his lips.

"Thank you for saving me, Nathan," I whisper. He moves his mouth like he is going to respond, but doesn't say anything. His brows are furrowed, worry still etched across his features.

"I didn't mean to scare you," he finally says, "I need you to know that. I just wanted to get your wet clothes off."

"I believe you," I quickly respond. "I just forgot where I was, I thought... I thought you were one of them for a second. But,

I'm okay, I promise."

"Did they..." He starts hesitantly but doesn't have to finish his sentence, I know what he's asking.

"No. One of them tried, but I sliced his face open," I say it with as much pride as I can muster, which isn't much in my current state of drowsiness.

It's barely there, but he smiles, just the small uptick of one side of his mouth. Shaking his head, he lets out a quiet laugh, not hiding his amusement. "Good girl."

My cheeks grow warm at his compliment. Eliciting a feeling I'm not ready to analyze yet. I turn back to the fire to sever the moment, still overwhelmed by everything that's happened. I focus on my breathing and relaxing all my muscles, finally feeling slightly at peace after the longest day of my life.

* * *

"Do you want me to move you to the couch?" He asks, but I shake my head in response, too comfortable to want to move. I don't know how long I've been lying here already, but I'm too content to care.

I sense Nathan's movements behind me as he shuffles back and leans his back against a couch that sits a few feet away. He stays on the floor with me, his legs stretched out just behind mine. The fire crackling is hypnotic, the warmth lulls me to the brink of sleep but my thoughts won't completely fade away.

Not wanting to ruin the calmness I feel, but needing to lift a weight off my chest, I wiggle my arms out of the blanket I'm wrapped in and turn my whole body so my back is to the fire and I am facing Nathan.

I take a second to absorb my surroundings -his living space. We're in the living room of a modern, but cozy, cabin. The only light coming in is from a big front window, and the fireplace behind me, casting anything behind the living room in shadows, making it too hard to see. From what I can tell so far, everything looks new, almost untouched.

He watches me closely as my eyes explore, making me self-conscious. I fidget, using my hands as a pillow to prop my face off the floor, mustering up the courage to ask the question that has been plaguing my mind.

"What are the chances they're still coming after me?"

Nathan sighs, "It's hard to say. They're injured, I made sure of that. But depending on how far they were from where you escaped…" He pauses, but continues, "I won't know until I go back out there and track them to see which direction they went.

Sitting up from my position, I assess him. "You can't go back out there, it's too dangerous."

"I'll be fine," he grunts. "I've been in worse places." He doesn't elaborate anymore, but stands up from his place on the floor, towering over me. It doesn't startle me, but I'm surprised at how large he looks now that we're inside.

"Nathan…" I start, but he cuts me off.

"I wanted to wait and make sure you were okay, but I still have an hour or so of daylight left, I'll be back before you know it. Get some rest, you're safe here." He goes to leave but I reflexively grab his hand- Quickly dropping it once I realize what I did. He has already carried me, held me, and stripped my clothes, but holding his hand feels too personal, too intimate. He probably already thinks I'm overstepping boundaries.

"Just be careful, please," I say, my voice timid even to me. I slide his jacket off, giving it back to him to use.

He looks at me for a few moments, like he's trying to analyze me, again. His eyes are intense, and calculating, like his thoughts are moving a hundred miles a minute. Finally, he acknowledges my request, giving a quick nod before grabbing his jacket. He's out the door quickly, without putting it on.

"Bye to you too, then," I mutter to myself. He also didn't exactly confirm that he'll be careful out there. I'll just have to hope his self-preservation skills are as honed in as his damsel in distress rescue skills.

The four-wheeler starts up, the sound slowly dissipating as he gets further away. Suddenly feeling vulnerable again, alone in his cabin, I get up to make sure the door is locked, tiptoeing across the dark wood floor.

I check the deadbolt, and of course, it's locked. I should have known, he doesn't seem like the type to overlook a security detail like that.

Grabbing the blanket from the floor, I lean against the pillows on the couch, feeling more secure with it wrapped around me. Taking a few needed deep breaths, I can't fight the yawn that overtakes me. I don't want to fall asleep yet, not until I know Nathan is back and okay. It feels odd being in his home, making myself comfortable when he's back in the woods, potentially with the bad guys.

Needing a distraction, I let my eyes wander around his home again. The fireplace sits in the center of the wall directly in front of me, with two armchairs facing it on either side.

The couch sits in the middle of the large room, dividing the space. Behind me it opens up into the kitchen, and a hallway off to the side. A big island sits in the middle of the kitchen with bar stools lining it. No dining table.

All his furniture and appliances look brand new. There isn't really any decor but the space feels homey regardless, maybe because of the fireplace being the centerpiece. I look in the direction of my thoughts and watch the flames flicker around the logs. My eyelids grow heavier, struggling to stay open.

My thoughts drift to Nathan again, who he is, what he's like. His home is earthy and simplistic, but very manly. I'd wager it reflects his personality quite well, at least from the little bits I've seen from him so far.

My last thoughts as I'm dragged into sleep are about how good the blanket I'm enveloped in smells. Like the freshness of summer rainfall and cedar wood... Entirely masculine...

Chapter Ten

Nathan

I walk back in the door as the last bits of light are fading outside, dusk turning to night. I immediately see Callie curled up on the sofa with the quilt from my bed, the one I gave her earlier. I'm relieved she was able to fall asleep after the day she had, though a part of me was worried I'd be returning to an empty home. A nagging pit in my stomach plagued me the whole time I was gone, worrying that she might be frightened by me and afraid to accept my help. Her opinion of me shouldn't concern me, yet I'm already spending too much time thinking about it. I've already become consumed with too many thoughts of her.

Her slow, steady breaths draw me in, giving me the chance to examine her unabashedly. Her fair skin is flushed, her cheeks pink from the warmth of the fire. Long lashes fan down, casting a shadow across her cheekbones. In the dim light of the fire, I can't make out the freckles that I know cover the bridge of her nose, and I'm not entirely sure why, but I feel a pang of disappointment. I watch as her lips part slightly, her soft breathing deepening with her slumber. My eyes linger on the fullness of her bottom lip, remembering how it looked while she was biting it earlier. Beautiful isn't complex enough of a word to describe her. She's ethereal.

Not that her looks matter, because they don't. She needed help, I'm helping her. I need to reign in my thoughts and focus. However, it doesn't stop me from brushing a loose strand of hair away from her forehead. The light casting from the fire makes it look more red than it did outside, hmm. That could explain the fair skin and the freckles. Moving the hair off her forehead makes another bruise visible, pissing me off all over again. I can't wait to find the fuckers who did this.

The image of sneaking up behind the man from the river who threw the rocks flashes through my mind. My fingers itch to wrap around his head, twisting hard enough to snap his neck. My arms jerk just thinking about it.

Not wanting to disturb her rest and needing an excuse to stop staring at her, I quietly make my way to my bedroom to shower. The cabin's small, and only has two bedrooms, but my main suite still has its own bathroom and shower, as well as another full bathroom in the hallway. I designed it that way in case I have a guest, but not encouraging people to think my home is an open house. Namely, my mom and sister. They mean well, but I learned a long time ago to set boundaries. They're still working on it.

I'm proud of the home I've built here though. Everything was hand-picked down to the beams of wood and the nails holding them together. The lot sits in the middle of the National Forest, in the heart of the mountains, right outside city limits. I only own about five acres, but I'm surrounded by hundreds of acres of woods and mountains, giving me all the space I need to breathe and reset my life. Or, so I thought.

I enter my room and discard my clothes directly into the

tub of the washer, a perk to living alone, not needing wasted communal space for a laundry room.

Once in the bathroom I get the hot water running and step into the walk-in shower. Another thing I customized, was a large walk-in with a stone bench and stone walls made of river rock.

I stand under the hot spray, letting it beat down on my neck and back. It doesn't help ease the tension though. I wipe my hand across my face contemplating what to do next.

When I went back to the clearing where I first saw Callie, I did my best to pinpoint exactly where I wounded both of the men. I found some traces of blood on the river bank where the short guy was, the one I shot when he was throwing rocks. My fingers twitch again thinking about getting my hands on him.

I followed his blood and it headed in the direction where the primary guy had been standing in the tree line with the gun. He's the one I really want to get a hold of. He almost killed her.

Their blood wasn't excessive though, it was only enough for me to track about 100 yards before I lost the trail. It means both of them weren't badly wounded and are long gone.

I lean over, bracing both of my hands against the shower wall, hanging my head. I don't know what's worse, telling Callie that the two guys who took her aren't dead or that without more information there is no way for me to find them. She deserves justice. Even if I don't ever get my hands on them, they deserve to rot in prison. Which reminds me that I still need to call the local Sheriff's department and let them know what happened. Fuck, this is a mess.

The thought of handing Callie off to a Sheriff puts a knot

in my chest, it feels like it's too soon to say goodbye. I feel responsible for her now, and I don't think she's safe yet. A deeper part of me just feels possessive over her. She chose to trust me, and I don't take that gift lightly. Trust is the difference between life and death where I come from, and even then, sometimes it's not enough to save someone.

Hell, she might not even be telling me the whole truth. I've put my neck out to help this girl and she could be lying about who she is, or her involvement. I don't think that's the case, I'm usually a pretty good judge of character, but it wouldn't be unheard of for a man to blindly follow a woman as gorgeous as she is. Her fear was too real, her tears too genuine, I don't think she's lying about anything, but I need to watch myself just in case.

Shaking off my thoughts of how goddamn pretty she is and how good she felt in my arms earlier, I finish my shower under a cold spray.

Deciding not to delay things any longer, I get ready knowing I need to talk to Callie, get some more answers, and discuss a plan.

Getting a t-shirt and some sweatpants out of my walk-in closet, I decide to grab a couple of things for Callie in case she wants fresh clothes once she wakes up. I walk back into the living room to find her still sleeping. Looking at her peaceful state I can't bring myself to wake her yet, so I decide to make some food since I haven't eaten all day. We'll eat. Then we'll talk.

* * *

I'm dumping pasta into the boiling water when the tingling on the back of my neck alerts me that she's awake. I continue stirring the noodles and dump a jar of spaghetti sauce into a pot on the stove, not sure how to start a conversation with her.

After I hear the faint sound of her clearing her throat, I finally turn around, trying not to act as awkward as I feel. I'm not used to having guests, my culinary efforts are proof of that.

"Which door is the bathroom?" She asks meekly. I realize as she stands there wrapped in the blanket that she isn't wearing pants.

"Here," I grab the pile of clothes off the bar stool that I brought from my closet and head down the hallway, "I know they won't fit but I thought you'd want some clean clothes until I can wash yours." I stop in the middle of the hallway and open the door to the right, setting the clothes down on the bathroom counter.

"If you want to take a shower, the towels are in the cabinet," I say as she eyeballs the tub longingly, her actions speaking for her as she slides past me into the bathroom. Our bodies don't make any contact, yet I feel her nearness like an electric current.

"Take your time, I'll save a plate for you when you're ready," I ground out, shutting the door. I blow out a deep breath before I turn to head back to the kitchen, overanalyzing our one-sided conversation as I walk away. I hear the lock click on the bathroom door. Not surprising after the day she's had that she might still be wary of being alone in a stranger's home. She doesn't know me, not truly, but I plan to make sure she feels safe as long as she's with me.

Chapter Eleven

Callie

I was so glad to see Nathan was back, though I was a little startled that he came in without me noticing. From the look of his dampened hair, I slept through him coming home and showering, only waking up once he was banging around in the kitchen. My stomach must have been more demanding than my need for sleep.

Now I am standing in his bathroom, not sure what to do. Well, pee, I definitely need to pee, but showering seems like a daunting task. I need to shower all the dirt and grime off of me though, so I might as well just get it over with. I strip the remainder of my clothes, suddenly feeling exposed even in the privacy of the bathroom. I make sure the door is locked one more time. I don't think Nathan would walk in on me, but it makes me feel better regardless.

Turning towards the vanity, I see myself in the mirror for the first time. I'm frozen for a second, looking at a reflection that I don't recognize. I look crazy.

My hair is a mess, so I tug on the hair tie, letting my auburn locks fall down my back. My temple is bruised from Tony's boot, and my lip is cut from who knows what.

Afraid critiquing myself anymore will make me cry again, I shift my focus. I poke through the cabinets until I find a towel, seeing a toothbrush and a couple of other travel-sized products still in their packaging, so I pull them out too. I'll pay Nathan back for the stuff I use, but the chance to use toothpaste and deodorant is too good to pass up.

I turn the water on and pull back the curtain to step into the tub. Noticing this isn't a standard-sized shower, the tub is more of a jacuzzi-type thing. I have always envied people who had bathtubs big enough to actually soak in. I mourn the chance to use it, knowing my muscles are going to ache tomorrow. But, I need to get in and out, I don't want to take advantage of Nathan's kindness. I'm already stealing his hygiene products.

While rinsing my hair, I realize how sore my wrists are. The hot water is making my raw skin sting, so I try my best to keep it out of the direct spray. Everything is sensitive, the skin on my forehead, my lip, the scrapes, and bruises all down my arms and legs. It could be worse, I could be dead right now. The thought makes me want to sob. I've never felt so mentally and physically fragile like the smallest thing might break me. Wary of my thoughts, I busy myself with showering before I end up as a puddle in the bottom of the tub.

A couple of bottles lining the shelf built into the wall of the shower catch my eye. Shampoo, conditioner, body wash, shaving cream, and a pink razor… I'm dumbfounded for a second, of course, a woman lives here. All of these products are women's, and I don't know why I hadn't thought about it before. Suddenly feeling like I am invading someone's space, I quickly use a little of each product, rushing through the process, feeling wrong about being here in another woman's home. Why wouldn't Nathan mention that?

Getting out, I try to dry off as best as I can without rubbing the towel against my sore spots, twisting it on top of my head to soak up the wetness in my hair. I pick through the clothes on the counter, feeling weird about wearing Nathan's clothes if he does have a wife or a girlfriend.

I wouldn't want my significant other loaning out their clothes to some woman I've never met, but I also didn't choose to be here. I'm doing the best I can with the hand I was dealt. Still, this whole situation is making me sick to my stomach. I feel like such an inconvenience, like an intruder in someone's home.

Begrudgingly, I pick up the black hooded sweatshirt, underneath it is a gray ARMY t-shirt. That makes sense, him being in the Army, and why he seemed so skilled back in the woods. I put on the t-shirt, then the hoody. There are track shorts, an army green color, and some sweatpants that match the black hoody. I choose the shorts, they'll fit better and be easier to wear, because the sweatpants look way too big.

I have to pull the drawstring as tight as it will go, and fold over the band of the shorts, but they seem to stay put, the mesh fabric stopping about mid-thigh. Putting on a pair of black socks that he left, I can't help but appreciate his hospitality. He didn't have to help me and he doesn't need to continue helping me. I'm thankful for it though, and I owe him my life.

Exiting the bathroom to meet him back in the kitchen, I try not to feel self-conscious about being here. Nathan is sitting on one of the bar stools, talking on the phone when I walk up, talking back and forth with someone.

Needing to busy myself while he finishes his call, I pull the towel off my head and continue drying my wet ends.

"...I'm not exactly sure where the incident took place, and neither is she. It started somewhere along the interstate... Yes, I-83. I intercepted them about a mile from access road 27... I was hunting... Yes, she's safe with me... Tomorrow... Okay, I'll call in the morning." He hangs up with a shake of his head, spinning his phone in circles on the countertop like he's still processing the call.

"Everything okay?" I ask, tentatively.

Of course, he doesn't seem surprised that I'm standing behind him like he sensed my presence, but he also doesn't turn to acknowledge me. I fidget with the towel in my hands, not sure what else to do or say.

"I called the county Sheriff's office to report what happened, but the Sheriff has already gone home for the evening. The deputy I just talked to said to call in the morning because he is the only one on duty. Apparently, he only handles emergencies, and doesn't take reports." Nathan finally stops his fidgeting, glancing my way, his eyes lingering on my clothes. Raking his gaze back to my face, I look away before his eyes meet mine, feeling a little awkward.

"He didn't even want to talk to me?" I ask, suddenly fixated on a speckle on the wood floor. I wasn't expecting the lack of urgency from the police after being kidnapped and assaulted. My mind races, unsure of what this means for me.

"Honestly, he sounded like he could be a teenager. I've never encountered the Sheriff's department, I've only lived here two months, but it must be a small town thing." He seems more confused about it than me.

"I can stay at a hotel for the night, you've done more than enough," I tell him, but my voice is weak and I still can't meet his eyes.

"Absolutely not." He sounds offended that I'd even mention it. I'd be lying if I said I wasn't relieved. The thought of leaving and going to a hotel at this point sounds miserable.

"I opened some of the products in your bathroom. I'll replace them or pay you back, I promise. I don't want to be a burden on you," I admit sheepishly.

"Callie, I don't give a shit about that stuff. You can use whatever you want. And you aren't paying me back." He gets up and rounds the island, grabbing a plate of spaghetti out of the microwave.

"Here, sit, eat. Stop overthinking everything. I'm helping you. You are going to accept my help, and not fight it. Got it?" He questions, mimicking his commands from earlier in the day. His insistence dampens some of the unease in my stomach, helping me relax.

"Got it." I scoot onto the bar stool, aware of every little noise I make with how silent it is. He stays standing, elbows leaning on the island opposite me, watching me. I realize he is waiting for me to eat my food. Just as he told me to. I pick up my fork, and take a bite, finally making direct eye contact with him.

"Happy now?" I ask, faking the courage I don't have. His undivided attention is intense, making the knots in my stomach tighten for other reasons. Even if he is married, I'm not blind, he's more attractive than any man should be. His attention makes me nervous. His dark eyes always seem to be searing into my soul.

"Almost." He responds with a gesture indicating he wants me to eat more. So I do. I don't know if it's delicious, or if I was just starving, but once I start eating again I don't stop until my plate is cleared. He stands there watching me the whole time. Normally, that would make me self-conscious, but I was too hungry to care. As soon as I finish my last bite, he takes my dishes and rinses them in the sink.

"I could have done that," I say. Nathan glances back in my direction giving me a "really" type of look. I'm not used to being taken care of, it's difficult to fight the impulse to do everything myself. I don't care what he says, I'll make everything up to him eventually. He's already done more than I could ever ask for.

"Do you mind if I use your phone?" I ask him. "My mom is probably worried about me. I was supposed to be home hours ago."

Chapter Twelve

Nathan

U nlocking my cell phone, I hand it to her, "Where's home?"

I don't know anything about this woman sitting in my home, eating the food I cooked, wearing my clothes. Looking damn good in them. I force my brain to backpedal out of that thought.

"Tennessee," she answers with a sad smile. "I was in Georgia for a few months, but my family is in Tennessee."

She dials the number she needs, walking over towards the couch while it rings, leaving me wondering why her answer seemed so sad. I turn towards the kitchen sink, trying to give her some privacy, but with no walls, it's hard not to overhear.

"Hi, Mom, it's me... Yes, I'm fine... I'm sorry I didn't call sooner, my phone died... No, I'm in North Carolina. My car broke down and I had to get a tow." She glances in my direction when she notices me looking at her now. I'm wondering why she lied, but she just shakes her head in my direction, continuing her conversation.

"I'm okay, really... No, I don't need you to come get me. I'm staying at a Bed & Breakfast here in the mountains." Glancing in my direction again, she shrugs.

"It's really nice, I might stay a few days... I accidently left my charger in my car so I'll get a new one tomorrow and call you back with an update... I'm using the B&B owner's phone... Yes, he's been very accommodating. Him and his wife."

This time her eyes beam in my direction. Not sure what that's about, or the wife comment. But I just raise my brow at her and turn back to the dishes.

"I'll call you tomorrow... Okay, love you too." She ends the call with a sigh, walking back towards the kitchen. I watch as she places my phone on the kitchen island, sliding it a couple of inches towards me with a nearly silent, "Thank you."

Waiting for an explanation for her fabricated story, I ask, "Me and my wife?"

"I didn't want to worry her by thinking I was alone in the mountains with a strange man. Plus, I don't know, you could have a wife." She speaks toward the countertop, not looking me in the face.

"What makes you think I have a wife?" I'm curious as to where this idea is coming from, because glancing around, this definitely looks like a bachelor pad. At least, according to my sister.

"Your bathroom is filled with women's beauty products. I don't take you for the type to use Cherry Blossom Pomegranate shampoo." Before I can respond, she continues, "It's okay if you do, I just need to know if I am overstepping in another woman's home. Using all her soap and wearing her husband's clothes is not cool. Even in a situation as messed up as mine." She looks at me then, her eyes focused intently on mine, searching for an answer.

I can't help the gruff laugh that escapes me. How sweet that she is worried about making my imaginary wife upset. Ridiculous, but sweet. It shows her character, another thing I am becoming acquainted with. Like the way she averted the truth to her mom, not wanting to worry her, she probably makes of habit of putting others' feelings before her own.

"No wife, I promise." I raise my left hand, showing my bare ring finger. She seems to visibly relax after that.

"So, you do like girly shampoo?" She asks with the most confused expression on her face like she is trying to solve a riddle. Smirking at her expense, I let her sit with her confusion for a few seconds before explaining.

"I don't mind it, but no it's not mine. My mom and sister stayed here before I moved in, making it livable." I shrug, "They left their stuff here, making it obvious that I'm supposed to let them visit."

"Oh. Well, that was nice of them," she says sheepishly, her voice soft.

"Yeah, nice. They had a field day with my credit card," I grunt, "but I didn't have to mess with it, so I didn't really mind."

She finally gives me a small smile and nods her head. Seemingly accepting my explanation of everything. She moves back over to the couch, collapsing into the cushions.

"Anything else I should know before my brain shuts down for the rest of my life…" Her head is leaned back, eyes closed, the perfect picture of exhaustion. I wipe my hand across my face, deciding to bite the bullet and fill her in on what else I know.

"Uhh, yeah I need to tell you what I found back in the woods," I say, waiting to see whether I should continue or not.

She sits up taller and looks at me as I round the couch to sit in one of the armchairs. She nods her head, so I take it as the signal to continue.

"They're still out there somewhere. There wasn't enough blood to indicate that they bled out after I shot them, so it's likely that they're not dead. I'm sorry, Callie." I wring my hands together, not sure how she'll handle that news.

She fiddles with the sleeves of her sweatshirt- my sweatshirt, folding her legs under her. Her hair has mostly dried now, leaving wild strands of curls falling over her shoulder. I thought her hair was dark before, but in the light of the fire, the waves shine like copper. God, she's beautiful. I'm itching to tuck the loose pieces away from her face, so I can see her more clearly.

"Do you think they're going to come after me, Nathan?" Her voice quivered as she asked. I can't help it, I move over to the couch to sit next to her, feeling the need to comfort her. I keep my hands clasped together on my knees, not wanting to overstep by touching her.

"I don't know what their plan is, but it would help if I knew more about what happened to you. More details could give me a clue of what they're capable of." I wait for her response, watching her drum her fingers against her lips.

After a couple of minutes, I give up on her telling me anything, accepting that all I can offer right now is my presence. To continue reminding her that she is safe. I stare into the fire, lost in my thoughts. Realizing that it's been quite a few hours since I first saw Callie, it seems like a lot has changed in that span of time.

"I'm sorry, I don't know where to begin." She sighs, pulling me out of my thoughts.

"From the beginning, any detail you can remember," I prompt.

So, she does. Step by step she fills me in on what they wore, how they spoke to her, how they spoke to each other. She tells me about the type of supplies they had in their van, indicating what type of work they probably did. When she started describing the one called "Bub", the short one, and how he attacked her and almost raped her, I had to clench my fists to school my reaction.

I try to stay calm, but the rage burns inside me hearing about what they did to her. An innocent human being, assaulted and chased down like an animal. It's inexcusable, they deserve to die for what they did.

When she chokes back a sob I can't control it any longer, I wrap my arms around her, pulling her head into my chest. She lets me hold her while she finishes telling me the rest. Once she's done talking, she doesn't pull away from me and I'm glad. Holding her like this gives me a false sense of control over this whole damn situation.

"I thought I was going to die. I looked right into the barrel of Tony's gun and thought that it was the last thing I was ever going to see. That sick twisted pervert was going to torture me before he killed me, I just know it," she sobs. I wrap my arms around her tighter, resting my chin on top of her head, desperate to blanket her in security, to ease her pain in some way.

"I wanted to put a bullet between his eyes when I saw him pointing that gun at you, but I was too far away. If I was even 20 yards closer, he would be a dead man. They both would have been. I'm sorry." I can't go back and change it now, but I'm still pissed about it. She pulls her head back to look at me.

"I didn't know what was happening yet. When he backed off I just got up and ran straight into the river. I didn't care if it was too deep, or too cold, I was willing to risk getting carried away in the current and drowning just to get away from them. Then I made it across and thought it was a miracle I hadn't been shot yet. But it was you, you were the miracle." She wraps her arms around my neck urgently, embracing me.

I hold her tightly, one hand around her back, the other on the back of her neck, offering as much strength as I can give her. Thinking of how scared she was, how willing she was to die instead of being caught by them... It solidifies my need to find the fuckers and kill them before they can hurt her or anyone else again.

Chapter Thirteen

Callie

It's too much, every emotion I've felt today is too heavy. I am going to fall to pieces at any moment. The only thing keeping me together is the hold Nathan has on me. I'm afraid if I let go of him, I'll lose the only thing that hasn't threatened to break me. I know my tears are soaking through his t-shirt but he doesn't let me go, he doesn't loosen his grip on me. If he holds me tight enough and long enough, all of my broken pieces might fuse back together.

It's hard to say how much time passes, with us molded together on his couch, but my brain finally quiets enough that I feel a sense of peace again. Easing out of Nathan's arms, my muscles are stiff but I force them to move. He hesitates, not loosening his grip for a moment, but once he realizes my intention he lets me go. I miss his embrace instantly, but I feel pretty foolish for breaking down on him. He has seen more tears from me today than I've cried in front of anyone. At least not since I was a child.

"I'm sorry for crying, and for getting your shirt wet," I say, wiping my wet cheeks.

"Don't apologize. Never for that." He looks at me so

seriously that I truly believe him. Never in my life has there been anyone to let me feel things so deeply, and with no apology for it. How is it possible that Nathan can elicit that from me within half a day? Is this some trauma bond we have together?

Maybe it's the forced vulnerability, maybe I am just out of my mind exhausted, but I don't think this connection we have is just circumstance. I push my hair behind my ears, suddenly feeling overwhelmed by my thoughts. My stinging wrists distract me. I hiss in pain as I move my sleeves up to my elbows, examining the raw skin the zip ties left behind.

"Shit, Callie. Stay right here, let me get something so they don't get infected." His concern warms me from the inside out. Is this how it feels to have someone truly care about you? I shake those thoughts away as quickly as they come. My ex did more damage than I thought if receiving basic compassion feels so unusual.

Nathan gets up and moves towards the hall bathroom, quickly returning with supplies. He sits down next to me again, so close that our knees touch. Grabbing my right hand hesitantly, he takes his time applying a thin layer of healing ointment, then wrapping it in a layer of gauze. He lays my hand down gently on my knee, repeating the same process for my left.

It hurts a little as he does it but I'm more distracted by his hand holding mine. I can feel the rough skin of his fingers against the back of my hand, his thumb pressed into my palm holding me steady. I can see the calluses on his palms from years of use. He twists my hand over slightly, steadily applying ointment to my left wrist. My eyes follow the veins on the tops of his hands that run up his forearms.

His forearms and biceps are strong, obviously so, but not in a way created at the gym, but by years of hard work. I haven't asked about his life in the Army, but I imagine he wasn't sitting behind a desk much. The way he holds himself and how calmly he behaved while saving me today, makes me believe he's seen some things.

My eyes drift to his broad chest, even through his shirt I can tell how solid he is. Nathan oozes strength. He could easily overpower me but I haven't felt an ounce of fear with him. Such a powerful man, and yet he has the lightest touch when handling me. He has shown me nothing but kindness and understanding during the most stressful day of my life.

I guess I'm not the best judge of character, Mark had me fooled long enough, but something in my gut tells me that Nathan is not that type of person. I do believe he is dangerous, deadly even, but not to me. He was willing to gun down those men before he even knew my name, not thinking twice about it. It probably wouldn't have been the first time he took a life.

My eyes continue up their path until I am looking right into Nathan's eyes. Not realizing he had stopped working on my wrists, he's watching me watch him. I should look away, and apologize for staring. But I don't, and I don't feel the need to. He's still holding onto my left hand and I realize I've absently curled my fingers around his thumb at some point.

I look down at our hands, drawing his attention there as well. He clears his throat, "You're all set. Keep your wrists clean and they should heal soon."

He slides his hand away from mine and stands up, taking the medical supplies back to the bathroom. As soon as he leaves the room I feel the oxygen return to my brain. What am I doing?

I need to sleep. I am behaving recklessly and not thinking clearly. Getting caught ogling a man I barely know. How embarrassing... He has done so much for me, it's probably natural for me to be developing feelings of admiration for him. It's just simple psychology. That's all.

"It's getting late. We'll want to get a hold of the Sheriff first thing in the morning and figure out what happened to your car. I got clean sheets on the bed if you want to follow me," he says from the hallway. He probably doesn't want to get within reach of me so I don't try holding his hand again. I'm so embarrassed.

I get up from the couch and follow him, trying not to make it more awkward even though I feel my cheeks flaming. He leads me to the end of the hallway, into what I would assume is his room. He seems to notice my confusion.

"I don't have a bed in the spare room yet, you can have mine. I'll sleep on the couch," he explains, grabbing a pillow and blanket for himself out of the closet.

"Nathan I can't take your bed. You've already done too much," I try to argue.

"You're injured and you're in an unfamiliar place, the bed will be more comfortable. I'll be fine on the couch," he insists. Sensing I'm not ready to give in, he interjects, "I won't be able to sleep if I know you're in the living room alone, Callie."

I clamp my mouth shut, stopping any excuse I have to make him take his bed back. The unspoken elephant in the room is that I'm not safe. Tony and Bub are still alive, so I might still be in danger. All I can manage is a nod, acknowledging him and my unsaid thoughts.

Walking over to the bed, I sit on the edge, defeat weighing down on me, all the way to my bones. Twenty-four hours

80

ago I was a normal girl, living a normal life, going through a rough break up. The only tears I expected to cry today were to the sappy love songs playing during my road trip home.

Nathan stands in the doorway, holding onto the handle like he isn't sure if he should stay or go. I'm not sure if I want him to stay or go either. It's so conflicting, accepting that I enjoy having him around but knowing that this is only temporary. I can't rely on him too much, because once I leave I'll be on my own again, like usual.

"If you need anything…" His sentence trails off. I give another nod in his direction. He closes the door and I listen to his footsteps fading down the hallway.

Suddenly feeling too warm, I take off the hooded sweatshirt and throw it over the bedpost at the foot of the bed. Still wearing Nathan's Army t-shirt and shorts, I peel back the blankets and crawl into the bed. I stare at the ceiling, for what feels like hours. Without my phone, and no clock in the room, there is no way for me to tell what time it is.

My mind is racing but I can't focus on any specific thought. It's like I'm stuck in a small room with a million people, being pushed and pulled in every direction, but never making it any closer to the door.

Giving up on solving any of my life problems tonight, I turn over and bury my head in Nathan's pillow, forcing myself to fall asleep knowing tomorrow will be another stress-filled day. The last thing I remember thinking before drifting to sleep is how much I enjoy the smell of his pillow, the smell of him.

Chapter Fourteen

Nathan

What the fuck am I doing? I left Callie alone in my room when I knew she wasn't okay. I could see the way her shoulders sagged, and I still turned and walked away. I'm a coward. When I was applying the bandage to her wrists I could feel her eyes on me, studying me. I felt it as intensely as if she were touching me, and when she gripped my hand so delicately, I felt like I'd been donkey-kicked in the chest. I ran away from it and was afraid if I got within reach again I wasn't going to be able to stop myself from touching her, holding her, wanting her.

I know I can't have her. She has been through too much and I refuse to make her feel like my help comes with strings attached. I blow out the breath I've been holding. What a fuckin' day.

I close my eyes and listen to the last remnants of the fire crackling. The couch is comfortable and I'd normally have no problem sleeping, but my thoughts keep drifting back to my house guest. Knowing she is lying in my bed, wearing my clothes... fuck me. Maybe this is a curse, the universe handed me the most beautiful woman I've ever laid eyes on, and there

82

is no way I can have her. Maybe all that I'm meant to do is to help get her back on her feet, repentance for all the shit I've done wrong in my life.

I spend the next few hours sleeping restlessly. I even dream about Chester for the first time in months. We were at the bar again, sitting next to each other drinking beer...

"You think you'll ever get married, Nate?"

"Doubt it. I don't think I'm the marrying type."

"Why not?"

"I don't know what the hell I want with my life. How am I supposed to bring a wife into that? A family? I'd fuck it up for sure."

Chester laughs, ordering us another round of beers, "You're a good guy, you won't fuck it up because you're too stubborn to lose. Trust me, I've been runner-up to you too many times to count."

I laugh, punching his shoulder. "I guess if you're there to tell me when I'm fucking things up, I'll be okay."

* * *

I wake up around 6 a.m. feeling the familiar ache in my chest that I get after thinking about my old friend. With no chance of falling back asleep, I decided to slip into my room to get fresh clothes.

I quietly open the bedroom door and look inside, making sure Callie's still asleep. She's curled up on my side of the bed with the sheets tangled around her legs, her arms are wrapped tightly around herself. Unable to help myself, I silently walk over and lift the blankets up to her shoulders, thinking she might be cold. She stirs slightly but doesn't wake up. Even in her sleep, she exudes a feeling from me that I'm not ready to face. I've never ached to lay in my bed like I do right now though, and it has everything to do with her.

I force myself over to my walk-in closet, shutting the door behind me quietly, the light flickering on automatically once I'm inside. Changing into jeans and a t-shirt, I pull out my sig, and the holster. I'm not sure where the events of today will lead us, but I'm not one to leave the house unprepared.

Tucking my gun into the holster inside the front of my waistband, it slides into place with a click. I'm pulling on my boots when I hear my name from inside my room, "Nathan?"

"Sorry, I was trying to be quiet so I wouldn't wake you up," I say, exiting the closet. She is sitting up clutching the blankets to her chest. Her hair is even wilder than it was last night. She looks tired still, her eyes slightly puffy and red, probably from all the crying yesterday. The bruise on her forehead is purple, but it looks like it's starting to heal. Aside from the cut on her lip that already looks to be healing too, she looks perfect. From injuries... perfect from injuries.

"My whole body hurts. I feel like I got run over by a bus," her voice still gravely from sleep.

"I was afraid that was gonna happen. How's your head feeling?" I ask. She tentatively reaches up and touches her bruise, but doesn't flinch which is a good sign.

"I have a little bit of a headache, but it's okay." She offers a sleepy smile that just about knocks me on my ass. What I would do to see her smile at me again and again? Fuck. I can't think like that. I leave the room to retrieve some pain reliever, needing a distraction so I stop staring at her.

"Take two of these and try to get some more sleep, it's still pretty early. I'll call the Sheriff's office around 8 a.m. to see if I can get in touch with someone about coming in to talk." I hand her the pills, "Do you want water? Or I can get you some orange juice."

"Orange juice would be great, thank you," she stretches, groaning in discomfort, causing the t-shirt to ride up, exposing her bare stomach. I try not to let her notice how my breath catches in my throat, so I quickly leave the room again to get a glass from the kitchen. I've never run away from anyone in my life, like a scared kid.

Put me in any hostile situation and I'll face it head on with a cool head. Tell me to jump out of a helicopter, I'll jump without any concern. Raid a bunker that houses a terrorist organization? Gladly. Communicate with a traumatized human being who looks like she could be the embodiment of all the good in this world when all I know is the bad? Totally foreign to me.

When I get back to the room she looks like she is zoned out, staring in the direction of the floor, but not focused on anything. I've seen that look before, from soldiers who have been through some terrible shit. I sit down on the edge of the bed, refusing to stay ten feet away from her anymore.

"You okay?" That is all I can come up with as I hand her the juice. She snaps out of it quickly, returning to reality.

"Yeah, I'm fine." Another soft smile.

"You don't have to fake it for me. If you aren't fine, it's okay. You went through hell yesterday. I've seen well-trained men go catatonic for days after being shot at, let alone having the barrel of a gun pointed in their face," I tell her honestly.

She takes a moment to swallow the pain pills back with her drink, "I think the only reason I haven't completely fallen apart is you."

I'm taken aback by that, not sure what to say. "I just got lucky being there at the right place, right time. You're stronger than you know," I tell her.

"I don't feel strong," she says with a tight voice. We sit in silence as she finishes her orange juice and sets the glass on the side table next to the bed.

"Try to get some more sleep, your body still needs to recuperate." I stand up, preparing to leave the room. Afraid if I stay, I won't be able to stop myself from touching her in some way. She's like a magnet I'm constantly feeling pulled towards.

"Will you stay with me?" She asks, her voice even quieter than the last time she spoke. It stops me in my tracks. I shouldn't stay, but there is no amount of willpower that could make me reject her.

"I'll stay," I respond, silencing the battle in my head telling me I shouldn't.

Instead of sitting next to her on the edge like before, I move to the other side of the bed so she can stretch her legs back out. Navigating this as appropriately as I can manage, I lay on my back on top of the blankets, hands on my stomach so I don't accidentally touch her. I feel the mattress shift as her body turns over in the bed, facing me now. I sense her eyes on the side of my face, but I continue staring straight ahead at the ceiling. Not looking at her is the hardest test of my strength, knowing how closely it would put our faces.

"I feel better with you here, with me," she whispers just loud enough to reach my ears. I can't help it, I turn my head to look at her. Her eyes are closed, and her face looks peaceful, even though I know she hasn't fallen asleep yet. She could open her eyes at any second, but I keep looking at her. My hands ache to touch her, brush the hair off of her face, and run my thumb across her cheek to feel how soft it is. But I won't, I'll live in this torture if it means she is content and feels safe.

I watch as her breathing slows and each muscle of her face starts relaxing as she falls asleep. I should get up. Go get something productive done, but I don't. I kick off the boots I just put on, deciding to soak in this feeling that I'm not accustomed to. Peace.

Once I give in and close my eyes, sleep comes quickly. The sound of Callie's soft breathing next to me is more potent than a damn lullaby.

Chapter Fifteen

Callie

My eyes are closed but I'm cognizant of the thoughts telling me to get up, like an internal alarm clock. My lids creep open against the light coming into the room from the window, making me bury my face deeper into my pillow. I'm confused immediately when my pillow doesn't feel like my own, and it's hard... Because it's not my pillow at all, it's Nathan's arm.

I know I wasn't this close to him when I fell asleep, I must have moved closer subconsciously. He's in the same position he was in when he first laid down, so it's definitely my fault. I look up at his face, making sure he is still sleeping and not aware of my unsolicited cuddling, luckily his eyes are closed.

He looks peaceful. His normally serious expression is relaxed. The hard plains of his face almost look soft. I don't know why I suddenly have the urge to run my fingers across the stubble on his jaw, but I have to physically remove myself from the bed to keep my hands to myself. Every muscle in my body is sore and my joints are stiff, but the pain reliever seemed to have dulled my headache.

Deciding to brush my teeth and do a couple of other things

to feel a little more human, I raid the cabinets in the spare bathroom. Finding stuff to tame my hair, I mentally thank Nathan's sister and mother for leaving this stuff behind. I slip a hair tie on my wrist in case I need it later, but I'm not eager to wear my hair in a ponytail again anytime soon. The feeling of almost having it ripped from my scalp has stayed with me more than the pain of my other injuries.

After splashing cold water on my puffy face, I brace my hands on the counter, looking at myself in the mirror. This version of myself that's new to me. Changed.

I survived yesterday, so I can get through today, no matter what happens. Unfortunately, I have a feeling talking to strangers about what happened to me is going to rip open all the emotional wounds Nathan has helped me heal so far.

Walking back into the bedroom, I'm startled when I see that he's sitting up and putting his shoes on, no longer asleep. Suddenly, feeling underdressed in just his t-shirt since I'm not wearing a bra, I throw the hoodie back on that I left on the bedpost.

"Hi," is all I can think to say, feeling shy.

"Are you feeling any better?" He asks, his deep voice calms me immediately, turning my nerves into butterflies.

"I'm still pretty sore, but I feel okay. Really," I confirm as he studies me trying to figure out if I'm telling the truth or not. I think I might melt under his gaze.

He nods his head, accepting my answer. I stand there awkwardly as he stands up and disappears down the hallway. I feel so lost, and I don't know what to do. I've never been in a situation like this where I feel so helpless. No car, no phone, no money. Do I offer to make him breakfast as a thank you? How do you repay someone when you have nothing?

He acts like and has said he doesn't expect anything from me. I'd be doomed if he wasn't so generous. Just as I am thinking that he walks in holding my dirty clothes from yesterday, throwing them into a washing machine that I hadn't noticed behind another closed door.

"I could have done that," I tell him, but he gives me that look. The look telling me not to even try arguing with him. So, I don't.

I wonder if he is always like this, or if it's a trait he picked up in the Army. Taking care of people, helping people in need, being bossy... I'm starting to feel like he's not used to anyone arguing with him.

"I'm gonna go ahead and call into the Sheriff's office again, see what he wants to do. Then we can figure out your car." His voice breaks me out of my thoughts, "You can check the closet in the spare room and see if my sister left any clothes here. I wouldn't put it past her to have a stash, but I haven't been through the drawers in there to check."

He starts towards the hallway again but turns to look back at me. "You're also welcome to any of my clothes. They're probably too big, but you can wear whatever. The stuff you have on now was from when I first enlisted. I was 18 and pretty scrawny then." He rubs the back of his neck with his hand, a seemingly nervous gesture, but I think it's cute.

For the first time, it hits me that I am probably making him nervous by being here. Not because he doesn't want to help, but because he hasn't been in a situation like this either. We are both doing our best to navigate this, and that makes me feel comforted somehow. Unless he makes a habit of helping women in the woods... but based on how he's acting, it's not likely.

"I'll see what I can find… Thank you." I smile at him softly but, genuinely. I feel the need to reassure him somehow. He gives me a curt nod and heads toward the living room. I stand still for a few seconds not sure what to do. I decided to check for clothes in the spare room, hoping that his sister left something comfortable and somewhat in my size.

The room is empty, aside from the small dresser and a couple of boxes. Checking the closet first, I don't find anything hanging, just some linens folded on the top shelf. The dresser next to it is more successful, housing a pair of women's socks, black leggings, and a sports bra that will be a size too small but will work for the time being.

The faded pair of jeans in the bottom drawer make me believe that Nathan's sister is at least a few inches shorter than I am, and a fan of Christmas based on the sweaters folded up in a neat stack. Not wanting to wear a snowman sweater in November, I leave the rest of his sister's clothes where they are and try my luck in Nathan's room.

I step into his closet, this one much bigger than the spare room closet. He doesn't have a ton of clothes, and most everything is a shade of black, green, or navy. I assume I'll find something that will work, but my curiosity leads me to peek through the dresser that sits off to the side, opposite the hanging clothes.

The typical stuff fills the top four drawers, but I'm shocked when I see the bottom two filled with medals, awards, and pictures. I don't touch anything, but I can tell just from the surface that Nathan is a decorated hero.

There are a couple of framed photos of a group of soldiers who hardly look indistinguishable from one another with their shaved heads and uniforms on, but another photo that stands out is a much younger version of Nathan with two guys his age. They have on regular clothes, and they're standing by a pool table.

I wonder why these are stored in his dresser and not on display somewhere in his living room. I hear the door to his bedroom creak open, and not wanting to be caught snooping I silently close the drawer and stand up as fast as I can.

"I'm gonna make some food. Come to the kitchen whenever you're ready," he says from the entrance to his room. I let out the breath I was holding, glad he didn't come over to the closet to check on me. He'd see the guilty look on my face, and then kick me out of his house for invading his privacy.

I need to stay in my lane, but I'm dying to ask him all about his life. It's not my business though, and we're not friends, I mean not really. Even thinking that in my head causes a pang in my chest. Has it really only been one day of knowing each other? Am I able to call someone who is practically a stranger my friend? Not likely. I'm getting way too emotionally invested in someone who probably can't wait to get rid of me.

At that thought, I hurriedly browse through his clothes, finding a crew neck sweatshirt that will be big on me, but perfectly oversized once I have it on with the leggings. It's dark green with a logo in the middle, signifying a wounded warrior 5k. Of course, he does charity runs, he's the perfect man. I roll my eyes to myself. It doesn't matter how perfect he is, it does not concern me.

But, even I can't quite convince myself of that lie…

Chapter Sixteen

Nathan

Callie walks into the kitchen and sits down on one of the bar stools. She's wearing another shirt of mine and I can't help the satisfaction it brings me. I'm sure she didn't have any other options, but that doesn't stop me from being pleased about it. I finish plating toast and eggs and hand one over to her. She digs in immediately, dismissing any worries that she might not like my food. I'm getting low on options and need to pick up some things when we go into town today.

"The Sheriff isn't available to meet until 3 o'clock." She pauses mid-bite after she processes what I said, setting her fork down.

"Am I crazy, or wouldn't you think he'd be more eager to meet with me? I was almost raped and killed right outside of town!" She looks at me incredulously. I swear I feel my eyes twitch at the *raped and killed* part, but I swallow back my anger. I hate even hearing those words associated with her.

"You're not crazy. I was pretty hot-headed with the secretary I talked to. I asked to speak to the Sheriff directly, but after waiting on hold for five minutes all she could tell me was to come in this afternoon. I ended the call more abruptly than I should have." I shrug, not mentioning the string of expletives I used before hanging up.

"So, now what?" She asks me.

"Finish your food. Then we will go get your car," I point to her plate, indicating we aren't leaving until she eats.

"Yes, sir." She mocks, her nose crinkling with a smile.

I know she's joking, but those two words stir something in me... Something that crosses the line from platonic to much more, but the thought of her using that phrase in a different context... My mind is deep in the gutter.

Shit. I need a cold shower, and all she did was innocently utter two words. Two words that have a deeper meaning to perverts like me apparently. Luckily she doesn't notice my inner turmoil. She finishes her food and I realize I haven't touched mine so I scarf it down quickly, barely tasting it.

"Where did you put my shoes last night? Do you think they're dry?" She asks, looking around.

"By the fireplace, the heat should have gotten them dry by now." As she gets up to retrieve them, I'm glad for the distance she puts between us. It still isn't nearly enough, my brain is reeling with need. She bends down to put on her shoes and I have to pry my eyes away from her ass. Her nice ass. Fuck, I'm screwed.

Needing a distraction, I grab the plates and wash them in the sink, completely ignoring that I could put them in the dishwasher. I have to keep myself busy.

A couple minutes later we are in my truck and headed down my driveway. Part of me doesn't want to leave, knowing that once she gets her car back she'll be one step closer to leaving. I shouldn't be worried about that. Of course, she's leaving, but I'd be lying to myself if I didn't admit that I want to spend more time with her.

I drive towards I-83, planning to drive until it looks familiar to her, hoping we can pinpoint where her car is. It takes about twenty minutes to reach the interstate and another twenty minutes of driving before she perks up in her seat.

"I think we're close," she whispers, fiddling with the sleeves of my sweatshirt, a nervous tick I noticed she did last night too. She seems stressed and it's hard to say if we'll even stumble upon her car or not.

Sensing she could use a distraction in the meantime, I ask, "How are your wrists?"

"Uhm, better this morning. I took the bandages off, the skin's just a little tender." She pulls her sleeves up to show me. I take her hand, examining her abrasions, but really taking advantage of the opportunity to touch her. Damn. Am I a pervert? I've never felt so creepy around someone. Like I *need* to touch her.

I sit her hand back down, reluctantly, and give it a squeeze as I let go. A gesture intended to calm her nerves, or maybe mine, I don't know. I shift my focus, trying to pay attention to the road, I see a small sedan up ahead parked on the right side of the highway.

"Is that it?" I ask, realizing she's looking at me and not toward the road. Her head starts nodding immediately though once she looks out the window.

I can feel the uneasiness pouring off of her as I pull up behind it and park, leaving the ignition running. The wood line is far away, but it's close enough that if dumb and dumber were staking out the vehicle waiting for us to return to it, this would be their opportunity to strike.

"I'm going to go check it out, make sure it hasn't been messed with. And then I'll change the tire if that's all it needs. You stay in here and lock the doors when I get out. Got it?" I ask her. She doesn't respond, but she's biting her lip nervously.

"Callie, stay in the truck, I can't be worried about you and watch over my shoulder at the same time. Tell me you understand," I demand, harsher than I mean to, but I need her to know how serious I am. I'm hoping not, but this could be a sketchy situation and all that I care about is her safety.

"Okay, I'll stay in the truck," she whispers again like she can't quite find her voice.

I feel shitty raising my voice like that, but her being safe is the top priority, and has been since I met her. I should apologize, or say something to make her feel better, but I'm at a loss of what to say. Not surprisingly.

Instead, I shrug off my jacket, preparing to get out of the truck, but she grabs my forearm before I can. It's a light touch but it stops me like a vice grip.

It's the same reaction I had this morning when I woke up to her head lying on my bicep. I told myself I wouldn't move because I didn't want to disturb her sleep, but really, I enjoyed how close she was. I laid there for a long ass time, hardly breathing, so she wouldn't wake up. But, once she did, I pretended to be asleep so she wasn't alarmed by how close we were.

Like a coward, I wasn't ready to confront her or the feelings she was eliciting in me. I have no control over it and it's pissing me off.

"Please be careful," she says, bringing me back to the moment, but the look in her eyes tells me she's terrified. The

96

last time she was in this exact spot, her world was turned upside down. I don't blame her for being afraid. I place my hand over hers, squeezing it again like before, but this time my hold lingers. Seeing her fear eats at me, making me want to keep her close, my instincts screaming to protect her.

"I'll be fine. Watch my back, if you see anything, or anyone, just honk the horn. I'll come back to you, I promise." Still not wanting to let go, I keep my hand covering hers, waiting for her to let me go first.

Still worried, she doesn't budge, her eyes clinging to mine like she's trying to draw strength from me. If only she realized how weak I am already when it comes to her.

I don't want to leave her, but I need to get this shit over with, so reluctantly I pull away from her, severing our connection. Her fingers trail down my arm as she releases her grip on me and I fucking savor it, missing the feel of her soft skin against mine immediately.

The road's quiet but it means we're pretty exposed like this, and with no witnesses. I'm just glad I'm doing it so Callie doesn't have to. I'd rather take the risk than her every time.

I check the driver's door and it's unlocked, the keys sitting in the cup holder. I don't know if that's where she left them, but it's a miracle the car wasn't stolen. I start the car to make sure it still runs, and that they didn't mess with the engine. It turns over right away, that's a good sign. Hopefully, nothing else has been messed with. These guys were cocky, they didn't anticipate her escaping, or running back to her vehicle.

I look around the inside of the car, making sure there are no surprises. The back seat is filled with two suitcases and a couple of storage boxes. There is a backpack sitting on the passenger seat beside me, and another bag on the floorboard.

The car is packed tight, but it doesn't look to be disturbed. I don't think they rummaged through her stuff after they took her, but she'll have to check later once we're somewhere safe.

I turn it off and pop the trunk, finding the spare tire and tools thrown into the trunk haphazardly. It looks like something they did as an afterthought, not wanting to draw attention to the abandoned car.

I scan the roadway and treeline again, making sure no surprises are lurking before grabbing the tire and the tools. Besides the eyes I feel on my back from the truck, things seem to be quiet, so I get to work.

Chapter Seventeen

Callie

The trembling has come back. My whole body is tense as I watch Nathan pull the tire out of my trunk. The tire I know was sitting against my car yesterday. My eyes keep bouncing around, to the woods, up the road, checking each mirror, waiting for an attack.

I'm incredibly anxious sitting here, but not daring enough to get out of the truck. Primarily because I don't want Nathan worrying about me, but I'm also too afraid to stand outside in the exact place I was assaulted. So much has happened since yesterday, it's hard to believe that it's only been a day.

Needing to calm myself down so I don't have a panic attack, I try focusing on what Nathan's doing. He's already jacked the car up and is working on taking the lug nuts off. Once he gets all of them off, he straightens up, checking his surroundings, including glancing in my direction. He catches my eyes through the windshield, so I give him a half smile, indicating that I'm okay, because I know that's why he's looking at me. He shoots me a wink before going back to his task, as if that simple gesture didn't just turn me crimson. He can not do things like that, my heart can't handle it.

I try my best to continue checking all of my vantage points for danger, but my eyes keep drawing back to Nathan, way more often than necessary. I try to convince myself it's for his well-being, but I can taste the bitterness of that lie.

He's wearing a black t-shirt, and my gaze lingers on his arms. His biceps strain against the sleeves where his muscles flex as he works on the tire. He lifts the old tire off with ease, making quick work of putting the spare on. When he kneels down to screw the lugnuts back on, I can see the rippled muscles of his back through the thin material of his shirt.

I take a deep breath, trying to ignore the visceral effect it has on me. My cheeks warm, and I can feel heat creeping down my neck to my chest. My stomach tightens just thinking about running my hands across his back, down his arms. How would he react if I slid my hands around his waist to his stomach? Then lower?...

Holy crap, I need to pull myself together, fantasizing about him is not helpful right now.

Luckily, while I've been distracted he's already lowered my car off the jack and is putting my old tire in the trunk. I watch as he stands there for a minute, examining it, before shutting the trunk and coming back to his truck. To me.

He looks lost in thought as he gets in and shuts his door, not saying anything right away. I don't say anything either, using the silence as a chance to let my cheeks return to their normal color. I just know he wouldn't believe the rosy tint is from the heat blowing in the truck, he'd probably see right through me.

"It wasn't an accident," he says, distracting me from my inner embarrassment. I look over at him, but he's still staring off towards my car, still in his own head.

"What do you mean?" I ask, but my gut warns me about what he's going to say. He finally looks over at me, studying me for a second with his calculating gray eyes.

"Your tire still had the spike strip stuck to it. Something like that would only be on the road for one reason, and it did its job. They might not have picked you out as a target intentionally, but they definitely intended for this to happen to someone," Nathan finishes speaking through a clenched jaw.

He looks angry, angrier than I've ever seen him. I'm not sure how to react, or what to say, I feel empty. My mind can't contemplate anyone being so evil, that anyone could really be brazen enough to set a trap like this on purpose. They intended to take someone, and they got me, but what was their plan once they had me? If I wouldn't have escaped out of their van, where would they have taken me? What did they want to do to me?

"What if it wasn't the first time?" I ask out loud, finally finding my voice.

Nathan doesn't look surprised at my question, probably thinking the same thing already. "They rigged a bunch of scrap metal together, and it looked very homemade, but it could've just been one of many. It's hard to say how many rounds of trial and error they went through before they got it right..." His voice trails off, seemingly lost in thought, his gaze lingers out the windshield toward my car still sitting in front of us.

Like lightning, his eyes snap to his side mirror as we both hear a vehicle approaching, his focus instantly lazer sharp. I turn around to see a truck coming up the road, slowing down as it approaches. Nathan pulls a gun from his waistband that

I didn't realize he had, holding it across his lap as the truck stops right next to our driver's side door. The driver rolls his window down, staring at me and Nathan expectantly.

"Do you recognize this guy?" He asks me quietly.

"No, I've never seen him before." Nathan nods at me, rolling his window down.

"Did you guys still need a tow? I meant to be by here a couple hours ago but got held up," The driver says loudly over the sound of his engine. Nervously glancing around, I finally notice the tow equipment on the back.

"We didn't call about a tow." Nathan's deep voice is completely calm, making me wonder if he ever gets rattled.

The driver looks up towards my car, and then back down at his paperwork, "Well somebody did, that's the right color and description."

The driver stares, like he's waiting for Nathan to change his mind, like we're the ones who have it wrong.

"We're all good here, we don't need it towed," he says plainly in a no nonsense tone. I imagine his face is just as convincing, because the driver clears his throat, setting his paperwork back down in his passenger seat.

"I'll mark it in the book, give the office a call if you need anything else." The driver doesn't wait for a response from Nathan this time, he pulls back onto the interstate without even checking for oncoming vehicles.

"So... Someone was trying to get my car towed?" I ask, rhetorically.

"Looks that way." Nathan wipes a hand across his face, turning to me as he reholsters the gun I forgot he was holding.

I unintentionally stare as his shirt raises a couple inches, exposing the bare skin right above his waistband. He pushes the gun into the holster until it clicks, his jeans tugging down slightly from the pressure, giving me a peak at the black band of his underwear and the trail of hair that disappears underneath it.

I swear my mouth waters. Why was that the sexiest thing I've ever seen?

But, more importantly, why am I obsessing over Nathan when I could still have people out there trying to kill me?

I know the answer. Nathan is the hottest man I've ever laid eyes on. I need him to do something terrible, kick a kitten, yell at me, anything to break this trance I'm in everytime I'm near him. I turn towards my window so he doesn't notice how red my cheeks are again.

"Are you gonna be okay to drive your car back to my house?" He asks me, All traces of anger are gone, back is the soothing deep voice I've come to crave.

I turn to face him, but it suffocates me. He's angled toward me, one arm thrown over the steering wheel, the other leaning on the center console. I feel like a little girl crushing on him like this, but he's so masculine, so breathtakingly good looking, I have butterflies constantly. A sensation I haven't had since I was a teenager, and I know those boys weren't anywhere close to impressive like Nathan is.

I'm such an idiot. I'm a grown woman and I shouldn't be nervous talking to a handsome man. Something I've never had an issue with, until now, since every other man I've met is put to shame by him. In looks and personality.

Realizing I still haven't answered him, I clear my throat, "Yeah as long as I can follow you so I don't get lost."

"Don't worry, I'd never let that happen," he gives me a small grin, making my stomach do a somersault. Does he even realize what he's doing to me?

Chapter Eighteen

Nathan

Walking Callie to her car, I can feel my chest tightening. "Stay right behind me. If anything seems wrong, honk at me and I'll pull over. Got it?"

She smiles at the use of my now regular catchphrase, "Got it."

She gets in, starting it as I shut her door, pointing to the lock. She understands my signal and hits her automatic lock buttons.

She's okay, she'll be okay. We just have to get back home where it's safer. My thumb digs at my sternum, trying to dislodge the pressure.

I get back in my truck and after looking both ways, I pull back into the interstate to head back the way we came, coasting until Callie gets right behind me. She's right there, yet she feels a mile away. The unpredictableness of what could happen, all the external variables, almost made me say fuck it, and tow her car so she could stay in the safety of my truck. With me.

I stay on high alert the entire way home, and luckily, we

don't run into any issues. We make it back to the cabin within the hour and I can finally breathe easier.

After we park, she looks through her stuff to see if anything is missing. Her phone and laptop are untouched, but she tells me that her center console and glove box have been rummaged through, and that her wallet is missing.

Callie grabs her back pack and one other bag and I let her into the house. She plugs in her phone to the wall outlet in the living room, leaving it to charge. She uses my phone to cancel her credit cards. If they're willing to kidnap someone, they're probably willing to steal her money too, but hopefully they didn't get a chance yet.

We eat lunch in relative silence. Callie seems lost in thought so I do my best to give her space to process everything. I know she's worried about retaliation, thinking they took her wallet to figure out where she lives.

I attempt to ease her worry, telling her that I don't think they're bold enough to travel across state lines to find her and that they might have given up after seeing a Tennessee address on her ID.

"Georgia," she says, her eyes downcast.

"What?"

"My address. I had gotten a new license in Georgia when I thought I was going to be living there," her hands rubbing up and down her thighs anxiously, "in the apartment I shared with my ex."

I hesitate to respond, not sure what to say. She told me she was in Georgia for a few months but didn't mention why. Her body language tells me this is a fresh wound though, and I'm annoyed at the jealousy I'm experiencing. I just met her, I have no right to feel this way. Yet, my jaw clenches a little bit when thinking about her with another man.

"If you're worried that they'll go to that address..." I try to choose my words wisely, "Do you want to call your ex?"

"No!" She says a little too loudly, making us both freeze for a second. "I mean, I just don't want to talk to him, I don't want to tell him what happened to me. Things ended poorly," she fidgets in her seat, tugging at the sleeves of her sweatshirt.

Her reaction is sending warning signals to my brain, telling me there's more to it. That something happened to make it more complex than just "ending poorly." I won't push her, she's been through enough already the last twenty-four hours, but I have to ask, "Did your ex hurt you?"

"He didn't hit me, no." We both stew in silent contemplation after that, her not elaborating has my imagination running wild with what she might have gone through.

I don't think she understands the lengths I'll go to keep her safe. The lengths I go to protect what's mine, my team, and my family included. The second I looked into her eyes back in that clearing, saw her fear, and held her trembling body, I knew she was mine to keep safe. But, not wanting to sound like a possessive asshole, I keep it to myself for now.

"How are you doing?" I study her silent form from across the kitchen island, not wanting to leave for town until I know she's okay mentally.

"I'm fine." She answers too quickly. Clearly, she's not fine. "Callie..."

"I'm just overwhelmed, and a little scared to be honest. I'll be fine though, I have to be. The sooner we get this over with, the sooner I can leave all this behind me," she pushes up from her seat, taking her bags to my room.

I know what she means, she's ready to leave yesterday's

events in the past. She wants to move on without being in fear. However, the churning in my gut reminds me that I'm a part of this story too, and once things are resolved she'll be out of my life also. The thought of saying goodbye to her leaves a sour taste in my mouth.

Even if I didn't want to, I'd let her have a clean break. I wouldn't reach out to her and risk stirring up all the negative emotions associated with being here. I'm not worth it.

She comes back into the kitchen, still wearing the same clothes as before even though I had assumed she was changing into her own things.

I hate how much I love seeing her in my sweatshirt, how my pride swells at the thought of her choosing my clothes over her own. Maybe she'll want to take it when she leaves, a small piece of me to remember. Hell, she can have everything in my closet if she wants.

"I'm ready," her voice pulls me out of my thoughts and I realize I'm staring at her. She fidgets, tucking her hair behind her ear like I've been dying to do a hundred times now. Noticing her pink cheeks, it takes me a second to recognize why she looks different. She put makeup on. Barely enough to notice, but I noticed.

I've never cared about shit like that before. I've known Callie one day and I can already tell if her eyelashes are a darker shade than normal... Am I losing my fucking mind?

"Let's go," I grunt, shaking myself for letting a woman have such a stronghold on me. I don't know if it's better or worse that she probably doesn't even realize the effect she has on me.

We get back in my truck and head into town. Our first stop is the local auto repair shop to see about buying a new tire.

The spare is only meant to last a few miles and she'll need a replacement before she tries to make the rest of the trip home. I try to push the thought of her leaving to the back of my mind.

The shop doesn't have the tire in stock since it's a small business. The owner explained that they only get so much inventory to have on hand. He writes my name down, thinking he might get it in tomorrow on their truck. We give him our thanks and leave.

Callie doesn't say anything else until we are pulling out of the parking lot. "Are you sure you don't mind that I stay with you one more night?" She asks, biting her lip, "You won't hurt my feelings if you want me to stay in a hotel tonight, I promise."

"Not happening," I insist, shutting down any argument she might have. She doesn't argue though, instead, she smiles softly and I'm transfixed on her mouth.

She doesn't want to stay in a hotel, she's just being polite and trying to give me an out, a way to get rid of her if I want to. But, I don't want to, not at all. Especially after she gives me that sweet smile, bolstering my belief that she may not be eager to get away from me either.

I pull back into the roadway, "I need to grab some groceries, then we'll go to the Sheriff's Department." She only nods, the mention of the Sheriff making her nerves come back.

I notice because she starts pulling at the sleeves of the sweatshirt, again. She might wear holes in it by the time she's done.

Reaching over, I grab both of her hands with one of mine, giving them a quick squeeze. It's the only touch I can give her that feels safe like I'm not crossing a line into dangerous

109

territory.

Before I can pull away, she twists her hand over, holding me in place on her lap. She doesn't say anything, doesn't look in my direction, just continues holding my hand to hers. That's all it takes to send me off the deep end. Her touch is like a drug and I'm an addict.

She needs comfort, that's all it is. But I'm soaking in this feeling. Holding Callie's hand as we drive down the road, like normal people. Pretending for a moment that she chose to be here with me, and that yesterday never happened to her.

However, I know the reality is that Callie would never go for a loner like me. She's too good for me, too pure. She deserves a normal guy who will take her out to a fancy dinner. I'm not a normal guy. I don't go to malls, I don't do crowds, I don't talk to people. I can't stand in a room full of people without pressing my back against a wall, too apprehensive to be surrounded.

What would happen if she knew how fucked up I am? If she knew half of what I see in my nightmares she'd probably never look at me the same. No, I'd never want to bog her life down with my problems.

Luckily, we arrived at the grocery store, glad for the excuse to stop my spiraling thoughts. She walks with me as I pick up the items I need. After encouraging her multiple times, she finally grabs a few snacks for herself. It's all very domestic, like nothing I've ever experienced before. I try to play it cool so she doesn't notice how new this is for me. My efforts are almost completely in vain though after we reach the cash register and I'm ambushed by the overly friendly, i.e. nosey, cashier.

The older woman beams a smile in my direction, "Is this

your wife? I've only ever seen you in here before!"

Never having said more than a few words to this lady ever, I'm surprised she recognizes me at all, and her question throws me off guard. My silence is awkward, but I am tongue-tied worse than I've ever been before.

What is Callie to me? I can't just tell this woman that I found her in the woods. She saves my ass though, jumping in to amend the conversation.

"Nope, not his wife. I'm just his friend, visiting from out of town!" She responds for me, matching the cashier's friendliness and smile as if she wasn't just a bundle of nerves in the truck a few minutes ago.

They continue with small talk about the weather and I'm relieved that I'm removed from the conversation, busying myself with loading the bags of groceries into the cart. Callie slowly follows me out of the store, but she and the cashier need at least 20 more seconds to finish telling each other goodbye and to have a nice day.

I start loading the bags into my truck when I hear her come up behind me, I can feel her nearness like a sixth sense.

"Are you telling me that big, bad, badass Nathan can save an innocent woman from two psychopaths in the mountains without a second thought, but can't handle talking to little Ms. Betty at the Piggly Wiggly?" I turn around to see her staring at me with a raised brow, hands on her hips. Despite her making fun of me, she looks fuckin' cute, as usual.

"I can handle Ms. Betty, I just choose not to," I shrug. "I also didn't know how to respond to the wife thing without telling her your business."

"You mean, you didn't want to tell her you found a helpless girl in the woods that you've been holding onto for safekeeping?" She snorts a laugh at me as she climbs into the truck. Yeah, pretty much, I think to myself.

"They probably already think I'm strange. A recluse, new-to-town… So that definitely wouldn't help my case," I say jokingly.

She laughs, shaking her head at me, "I doubt they think you're weird, more like the mysterious, handsome, rugged stranger that comes into town once a week for milk and eggs." She makes a fake swooning gesture, her hand clutching her chest dramatically.

It's ridiculous, but I still laugh at her joke, not missing the part where she called me handsome. Seeing her so carefree fuels my need to see her happy, a smile belongs on her face all the time. I'm determined to make that happen.

I finish packing away the cold stuff in a cooler I keep in the bed for longer trips to town like this and return the cart so we can leave.

Without saying anything, as soon as I pull out of the parking lot I see the tension return to her shoulders. She knows what stop comes next.

She's about to relive the terrible things she went through yesterday to a complete stranger, again. Not that I'm a stranger to her anymore, hell, she told the cashier she was my friend. She might not have meant it, but I hope she did.

Her earlier words ring in my head- *mysterious, handsome, and rugged…* There are worse ways to be described, but it doesn't matter. She's one foot out the door to never being seen again. That's always been the reality of this situation, so why does it feel like she's slipping through my fingers?

I pull up in front of the old building that holds the Rollins County Sheriff's office. I haven't been to this area yet. It appears much older than the part I'm used to. It looks like it's been here for a couple hundred years or more. All the neighboring buildings butt up to one another looking like something from a Western. It could have been used as the set for Mayberry for all I know.

Turning the ignition off, I look over at Callie. She's clutching her seat belt with both hands, biting her bottom lip as she stares out her window at the building.

"Hey, stop that, you're gonna open your cut back up," I reach over and tug lightly at her chin, making her release her lip. She looks at me then, with big doe eyes, clearly on edge.

I realize I haven't let go of her chin yet, and drop my hand back to my lap, "Don't be nervous."

"What if he doesn't believe me?" She asks, softly.

"He will. But, if he gives you any trouble, I'll kick his ass," I say in all seriousness. Despite my blank expression, a smile slowly spreads across her face, breaking me, and making me smirk.

Goal achieved, I hop out of the truck and round to her side, opening her door, "Ready?"

"Nope." She answers, but slides out of her seat anyway, meeting me on the sidewalk.

Chapter Nineteen

Callie

The pressure in my chest is tight, making it difficult to take full deep breaths. All I feel is dread, and I don't entirely know why. I don't want to talk about yesterday, I don't want to cry again, and I know it's inevitable. I'm too emotional as a person to get by without breaking down again.

Nathan has been good at keeping me distracted today, I've even caught myself feeling happy. But, being here to meet with the Sheriff is forcing reality to sink back in. I'm a victim. I was attacked, and the men who did it are still out there. Two men who are probably angry and plotting a way to kill me so they don't get caught. I shudder at the thought.

Part of me wants to test my luck and get the hell out of town, see how far my spare tire takes me. The more sensible part of me knows that I need to tell law enforcement what happened before Tony and Bub try to take another innocent woman. Not to mention, my luck hasn't been that great, and I'd probably end up stranded on the side of the highway again with one less spare tire.

Nathan walks into the front office, holding the door for

me as we enter. Reminding me that in one way I have been pretty lucky. I don't think there is anyone more perfect that I could've come across out in those woods. He's shown me so much patience and kindness and made me feel so safe. There is a soft spot in my heart now, solely reserved for him. No matter what the future holds.

We walk up to the receptionist's desk and unlike the grocery store, I'm too nervous to speak. Nathan doesn't skip a beat, taking the lead and telling the receptionist why we're here.

I take the opportunity to glance around the small space. Just past the front desk are a handful of filing cabinets and a couple of empty desks. The walls are covered in old photos and newspaper clippings, and in the far corner is an empty jail cell. It's probably the most stereotypical-looking police station that exists. However, I guess I'm not the best judge since this experience is a first for me.

"I'm surprised there isn't an old bloodhound sleeping in the corner," Nathan whispers in my ear, making me jump. I spin to face him, glad for his distraction once again.

"I'm disappointed not to see the town drunk sleeping it off," I point over my shoulder at the jail cell, playing along with his joke.

"I could go down the street to the bar, knock a few too many back, and fulfill your dreams," he teases, feigning pain when I elbow him in the arm, laughing at how absurd he is. Making silly jokes seems out of his wheelhouse, so I appreciate his attempt to lessen my unease.

My eyes meet his and I feel like we're in a bubble. It's only me and him, smiling at each other, laughing at our silly inside jokes. He reaches up, brushing the hair off of my temple, his fingertips dragging across my skin, making me shiver. My obvious reaction to his touch makes me blush.

I have the strongest urge to lean into him, lay my head against his chest, and soak in this moment. Instead, I simply shoulder up to him and rest my cheek lightly against his arm, only feeling so brave.

The contact is minimal, but it's everything I need at this moment. Enough to feel his solidness against me, the embodiment of his support that never seems to waver.

Content to stay like this for eternity, I'm disappointed when our bubble bursts as the Sheriff plows through the back entrance of the building.

He is an older man, with gray hair that's balding at his temples, and a thick mustache to match. His gun belt hangs snug around his hips, just under his significant beer gut. He doesn't even look in our direction, he marches up to the receptionist and drops a box of papers on her desk.

"Get these filed before you leave," he orders, without an ounce of politeness. He turns around then, eyeing me and Nathan.

"Are you the ones who called about a situation on I-83?" He asks gruffly. His uncouthness leaves me stuck, my mouth not able to make any noise.

"Yeah, I called last night, and again this morning." Nathan's answer matches the Sheriff's unfriendly tone. He takes notice, standing up straighter, trying to be bigger than Nathan. There's no chance, Nathan's presence dominates the space.

Clearing his throat, he finally introduces himself properly, "I'm Sheriff Donahue, been in charge here for 15 years," reaching his hand out to shake Nathan's. Still completely ignoring me, which I'm fine with.

"Nathan Wolfe, I've only lived here a few months. This is

Callie," he indicates to me, forcing the Sheriff to look at me finally. I still can't speak, my tongue feels like it's covered in cotton.

"You the one who got attacked?" He asks me, squinting at me like he is analyzing me -or rather, sizing me up.

"Yes, sir," I barely squeak out. "My name's Callie Richards."

"Alright, come with me, I'll take your statement in my office." He doesn't wait for me to respond, he steps around me and walks towards the back of the room to a door with a frosted glass window. His name and badge are etched into the glass. We turn to follow him, but once he reaches his door he turns to look at us and puts his hand up, halting our steps.

"I need to talk to the girl alone, you need to wait out here," speaking directly to Nathan. I'm too anxious to be pissed about him referring to me as "girl", as if we didn't tell him my name, twice. I look at Nathan, realizing just how dependent on him I've become.

"She's already told me everything," Nathan says, "I'm not leaving her alone." He insists, not moving an inch from my side.

"I didn't ask your opinion, boy. She either comes in alone, or I'm not taking her statement. I run things around here." He rests his hand on the butt of his gun, either as a threat, or just a show of power, I'm not sure.

Feeling the tension in the room escalating, my hands start to sweat. I can't handle conflict right now, I'm already too on edge.

"It's okay, Nathan, I'll be okay. I know you'll be right out here," I say to him, squeezing his hand. Reassuring him, like he's done for me so many times today.

Afraid I won't have the courage if I think about it any longer,

117

I walk through the door the Sheriff is holding to enter his office. I get a quick look at Nathan as the door shuts and he looks worried, or maybe angry. I can tell that he doesn't like this guy, and neither do I. I just want to get this over with.

He sits down roughly in his seat behind his desk. He doesn't offer any direction, so I pick one of the two seats opposite of him and sit down. I shift nervously, feeling claustrophobic being sandwiched between the desk and the closed door behind me. Sheriff Donahue shuffles papers around on his desk. The entirety of it is incredibly messy.

The office itself is cluttered with boxes, papers, and mismatched furniture, not to mention the empty coffee cups scattered throughout. It is definitely not a welcoming environment. He finally stops what he was doing and leans back in his chair, resting his hands on his stomach, very casually. My initial thought is that he doesn't know the extent of what happened to me. If he realized how serious the crime was, he would be behaving a lot more professionally.

"Go ahead and tell me what happened." He prompts with a wave of his hand, so with no further instruction, I start from the beginning.

I give him the timeline of events as it happened, giving enough detail to explain what transpired, but leaving out the more emotional bits that I know would send me into a crying fit. Crying in front of this man would be pure misery, I just know it.

I finish my story on trembling lips, but he doesn't say anything. He just sits in his chair, staring at me. I'm worried that I missed something, like he is waiting for me to say something else, but nothing comes to mind, so I stay silent. My anxiety is climbing, I can feel the sweat trickling down my spine, dampening my shirt.

"So let me get this straight. You were taken off the side of the road, thrown into the back of a van, driven into the middle of the woods where you escaped on your own, and then outran two grown men until you found help? Did I get that right?" He asks rhetorically, like he doesn't actually care for clarification.

"I mean that's the simplified version I guess," I say defensively. My walls are going up, my senses telling me that he is going to try to discount everything that happened to me.

"Tell me what you know about the two men," he grumbles, chewing on a toothpick he picked up off his desk like he couldn't care less what I'm about to say.

"They were brothers I think, in their mid thirties maybe. One was tall and skinny, Tony was his name. He called the other one, Bub, he was shorter and fat." He stops chewing on the tooth pick and leans forward on his desk, eyeing me harshly.

"You're sure about this? I'd hate to see you ruin any lives if you've got this wrong," he accuses, and I'm taken back by his lack of empathy.

"Of course I'm sure. I wouldn't be here if I wasn't," I snap at him, my patience wearing thin.

"And just how did you end up escaping this Tony and Bub? I must've missed that part of the *story*." He might as well have done finger quotes, clearly dismissing what I've already told him.

"I made it across the river and ran into Nathan," I indicated over my shoulder towards where I know Nathan is waiting outside the office. "He shot at them, giving me cover so he could help me get away. He's the only reason that I'm alive."

"He shot them?" He sits up fully, like he's finally taking this seriously.

"I think, but they got away. He was too far away to get a good shot," under my breath I add, "Unfortunately."

Chapter Twenty

Nathan

I feel like crawling out of my skin, being so close to Callie but not in the same room with her. My first impression of the Sheriff was not good. He's an old school cop who thinks his badge makes him superior to everyone. I've dealt with shit like that before, but I don't like the way he was talking to Callie either. He hardly acknowledged her existence.

I pace back and forth between the empty desks. There's no one else here besides the secretary. She watches me over the rim of her glasses, the frames sitting on the tip of her nose absurdly. She's older, probably close to the Sheriff's age, her gray hair is pulled back in a tight bun. That paired with her outdated wardrobe and she looks more like a librarian. I can feel her unease about being left alone with me though. Normally I'd reign it in so I don't startle her, but I just can't seem to care enough.

I'm used to people being nervous around me, something about my ever present scowl probably. It didn't always used to be like that, I remember being carefree once, never meeting a stranger. Chester used to joke that I only joined the Army to make friends. I wonder what he'd think of me now... Living in the mountains, utterly alone. At least, up until 24 hours ago.

Damn, I hope Callie's doing okay in there. The thought of her breaking down while talking to that pea brain Sheriff makes my blood boil. I should be in there. I told her I'd help her through this, but I'm stuck out here not doing shit to help. I know what it feels like to relive a horrible experience over and over, how it chips away at your soul a little at a time, every time you have to relive it.

Chester's death was the first for me. I sat in the police station that night and had to tell three different detectives what happened. I had to keep remembering how his blood soaked through my shirt as I held him, and how my friend, Robby, fell to the pavement sobbing. His cries sounded hollow, like they were coming from somewhere else, and not from right beside me. My own tears were silent, rolling down my face into Chester's hair as I clutched his body to mine.

I think I ran out of tears that night. The grief I felt was the heaviest thing I'd ever experienced, his death was so sudden and unexpected. I told myself I'd never be caught off guard again. That's when I started living with the mindset that the worst was always yet to come. I went into every mission thinking that if I didn't die, someone on my team would die. That was just the price we paid.

My mom cried when I made her sign the papers explaining what would happen in the events of an untimely death. It was hard on her after losing my father only a few years prior. I focused on the splotches her tears left on the papers, wishing I felt a single drop of moisture roll down my own cheek. But, there was nothing left, I knew then that I'd never cry again. My heart was only an organ, not a vessel for emotions, my brain a steel trap, absorbing bad things with no way to escape.

Four years into Special Forces, I was used to the void left by my hardened perspective on life. By that time I had lost two teammates in the line of duty. I felt their loss, I grieved for them, but never shed a tear. I knew that I was broken beyond repair, so I continued doing the job. I continued risking my life for my country. Better for something to happen to me than someone else.

On multiple occasions injuries in the field left me hospitalized. Shrapnel, bullet wounds, torn muscles and tendons. But, I kept returning for duty. If it wasn't me out there, they'd find a replacement, another guy who could lose his life too early. It's a backwards way of thinking, rationally I knew I wasn't actually saving anyone from their fate. The Army would simply assign them somewhere else, to another unit, and they could still die. Another life snuffed out before their time.

Worst cases in my eyes were the innocent lives lost. Like Callie, the ones who didn't ask to be a part of a conflict or the ones who didn't choose to be thrust into the middle of a war. The ones who still haunt me when I close my eyes.

The day that I came the closest to my emotional dam breaking was a few years back. My team and I were tasked to sneak into a small town in South America under the radar, extract a small group of American missionaries who were being held hostage by one of the drug cartels, and get them back to the States without a peep. Easy enough, a mission we'd done countless of times for varying reasons.

* * *

Six years ago...
   Classified location, South America

I don't know what's worse, the feeling of water stuck in your ear, or knowing it's sweat. It's so humid in this jungle, even in the dead of night, I haven't stopped sweating since we crossed the border. Wearing 30 pounds of gear isn't helping either. Fuck, this is miserable.

In formation, we are trekking through the overgrowth silently, well prepared for a situation like this. We were dropped off by our helo a few miles back, not wanting to risk being heard by our targets. The cartel is operating out of a farm, transporting drugs in the same trucks providing food to the community.

I hear voices chirping in my ear, my guys calling out what they see as we get closer to the crops surrounding the property. Brandt readies the drone, sending it up in the sky to scout the area for hostiles. It detects heat signatures, telling us that besides six warm bodies in an outbuilding on the other side of this food crop, the coast is clear.

Our hope is that the hostages are being kept in that outbuilding, the six bodies could be our six missionaries. Worst case scenario is they're being kept in the main house on the north side of the property, which would require a lot more effort to extract them, and it definitely wouldn't go down quietly.

According to the United States government, me and my team aren't here right now. To them, we don't even exist.

They'd probably sell us out before they'd take accountability for the risk of sending us here. U.S. armed forces on foreign soil is not a good look, but neither is leaving six Americans to the mercy of a notorious drug gang.

Jesse slaps a hand on my shoulder, the silent "go ahead" signal distracting me from my overheated misery. We start through the corn field, slowly weaving through the rows of stalks, trying not to make our approach obvious. We halt at the edge of the corn, looking onto the property ahead of us. There doesn't seem to be any movement anywhere other than the house. The music is loud enough to be heard from where we are about 100 yards away.

We know from the drone coverage to approach the out-building closest to us with caution, there should be six people occupying it. It looks like an old barn, bandaged with rusted sheet metal, probably used to store a couple of small animals at one time. It's pitch black and utterly silent, even with the full moon, I doubt whoever is inside can see more than a couple inches in front of them. It's got to be our hostages. We surround the building, hiding in the shadows, simultaneously looking for a visual and a way inside.

"Got a door on the south side, looks unlocked, it's probably our best entry point. It'll keep us out of the line of sight from the house," Jesse relays over the comms.

"Copy." One word of confirmation, and within seconds we're all prepared to breach the door.

We're going in blind, no one was able to get a look at who is inside. So we set up, prepared to encounter six hostiles, always ready for the worst-case scenario. Another hand to my shoulder, and it's a go. With a twist to the door handle, the unlocked door swings open and we enter in a flash, staggering our entries to sweep the room. Our night vision goggles give us the advantage, the occupants know we've entered but can't tell who we are, or where we're standing.

"HANDS! HANDS! HANDS!" We shout as we enter, I immediately notice the group of people bound to a support beam in the middle of the room, their limbs are tangled, their bodies tightly pressed together, bound with rope. They cower away from our approach, straining to raise their hands against the ties binding them together.

I count the heads I can see -One, two, three, four, five...

My face flinches when the sound of a shot being fired goes off right above my shoulder, the silencer is the only thing keeping it from bursting my ear drum. Jesse dropped a man who was pointing a gun right at me from the opposite corner of the room. Six. The six warm bodies have been accounted for, but we're still missing one of our hostages.

I glance back at Jesse, a silent thanks for covering me. He nods, a smug look on his face because he knows he just saved my ass. If we had a running tally of how many times we've saved each other in situations like this, we'd probably be neck in neck, but neither of us really want to know how close we've come to going home in a body bag.

We start untying the kids in the room, which is exactly what they are, teenagers, not a single one older than 19 probably. I wonder if they pictured hell to look like this when they preach about it from their Bibles... Bound and gagged, covered in dirt, blood, and their own waste, like pigs being prepared for slaughter.

"Please, you have to help my sister. They took her. Please!" A young woman pleads as soon as we remove the gag from her mouth.

It makes things complicated because now it's not going to be a quick recovery as we hoped. Adding unknowns to a stealth mission like this makes it more dangerous.

"Where is she?" Jesse asks, and I relay back to command that our sixth hostage is not with the rest of the group, but suspected to still be alive.

"They have her tied to the back porch, up at the house!" Her words are frantic, the panic clear on her face.

"How do you know?" My voice is completely void of emotion, my tools for empathy are long gone and I'm not in the mood to be led on a wild goose chase. We've been on this property too long already, it won't be long until they notice we've stolen the hostages back.

"Because that's where they had me," her voice quivers. I don't know what I was expecting her to say, but that wasn't it. I take a second to really look at the girl in front of me, trying to decide if she's reliable enough to put ourselves at risk by going into the lion's den.

She's filthy, they all are. Obviously, they've been tossed around in the dirt quite a bit in the few days they've been here. Her hair is knotted, and tangled so badly I wouldn't be surprised if they have to shave it once we get her home. They've all got splotches of blood here and there, a fat lip or two. The four guys all look like they've been clocked a few times.

"They had you up at the house then they just let you go?" I ask skeptically. It feels like I'm missing a piece of the puzzle, and I hate needing a clue. This whole mission has been a giant question mark. Why would they take these kids as hostages? What good would it do for a drug farm to keep extra mouths to feed and keep alive?

"They said I was ruined, they needed fresh meat." Her words are so quiet I can hardly hear her, her eyes peer vacantly towards her feet. "Demasiada sangre." *Too much blood.*

I'm not fluent in Spanish, but the word blood catches my attention. My line of sight follows hers, the stream of light from my flashlight illuminating her bottom half. Something coils in my gut as I comprehend what I'm seeing. Her linen pants are soiled with blood, deep red originating from between her thighs.

"God damn…" Jesse whispers from beside me, his words echo my own thoughts. This girl was brutalized, clearly raped, dragging out her torture repeatedly, and now they have her sister.

Chapter Twenty-One

Callie

He slaps a couple of blank papers down on the desk in front of me, "Fill these out with your statement. Include every detail. I need to go talk to your boyfriend."

He stands up, not even giving me a chance to react. What a pig. He's probably going to listen to Nathan's side of the story, completely disregarding me and everything I just told him. He seems like a typical misogynist, so I guess I shouldn't be entirely surprised if he hates women.

I glance around his desk, looking for a pen because he forgot to give me one, of course. I look back to where the two men are standing, Nathan looks pissed. I don't blame him. This Sheriff Donahue is hard to like. Not wanting to interrupt them, and not wanting a reason for the Sheriff's sights to be set back on me, I move to the other side of his desk to look for a pen.

I nudge a couple of papers around, seeing if there is one hiding under the mess. There's a small drawer under his computer monitor, but when I reach for it I freeze, my blood running cold in an instant. My stomach sinks.

Sitting right beside his monitor is a framed photo. The Sheriff is posing next to a large, freshly killed deer, with two other men posing on its other side. I stare at it, hoping my eyes are playing tricks on me and I'm not really seeing what I'm seeing. It doesn't matter how long I look or how many times I blink, it's definitely a younger version of Sheriff Donahue and the two men from yesterday, Tony and Bub. They're probably five years younger in the picture but it's definitely them, it's unmistakable. Their slimy grins are burned into my memory, haunting me every time I close my eyes.

I can't breathe.

My thoughts go spiraling. Who is the Sheriff to them? Could he be old enough to be their father? A brother? They don't look alike at all, but maybe.

I told him that I knew their names... I just sat here and told him that Nathan tried killing them. Now he is out there talking to him. Oh my God. What have I done? We need to leave. Now.

I rush around his desk and out of his office, Nathan sees me coming right away and gives me a questioning look. Of course, he can tell something is wrong, he reads me like a book, and I am incredibly thankful for that right now. The Sheriff notices Nathan looking toward me, pivoting to look at me also.

"You're done with your statement already?" He squints at me, his mustache twitching while he scrutinizes me.

"Yep, all done." I channel every ounce of courage I have to remain calm, to pretend like I'm not panicking. "Can we go now?" I look directly into Nathan's eyes, his eyebrows pinching together, knowing something is wrong with me but not knowing what.

"I still need your boyfriend here to write his statement, and I need both of you to write down your information." He positions himself between us and the front lobby, clearly trying to keep us from leaving.

I don't refute the boyfriend comment, I play into it instead, grabbing Nathan's hand and squeezing it, "Honey, can we come back later, I'm really not feeling well."

I stare into Nathan's eyes, praying he is reading into my act. Hoping he understands that something is wrong and I need him to get us out of here. He looks deeply at me and I can sense the wheels turning in his head. He reaches up and runs his knuckles across my cheek, cupping my jaw in his palm, "Yeah baby, let's go."

I can't help but melt under his touch. Even though he's just playing along, it grounds me. He wraps his arm around my shoulders tightly, facing the Sheriff head-on, making me relax slightly now that I'm safely tucked into the side of his body.

"I'll come back tomorrow, she's had a rough couple days. I don't want her to make herself sick," the lie slips effortlessly through his teeth.

"You can't go anywhere until I get your information." The Sheriff straightens his shoulders, again trying to stand tall against Nathan, but failing. I am gripping Nathan's side just above his hip, probably breaking skin with my nails even through his shirt.

"We're leaving, we'll come back tomorrow. You've got my word, *Sheriff*," Nathan finishes without even a trace of sincerity, not caring if the Sheriff knows he's lying or not. If only I had an ounce of his confidence.

Not waiting for a response, he sidesteps him and walks

towards the exit, shuffling me along. The receptionist stares at me from her desk, looking confused about what's going on but aware that there's some sort of tension in the room.

Nathan holds onto me, shielding me under his arm until we reach his truck. He opens my door for me and shuts it once I'm safely inside, rounding the front quickly to get in on his side.

Without saying anything, he takes off. We make it down the street and take the left to get us out of town and back to the mountain roads before he finally speaks up.

"You want to tell me what the hell that was about, *honey*?" He uses the pet name I gave him back to me, his voice full of curiosity.

"He knows them, Nathan. Sheriff Donahue knows Tony and Bub. There was a picture on his desk," I barely finish speaking before feeling the tears running down my cheeks.

I don't know if I'm mad or upset or both, but I do know I feel helpless. This situation just became so much worse, and I've dragged Nathan even deeper into it. I cover my face with my hands, feeling so defeated.

"That fucking bastard." Nathan slams his hand against the steering wheel, reacting harsher than I've ever seen him before. "He fucking knew. He was asking me where I shot them, and if I was trying to kill them. I thought he wanted to know for law enforcement's sake, but he was more concerned for their well being."

I watch him as he rubs his hand across his chin, then through his hair, clearly distressed about this new development. "I'm so sorry, Nathan, I didn't mean to drag you into this. I'm sorry." I sob quietly to myself, the guilt ripping a hole in my chest. This is bad, this is all so bad.

He doesn't deserve this, I've done nothing but bring problems into his life. I have to cover my mouth with my hand to stop the cries from escaping my throat. He doesn't speak right away and it's killing me. We drive the rest of the way to his cabin in silence, my head is throbbing by the time we pull in his driveway.

I jump out of the truck before he even has it in park and fall to my knees, throwing up the contents of my stomach into the grass. I squeeze my head with both hands, trying to dim the piercing pain that's stabbing my brain. I don't know if it's from the tears, or the stress, or maybe I've finally burst an aneurysm and this is the end, but I feel like I'm being punished for something. I'm really starting to take all of this personally, why me?

I feel Nathan's hands pulling my hair back, making sure it doesn't fall in my face. It's too gentle, too nice, I don't deserve it. I push myself up, ignoring the icepick in my frontal lobe, and go to the front door, pacing back and forth until he unlocks it. I rush past him into the living room, grabbing everything that I brought in, and retrieving my bags from the bedroom within a few seconds.

I can't believe I'm suddenly on the wrong side of law enforcement, not that this is lawful, but how am I supposed to stand up against a cop? He knows exactly how to make a person disappear. If it's between me or his family, or however he knows Tony and Bub, I guarantee he'll pick them. I need to leave, I need to get as far away from Nathan as possible to keep him safe. I'll die if it means he's safe, that I didn't get him killed. I turn towards the door and run smack into Nathan's chest.

"What the fuck are you doing?" He asks angrily. He's never

directed any level of anger towards me, and I'm stunned for a moment, unable to speak.

"I have to go. I can't stay here," I finally say.

"And why's that?" He doesn't budge from his spot, my face is still directly in front of his chest. If I leaned in just a few inches my nose would touch his sternum.

Not able to look him in the eyes, I manage to whisper, "I don't want you to get hurt because of me." My jaw is trembling, my whole body is shaking, I think my knees are going to give out any second standing here. "Please Nathan, just let me go, you don't have to feel obligated to help me," I stutter out.

"Sit down. Now." His command makes my knees immediately buckle. My butt lands in the living room chair that I'm closest to. Pulling the backpack from my shoulder, he discards it on the couch before leaning towards me, caging me in. Each of his hands brace the arms of the chair, one on either side of me, and I can't help but notice the strain in his grip.

"Callie, I'm going to say this one time and don't argue with me. You. Are. Not. Leaving," he says, enunciating each word. "Do you really think I gave a shit about that little podunk Sheriff? I promised to keep you safe, did you think I was lying?" He stares at me, waiting for a response, "Callie?" He prompts me again to answer him.

"No," I squeak out.

"No, what?" He doesn't yell, but his voice is elevated, stern, like a drill sergeant.

"No, sir," I respond, but immediately scold myself. Why the hell did I call him sir? That's not what he was asking. I'm afraid to meet his eyes, but he hasn't said anything yet, so I slowly look up into his face.

Expecting to see anger, I'm taken aback when I see a fire burning in his eyes. My body reacts immediately to his proximity, to the heat of his gaze. Warmth pools between my legs, my desire for him uncontrollable. We both stare at each other, neither of us saying anything, neither of us moving.

It's like walking a fine line. Both of us uphold a sense of decency around each other based on the events that led me here, even though attraction has been sizzling between us the whole time. I hoped it wasn't one sided, and now seeing the way he's looking at me… It makes me hope for things I shouldn't.

Finally, Nathan clarifies his demand, "Tell me that you're not going anywhere." His voice is like velvet against my insides. My brain responds immediately, like it couldn't wait to answer him.

"I'm not going anywhere," I whisper, still not having full strength in my voice.

Chapter Twenty-Two

Nathan

White knuckling the arms of the chair is the only thing stopping me from grabbing her. Crushing my mouth against hers, showing her just how much I really want her to stay. I lurch away from her before I do something stupid, something to scare her off.

I've never felt this much need for a woman, it's the first time I've ever had trouble controlling myself. It takes all of my willpower to walk away, to stop acting like a fucking animal.

I keep walking until the front door shuts behind me and I'm standing on the porch. I suck the cool evening air into my lungs, needing to clear my head.

Being near Callie is all consuming, and I can't fight it. I really don't want to, but I have to for her sake. She's too vulnerable, her emotions have been scrubbed raw, and she'd never forgive me if things between us escalated before she was truly ready. She holds all the power between us, whether she knows it or not.

Twilight fades to darkness while I stand here against the porch railing, trying to sort my thoughts. One thing for sure, Callie is staying with me. She doesn't get to leave on the basis of guilt.

She thought she would be doing me a favor, protecting me by leaving, but she doesn't realize how unnecessary that is. If she did leave, I'd follow her. I'd follow her all the way to Canada if it meant she was safe. I sound like a stalker, but I really don't give a fuck anymore. Protecting her is the only thing that has made sense for me in a long time. The only thing that has felt right.

I know saving her was the right choice, I just wish I knew what happens next. Now that we know there is a connection between Sheriff Donahue, Tony and Bub, it's hard to guess their agenda.

Two options stand out in my head, either the Sheriff is going to find Tony and Bub and make them disappear, figuratively. He doesn't seem the type to actually make them pay for their crimes if he has a relation to them. He'd probably pay for their tickets to Mexico. The other option, the one I'm worried about, is the Sheriff coming after us to make us disappear, literally. More specifically, Callie.

I need to call the state police, let them know what's going on and that there is a conflict of interest. I'm not familiar with the jurisdictions and the reach of law enforcement in this area yet, but calling them seems like the only option at this point.

Focusing on Callie's safety is easier than thinking about the other feelings I have. I don't know how it's possible to care about her this much in the short span of time that I've known her, but it's screwing my head up. I need to go back inside, let her know my plan, give her some sense of comfort. We can figure out the rest tomorrow.

Stalling a little longer, I grab the groceries from my truck that were almost long forgotten and take them in with me. I go straight to the kitchen, but not before casting a glance over to the living room. She's still sitting in the same chair that I left her in, holding her head in her hands with her eyes squeezed shut.

My chest aches seeing her like that. I resist going over to her, needing to keep the clear head I just achieved by standing on the porch for so long. I take a couple minutes putting away the groceries, trying to decide how to handle things going forward.

I can play the part, pretend like I'm not falling for her, even if it pains me to do so. The last thing she needs is more complications, but regardless of my feelings, she's still a wreck and I need to do something to make her feel better.

Not knowing the best way to do this, I go down the hall to the bathroom and run hot water in the tub. I leave it running while I return to the living room, without saying anything or giving her a chance to protest, I pick her up and cradle her to my chest. A perfect parallel of how I carried her through the woods yesterday, reminding me yet again that I've only known her a day. She lets out a small noise of surprise, but doesn't fight it. She's either too defeated to care, or she trusts me enough that she doesn't question what I'm doing. I hope for the latter. I sit her down on the counter next to the sink and turn the bath water off.

"I know everything that's happened seems like too much to handle, but you will handle it. We will get through this. But, for now, take a bath, I'll make dinner. We'll start trying to save the world tomorrow." I try joking, hoping to loosen some of the tightness in her posture, but she still won't look at me. Her head is downturned towards her knees, her eyes are still squeezed shut.

"What do you need, Callie, tell me what I can do," I plead, tipping her chin up to look at her face. She turns her head, resting her cheek in the palm of my hand, so sweetly, so delicately. My calloused hands are like sandpaper compared to her soft skin.

"My head... I think I'm getting a migraine," she whispers, her forehead creasing, cringing with pain. I slide my hand to the back of her neck, just under the base of her skull, and massage gently.

"I'll get you some medicine," I whisper against her forehead, my lips brushing against her skin lightly.

I pull away, chastising myself for doing that, for being too intimate. I'm already breaking my own rules and it's been five minutes.

Retrieving the pain reliever I'd given her earlier this morning and a water bottle from the kitchen, I return to the bathroom to find her standing, facing the mirror, her hands braced against the counter. Coming up beside her, I set the pills and the bottle on the counter.

"Drink the whole bottle if you can, you might be dehydrated," I tell her through the mirror.

"Should I thank your mother or the Army for making you, you?" She asks, studying our reflections.

"Depends... What do you think I am?"

"So far... too good to be true," she says with such a serious face, I'm not sure how to react. I could take it as a compliment, but instead, it feels more like a challenge. Like she is waiting for something to be wrong with me, waiting for a reason not to trust me.

"There's plenty of bad in me. But never for you," I match her tone, wanting her to know how serious I am. She analyzes me in the mirror, and I let her. If she wants to pick me apart piece by piece, she can. If it means she'll feel better, that she trusts me, I'll do anything, tell her anything she wants to know.

"Why don't you keep any of your pictures on the wall?" She asks, the question seemingly out of the blue. "The one's in your closet," she clarifies.

She's been snooping, not that I blame her since she's been staying with a relative stranger. I think about her question for a second, not really knowing the answer myself, "I'm afraid to look at them too often."

"Why?" She asks, a curious tone in her voice.

"Remembering makes the nightmares worse," I tell her honestly.

She doesn't ask anything else, she doesn't even give me a pitying look, something I wouldn't want from her anyway. She looked at me with understanding, like all she wanted was to understand me better. I think I passed the test.

She turns around to look at me directly, "Thank you for telling me."

"Thanks for staying," I respond, meaning it wholly, hoping she realizes how much her staying means to me. How much keeping her safe means to me. She wraps her arms around my waist, burying her head into my chest and I feel fucking victorious. I don't hesitate to wrap my arms around her too. She exhales deeply, forcing her body to relax.

I can easily stare over her head into the mirror and she looks so small in my arms. Not in a petite way, but because she's burrowed so snuggly against me, my arms envelop her. It feels right.

Having her so close is torture, but the best fucking torture there is. If this is all I get if Callie's world is fixed tomorrow and she leaves here healthy and happy, I'd feel empty, but I would hold onto this moment forever.

I feel her cringe against my chest again, her head still hurting. I pull away slightly, just enough to look at her. She's got a frown on her face. "Take the medicine. Take a bath. I'll be in the kitchen when you're done."

She nods slightly. "Okay, okay… Bossy," she mumbles that last part under her breath, but I see the smile in her eyes as she says it.

She jokes, but I can tell she likes it, she likes it when I take away her need to second guess or argue. When I take away her choice, it's for her own good, and she knows it. She is used to being polite and apologetic for taking up space, and not being taken care of. That shit won't fly around me.

I turn away, filling the tub the rest of the way up with hot water, trying my best not to imagine her five minutes from now, laying in the hot water, naked, her light skin turning pink from the heat. Fuck me.

"Take your time," I manage to spew before hurrying out of the bathroom, and shutting the door behind me. I take a deep breath and adjust the front of my pants, hoping like hell Callie didn't notice the raging hard-on I have now.

She didn't even have to do anything, I look in her direction or think about her, and all the blood in my head rushes south. I'm worse than a fucking teenager.

Chapter Twenty-Three

Callie

I do exactly as Nathan says, take the pain pills and get in the bath. I don't know how he knew a bath would be perfect for me, but laying in the hot water feels incredible on my aching body. I might actually wake up tomorrow feeling semi back to normal.

I rest my head against the edge of the tub, my thoughts keep going back to the photo in Sheriff Donahue's office. How do they all know each other? And what is he going to do now that he knows that I could ID my perpetrators?

He had to have realized something was wrong as soon as we left. Did he know I would see the photo? He didn't exactly have it hidden, so it wouldn't be a stretch that I'd come across it. Then again, he wasn't paying attention to my story at all until I brought up Tony and Bub's names. He jumped up so quick to talk to Nathan after I told him they were shot, he probably hadn't spared me a thought.

The unknown is making me anxious, I can feel the jitters coming back. I try to clear my head, and distract myself with anything else so I can actually enjoy this bath. It doesn't take long to remember the feel of Nathan's arms around me, his hard body pressed against mine.

When he pulled away from me earlier I was disappointed, not ready for our hug to end, but he quickly redeemed himself by getting the hot water going again in the bath. I imagine his lips against my forehead, firmer than the butterfly light kiss he gave me earlier. Would he kiss me if I asked him to?

What if I asked him to stay? To join me?

I shouldn't be thinking these thoughts, it's only going to hurt me in the long run, but I can't stop. I imagine his body lounging in the tub underneath me, his masculinity on full display, gazing at me with that heat in his eyes that I saw before.

I would straddle his hips, grinding my hot center over his hardness. And I'd kiss him with every ounce of passion I have, showing him how much I truly want it, want him. I definitely want him. I've been attracted to him from the start, but that is only the beginning of what I feel for him now. He shows me over and over again how kind and compassionate he is, how dependable and brave he is. Qualities of a man that I know I can trust.

The responsible part of my brain knows that this is crazy. I have full-blown feelings for a man that I barely know. But I can't stop thinking about him in all of the ways I shouldn't. I wonder if he is thinking about me this way too? Probably not. It's hard to imagine when he's seeing me at my lowest, always crying, always panicking, he probably thinks I'm a basket case. Ugh. But he's been so tender towards me, it's hard not to hope he likes me too.

Glad for the reprieve from my thoughts about being killed or kidnapped again, I let the water turn to ice while thinking about Nathan. It takes all of my willpower, but I finally get out and dry off.

Suddenly, I realize all of my sleep clothes are still packed away in a suitcase in the back of my car. None of the bags I brought in have pajamas in them, and even if they did, they are on the living room floor, haphazardly dropped in the middle of my panic attack earlier.

Contemplating what I should do next, either I put on my dirty clothes from today, or I sneak into Nathan's room and raid his closet for something new to sleep in. The latter option wins.

I walk into the hallway with my towel wrapped tightly around my body, glancing toward the kitchen. I don't see him but I hear the TV in the living room. Assuming he is watching it, I enter his room. I'm halfway to the closet when I hear the dryer click shut behind me, I spin around and see Nathan standing next to his laundry machines, staring at me.

"I forgot to dry your clothes…" He clears his throat, "I had to rewash them," he finishes, his voice sounding hoarse.

"It's okay, I was just going to get something to sleep in." I don't move, feeling like I just got caught doing something I shouldn't be, a little on edge standing here with nothing under my towel. I swear I see the muscle in his jaw flex like he's grinding his teeth. His eyes bounce around the room, landing everywhere but on me.

I want them on me though, I want his eyes to burn a hole right through me like they did earlier, I crave it. I take a small step forward, drawing his focus back on me, hoping I'll be met with the desire in his eyes that I know was there before.

"Is that okay? If I wear your clothes to bed?" I utter with a small voice, my tone not matching the brazen thoughts in my head. I wanted it to come out playful, but I'm not as brave out loud as I am in my imagination.

Through clenched teeth, he forces a "Yes" out of his mouth, but doesn't say or do anything else. Not feeling as bold as I was before, I don't push him anymore. He's clearly keeping himself at a distance for a reason.

A small part of me is worried that I am reading this all wrong, and that he is *just* being a gentleman, taking care of a lost puppy until it gets the hell out of his house. He's a man, and I'm a woman, maybe that's all there is between us. Maybe this connection I feel we have is all in my head. I turn to the closet, ending this false moment I created.

"Callie…" He starts but doesn't continue after I look back at him. Still flexing his jaw, finally he mutters, "Food is in the kitchen."

He doesn't wait for a response before he is out of the room and all but fleeing away from me. He's attracted to me, but maybe that's all it will be. I laugh to myself, needing to find humor in this crazy situation I ended up in.

Two men assaulted me and kidnapped me off the side of the road. Now I'm obsessing over the man who saved me from the bad guys. The only thing that would put the icing on the cake is if Nathan was riding a horse when he did it, a real knight in shining armor. He is going to be the star of my fantasies for the rest of my life, it's inevitable.

I continue daydreaming about Nathan as I sift through his closet, enjoying the warmth that thinking of him brings. Not seeing any more shorts that would fit me, I boldly pull on a pair of his black boxer briefs and throw a flannel button down shirt over it. It's long on me, hanging down to mid thigh, and I have it buttoned high enough that I don't feel exposed. It's comfortable and smells like him, so I'm content.

A little nervous to enter the kitchen after our awkward stand off in the bedroom, I take my seat at the kitchen island without saying anything. He doesn't say anything either, simply tracking my movements as I enter. Without a word, he sits a plate of food down in front of me. I smile at the plate of grilled cheese, a little bowl of tomato soup in the center. Another simple comfort food, something that is much appreciated right now.

"I love grilled cheese." I smile at Nathan, genuinely pleased. He doesn't say anything still, but he responds with a small smile. A smile that would make me weak in the knees if I was still standing.

He starts eating his own food at the same time as me, tugging on my heart strings that he waited for me. I swear if he doesn't cut this shit out, I'm going to fall in love with him in no time. Apparently I have no willpower when it comes to this man.

Chapter Twenty-Four

Nathan

Bullets flying past my face in war zones, helo rides being targeted with missiles, and hand-to-hand combat with terrorists. More of the worst things I've experienced, yet walking away from Callie back in my bedroom was the hardest. When I saw her standing there, only in a small towel, I thought I was going to cum in my pants at the sight. I wanted to throw her down on my bed right then and bury my face between her thighs. Grab her full hips and make her ride my face. It'd be too easy to lose myself in her soft curves, I'd suffocate, never wanting to come up for air again. She's worn nothing revealing since I met her, and the towel did little to hide her full cleavage. I almost cracked a molar trying to restrain myself. It's been too many times now I've felt out of control around her, something I cannot let happen.

I had to get away from her before I did something I'd regret, and I'm glad I did. She doesn't need me coming onto her, I'm the last thing she should be worried about. So I splashed cold water on my face and downed a beer while I waited for her to come eat. One drink will only do so much to ease my pent-up tension, but I won't risk over drinking and letting the alcohol cloud my judgment.

Then, she walks into the kitchen wearing nothing but my flannel shirt, fully covered, but still, my fucking cock jumps at the sight.

Gorgeous, she's fucking gorgeous with her long hair falling over her shoulders. The curls are still full and wild, only the ends look damp from her bath. I know I don't know much about her, but she could tell me she's a swimsuit model and I'd believe her, easily. Hourglass curves, long toned legs, pouty lips I'd love on my...

"I love grilled cheese." I don't finish my thought, her beaming about the simple dinner I made distracting me. Her smile is contagious, radiating through me to my core. A smile the world deserves to see, but that I selfishly hope she only gives to me. Man, I'm in deep.

Trying to keep the atmosphere light, and not like I'm crawling out of my skin wanting to touch her, I ask about her family as we finish eating.

"I'm an only child, so it was pretty lonely growing up. My parents are great though, they were always my biggest supporters. They made sure I was early to every practice and attended any and every school event that I needed to. They moved me into my college dorm with tears in their eyes." She laughs, obviously fond of the sappy memory. We end up on the couch, appropriately spaced with one empty cushion between us.

"They were sad to see you go?" I ask, already pleased with how much it sounds like her parents love her.

"Definitely, but they were so proud of me. They still are, even though my life has turned into a dumpster fire." She blows out a breath, drawing my eyes to her lips.

"What happened to you isn't your fault. Things will get back on track," I assure her, sensing she needs a little bit of optimism right now.

"I hope so. But, unfortunately, things turned bad before yesterday. I mean everything was great a few months ago, then I got restless. I felt like I needed a change, like was missing out on something in my life. That's when I decided to move to Georgia with Mark... My ex. It turned out to be a disaster. Then I decided to leave and things just kept getting worse. It's been one blow after another for a while now..." She trails off, her eyes downcast. "Until you," she whispers. "You're the one positive in all of this." She shrugs, giving me a small smile. It nearly makes me snap. My fingers twitch, I'm aching to touch her. So, I do what any good self destructing person does, I ruin the moment.

"What did your ex do?" I don't know why I choose right now to ask a hard hitting question, but before I can rethink it, the words are already out. Her smile instantly vanishes and I hate myself for it. This isn't a topic I'm going to be fond of, but I can't help myself. I need to know.

Luckily, she seems comfortable enough to talk about it with me. She explains why she left and the anger he was susceptible to. After detailing all the damages he inflicted on the apartment they shared, I made a mental note to kick his ass if I ever have the chance.

"It was the first time in my life that I truly felt unsafe. I don't know, I guess I didn't realize how lucky I'd been most of my life. I had a few relationships in high school and college, but even when they ended there was never any drama. They were normal, boring even. I never expected to be in that situation.

I feel like such an idiot. I upturned everything all because I didn't feel like I belonged anywhere." She wipes a tear from under her eye before it can roll down her cheek. "I still don't know where I belong. Do you know what I mean?"

"Yeah," I confirm, my voice thick with emotion. I do know what she means. All of my life I've been making decisions, just trying to find my spot in this world, but never quite figuring it out. "I quit Special Forces and left the army because I needed something different. It might have been the worst fuckin' mistake of my life." I laugh humorlessly.

"How so?" She asks, her voice full of curiosity like we both are trying to find the answer to life tonight, sitting here on the couch together. I wish I could give her that, but I'm still clueless.

I don't want to tell her about the death I've seen, or the people I've killed, so I keep it simple. "I miss my team. I miss having a purpose. It was miserable at times, and I witnessed terrible things. Way more bad than good, but at least I had something. I don't know. I thought if I tried out civilian life, I'd get some clarity. Now I'm more lost than ever." I shrug.

"Can you go back? Would you want to?" She asks, reminding me how little I've talked to another person about my issues. She's too easy to talk to. It'd be easy enough to spill my guts, tell her all the dark shit that I can't escape, but I can't burden her with that.

"Maybe." I watch as she curls her legs up onto the couch cushion between us, angling her body towards me, erasing some of the distance between us. It's an innocent gesture, her body telling me that she's interested in what I have to say. It just makes me want to pull her into my lap and never let her go. "I felt like I was drowning in the darkness that surrounded me. I wasn't sure that I would survive another year, let alone until retirement."

"Retirement?"

"You can retire with benefits at 38," I admit. Saying it out loud makes me feel like a failure. All I needed to do was make it seven more years, but I gave up.

"You didn't have anyone to lean on? No one to throw you a life vest when it got really bad?" Her eyes look achingly sad on my behalf. Her concern is so real, her empathy for me so raw, it's like nothing I've ever experienced. Maybe this is what I was missing all these years. Someone in my life to grab onto when I felt like my head was going underwater.

I've lived so stubbornly alone, that I didn't realize it was the thing that was killing me. It seems unfair now, to receive a beacon of light when it's too late. Callie would have kept me grounded, she could have saved me.

"My mom was lost in grief after my dad died. My sister…" I shake my head just thinking about the ray of sunshine that is my sister. "Thea is my baby sister. She's so smart, so kind. I'd never bring my problems into her life. She doesn't deserve it. She deserves nothing but happy thoughts." I give Callie a small smile, trying to break some of the tension. Stopping myself from admitting that I feel the same way about her. She doesn't deserve to have someone like me cast a shadow over her life.

"I'm sure they'd want to know. To help you, if you want it." She assumes correctly.

"I know." We sit in silence for a few minutes, thoughtfully contemplating everything that was purged between us. I'm worried that she'll see me in a different light now. That she'll know that I'm broken.

151

"Why Special Forces? Why not a different unit? Something easier," she says with a laugh. I appreciate her attempt to stay lighthearted with her question, but it just reminds me of one of the darkest memories I have. Even though I promised to be as open as possible with her, I still hesitate to answer. I get up and grab another beer, needing more liquid courage to get through this.

Stalling, I don't start talking until I return to the couch, trying to bolster the courage to talk about Chester. I never talk about him, not to my family, not to my friends, even though his death was the hardest I've ever encountered.

After taking a long drink, I tell her about him, from the beginning. I explain our friendship, talk about the bar, and how it was his goal to be in the Special Forces unit. I smile to myself at the good memories, Callie mirroring me with her own smile as I talk. Reluctantly, I tell her about the night he died.

"I never felt the same after that night. I woke up the next day and hardly recognized myself in the mirror, I don't know if it was grief or what," I pause to take another swig from the bottle. "Anyway, it wasn't long after that day that I applied for the team. I wanted to fulfill Chester's dream for him."

I stare at the TV, lost in thought. When I finally look at Callie, she has tears in her eyes. One droplet escapes, rolling down her cheek.

"Don't do that, don't cry. Not for me." I wipe the tear away with my thumb.

"I'm sorry you lost your friend," she says sweetly. So, so sweet.

"That's one of the pictures in my closet, me and Chester," I say, managing a small smile, not wanting her to waste any

152

sadness on me.

She reaches over and grabs the beer bottle from my hand, taking a small drink. My eyes are glued to her lips as they press to the opening, then her tongue when she subtly licks her lips, handing the bottle back. A nice distraction from the topic we're discussing.

"You get nightmares about the night he died?" She asks. I hesitate, not sure what to say.

"Sometimes. Sometimes it's about other things." I leave it at that, not wanting to talk about my other demons, but willing to tell her if she asks. She doesn't, and I'm grateful.

Instead, she jumps up and stands in front of the fireplace on the brick hearth. The fire's not lit, so it's not hot. She turns to face me, looking carefree and happy, and as gorgeous as I've ever seen her. Instantly lifting the heavy atmosphere from around us.

"When you're ready," she sounds enthusiastic, and the contagiousness of it is appreciated after such a dark topic. "You should put your pictures up here. It'd be perfect, you could put Chester here, and your team pictures here and here," she says, indicating to each spot on the mantle as she goes.

"Then you need a picture of your mom and sister, or I'm sure they'll be disappointed." She finishes with her hands on her hips. I smile at her, enjoying her enthusiasm and how lighthearted she is.

"But that leaves one empty gap," I point to one spot she hadn't filled with her imagination, teasing her.

She thinks for a second, "I guess you'll need a picture of me too." She shrugs, "So you'll remember me always." She flutters her eyelashes, feigning innocence. I laugh, a real full belly laugh, incredibly entertained by her whole display.

"I'm offended!" She scoffs, jokingly, I can see the smile in her eyes.

"I don't need a picture to remember you," I joke. "You're too hard to forget."

She squints her eyes at me, "I don't know if you mean that as a good thing or not."

I laugh again, "Good. Definitely, good." I grin at her, watching the smile that spreads across her face.

I take the last drink of my beer, remembering that her lips were just on it. Her eyes linger on the bottle at my mouth, like she realizes it too. The playfulness we were feeling suddenly dissipated, replaced by something thicker.

"I'll never forget you either, Nathan," she admits quietly.

Both of us know that our situation is temporary. We're two strangers that weren't supposed to cross paths, that have two separate lives, in two different states. Even the likelihood that we could continue being friends over long distance seems unlikely.

Mostly because I'm never going to be content being just friends with Callie. If I ever had to see her with another man, I think I'd lose it, and I have no right. I have no right to be possessive of someone who isn't mine. It'll be better for both of us if we completely sever ties once she's safe to go home. We can go back to living our separate lives, even though the thought of that kills me. I'd never want her to feel guilty leaving behind a guy like me, forcing herself to maintain a friendship because I saved her life.

I move to stand in front of her. She's still standing on the hearth making her taller than normal, but I barely have to look up to meet her eyes. I cup her cheek with my hand, hoping it's not the last time but scolding myself for touching her again when I keep telling myself not to.

My thumb brushes her cheekbone. "You should. Forget me and this whole damn mountain. You deserve nothing but happy memories in this beautiful head of yours."

She pinches her eyebrows together but doesn't say anything. Her eyes are filled with so much endearment, it's hard to believe it could be directed toward a guy like me. I'm inches away from kissing her, her eyes dance across my face landing on my lips, silently giving me permission when she leans just a centimeter closer to me. Even though the temptation is unbearable, I can't do it. Even though everything in me is telling me to take the leap, I back away.

"I'm gonna take a shower, you can stay out here and watch TV if you want." Like a coward, I flee from the living room. Leaving the girl of my dreams in my wake.

I'm doing the right thing by not crossing a line. Right? So, why do I feel like a fucking asshole every time I walk away from her?

I'm either making the biggest mistake of my life, or I'm just a pussy who doesn't know how to handle his emotions. That's probably all it is. I keep telling myself that as I go into my bathroom and punish myself with scalding hot water.

Chapter Twenty-Five

Callie

What the hell just happened? The roller coaster of emotions that went through me in the last few minutes has my head spinning. I plop down on the couch and stare at the ceiling. We had such a nice evening, really getting to know each other and laughing. I got real genuine laughs out of Mr. Serious. The second it seemed like he might actually cross over the proverbial line we both walk on, he doused us with water. Snuffing out the flames.

I saw the heat in his eyes when he looked at me, and then the way he actively put the wall back up between us. I'm confused, and kind of hurt. Our teasing back and forth had felt flirtatious, at least to me, but maybe I read it all wrong again. He's had bad things happen in his life, there's a chance he doesn't have room in his heart to have feelings for me. I've so easily fallen for him, but he might not want me at all.

I wish I could stop thinking about him, but it's hard to do when you're stuck in the same cabin. Not that I want to go anywhere else, that's the last thing I want.

I blow a hair off my face, not sure what to do now. The TV is showing the news, though the sound was muted a while ago and with no clue where the remote is, I can only watch as it switches between segments. I lean my head back against the couch, looking off to the side toward the front window. The living room lights are dim, still allowing me to see outside into the yard. It's incredibly dark though, the glow of the moon only making the trees that surround the property faintly visible. It's eerie how isolated it is up here, with no one around for miles. It's definitely not a place I could ever live alone. Nathan must not be afraid of what lurks in the night but, me, I'm afraid of the dark.

Even looking out into it from the safety of the cabin is putting me on edge. I imagine how much worse it would've been if Tony and Bub took me closer to dark, and if I would have had to escape into the woods at night. It's hard to believe I could be any more terrified than I was, but being chased through the forest in the pitch black would definitely have been worse. I sigh, still in denial that yesterday happened.

I've watched true crime documentaries, and I've seen news articles about people being abducted, but I've never believed it could happen to me. Of course, now it's even worse that the town I ended up in has a Sheriff who may or may not be related to the guys that took me. UGH!

I'm not sure how all of this can be resolved, but I am glad to have Nathan in my corner. Thank goodness for small miracles.

He told me during dinner that he was going to call the State police for advice tomorrow. See if they have an opinion on what we should do moving forward. Now it's just a waiting game, we'll see if two criminals will be taken off the street and I get justice, or if the system will fail and they roam free. Best case scenario, I wake up tomorrow and I see on the news that Tony and Bub have been arrested. I don't know how that would happen, but it's just wishful thinking. Then, this nightmare would be over.

Then, what?

I just go home?

Return to Tennessee and pretend like nothing happened. That doesn't seem plausible. I'm forever changed by what happened to me. I'll never feel safe traveling alone again, I'm never going to trust strangers. I don't want to live in constant fear, but Tony and Bub took that choice from me. They ruined the sense of security in my life, and that makes me so angry. How dare they?

How do they think they have the right to do what they did and get away with it? Fucking psychopaths.

Then there is Nathan. When I tell him goodbye is it going to be like we never met? Go back to being perfect strangers even after he's carved a piece of my heart out. Part of me feels like that piece will always be here, with him. Once I leave these mountains, I'll never truly feel whole again.

Still gazing out the window, I jump when I see a bright light sweep across the front yard, dragging me from my pity party. The yellow light bounces off the trees until it comes to a stop, leaving the woods aglow across from the direction it's coming from. I scamper to the front door, peeking out the peephole.

I see the headlights from a car idling in the driveway, just at the edge of the yard, flanked by the wood line. The creeping feeling on the back of my neck tells me this isn't good, it's too late for anyone to be stopping by. But, this is Nathan's home, maybe he was expecting someone and didn't tell me. The car slowly starts forward, getting closer to the cabin like a scene from a scary movie.

I don't hesitate, running down the hallway to get Nathan, half-yelling his name once before I even reach his bedroom door.

"Nathan…" I shout again, raising my hand to knock.

Before I can even make contact, his bedroom door swings open. My hand freezes in midair, stunned to see him standing in front of me shirtless. His hair is still wet from his shower, a towel wrapped around his waist. Temporarily forgetting how to function, all I do is stare at him.

"What's wrong?" He asks, clearly concerned.

"A car… There's a car… Outside," I choke out finally, stumbling on my words a little.

"What the fuck?" He disappears behind his door for no more than five seconds, cluing me in that he was not expecting anyone, and this likely isn't a social visit.

Nathan returns wearing nothing but a pair of sweatpants, grabbing my hand and pulling me down the hallway toward the kitchen. I don't have time to process what's happening before he drops me off behind the kitchen island. "Get down, stay out of sight." His tone leaves no room for questions.

He goes to the front door, looking through the peephole just as I did, and that's when I see the handgun sticking out at his lower back, tucked into the waistband of his sweats. Storing the mental image of how incredibly sexy that is for later, I look away, too nervous about what's waiting on the other side of the door. Nathan glances back at me to make sure I'm hidden, eyeing me when he sees I'm standing here still just staring at him. I startle after realizing he's waiting on me, making me crouch down so fast I fall on my ass.

He opens the door suddenly without ever hearing a knock.

159

"Sheriff."

His voice is low, but loud enough that I can hear. I breathe a silent sigh of relief, thinking for some reason I was found by Tony and Bub, even though logically I don't know how they would've even found us.

Almost as quickly as I have that thought, it dawns on me that the Sheriff would be the way they would find us. The Sheriff is the only one that would know and could easily tell them. I can barely breathe, and my heart is beating so loud in my ears it's hard for me to hear the conversation happening at the front of the house.

"I'm looking for the girl," the Sheriff states.

"Why?"

Sheriff Donahue, "None of your concern, boy."

"She is my concern."

I shiver, hearing those words and how seriously he said them, putting a lump in my throat. Maybe he truly cares about me. Or maybe he's just faking it for the Sheriff's benefit.

There's a long pause, I imagine them standing there, sizing each other up. God, I don't want this to turn into a shoot-out. Not over me.

I should show myself. The Sheriff will get what he wants and then leave. It'll keep Nathan from doing something crazy just to protect me. From getting hurt.

"She never filled out her statement. It's a problem," the Sheriff counters Nathan's earlier response. His callous tone keeps me from budging, my ass is practically glued to the floor.

The rational part of my brain knows to listen to what Nathan said and stay hidden. He has done nothing but keep me safe since the moment he met me, I know I can trust his judgment. If he thought it was safe for me to confront Sheriff Donahue he wouldn't have told me to stay hidden.

"I told you we'd come in tomorrow," Nathan gives a curt response, clearly annoyed.

"I'm startin' to believe she made up the whole thing. She's not turning out to be a very reliable source," Sheriff Donahue says, arrogance lacing his words.

"Is that so?" Nathan states plainly, not giving the Sheriff any fuel for his fire.

"Where is she?" He asks sternly.

"Not here," Nathan lies.

"Then, why is her car here?" Shit. That must be why he was in the driveway so long, he was running my plate, making sure it was my car.

"It's not safe to drive, I dropped her at a hotel in the next town over after we left your office earlier," Nathan lies again. It's effortless, he doesn't even hesitate between each answer, not leaving any room for the Sheriff to question him.

"Which one?" The Sheriff grunts out, obviously frustrated.

"Not sure, it was off of the highway."

"THEY'RE ALL OFF OF THE HIGHWAY BOY!" The Sheriff shouts, startling me. My trembling returns, my whole body quivering even though I'm doing everything to remain still.

"Sorry, guess you'll have to go ask around," Nathan responds, not sounding even slightly fazed by his outburst. "Have a good night, Sheriff."

He shuts the door, not giving him a chance to respond, ending the conversation.

I don't move, still listening to see if it's really over.

Chapter Twenty-Six

Nathan

He knew I was lying. He's an old fuck, but he isn't dumb enough to think I wouldn't have Callie here with me. He's also not dumb enough to do anything that's going to get him killed. Man to man, even an arrogant piece of shit like him knows that I'd win. I watch him through the peephole, seeing the options run through his mind like they're written on his face.

He could try to strong-arm me and use the law as an excuse, but we both know he's not here because he's enforcing any laws. No, he's here to get more information out of Callie, if not more. At minimum he wants to scare her into silence, already making that clear by questioning her validity, accusing her of lying about everything. My biggest concern was that he was going to try to take her. Whatever his plan was, he realized he wouldn't be able to get through me without a fight.

Seeing the uncertainty play out across his face tells me that he doesn't know what to do either. He wants all of this to go away, but does he have the balls to risk his livelihood for it?

That question is answered for me when he finally turns to

leave. Rubbing a hand across his face, and muttering under his breath, he descends the stairs of the porch and returns to his cruiser.

I wait until he leaves, flipping a u-turn right through my grass -fucker- before releasing the breath I was holding. That could've been ugly. I didn't want to get into a shootout but I wouldn't hesitate if it came to it. I wasn't going to let him even an inch through this door, not with Callie hiding just in the kitchen.

I turn towards the subject of my thoughts, still tucked behind the kitchen island. I walk over and crouch down in front of her, her big doe eyes following my every move.

"He's gone."

"Was he here to hurt me?" Her voice trembles.

"Only over my dead body," I say with absolute certainty.

"Nathan..." She scolds me, not liking my callousness about losing my life. She continues, "I wasn't going to let him hurt you. I would've given myself up."

I grab her face gently with both my hands, needing her to listen to me, to hear me. "Never give yourself up for me. Never." I stare deeply into her eyes, needing to see it click. I need her to know how serious I am.

"But..."

"No buts, Callie. Promise me," I demand sternly.

"Fine, I promise," she grumbles. She does not look thrilled about it, but I'm willing to upset her if it means she won't do something stupid by wasting her life for mine.

"Good." I pull her up to stand, wrapping my arms around her, needing to hold her. She doesn't hesitate at all to wrap her arms around my waist, burying her head into my chest.

Her arm bumps the handle of the gun still tucked into my

waistband. It clears my senses enough to remember that I'm still shirtless, and now I have Callie wrapped in my arms, pressed to my bare skin.

I should pull away, but she feels too damn good. Her hands flatten on my back, pressing me firmly against her, needing the connection as much as I do.

Unfortunately, another part of me is also obvious in its needs, and I'm only wearing loose sweats. I angle away, slightly separating our bodies, trying to keep her from noticing how hard I am. She either doesn't notice or doesn't care, because she closes the millimeter of space instantly.

I grit my teeth, trying to calm the raging thoughts in my head. I want Callie so bad, more than I've ever wanted anything. It's more than taking her to bed, I want all of it. I want every laugh, every smile. I want her to stay here with me.

Like a glutton for punishment, I let my brain entertain those thoughts as I stand here running my fingers down her hair. I'd turn the spare room into an office, her office. Hell, I'd make every part of this house different if it pleased her. I'd put those damn pictures up on the mantle in any way that she wanted. Maybe then this house would actually feel like a home. I sigh, releasing her slowly from our embrace. Those things won't ever happen.

"Are you okay?" I ask, not knowing what else to say.

"I'm okay." She gives me a fake reassuring smile. "I mean, a little worried I might get taken out by a crooked Sheriff and, or, his two cronies." She laughs humorously, "But other than that. Totally fine."

"I'm not going to let that happen," I promise her, worried that the pieces I've helped her meld back together the last 24 hours might start cracking again. She just nods her head in response, unable to give me anything else.

"Come on, you need some sleep." I usher her towards my room without any objection after subtly tucking away my obvious attraction to her.

She goes into the bathroom, giving me a chance to put on a shirt and some briefs under my sweats, needing the extra barriers to keep me from doing something rash. When I step out of my closet she's sitting on the bed, staring off into nothing, like she did last night. Zoning out, lost in her own thoughts, I'm not sure what to do.

Thinking maybe she needs room to process her thoughts, I start towards the hallway, but almost to the door, I hear my name. "Nathan…"

She spoke so faintly, I almost missed it. I turn towards her, and my heart rips in two. She looks so defeated, her shoulders are slumped with the weight of the world resting on them. I can see it on her face that it won't take much to break the dam that she's had up, she's starting to crumble right before me.

Tired of second-guessing myself, I flip off the light and crawl into bed next to her. Unlike this morning, I pull back the blankets, not intending to leave any space between us. Laying flat on my back, I raise my arm, indicating for her to tuck her body into mine.

It's probably a bad idea, but I don't care, she's been through too much. She needs comfort, she needs me. And I intend to provide just that, even if it leaves me aching for more. She nestles into my side immediately, laying her head on my chest. Now that I have a shirt on, I miss the feeling of her cheek on my skin, but this will do. I feel her body shake, exhaling all of

165

her pent-up anxiety, relaxing into my embrace.

"Thank you," she whispers against my sternum. I kiss the top of her head in response.

I'm whipped. This woman is going to ruin all other relationships for me and we aren't even in one. How will I move on from this when I feel so much for her already?

I tighten my arms around her. "Any time."

Damn, and do I mean it. She has me, whenever she needs me, I'm at her mercy. I don't say that out loud though, afraid I'll scare her off. The intensity of my feelings is even scaring me.

I've had girlfriends, and flings that weren't even serious enough for goodbyes. Nothing compared to what I'm experiencing right now. How is that even possible in such a short amount of time?

When I notice her breathing has slowed, and her fingers twitch slightly where they rest on my chest, I sigh. Maybe my concern with her well-being is clouding my judgment. I've never felt responsible for a woman before, never so invested in keeping someone safe.

My team depended on me, sure, but that was different. They were all guys that made the commitment to enlist, they knew the dangers they signed up for. I'd die for any one of them, and I know they'd do the same for me, but it's not the same. Callie is different. I wouldn't be able to live with myself if something happened to her.

I contemplate staying awake, in case the Sheriff decides to grow some steel in his spine and come back. The lull of Callie's breathing is too much though, and I feel my eyelids getting heavy. I could fight it, or even try to get up now that she's asleep, but I don't have any real desire to. The house is locked up. My gun is on the nightstand. I learned how to sleep with one eye open a long time ago, so I let myself drift, content holding onto Callie for as long as she'll let me.

Chapter Twenty-Seven

Callie

Thump… Thump… Thump.

What the hell is that? My head keeps knocking against something. Thump… Thump… Thump… Why won't it stop? I use all my strength to turn my head, my neck feeling stiff as a board. I blink the blurriness out of my vision, trying to focus on what's in front of me. I squeeze my eyes shut, willing them to cooperate. When I finally open them, I'm staring directly into Tony's grimy face, in the back of their van.

"AHHHHHHRRGG!" I try to scream but it's muffled by something. Duct tape. They put duct tape on my mouth this time. No, no, NO! This can't be happening. Where's Nathan? Do they have him too? I lash my head back and forth trying to get rid of the sight in front of me. I can't tell where I am, we're surrounded by darkness.

"Shh, shh, shh, don't cry little girl, I've been looking for you," Tony leers. All I can do is buck and roll, trying with all of my might to get away. My muffled cries are all I hear before my world goes black.

Suddenly, I'm thrust into the river, blackened by the night

sky -soaked up to my thighs in the biting, icy water. I look behind me and see Bub standing on the river bank illuminated by the moonlight, crouched on all fours like a wild animal.

I turn to run, but the current is too strong, I'm pumping my legs but I'm getting nowhere. Finally, I see Nathan up ahead of me. Yelling for me, beckoning me to follow him.

"I'M TRYING!" I scream, tears pouring down my face, soaked from the river.

I keep running even though I don't feel like I'm making any progress, the river bed thick with mud. Chancing a glance over my shoulder, I barely have time to register the gnarly-looking man about to pounce on me. Bub is coming at me full force, jaws stretched open inhumanly, saliva dripping from his teeth. I scream at the sight, falling forward from the impact of him tackling me.

Instead of my face landing in water, it lands in sand. I look up, hoping to see Nathan in front of me, hoping that he's here to save me once again, but instead, I'm met with a demon-like figure that resembles Tony. Its neck twisting and contorting, his red eyes bugging out of his head.

"Gotcha!" He says before he lunges at my face.

"NOO!" I wake with a scream, panting uncontrollably while I take in my surroundings.

"Callie, are you okay?" Nathan is right beside me, face filled with concern, his arms tightly wrapped around me. I bury my face in his chest, catching my breath after that horrifying nightmare.

I twist my hand into Nathan's shirt, needing something to hold, to ground myself. The gruesome images of the demonic version of Tony and Bub litter through my mind again, making me grimace against Nathan's chest.

"It was horrible," I finally say. "I was so scared."

My heart is still beating out of my chest, and I'm suddenly aware of the sweat dripping down my back. I sit up, needing to stretch my limbs, swiping the loose hairs from my sweaty forehead. He follows my movements, sitting up next to me, and rubbing the sleep from his eyes.

"Was it about them?" He asks, not needing to say their names. I nod in confirmation.

"They were chasing me again, but they looked like monsters," I sniff back the tears threatening my eyes.

"I'm sorry, baby." He pulls me into his chest, not caring about my clammy skin, my heart melting from his term of endearment. "I know how real nightmares can feel."

I nuzzle my face into his neck, wanting to be close enough that my bad dream becomes a distant memory. This is what I needed. I needed him.

My heart eventually finds its normal rhythm again, or as normal as it can be when I'm this close to Nathan. We stayed cuddled together like that for a long time, him holding me, my face buried in his neck. Eventually, I feel the need to pull away, overheating in the flannel I had put on earlier.

"I need a different shirt," I tell him, pulling at the fabric, and trying to cool off my skin.

"Here." He pulls the shirt off of his body and hands it to me, "I'm not used to sleeping in a shirt anyway."

Thoroughly distracted, and hot all over for different reasons, I take the shirt from him. Getting an eye full of his bare chest, I'm frozen in place. His broad shoulders and chest make me weak just looking at them. His stomach is firm, obvious that it's all muscle, but not overly defined like he starves himself. A sprinkling of hair across his chest trails down his stomach to below his navel, disappearing under the sheets. I groan inwardly, dying to see all of him. He's magnificent, perfect even.

"Thank you," I squeak out, turning my back to him, not bothering to get out of bed, but very aware of him right behind me.

I unbutton the flannel, shrugging it off my shoulders. Nathan pulls it the rest of the way off my arms from behind me so I don't have to, his fingers skimming across my skin. My stomach clenches with desire, feeling butterflies all the way to my core. The trail that his fingers left on my skin is going to be etched into my memory forever.

Being topless and exposed when he is so close is liberating, but terrifying at the same time. I desperately wish that he would make the first move. Grab me, touch me, kiss me, anything.

I clutch his t-shirt to my chest, hesitating to put it on, knowing that he's not going to do what I want him to unless I say something. He's the king of consent and I'm dying because of it.

I quickly put his shirt on, not brave enough to voice my desires. Before I have the chance, he's pulling my hair from the collar of the shirt, away from my sweaty neck. He smooths it down my spine, making me shiver. Turning back towards him, I can see how affected he is by all of this too. His eyes are hooded with lust, his jaw clenched like he's having trouble keeping words from coming out of his mouth. It's a standoff, neither of us making the first move.

The only light coming in is from the window, casting moonlight across the room. It somehow makes all of this feel like a dream like there is no possible way that I'm here right now. I reach out and touch Nathan's hand, his eyes focusing on where they're connected.

"Just making sure you're real," I joke.

He closes his hand around mine, holding it, "Were you worried I wasn't?"

Yes. I answer to myself, but instead say out loud, "I told you, I think you're too good to be true." I smile, trying to ease the sexual tension I'm consumed with.

Whether he wants to take it to the next level or not, I'm truly happy being here with him. Regardless of all the other bad shit, meeting Nathan has been incredible. Being with him has been a fairytale.

He smiles at me, "I know you're too good to be true."

We both sit there, face to face, smiling at each other like nothing else in the world matters. Suddenly, feeling shy, I duck my face. These feelings are so overwhelming, but so good at the same time. He tips my chin back up and cups my cheek, making me look him in the face again. He leans in slightly and my breath hitches.

"Tell me to stop," he whispers, slowly drawing closer to me.

"Never," I respond, barely taking a breath before his lips melt into mine.

His mouth is slow but intense against mine, giving me exactly what I need. My lips part slightly and he slips his tongue in my mouth, lightly caressing mine. I push back, needing to explore him too. Kissing him feels so right, it takes my breath away. I run my tongue along his bottom lip before tugging it between my teeth and biting down gently, wanting more.

He moans into my mouth, "Callie..." He scolds.

I pull away, surprised at his tone, afraid that I did something wrong.

"If you keep kissing me like that, I'm not going to be able to control myself," he sounds like he's in pain, but he registers the hurt expression on my face instantly, pulling me in closely again, his lips barely touching mine.

"I want you more than I've ever wanted anything in my life, Callie, but I need to do things right so you won't regret it." He brushes a feather-light kiss to my lips, then nose. "So, you won't regret me," another kiss to each cheek.

He rests his forehead on mine, "Please, say something."

My mouth moves, but no words come out. I'm hurt and relieved at the same time. Hurt that he stopped kissing me so suddenly, but relieved that he finally admitted he wants me. The confusion is too much this late at night, my brain isn't working as quickly as it usually does.

Which is exactly why he pulled back. Of course.

He wants me to make clear-minded decisions, he doesn't want me to wake up tomorrow with a different perspective… Dammit. It's annoying, but so damn thoughtful.

Feeling bold and more clear-headed, and wanting to act on it, I move before he can stop me, straddling his hips. I trap his thighs between mine, slowly sinking down onto his lap, feeling just how much he wants me. His hard, significant, length is nestled right in between the apex of my thighs. He can probably tell how wet I am, and feel the warmth of my pussy even through our clothes.

"I understand, Nathan. But, you need to understand that I want you. I have wanted you since the moment I met you. This is not a rash decision. I have fantasized about you kissing me, fucking me, making love to me…" I rock gently against him, rubbing his cock against me, wishing we weren't clothed.

He lets out a strangled moan but doesn't stop me. I love having this effect on him, it makes me feel powerful. Spurred on by his reaction, I continued, "If I weren't wearing your underwear right now, you could feel just how wet I am for you. How much I want you."

I keep grinding against him, rubbing my clit against his hardness. "So, I am going to stop. I won't let you make love to me. Not tonight. Because I want you to know, with my full heart and soul, that I will never regret anything that happens between us. Got it?" I finish with the phrase he always uses on me, demanding that he understand me.

Not wanting to stop, I keep grinding on him, but put my finger under his chin, forcing him to make eye contact with me. "Got it?" I repeat, my lips just a whisper from his.

"Yes, Ma'am." He crushes his lips against mine, devouring my mouth. Using his hands on my hips to keep rocking me back and forth, creating the friction that my clit so desperately needed.

"Nathan." I gasp, this time it's my turn, strangling his name from my throat.

"I agree, no sex. But you're going to cum for me. I need to see you cum for me baby," he insists.

The use of his pet name for me makes me whimper, feeling delirious, the sensation is too much, but in the best way. My arms are wrapped around his neck, holding on for dear life, putting my chest at the perfect height for his mouth. He bites my sensitive nipple through the fabric of the t-shirt, making me gasp again.

The next bite on my other nipple sends me over the edge, all of the pent-up tension from the last two days making me orgasm hard, moaning his name as I cry out. I cling to him while I ride the wave of euphoria, feeling him gently thrust against me, prolonging the blissful torture.

Chapter Twenty-Eight

Nathan

I can't stop kissing her. I press my lips against her neck over and over, trailing up and across her jawline, up her chin where her mouth meets mine. Her kisses are slow and lazy, coming down from her climax. I savor every second of it, never feeling more alive than in this moment. I'm still rock hard under my sweatpants, but it doesn't matter, I just witnessed the most beautiful woman I've ever seen crumble in my arms with pleasure.

My body is already aching to see it again, to feel her convulse around me, to hear her cry my name out again. When my name left her mouth as she lost all control, I thought I was going to cum right then.

If I wasn't hooked before, I'm definitely hooked now. It'll never get better than this, nothing will ever compare to Callie.

She rubs the tip of her nose across mine, tenderly, and a small smile plays on her lips. "That wasn't part of my plan," she teases.

I laugh, not able to hide my amusement. I run my hands up and down her back, the compulsion to touch her too strong to stop. They trail down her hips, my fingers tracing the seam of my briefs around to the back of her thighs, moving up to palm her ass with both of my hands. She's fucking perfect. I squeeze and massage her soft skin, working my way back up to her lower back.

"You're perfect," I admit, voicing my thoughts out loud. I look into her eyes, seeing the doubt in them. "Callie, you're fucking perfect," I insist, kissing her again.

Both of us long past the stage of hesitation, she kisses me back eagerly. We both want this, and kissing is safe. For tonight. As much as I want more, I can wait.

I would wait forever for her if she needed me to, but I can tell she doesn't want to. Thank fucking god for that. Maybe tomorrow, I'll take her on a date, and treat her like a man should. Like a normal couple would do. Like two people who aren't single-handedly trying to navigate a potentially corrupt Sheriff and everything else she's gone through. Yeah... maybe a dinner date should wait, but staying secluded in my cabin with her sounds just as good if not better.

"If you keep kissing me, I'm going to combust," she moans against my mouth, my hips involuntarily thrust forward, rubbing my hard cock against her ass.

"You're right, I'm dying too." I smile at her, feeling immense satisfaction that she is as needy for me as I am for her.

She scoots further down my legs, her fingers trailing down my stomach towards the waistband of my pants making my muscles clench. "Can I?..."

Before she can finish, I grab her hands and flip her onto her back, pinning her below me. She lets out a surprised gasp, not seeing it coming.

"If you touch me, I won't be able to stop, and I agreed to no sex. I'm hanging on by a thread baby." I keep her wrists pinned with one hand, using the other to pull her face gently to mine, kissing her again, never getting enough. Her lips so soft against mine make me crazy. I lick her bottom lip, needing to feel the softness on my tongue, tasting her.

"Nathan…" She moans again, "You're torturing me."

I release her while I can still think clearly, turning to the side and tucking her body into mine. I kiss her forehead. "So the seductress can't handle a little teasing," I joke.

"Me? A seductress? Never." She feigns innocence.

"Oh so, grinding against my cock until I almost came in my pants, that wasn't you?"

She giggles, burying her face into my neck, "Nope, wasn't me." Her sweet, shyness returned. I kiss her head, again, like it's a reflex. Now that we've crossed that bridge I don't think I could ever go back to keeping my distance, she's too addicting. She's going to have to beat me off with a stick to stop me from kissing her.

She pulls her face away from my neck slightly, "Nathan?"

"Yeah, baby?"

"I'm not usually so forward," she clears her throat, "but I need you to know that I meant it. I won't ever regret anything that happens between us." She seals her statement with a soft kiss on my neck, right above my collarbone.

I don't respond right away, because I'm not sure what to say. I hope she's right, I hope she doesn't wake up tomorrow thinking this was a mistake. The pessimist in me is telling me there is no way this could end well, there is no way either of us is going to walk away from this unscathed.

I don't say any of that out loud though, preferring the version of reality we're in right now. One thing I know for sure is that I will never regret meeting Callie. I would have preferred to meet under different circumstances, sure, but the only thing that matters is I found her. I kept her safe when she needed me.

Still not knowing what to say, I simply hold her close, deciding not to say anything. Not tonight at least.

I run my fingers through her hair, feeling her relax, and her breathing slow until I know she's fast asleep. I lie awake for what feels like hours, thinking about everything. Thinking about Callie, thinking about what I'm going to do tomorrow to make sure she's safe. I wonder if tonight has changed anything, if I could ask her to stay here with me a little longer, or if that's insane to even think about. If I were by myself, I'd be tossing and turning, but with Callie in my arms, I lay perfectly still hoping she can get enough rest for the both of us.

After what feels like only a couple minutes of sleep, I wake up to the morning sun streaming in the window. I'm usually awake by dawn out of habit, so I never bothered to put curtains up.

Callie's bare leg is draped over mine over top of the sheets, giving me a chance to admire it. Her smooth skin tempts me, I can't help but run my hand along her thigh, knee to hip, back and forth. I pause, afraid I woke her up when I feel her fingers twitch against my stomach. Her eyes stay closed, so I continue my caress, this time going further down to her calf. Memorizing every inch in case she wakes up and comes to her senses, leaving me in the dust.

Those fears are quickly squashed when she stirs slightly, pulling herself closer to me, nuzzling into my chest. "Good morning," she mumbles sleepily, her lips pressed to my skin.

"Good morning, beautiful," I respond with a kiss on her

head.

She giggles, "I've always wanted someone to say that to me." She looks up at me, smiling, her sweet face so close to mine, "Like the country song."

How the hell has she never had someone say that to her before? She told me about her ex, he must be a bigger piece of shit than I thought. "You deserve it, and a lot more, every day," I tell her honestly, closing the distance and kissing her earnestly.

She matches my kiss with her own, deepening it. She's like a magnet pulling me in. I can't stop touching her, kissing her, and I don't want to. My hand is tangled in her hair, holding her to me. The other hooks around the back of her knee, pulling her body all the way on top of mine. Needing to feel all of her on me, like a compulsion, I can't stand any space between us. She doesn't protest, anchoring her elbows on either side of my head, putting her in the perfect place for my lips to reach hers.

She pulls away, just an inch, studying my face, "Are we crazy?" She asks me, genuinely, wondering the same thing I am.

"Definitely." It's all I can muster up as a response, needing to take control of something because I feel like I'm drowning, I flip her over so I'm on top.

I brace my arms on the bed so I don't crush her under my weight. "I'll call up any loony bin you want if you promise to be my roommate," I joke, kissing her all over her face, and making her smile. I keep kissing her and I'm rewarded with a full belly laugh, the kind you can't fake. The kind that you can't help but laugh along with. I watch her as she comes down from her laughing fit, feeling incredibly fortunate to witness her happiness.

"Maybe we can just be crazy together here, in the comfort of your home?" She jokes, still catching her breath from laughing so hard.

Damn, the words *together* and *home* stir up a deep aching in my chest. The thought of my home eventually being her home sounds fuckin' nice. I want her to stay, I really want her to stay. Instead, all I say out loud is, "Deal."

We lay in bed talking for a while, neither of us eager to start the day. The sexual tension is still heavy in the room, my eyes and hands continuously lingering on her body. Hers do the same, tracing the veins in my arm, her fingers skimming so lightly across my skin at some points I feel like I'm going to catch on fire.

Especially when her fingertips trail along the exposed black waistband under my sweatpants, teasing me relentlessly.

"I don't think I've ever wanted anyone as much as I want you. I also don't think I've ever felt as safe, or as comfortable with anyone, and I barely know you," she admits. "What have you done to me?" She laughs, but her eyes are full of desire, cluing me into the dirty thoughts in her mind.

"You're making it really hard to be a gentleman when you say things like that. Be careful," I warn. "I might not ever let you leave my bed."

"Is that a threat, or a promise?" She bats her eyelashes at me and I swear it takes everything in my power not to spank her ass.

I keep it reigned in though, happy to have her in my bed, in any form. Especially when I'm trying to do things the right way like she deserves. It helps that I'm eager to hear every word that comes out of her mouth, dying to learn all of her thoughts, her secrets.

Joking around and getting to know each other is just as addicting as the physical stuff, I want to know everything. I want all of it.

Chapter Twenty-Nine

Callie

My cheeks hurt from smiling so much, I can't recall a time I've ever felt this comfortable and happy. Nathan looks so carefree and relaxed, I've lost count of how many times I've seen him smile. He tells me a couple of stories from his childhood, all silly things, like trapping his sister in her treehouse for stealing his GI Joes. We talked about school and some of the things we did as embarrassing teenagers. He was shocked when I told him about not having a date to my senior prom and promised he would've taken me if he was around. We both laughed, realizing that when I was a senior in high school, he was already five years into his Army career. Now the age gap isn't weird, but back then it would've been creepy. When I told him that I'm almost 27, that my birthday is next month, he promised he was going to buy me the best present I've ever had. I laughed at that, but inwardly I realized I'd probably be back in Tennessee by then.

Not wanting to kill my mood, I don't dwell on the what-ifs. Instead, I list off some of the best presents I've ever received, so he knows how strong the competition is. I swore that he'd never be able to compete with the razr flip phone I got for Christmas one year.

"I really wanted the pink one, because all of my friends had one, but I got silver instead. It was still one of my favorite presents, so you'll have a hard time topping it," I joke with a shrug.

"Baby, I would scour the Earth for a pink razr flip phone before I'd ever lose a challenge," Nathan retorts, cockily, making me laugh.

We are bantering back and forth about which flip phone was better growing up when we both hear a loud crash come from the front of the house. I freeze, not knowing what it is or what to do. My fight-or-flight response is not kicking in at all.

Nathan, however, his eyes go from joking and playful to hard as stone in a second. He jumps out of bed, grabs his gun from the nightstand, and pulls me up with his free hand, dragging me into the closet.

"Here, you know how to use this?" He asks while handing me his handgun. I'm still frozen, not reacting. He pries my fingers open, wrapping them around the handle of the gun.

"It's loaded. You point and shoot, got it?" His voice is harsh and commanding, so different from how he was just moments ago. It does the trick though, snapping me out of my funk enough to let him push me down to the floor, hiding me behind the dresser.

"Stay here, shoot anyone that walks through that door." He pauses, "Besides me." He pulls a rifle out of his gun locker, racking it once to make sure it's loaded.

He turns to exit the closet when my body and my brain finally catch up to one another, I scramble up from the floor, grabbing his arm, "I don't want you to get hurt."

He grabs my face with his free hand, pulling me in for a chaste kiss. "I won't baby. Besides, it's probably nothing." His smile doesn't reach his eyes. He knows as well as I do that there could be someone out there coming to finish the job, coming to kill me.

"Stay hidden." He leaves, closing the closet door behind him. I start to panic instantly, slumping back to the ground. What the hell is going on with my life? Why are all these bad things happening?

I try to calm my breathing, inhaling and exhaling slowly so I don't have a full-blown panic attack. My fingers grip the gun so tightly their shaking and my knuckles are white. I'm so afraid for Nathan. Why does he have to be all tough and brave, running straight into danger? I want him here with me, holding me, instead of out there with who knows what?

A loud gunshot sounds off, close enough for me to hear but muffled enough that it sounds like it came from outside. Agony rips through my heart, terrified that Nathan's hurt, or worse, dead. I will never be able to live with myself if he gets hurt because of me, if he dies it would kill me too. The realization that I'm falling in love with this man makes tears burst free from my eyes.

I don't know how it would be possible to start falling in love with someone so quickly, but Nathan makes it so easy. He's such a good man, and I fed him to the wolves by bringing my problems here. I sob, trying to contain the sound with my free hand. This is all so fucked up.

I hear the door to the bedroom open with a creak, but it's barely audible so I hold my breath, trying to listen. Footsteps approach the closet, and I squeeze my eyes shut, preparing for whatever happens next.

"Callie, it's me." Nathan throws the door open, not even slightly concerned that I was going to shoot him. His voice is like music to my ears.

I launch at him, discarding the gun on the floor where I was hiding. I wrap my arms around his waist, burying my face into his chest. "I heard a gunshot." I sniffle, still not completely able to stop my tears from escaping, "I was afraid they got you."

He kisses my head tenderly, running his hands up and down my back. "I'm okay, baby. It was just a bear."

I whip my head up to look at him, "A bear?"

"Yeah, apparently I need to lock up my trash cans better," he squeezes me tighter.

"Oh my god, I thought they found me." Burying my face into his chest again, "Instead you could've been killed by a fucking bear." My tears continue running down my face, I don't know if they are from fear or frustration, but they keep coming.

"Hey, don't cry. I'm okay, the bear was just making noise. I shot my gun into the air to get him to leave, nothing more." He pulls me away so he can wipe the tears from my cheeks. "Besides, I don't know what the Sheriff's intentions are regarding Tony or Bub, but if any of them come onto my property, I'll win. Every time."

"I'm sorry," I say as I wipe the wetness from his chest that my tears left. "I panicked when I thought I might lose you, I don't... I don't want you to get hurt."

I want to tell him how badly I don't want to lose him. I don't want our relationship to end once my car's fixed. I don't want it to end at all.

I don't even know if you can call what we have a relationship, we haven't even known each other long enough to be able to put a label on it. I continue wiping the trails of wetness off his chest, moving down to his stomach, enjoying the feel of his bare skin under my fingertips.

I'm mesmerized by his firm build, and how his muscles tighten as my hands trail lower. His body is a distraction I so desperately want. My tears all but forgotten, I scrape my nails down his stomach until they meet the waistband of his pants.

"Callie..." He choked out my name. I look up into his eyes and am met with a beautifully pained look on his face. He's restraining himself, holding back again, like he was last night. Trying to be decent. I don't want decent, I want him. I sneak my fingers under the elastic, prepared to tug them down. I maintain eye contact the whole time so there is no question of my intent, when he catches my wrists with both of his hands, halting my movements.

"Please, Nathan, I thought I might lose you." My plea sounds so desperate that I should be embarrassed, but I'm not. Not with him. His jaw ticks, the war raging behind his eyes of what he wants and what he thinks is right. But, this is right, he's just fighting harder than I am, trying to protect my feelings. I lean up on my tip toes, and plant a kiss on his lips, needing to feel him, to connect with him.

He doesn't resist me, immediately sliding his tongue into my mouth, simultaneously releasing my wrists. Before I have a chance to continue my work on his waistband, he wraps his arm around my waist, lifting me, using his other hand to secure my legs around his hips. *Yes.*

He carries me to his bed, never breaking our kiss, squeezing my ass roughly. My pussy is already throbbing, craving Nathan's touch. He lays me down across the bed, pinning my arms above my head immediately, "You want me to fuck you, baby?" He whispers between kisses that have turned sloppy and breathless.

"Yes," I breathe out, just barely.

"Yes, what?" He demands.

"Yes, Sir," I answer immediately, the term slipping easily off my tongue knowing the effect it had on him last time.

"You're going to do exactly what I say, got it?" He asks rhetorically, knowing what my answer will be. He knows just how badly I want him. How badly I want this.

"Yes, Sir," I respond, but in my head, I'm screaming hell yes, yes, yes, yes.

"Good girl." He seals it with a soft kiss. Letting go of my wrists, he stands in front of me at the edge of the bed. "Come here," he commands. I don't hesitate, rising on my knees in front of him. I'm breathing rapidly, my need for him so intense, my body trembles with anxiousness, the mattress making me wobble slightly. He steadies me by grabbing my hips, dragging his hands up to my waist, and taking the hem of my shirt with him. His movements halt with a squeeze to my waist, not going any further.

"Shit. Callie, I don't have any condoms." He clears his throat like it pains him to say it. "I wasn't exactly expecting any guests when I moved out here." I have to process what he's saying, my mind is a little foggy.

"I have the arm implant," I pause, feeling a little vulnerable, unsure how he'll react. "I've never not used a condom, but I got checked a couple of weeks ago when I thought my ex had cheated. Just in case."

"I've always used condoms, and I haven't been with anyone in a long time. I'm clean." He flexes the muscle in his jaw again, clearly distraught. "We can stop, I don't want you to feel like you have to."

Always such a gentleman...

Chapter Thirty

Nathan

My heart is pounding in my ears waiting for Callie to respond. I meant what I said, I don't want her to keep going just because she feels obligated.

She presses her hands to my chest, running them upward to hold me around my neck, pulling me towards her until our foreheads press together. "I trust you. I need you, Nathan. All of you." She kisses me gently, giving herself over to me.

I want to fall to my knees in triumph hearing her say those words. Pride courses through me for having the privilege of Callie's unyielding trust. I kiss her harder, feeling almost feral at the thought of getting to make love to this perfect woman in front of me. Our tongues clash, teeth scraping each other's lips, and when I thrust my tongue into her mouth she takes the opportunity to suck on it, making me crazy. I drag her shirt off the rest of the way, pushing her back down on the bed in the process.

I'm floored from the sight of Callie's perfect body, wearing only my black briefs, she looks so fucking sexy. My mind would never be able to conjure anything, anyone, as hot as she is. She's unreal.

I cup her full chest with each palm, bringing my mouth down to one of her taught pink nipples, reminding me she is very much real. I massage the other side, loving the weight and fullness, and how her soft skin feels in my hand. I lick and nip at the tight peak, eliciting moans from her, getting high off her sounds.

My dick is rock hard and desperate to be inside her, but I want to take my time and enjoy every second of this. After a long, hard, suck, I pop her nipple out of my mouth, making it glisten from the attention. "You're so perfect, baby," I tell her honestly.

"Nathan…" She moans breathlessly. My name sounds so goddamn good coming out of her mouth, it's something I've never cared for before, but having Callie say my name in pleasure is becoming the best thing in my life.

I eagerly continue, sucking the neglected breast into my mouth. I bite and suck the firm mound, teasing her, before finally pulling her nipple between my teeth. Tugging gently, I am rewarded with another moan. The sound goes straight to my cock, and I can't stop from grabbing my hard-on through my pants, giving it a tight squeeze to calm it down.

No luck of that when Callie is still lying before me, hot as hell, and I've only just started. Dragging my lips down her torso, I find her waistband and pull the underwear down her legs, tossing it away. I'm greeted with the prettiest pussy I've ever seen. Her small patch of trimmed hair is like a beacon to her warm, pink folds.

"So, god damn, beautiful," I breathe against her, before diving right in.

Not enough patience to take it slow, or tease her, I eat her pussy like a man starving. I lick her slit with my flattened tongue, leading me to her swollen clit. I flick it back and forth, moving my head in momentum with my tongue, hitting her most sensitive spot. She tastes like heaven. She tastes like *mine*.

Callie's reactions spur me on, her thighs are clenched around my head, her hips bucking off the mattress. She's breathing heavily, mumbling my name, and our lord and saviors', over and over.

"God's not here, baby. Just me," I tease her, getting a breathless giggle from her, so I nip at her clit as punishment, making her jump.

"Fuck, Nathan…" Another moan that goes straight to my raging dick. I hold onto her hips tighter, keeping her right where I want her, traveling lower to fuck her tight hole with my tongue, just like my cock will.

I inhale her scent, using the tip of my nose to continue applying pressure to her clit, while I penetrate her opening, licking her like I'm deranged.

"Oh my god, it feels so fucking good!" Her hands clench the bed sheets, holding on for dear life. Exactly how I want her.

I raise my hand to her mouth, sticking two fingers in. She sucks them greedily like the good girl she is. A good little slut. I pull them out with a pop, making her release the suction she had on me. Using the wetness, I stick one finger into her tight pussy, then the other. My hips involuntarily thrust against the side of the bed when I feel how warm and tight it is. I'm practically humping the mattress, my cock dying to be inside her.

Curling my fingers slightly to rub her inner walls, I pump in and out, continuing to attack her clit with my tongue. She runs her fingers through my hair, barely long enough to hold on to, something I am regretting right now. Her nails scratch my scalp as she grips my head, keeping my face right where she wants it. Happy to oblige, I keep devouring her pussy until I feel her start to twitch, signs of her impending climax.

"I'm gonna cum, Nathan… Please…" She begs, her mumbles start becoming incoherent, telling me she is right on the verge.

I suck on her clit as I fuck her with my fingers, until I feel her walls tighten, clenching me repeatedly through her orgasm making me throb with need. Her moans turn to heavy breaths, in and out. Her muscles relax once the waves of her release cease.

Slowly, I slide my fingers out of her, enjoying the look of bliss on her face. She watches as I stand up from my kneeled position, sucking her juices off of my fingers. Her eyes darken with lust.

"You still with me, baby?" I ask her, seeing how serene she is after cumming around my fingers.

She doesn't respond. Instead, she sits up, leaning back on her hands. Her hair is wild and her skin is flushed with arousal. She looks like the goddess of sex, a wet dream.

Her eyes are telling of her intentions, the boldness returning that was in them last night when she crawled on my lap and rode me. She crawls towards me, sitting on her knees right before me, slightly spread. Yeah, definitely the sexiest woman I've ever seen.

She grabs my waistband, and even though I'm supposed to be in control, I'm no saint, so I let her pull my sweats down until they fall to my feet. I step out of them and kick them away, while Callie sits in front of me fully exposed and submissive, staring at my cock. I grab it, rubbing it loosely as I watch her eyes track my movements. Her tongue sneaks out, licking her lips.

"You're huge," she breathes. "I had a feeling you would be, but wow."

My ego explodes at that comment, like any man, but to have it come from a girl you're becoming obsessed with, yeah, that's fucking nice.

"It's yours baby, all yours." I watch the fire ignite in her eyes at my comment, my balls tighten in anticipation. She raises up on her knees so our faces are level with one another, wrapping both hands around my dick, pumping it up and down, slowly. She snakes her tongue into my mouth and I welcome it greedily, tangling my hands in her hair, and kissing her back fervently.

Her slow, methodical, movements are torturing me in the best way, making me afraid that I'll cum before I want to. She pulls away before I can, descending lower, her mouth wrapping around the head of my cock. I should stop her, I'm almost a goner already, but I have no willpower. I choke back a moan when she tightens her lips around me and sucks. I swear I can feel the sensation all the way up my spine as her lips drag along my length.

I need to take back the reins before I'm too far gone. Before I get lost down the back of her throat and miss my chance to fuck her like I want to. Like an idiot, instead of pulling her away, I use the hands that are in her hair to slowly pump her head back and forth, fucking her mouth. I can't resist.

She hums happily, but I'm on the very edge of exploding so I pull out, tugging her back up to my face. I crush my lips against hers, "I need to be inside you. Now."

She whimpers at my words, wrapping her arms around my

neck, "Yes."

That single breathless word is all the confirmation I need, I lean into her, fucking her mouth with my tongue, urging her back down to the bed so she's laying beneath me. I kneel between her legs, the head of my cock right at her entrance. Looking at her is surreal, having her open to me, physically and mentally. I'm never going to get over this, over her. She's it.

"You're mine, Callie. This is fucking mine," I slide into her tight pussy slowly. She gasps as I push deeper into her. The feeling of her tightness surrounding me is enough to make my eyes want to roll back into my head, but I don't want to stop looking at her face. Her expression is beautifully anguished, accepting every inch of me. She bites her bottom lip like she's the epitome of sin and lust.

Her eyes stay on mine, not breaking contact, an unsaid promise in them. The way she looks at me, like we've known each other an eternity and we've finally found our way back, not like someone who was a stranger two days ago. Full of trust and adoration, things I hope to never screw up.

Mine, she's fucking mine. I slam into her to the hilt, filling her completely. She cries out, and I keep going pumping in and out, fucking her hard. I should slow down, and savor this, but I can't. I'm delirious with pleasure, she feels too good and I've wanted her so fucking badly.

She doesn't seem to mind, meeting me thrust for thrust. I hold onto her tits, squeezing them. Her nails scrape my biceps, holding onto me for leverage as I drive into her. Not being able to keep my lips from hers, I lean into her until we're chest to chest, sucking on her bottom lip.

She cries out again, the sound muffled by my mouth as I

rock into her deeply, rubbing her clit with the front of my pelvis. She's clawing my back, holding onto me as I take us to the edge of release. I'm so fucking close, but I want Callie to cum again. I want to feel her pussy contracting around my cock. Her lips are still against mine, unable to focus on anything but the build up of pressure between us. She exhales roughly, whimpering into my mouth, "Fuck, I'm gonna cum."

Those words make me drive into her like a madman over and over. I don't relent, fucking her senseless until she gives me what I want.

She gasps and I feel it, her walls clenching around me, squeezing my cock so tight I couldn't prevent my own release even if I tried. I cum hard, filling her, my gasps are barely audible because of hers.

I stay seated deeply inside her, relishing the final waves of her climax clenching me.

Chapter Thirty-One

Callie

Literal heaven on Earth. That's what having Nathan inside me feels like. I've never been mind blown by sex, until now. I couldn't have conjured up a better fantasy for our first time together, I'm completely and utterly satisfied. Our kissing has turned slow and unrushed, neither of us ready to separate. Nathan has me wrapped in a cocoon of his body, his arms encircling my head, the weight of his torso resting on mine. His heaviness feels good and relaxed like he's just as satisfied as me. He kisses my face, leaving no part of it untouched by his lips, making me giggle. I know I have the cheesiest smile on my face, I can feel it, but I don't care because Nathan looks at me and smiles just as hard.

"I think we have a problem," I tell him, feigning seriousness.

"Mhm," he kisses me again, "and what might that be?"

"That was too good. I don't think you could ever top that performance," I say jokingly, not able to hold back my smile.

"HA!" He barks out a laugh into my neck, the direction his kissing had gone. "Baby that was just the beginning of what I plan to do to you," he finishes, fully serious. My stomach does a little flip, excited about the prospect of what is yet to come. "Can't wait," I say, my smile never fading.

"Come on," he picks me up by my waist, still buried deep in me, and carries me to his shower. "I've been waiting to see you naked in my shower since you got here."

I act astonished, "Nathan Wolfe, were you fantasizing about me?"

"Only every second," he admits, setting me down on my feet in the bathroom as he slowly pulls himself out of me, leaving me feeling empty. He turns on the shower, adjusting the temperature before holding out his hand to me, inviting me in with him. I follow his lead, stepping under the spray, and sighing against the hot water. Nathan presses up against me, his chest to my back, wrapping me in his arms.

Turning my head to the side, I whisper against his jaw, "I fantasized about you while I was in the bathtub last night."

His arms tighten around me, growling into my neck. "Don't tease me, sweet girl." He finishes with a kiss on my neck, right below my ear, eliciting a small moan from me. Everything he does makes me weak. His kissing continues down my neck, to my shoulder, and I'd swear he's making it his life's mission to cover every inch of my skin with his lips. Something I don't mind at all.

"Any of your fantasies include cumming on my fingers in the shower?" He asks as his hand trails down my stomach, cupping my sensitive mound.

"Not until now," I squeak out. I can feel his hardness pressing into my back.

"You like it when I touch your pussy, baby?" He whispers into my ear.

"Yes," I responded breathlessly. He separates my wet folds, pressing two fingers to my clit, and starts softly massaging me. His other hand kneads my breasts, taking turns pinching each nipple, my skin slick from the water.

"You like being slutty for me?" He continues his movements, speeding up his fingers, and making me twitch. I'm so sensitive already, I feel like I could cum any second.

"Yes," I answer him truthfully.

"Yes, what?" He demands.

"Yes, sir." He bites my neck, making me gasp.

"Good girl," he praises, making my pussy clench. I'm so close.

"Nathan..." I mumble. Trying to beg him to make me cum, but not able to get the words out because I'm overwhelmed with sensation.

"Cum for me baby, cum all over my fingers like my good little slut," he's breathing roughly, like he's just as overwhelmed with arousal. The evidence of that, I feel flexing against my ass.

"So... close..." I manage to whisper out. He pinches one of my nipples, hard, making me scream, my release following instantly. His fingers are buried deep in my folds as I cum, holding me as all of my muscles clench around him. The waves of my orgasm make my legs so weak that I would fall if it weren't for Nathan's arm around me.

He holds me to him, still cupping my sex in his hand. "You're so beautiful when you cum, so fucking beautiful." He continues whispering sweet words in my ear until my body stops contracting and I fully relax against him.

After I catch my breath, I turn so I'm facing him, wrapping my arms around his neck. I press my body flush against his, feeling his hard cock against my stomach. His perfect, incredible cock. It matches him perfectly, long and thick, hard as a rock. He reaches behind me, grabbing a bottle of soap. "Are you sure you want to get clean already?" I ask suggestively, sliding my body against his. He laughs but squeezes soap out into his hands and starts rubbing them on me, paying extra attention to my ass.

"I'd love to keep fucking you all day," he sighs, "but we have things that need taken care of today."

I can't contain my pout, and he laughs again. He grabs my chin with a soapy hand and kisses my protruding bottom lip, "Don't do that to me, my willpower's holding on by a thread already."

"Will you at least let me wash you too?" I ask, innocently, hoping I can put off our real-world problems a little longer.

He cocks an eyebrow at me, but relents. "Fine, but don't take advantage of me," he says sarcastically. I lather soap between my hands and start washing his body. I take my time, massaging him as I go, enjoying the soft sounds he makes when I knead into his muscles.

I want him to feel good, in more ways than just sex, I want to pamper him the way he deserves. The strength he carries in his shoulders shows me he's worked hard, and the tension in his back probably never fully goes away, but I can try to ease it. My lips brush against every rough scar I come across, making me want to know every story and learn about every injury. I can't imagine the things he's been through, but I can't help but want to be his rock now.

After spending a couple of minutes on his lower back, my hands linger on his firm ass, trailing down the outside of his thick, muscular thighs. Not being able to help myself, I lower myself to my knees before him, continuing to massage my soapy hands into his calves.

"Callie…" He says my name with a warning. I look up through my eyelashes at him towering above me, my view obscured by his raging hard-on.

"I'm almost done," I answer innocently, fully aware of what my attention is doing to him. Maintaining eye contact with him, my hands trail up to his knees and then start massaging his thighs. My hands creep higher, pausing just shy of his erection. I blink at him, not wanting to "take advantage," but waiting for his queue.

"Keep going," he grits out his demand, knowing exactly what my intentions were. I happily oblige, cupping his balls in my soapy hands, and his jaw clenches at my touch. I work my way up, gripping his shaft with two fists, slowly working it from base to tip. Watching me pump him, his eyes burn into mine.

I want to put him in my mouth, I'd love seeing his reaction as I choke on his cock, but there's too much soap everywhere. Seeing a man as strong and as in control as he is, affected by the pleasure I give him is such a turn on. Watching Nathan come undone by my touch has made me feel sexier than anything else I've ever experienced in my life.

Luckily, he doesn't seem to mind that I'm limited to my hands, his hips flexing with my movements. I admire his body as his muscles tighten across his stomach, the 'v' below his belly button becoming more pronounced. His strong arms bulge as he braces himself against the shower wall. My eyes move back to his face, and I realize he likes me ogling him, his own eyes hooded with lust as he watches me. He lifts me to my feet, not interrupting my efforts, kissing me roughly as I grip and rotate my hands, moving erratically up and down his cock. The passion he kisses me with makes me drunk, leaving me dizzy.

"You're so fuckin' sexy," he pauses, on the verge of his orgasm, "and you're mine." He breathes the words into my mouth, making me moan. It's not the first time he's said it and even though it terrifies me, I want the words to be true. I want him to mean it.

"I'm yours," I respond breathlessly, and I swear I hear him sigh in relief. One final thrust into my hands and he moans against my mouth at the same time that I feel the warmth of his release. He rubs the head of his cock along my soft skin, smearing his cum across my stomach. My hand lingers, slowly pumping him up and down, emptying him completely.

The post orgasm makeout has become my favorite type of kiss, and he delivers, kissing me slowly, both of us catching our breath. "You're gonna kill me, woman," he says between breaths. I laugh, feeling the same way about him. I never imagined I could experience this type of pleasure from someone. Even after three orgasms this morning, watching him cum made my pussy throb, uncontrollably turned on by him.

"And what a sweet, sweet, death it would be," I joke, giggling into his neck. He kisses my temple, reaching around me to shut the water off now that the soap and cum have been rinsed away. He wraps me in a fluffy towel when we get out, drying the ends of my hair for me with his own towel, before wrapping it around his waist.

The sex was mind blowing, but the gentleness he shows me is more than I could ever ask for. I get a pit in my stomach though, worrying about the depth of my feelings for Nathan. The overwhelming happiness that being around him makes me feel, is like I'm bubbling from the inside out, unable to control how giddy I feel in his presence.

The words, 'I love you', feel like they're on the tip of my tongue after every smile, every laugh, and I'm afraid I wouldn't be able to stop them from tumbling out if it weren't for how truly insane it makes me feel. It doesn't seem possible after such a short amount of time, we hardly know each other, yet... No, absolutely not.

Falling in love with a stranger is illogical, and I always listen to logic.

Chapter Thirty-Two

Nathan

We collapse onto the bed, still in our towels. The turn of events this morning was unexpected but not unwelcome. After finding the bear outside knocking over all of my trash cans, somehow bypassing the trash cage I had them in, I never expected Callie's reaction. Before she knew it was just an over curious black bear, she was genuinely worried about me. She feared for my safety, for my life, and it gutted me to see her face when I returned to her in the closet. Though it warmed my cold heart a bit to see how much she cared, I never wanted her to waste her tears on me. When she told me she needed me, I had no power to resist her, and I didn't want to. Of course, she's fucking amazing in bed, my sweet, sweet Callie. I swear she can bring me to my knees with one fucking look.

After she rubbed and massaged every muscle in my body during that shower, I'm whipped. I just want to lay here all day with her, exploring every fuckin' part of her. But, I notice her mood has already turned somber with the impending doom of what today will bring. Or maybe I went too far with the possessive shit, even though I meant it, maybe I pushed things too far. Whether she knows it or not, I'm hers. I'm not sure what tomorrow will bring, or even today, but I know that I want Callie.

The reality though is that she'll more than likely leave, go back home to Tennessee, and I'll be here with no desire to ever find anyone else. No one could ever compete with her.

My worries are momentarily forgotten though as she rolls to her side, laying her head on my shoulder. My arm goes around her instinctively.

"So, what's the plan today?" She sighs as she asks, her fingers lightly playing with the short hair on my chest. Every touch she gives me makes me hopeful and makes me crave a future with her in it.

"I'll call the State Police while you're getting ready, see what they think we should do. Then we need to go back into town to get your new tire. I'll put it on once we're back home," I wince slightly at my phrasing. I don't want to push things too far and scare her off. Even though, if it were up to me, this would be her home too. I don't want her going anywhere.

"What about the Sheriff?" She asks under her breath like she is afraid to speak the words out loud.

"I'll see what the Staties say, but it's probably best if we avoid him for now until I can gauge his next move. So far, he hasn't left me with a good feeling," I tell her honestly. I don't want to scare her, but I also need her to know the truth. I continue, "I can tell he wants all of this to go away, I just don't know how he plans to do it."

"You mean, whether he is going to make me 'go away', or just the crime?" She asks, emphasizing the words' meaning, to make her disappear. I squeeze her body to mine tighter.

"Yeah, that's exactly what I mean," I answer, kissing her

temple. We lay like that for a couple more minutes, still not ready to leave our bubble and go back to reality.

"What happens after you fix my car?" She asks thoughtfully, breaking the silence.

I know what she's asking, she wants to know what happens next, with us. Once her car is fixed, she doesn't necessarily have a reason to stay. Hell, it'd probably be smarter for her to get out of town with the Sheriff acting the way he is, but I'm too selfish to suggest that. I still think I can keep her safe here, with me. I also just want her to stay.

Technically, if there is an active investigation then she should stay until the police tell her it's okay to leave, but I don't even know if the state police can even help if the crime happened in the Sheriff's jurisdiction. Hell, they might not even believe me when I tell them my concerns regarding the Sheriff. My biggest fear is that they choose not to believe Callie, and make her out to be the bad guy in all of this. I know how the military can be, brothers protecting brothers, brushing things under the rug. I imagine law enforcement isn't much different.

Tip-toeing around her question, I give her an answer but not *the* answer. "After I fix your car, I'm going to fuck you nice and slow, in every room of this house if you let me."

I feel her smile, "And, what makes you think that I wouldn't let you?" She asks, the tension from earlier evaporated, replaced with playfulness.

"You hold all the power here, baby. I'm at your mercy," I tease her, but it's not a lie, she holds all the cards. I'll do anything for her, give her the world, but only if she wants me to.

She ponders what I said, not responding right away. Finally, she props herself up on her elbow, resting her chin on my chest so she can look at me. "I told you already, I'm yours. You can have me any way you please."

She kisses my chest lightly as if her admission didn't just knock the air from my lungs. Calling herself mine in the heat of the moment is one thing, but telling me now like she means it, fuck, that's like music to my damn ears. I study her eyes, looking for any signs that she's joking, that she's just being playful. Instead, her beautiful hazel eyes stare unwavering into mine, burning her words into my soul. I don't deserve to feel this fucking happy, and I definitely don't deserve this gorgeous woman. But, I kiss her anyway, sealing a promise that I'm not ready to admit out loud, that I'll follow her to the end of the Earth if she'll have me.

Having the newfound motivation to get shit taken care of for Callie's sake, and before I can put off the inevitable anymore, I peel myself away from her and the bed to throw on some jeans and a shirt, giving her a final kiss before I head to the kitchen. I google the number I think I'll need and start some coffee while I wait to be transferred to a State Patrol Officer.

Finally, after waiting for five minutes, the line picks up and Trooper Malec introduces himself, asking who I am and what the call is regarding. I give him the cliff notes version of events, highlighting that the two attackers are somehow related to the town's Sheriff, and wondering what we need to do moving forward. Trooper Malec remains relatively silent, repeating a couple of things back to me as if he is taking notes. After I finish talking, he starts his follow-up.

"So, the girl from the attack is safe with you now. Staying with you?" He asks, his tone giving nothing away.

"Yes."

"How sure are you that the individuals she identified in the photo are the same ones from the attack?" Again, his tone remains calm and even. Not giving me a clue to his take on all of this.

"She's 100% sure."

"And, what about you?"

"95% sure," I reply honestly.

"Why the minus 5%?" He asks, sounding genuinely curious.

"I believe her, but I didn't see the photo myself, and when I saw the two men back in the clearing it was through my scope at 100 yards. Statistically speaking, I can't be 100%," I clear my throat, hoping I didn't just fuck up this whole conversation. I hear the trooper writing notes in the background before he asks to put me on a brief hold. I hit the mute button and let out a heavy sigh, wiping my hand across my face to relieve some tension.

When I open my eyes, Callie is standing there. Her eyes are downcast, "It was them."

Shit.

"I know baby, I believe you, I promise." She nods her head at me without saying anything else, grabbing her phone from the wall charger.

"I need to call my mom." She walks back down the hallway to my room, not giving me a second glance. Fuck. I don't want her to think I don't believe her, she never needs to worry about that, not from me. I silently beg for this cop to finish talking to me so I can go to Callie.

Trooper Malec chimes back in. "So," he sighs. Shit. "I understand and I hear your concerns regarding local law enforcement, but I am running into the issue that it's going

208

to be your word versus his. I would advise you to continue documenting anything that seems suspicious or threatening from Sheriff Donahue, but in the meantime, I am going to have to contact him. My sergeant needs me to get his side of the story before my agency can look into the crime further. If there is evidence that he is covering up any involvement, or the involvement of others, the State Patrol will step in and take over."

The officer goes on for another couple of minutes, taking all of my information, and asking for Callie's information. Of course, I could only give him her last name and her home state, still not knowing her phone number or anything. He tells me not to worry about it, I can call back this afternoon and it will give him a chance to look into it.

I finally hang up with him and it hits me how much I don't know about Callie. We've talked nonstop for days now, yet I still don't know basic things. I don't even have her number in my phone. These last couple of days have been a whirlwind.

I go to check on her, listening against the door for signs that she's still on the phone. Hearing nothing but silence, I push the door open and glance inside. She's sitting in the center of the bed with her knees pulled up to her chest, her face tucked in so I can't see it, looking small and so fragile.

Gone is the confident, sexy woman from this morning who knows and takes exactly what she wants. In her place is the shell of a person who was left behind once reality came rushing in.

Chapter Thirty-Three

Callie

"Callie?" I hear my name called out, softly. I know it's Nathan, but I have no power to lift my head to acknowledge him. I feel the bed dip, as he sits down next to me. "Callie?" He says my name as a question like he isn't sure what else to say. I lift my head, resting it on my knees, and look at him. The sun is shining in from the windows, surrounding his silhouette with a halo of light, making him look like every bit of the savior I know him to be. I still don't know what I did to deserve it. To deserve him.

"I told my mom the truth about what happened to me. It broke her heart," I admit to him, picking at the bed sheets, making little peaks with the thin fabric.

"Like it was her fault that she didn't protect me." I roll my eyes at the absurdity. "She meant no harm, but I still feel guilty for making her cry."

Nathan's hand covers mine, stilling my nervous movements. "She cares about you, she's probably just worried to death."

"I know." I sniffle, trying to hold back my tears. "She wants me to come home."

I don't look at him for a few seconds, anxious about what

he'll think about that statement. He doesn't say anything, forcing me to look up at him. His brows are furrowed, and he's looking at me so intensely, that it's making me more nervous.

"And, what did you say?" He finally asks, his voice low, just above a whisper.

"I told her that the Bed and Breakfast owner was helping me fix my car and deal with a couple of things regarding the police. That I was okay, and I'd let her know when I could come home."

The corner of his mouth ticks up in a grin. "Bed and Breakfast owner?"

I feel the heat on my cheeks. "Well, I didn't tell her everything."

He laughs a full belly laugh, making my whole body flush with heat. "Don't laugh at me! I've been through enough, I didn't have the heart to tell my mom. What was I supposed to tell her? I've been thanking my rescuer by banging him?" I ask him, not able to hold back my own laughter, but glad for the shift from the heavy atmosphere.

He pulls me into his arms, kissing me softly on the lips. "You can tell your mom whatever you want, but please tell me I'm more than just the rescuer you're banging?"

Of course, he's more than that. I know that. But we also don't really know what we are, at least I don't. I search his eyes, trying to decide what I should say, but I take too long. I see the warm teasing in his eyes turn cold like he put a blanket over the fire. He doesn't move away from me, but I feel his body stiffen. "Come on, let's go get your tire, I'll fill you in on my phone call on the way,"

He stands, pulling me up from the bed. He gives me another

soft kiss, but it's lacking something from before. The last thing I want is to hurt him, or to miss out on something special because of my fears, and preventable miscommunication.

"Nathan?" I call quietly to him as he moves toward the door. "You're more than just my rescuer."

Much more, but I don't say that, only feeling so brave. He gives me a nod, but continues towards the kitchen, leaving my stomach in knots.

How can I feel so safe with someone, yet so vulnerable? Admitting my feelings out loud to him feels like stepping off of a cliff, like something I'll never come back from.

* * *

We leave the cabin, getting in his truck to go into town and I breathe a little easier once he reaches over to grab my hand, his thumb rubbing gentle circles against my skin. He tells me about the phone call with the State Patrol Officer, and so far my expectations aren't high for how much help they might provide.

He asks me to add my phone number to his phone, a simple gesture that seems silly after all we've been through. I add my name, with a heart, and it draws a small smirk from him once he notices. A simple reaction that somehow still causes the butterflies to erupt inside me.

The trip to town is relatively uneventful. We get my tire and stop at the local hardware store so Nathan can get a better chain and padlock for his trash cage, not wanting a repeat visit from the black bear. It's all very domestic, and I take comfort in the normalcy.

When we take the turn that will take us back up the mountain road, I notice Nathan repeatedly glancing into his rear view mirror, his relaxed state long gone.

"What's wrong?" I ask him, suspecting that he isn't saying anything so he doesn't make me worry. His knuckles are white, gripped on his steering wheel, and his right hand is tensely gripping my thigh.

"Sheriff Donahue is behind us," he replies flatly, focused on the road behind us more than in front of us. My blood runs cold, realizing that if Nathan's worried, it's not a good sign. He told me what the State Patrol Officer said about documenting interactions, and that we shouldn't make contact until we know he's not involved with Tony and Bub in some way.

So, why is he following us? Has he not talked to Trooper Malec? Or does he just not care? Either way, my hands mimic Nathan's, gripping my seat belt until my knuckles grow pale.

"What are we going to do?" I whisper as if he could overhear us.

Nathan gives me a half smile, not even close to reaching his eyes, the ones that are still glued to the rear view mirror. "We'll just keep going. He might just be trying to scare us."

"Well, it's working," I mutter to myself. My arms are starting to tremble, the telltale sign that my adrenaline is rising. We keep driving, my fear only growing the closer we get to the cabin.

We round the last curve, the cabin's driveway in sight. "Listen, I'm going to stop and tell him he can't come on my property. You stay in the truck unless I tell you. If I say run, you run straight up to the cabin and lock yourself inside. 3321 is the code for the padlock on the door."

"Nathan..." I utter his name in worry, not liking this at all. My heart feels like it's beating out of my chest.

"Callie?" He says my name as a question, clearly wanting me to confirm that I'll do what I'm told. He breaks hard at the bottom of his driveway, throwing it in park, trying to catch the Sheriff off guard. He looks at me quickly, expecting an answer.

"Yes, Yes. Got it," I stutter out to him, he doesn't hesitate, getting out of his truck and walking towards the cop car, not sparing me another glance. He trusts me to do what I'm told, and I trust him to keep me safe, there is no need for debate.

I'd walk through fire if he told me it was safe because I have the feeling he'd lay himself down on the flames just so my feet don't burn. If it makes me insane, or naïve, so be it, but he hasn't failed me yet.

I'm terrified to look, but I need to see what's happening. I realize it was probably incredibly unsafe for Nathan to leave the truck, and especially walk towards a suspected malicious Sheriff. He could have shot him, pretended like he was being threatened by us, anything. But, I know Nathan only left the truck because I'm in it. If there is going to be an altercation, he wants it to happen the furthest away from me, to give me a chance to run. UGH! Stupid, selfless Nathan, putting himself in danger for me, AGAIN!

I can't hear what is being said, but the Sheriff has exited his vehicle, and they look to be having a heated debate. Nathan is standing his ground, while the Sheriff is throwing his hands into the air, clearly upset. Finally, he points his fingers in Nathan's face, his pointer and thumb like a finger gun, before spitting at his feet and getting back in his cruiser. Nathan's feet stay planted where he's at, glaring at the Sheriff as he flips a U-turn on the narrow roadway, almost going into the ditch. His tires squeal as they peel down the asphalt back toward town.

After a couple of seconds, Nathan finally returns to the truck. I'm sitting sideways in my seat, waiting to hear what happened, but my questions are stuck in my throat when I see how hard Nathan's face is. He looks more than angry, he looks deadly. The air in the truck turns thick as he drives up towards the cabin, neither of us speaking a word.

"Go inside," he demands through gritted teeth. I have never been afraid of him, but his tone is frightening. I jump out and run up the cabin steps, fumbling to type the code in before shutting the door behind me. I peek through the peephole, still able to see him sitting in the truck, his hands are ringing the steering wheel so hard it looks like it could break. He gets out of his truck, slamming his door, once, then twice. Each slam making me jump. He starts to round the front of his truck, like he's going to come inside, when he stops, bracing both hands on the hood and hanging his head. My heart breaks, knowing that I'm the cause of this. No matter what he says, it's my fault he's in this mess.

He stands up straight and starts walking towards the front door again, so I jump back a few feet, lingering by the couch. I sit down on the arm, not sure what to do with myself, but preparing to be ambushed by a cloud of doom.

This is it. This is the moment that the veil will finally be snatched away, and our perfect reality together will turn into nothing but another painful memory. I can't blame him, he has every right to be angry with me, for involving him in this.

My ex would have already taken it out on me by this point, screaming at me, telling me I'm worthless. He would have made sure I felt the brunt of his frustration... But, Nathan isn't Mark. Mark punched holes in walls and tore doors off of their hinges, he lied about everything, never caring about me like he should have. Nathan isn't like that, he actually cares about me.

Right?

Chapter Thirty-Four

Nathan

That stupid mother fucker. Stupid, fucking snake. I don't think I've ever wanted to kill a man as much as I want to kill a man right now. I wasn't sure what I was going to get when I confronted Sheriff Donahue at the bottom of my driveway, I was just hoping it wouldn't lead to a bullet to my head. Instead, I listened to that slimy son of a bitch threaten Callie right to my face. I'm a reasonable man, and I've been in hostile confrontations before, but nothing could prepare me for the level of restraint I had to use today. It didn't matter that he was a Sheriff, it didn't matter that we were 10 yards from my property. The only thing that kept me from shooting him between his eyes was Callie sitting right behind me in the truck. She would have seen pure evil in me, the evil that I've worked hard to keep tapped down. The darkness that lurks in me would scare her away, but I need her to stay with me, not run from me. It's not a question anymore, she's not safe.

Trying to calm down, I sit in the truck for a full minute before getting out. I have to shake my head to stop hearing his sick voice, *"Tell that whore of yours to get out of town... If I come back here and she's not gone, I've got a bullet for both of ya."*

He slurred his threats in my face, the alcohol evident on his breath. Thinking he has the upper hand, he has no idea how close he was to dying at that moment. To threaten what's mine? The man now has a death sentence on his head. My only resolve is that with him alive, he'll eventually draw out the other two. When the time is right, there will be no stopping me. Callie doesn't need to know, she'll never be involved or suspected, and she can continue living her normal life. She'll finally be free of this nightmare.

I knew she was in danger, I knew shit could get bad, but to hear the words come out of his mouth... I have to grit my teeth to bear it, the thought of Callie lifeless, dead at the hands of these fuckers. I'll never allow it.

I need to get a grip, I'm still on the edge of losing it, my rage is eating at me. *My sweet Callie, she's okay, she's inside.*

She needs me to be in control, not this feral animal ready to snap necks. I brace my hand on the doorknob of the cabin, hesitating. She needs me, I'm in control, I'm good. She doesn't need to know how serious the threat to her life is, not right at this moment. I'll break it to her slowly, and prepare her for what needs to come next.

I run it through my head, needing my plan to calm me down even more, to put the chaos out of my mind. The first thing I'm going to do is fix her tire, that way if she needs to run, she can do it safely. Second thing, she's keeping a gun on her every time she leaves the house or my side. Third, or actually swap this with number two, make sure she knows how to shoot and shoot well. I need her to be able to defend herself, even if I'm not around. I plan to be by her side every step, but I need to know if I die trying to save her, she still has a chance. Fourth thing, we need to consider getting her back to Tennessee as soon as possible. No, scratch all of that, Tennessee is safer. There's no way they have the nerve to go after her across state lines. But, I still need to hear back from Trooper Malec, fuck.

Based on my conversation with Sheriff Donahue, he knows I called them. The first thing he said to me during our standoff was, *"You called the fuckin' staties on me boy? And here I thought we would be handlin' this as men."*

Clearly pissed about it, he most likely lied about his involvement. Now, I'll have to wait to see whether Trooper Malec believed him or not. God dammit, I hate not being the one calling the shots. I feel powerless as a civilian, at the mercy of these fucking police agencies. I'll tell Malec that I made her leave for her safety, and he'll just have to be okay with that. Who knows how long it will take them to do an investigation and work things by the book, she might not have that long.

At least as Special Forces, it was simple; find the bad guys, take them out, repeat. All they asked was that we stay under the radar, not make the news. That made me good at stealth. I could get me and my entire team in and out of a building without ever being seen. We could disarm and kill targets without making a sound, a skill that I can't wait to use again. My palms twitch thinking about strangling Sheriff Donahue with my bare hands.

I roll my shoulders, take a deep breath, and go through the plan in my head again. Fix her tire, *check*. Teach her how to shoot and carry a gun, *check*. Get her the fuck away from here and back to Tennessee, *check*. Kill the fuckers that want to hurt her, *check*. Bring her back home to me. *Check*.

Feeling in control enough to go inside, I push the door open. The first thing I see is Callie, sitting on the arm of the couch, playing with the sleeves of her sweatshirt. Her nervous tick.

Seeing her in front of me brings out my rage at Sheriff Donahue again, all the control I just worked on maintaining outside has flown out the window. How dare he threaten to take her from me, from this world?

I need her. I need to hold her in my arms so I can feel that she's safe since my mind can't convince me, but I move too quickly. My need to touch her comes out too aggressively, making her flinch. It halts me in my tracks. The panic that sweeps across her features is instantaneous, but it's there. It's like being doused in ice water, making me hate myself for scaring her. I stay rooted in my spot, not in control of myself enough to behave rationally.

I'm terrified to move, not wanting to scare her anymore, but my body is trembling with my need to touch her. Touching her will quiet my brain, confirming that she's okay, that she's safe.

"Nathan?" She whispers my name, confusion marring her features, all traces of fear long gone. My eyes squeeze shut, hearing her voice helps me breathe a little easier.

"Are you afraid of me, Callie?" I ask, needing to know. I need to hear her say it.

"No," she answers right away, chipping more of my rage away. I need her. She's the only thing that will make me sane again.

"I promise I'll tell you everything, but right now I can't think straight. I need... you," I admit to her, raising my hands slowly so I don't startle her again.

She jumps up from her seat immediately and throws her

arms around my neck, "You have me."

The air escapes my lungs in relief, finally clutching her body to mine, feeling her heartbeat against mine. Those mother fuckers will never take this girl from this world, she's too good, for all of this. I bury my face in her hair, inhaling her scent, needing it to clear my head. My thoughts are still racing. I need to keep her safe. I need to eliminate the threats. I need to kill someone.

My hands graze over her bare midriff, her sweatshirt riding up as she hugs me. I tug it the rest of the way off, not wanting it between me and the rest of her body. She lets me remove it, raising her arms in assistance.

I thought touching her soft skin would ground me, calm me down, but seeing her in front of me now with just her bra on... It's making me unhinged in a different way.

I wrap one arm around her waist, lifting her to me so her face is in line with mine. My hand is gripping her hair, holding her in place so I can crush my mouth against hers. She accepts my kiss with a gasp, opening her mouth when I slide my tongue across her bottom lip.

"Callie, I'm gonna fuck you now. I'm gonna bury my cock in you until I can't think about anything but your tight pussy." I set her down on her feet and take a step back. She looks hot as hell standing there with her hair tousled and her lips swollen from kissing me. "I can't be gentle, not right now. If you don't want this, you have to say no."

I stand still, waiting for her response, feeling like I might combust at any moment. The rage, the fear, the lust, the love, I'm feeling right now is all too much. My nervous system is going haywire. Once I start fucking her, I'm going to be lost in her, and I know it's not fair to her, but it's exactly what I need.

Instead of responding, she slowly slides her pants down, kicking them toward her sweatshirt that was already tossed away. "Fuck me, Nathan."

My cock jumps at her words, already painfully hard. She said it so confidently, she knows how much I need her right now, her boldness spurring my need to take her. I feel like crawling out of my skin, I want to crush my body to hers again, not let any space between us. But, I need to fight for control, that's what I need to restore my equilibrium.

"Take the rest off," I demand.

She unhooks her bra from the back, letting the straps slide down her arms, before dropping it to the ground, "Yes, Sir."

Her perfect tits are finally exposed, her nipples tight with need, making me want to bury my face in them. The thin band hugging her hips makes my mouth water, but watching her slide it down her thighs makes me almost come undone. She maintains eye contact while her panties fall to the floor, waiting for my next move.

I pull my shirt over my head, discarding it on the back of the couch. "Come here," I order and she steps immediately to me, "turn around, lean over the cushions."

She doesn't hesitate, angling her body exactly how I need her to. Her ass is up, the perfect height for me to fuck her, the rest of her torso hovering above the couch cushions, facing away from me. If I wasn't so out of my mind with need, I'd take a picture of her bent over with her legs spread, and hang it in every room of this fucking house. So fucking beautiful.

Chapter Thirty-Five

Callie

My pulse is racing. The energy in the room is crackling because of Nathan's intensity. I know he's upset about his conversation with Sheriff Donahue, but I still don't know what was said. My worries are forgotten though, because right now Nathan is all I can focus on. His piercing gaze is glued to my exposed body, radiating with dominance. Something I am starting to crave from him.

Feeling his eyes trail along my nakedness makes me feel open and vulnerable but in a good way. There is no hiding from him, and I don't feel any need to. He makes me feel beautiful but sexy, and powerful in my own way.

"Spread your legs wider," he orders, his voice low, filled with lust. I quiver at the sound of it, immediately shuffling my feet further apart, leaving me wide open and at his mercy. Exactly where I want to be.

He had asked me earlier if I was afraid of him, and I would have laughed if it weren't for his obvious distress because I realized right away he wasn't the same as my ex. He'd never do anything that could harm me. The power he has over me is comforting. It's safe.

When he cautioned me he wasn't going to be gentle, he presented it as a warning, but I hoped it was a promise. Being rough isn't going to scare me off, it's going to make me want more. It's the comfort of being yourself and exploring pleasure with someone because you know you're truly safe to do so. I'm safe to let go and enjoy the pleasure that I receive because there's no act. Sex with him isn't a performance that I'm putting on to satisfy him. It's a raw connection that we've found within each other.

So, I stand here, bent over the back of the couch, waiting for his touch, yearning for him. My anticipation is making my breathing unsteady, and when Nathan finally kneels behind me and grabs both sides of my ass in his hands, I gasp. "So, perfect," he whispers, slapping one cheek, leaving a sting of pain behind making me whimper.

He slaps the other side, and another small noise escapes my lips. He kneads my ass cheeks, rubbing out the stinging his hands left. I feel his warm breath on my center and I swear I convulse at the proximity, my pussy begging for his touch. He answers my wish, his tongue gliding from my clit up to my second hole, something I've never experimented with before.

He buries his face in my pussy, and I swear he'll suffocate. There's no way he can breathe, but the thought is lost as soon as he starts devouring me. He licks, sucks, bites, and eats me out like he's starved. I have to brace my hands on the couch cushions below me to keep from toppling over.

The extra leverage allows me to grind back against his face, desperately seeking every sensation. The stubble on his face scrapes across my sensitive flesh, making me cry out. The pressure inside me is increasing rapidly, each second of his attention bringing me closer to exploding.

"Ride my face, baby," he demands, diving back in, his tongue fucks me while I grind against him. His face is pressed so deeply into me, his chin brushes against my clit as I buck against him. I'm so close to cumming, but I can't make any coherent words, everything leaving my mouth is a mix between a moan and a plea for more. He stands up suddenly, leaving me on the edge of release, making me groan in protest.

"Be a good girl and hold on tight," he orders with another slap to my ass, his fingers grazing my folds, making me whimper. Without another word, Nathan drives his cock deep inside me, taking my breath away. I hardly have a second to adjust to his invasion when he starts fucking me hard. I have no choice but to grip the couch cushion under my hands, hopelessly trying to stay in place. Nathan grips my hips, keeping me right where he wants me, pounding into me like a man possessed.

His brutal thrusts are making me lose my mind with pleasure, his balls slap against my clit over and over, tipping me over the edge. I finally cum, hard.

"OH, GOD. YES!" I scream, my walls contracting around his hammering cock.

Pulling me up by my arms, so my back is pressed against his chest, he grabs my neck, holding me close so he can whisper in my ear, "Such a good girl." He bites my ear lobe, making me whimper.

Having Nathan wild over me is something I can't get enough of, and I love every second of it. His hands move to my breasts, cupping them so he can hold onto me while he continues driving into me, harder with each thrust. His hands keep roaming, like he can't stop touching me, they caress my stomach, my hips, and my back. He drags his palms from my shoulders down to my wrists, pulling them back toward him.

"Spread your ass for me, baby, I wanna see it." I do as he says, grabbing each cheek and exposing my tight hole to him. He spits, the warm moisture trailing down to the puckered hole. "Put a finger in," he commands, his thrusts slow down but don't stop. His focus is lasered in as I hesitantly slide my middle finger in the tight opening, just to my first knuckle. It's a new feeling, but not bad, just full. What's more erotic is having Nathan's eyes on me while both my holes are penetrated. I wonder what it would feel like to have him fuck me here? I shiver at the thought, anticipation filling my gut.

I faintly realize that he's grabbed the t-shirt he had tossed onto the couch earlier, twisting it until it's rolled tight, like a rope. He loops it around my neck, and I know exactly where this is going. Another first, but not unwelcome. Nathan is putting every fantasy I've ever had to the test, and I'm eagerly along for the ride. The shirt tightens around my throat, not suffocating, but enough to make my breathing shallow.

"Every part of you is mine, Callie," he says through gritted teeth before picking up his pace, pounding into me again with no restraint. My body is at his mercy, he's possessing every part of me. My hips are pinned between him and the couch, the cushions softening the blows I'm receiving from behind, and the tightness of the t-shirt around my neck is cutting off blood flow, making me dizzy. Or, it's the overwhelming sensation of his cock driving into me, his head rubbing my g-spot over and over. I have to pull my hands back in front of me to brace myself, afraid I'll fall from how intensely he's fucking me.

He releases the shirt from my neck, leaving me gasping for

breath, the rush of blood returning feels euphoric. He pushes his own finger into the tight opening I just vacated, making me cry out at the intrusion. His finger is bigger than mine, making me feel fuller than before.

"I can't wait to fuck your tight ass," he says between breaths, "but I need to fill your pussy. You want me to fill your pussy, baby?" He asks rhetorically, obvious that I'll let this man do anything to me.

"YES!" I scream, "Fill me!" His finger penetrates my ass deeper, the fullness making my walls tighten. The overwhelming pleasure sends me over the edge again, making me scream his name with my second orgasm, "NATHAN, YES!"

"FUCK!" He yells as buries himself in me to the hilt, my release milking him, making him cum. I feel the warmth fill me, my pussy still convulsing around him. He pulls me up by my shoulders, wrapping his arms around me so I'm pressed tightly against him, my back to his chest. We stay like that, riding out our orgasms together. His lips press to the hollow spot between my neck and shoulder. "You're amazing, thank you," he whispers.

I turn my head to look at him better. "Me? You're the one I should be thanking." I nuzzle my face into his jaw and he chuckles, the vibrations of it tickling my spine. Becoming more aware of his body against mine, I feel the coarseness of his jeans pressed against my legs. "Are you still wearing pants?" I ask him, surprised I wasn't aware of it before.

He laughs again, sheepishly. "Uh, yeah, I still have my shoes on too. I was a little frantic to get inside you." He kisses my neck again, his arms still hugging me close.

He sighs, "I hate to ruin this moment, but we need to talk."

My stomach clenches with anxiety, I'm reluctant to come down from this high, but I know Nathan wouldn't worry me unless it was serious. We pull apart slowly, gathering our scattered clothes, and silently get dressed. He motions for me to sit down next to him before he tells me what happened with the Sheriff, and why he was acting the way he was afterward.

"I wanted to kill him, Callie, I still do." His hands clenched against mine. I crawl into his lap, needing him as much as he needs me. I don't say anything, still processing everything, that there are legitimate people out there that want me dead. I could die. I bury my face into the crook of Nathan's neck, hiding my trembling lip. He holds me, running his fingers down my hair, trying to comfort me. "I'm sorry, baby. I should have told you before, but I got carried away. I was drowning and I needed you. I was afraid I was going to do something stupid," he admits, his lips pressed to my forehead.

I pull back to look at him, feeling slightly in control of my impending tears again. Hearing how badly he needed me at that moment makes my heart thump harder in my chest. Especially knowing how much I've come to need him too.

"I'm glad we found each other, but I'm so sorry I got you mixed up in this. It's infuriating that it's even happening... How could they do this? I didn't do anything wrong! *They* attacked *me!*" I shout.

"I know, and they're gonna pay," Nathan says, his tone so flat, it's ominous.

I study his face, looking for a clue. "Nathan, what are you going to do?" He doesn't answer me right away, but he brushes a loose strand of hair behind my ear.

"I'm going to keep you safe, that's all there is to it," another flat statement, making my stomach somersault. I have my theories, but I don't know how dangerous Nathan is, I don't know what he's capable of. At this moment, I worry that he's capable of way more than I could ever imagine.

Chapter Thirty-Six

Nathan

"I think you should go back to Tennessee." It takes everything in me to say those words. It's the last thing I want, but the rational part of me knows she'll be safer far away from here. At least until the threat is neutralized, but once she's gone, will she ever want to come back? Like a knife to my heart, I watch her eyes fill with moisture.

"You want me to leave, now?" She whispers as if it pains her to say the words. A sick part of me is relieved that she seems reluctant to leave. Maybe I can convince her to go back home, until it's safe, then ask her to come back to me. How could I though? Ask her to take a chance on me, uproot her life again, for what? A jobless, recluse, with no social skills and a propensity for violence. I don't say any of that though, instead, I brush my thumb along her cheek, memorizing the way her skin feels.

"I don't want you to leave, but I need you to be safe," I admit, my voice hoarse. My brain and mouth, battling over what I need to say and what I want to say.

She touches her forehead to mine, "I'm not ready to leave you, not yet, not like this. They can't take this from me too."

I squeeze my eyes shut, knowing that looking at her will make me crumble. I'm too soft when it comes to Callie, she's like kryptonite. Her hands cling to the back of my neck, holding our heads together. "Nathan?" She whispers at me, pleading.

"I'm sorry," I utter the words through gritted teeth. Still not looking at her, I feel her hands release my neck and my body immediately misses the connection. She pushes herself to her feet in front of me, and all I can do is hang my head. She stands there for a second, waiting for me to acknowledge her. I don't. I can't. Not without giving in to her. God, I want to. I don't want her to leave.

"I've never quite understood the phrase 'hit it and quit it' until now. It really fucking sucks," she utters. The words come out shaky, like she's holding back tears and it guts me. I grab her hand to stop her from walking away.

"No, baby, it's not..." She cuts me off before I can finish, before I can defend myself, she pulls her hand from my grip.

"You've obviously made up your mind, I'll go get my stuff together," she mumbles, hurt lacing her words. She leaves the living room and I bury my face in my hands, my head suddenly throbbing. She'll never forgive me for sending her away, and I'll never forgive myself for hurting her. I get up and go outside, still needing to change her tire, and using it as an excuse to put more space between us. Hearing her just down the hallway, knowing she's packing her things is breaking all of my resolve, and I know I'll end up begging her to stay if I don't get out of this house.

I get to work changing the tire, but my head's not in it. The tire iron slips off the lugnuts so many times as I'm loosening them, I almost chuck the damn thing into the woods. Every

231

curse word in the book leaves my mouth while I'm swapping the tires, especially when the spare goes rolling down the driveway, crash-landing in the tree line. Fucking, great. My thoughts keep bouncing back and forth between Callie in the house, and Sheriff fucking, Donahue. The quicker I kill him, and the other two, the sooner I get my girl back. The only thing I can do is watch him, wait until he leads me to his buddies, and take them all out before they ever know I'm onto them.

I lower the car off the jack stands and put the jack back in the trunk just as Callie walks outside. She walks down the steps slowly, her bags thrown over her shoulder, stopping in front of me. "So, this is it…"

"It doesn't have to be," my voice sounds foreign in my ears, speaking on its own accord. "When it's safe, I want you to come back to me." My admission sparks something in her eyes, but she doesn't respond right away. Her posture is still guarded like she doesn't want to get any closer to me, and it's killing me.

"I…" Telling her that I've fallen in love with her sits right on the tip of my tongue, but the words don't feel right. This moment doesn't feel right, she doesn't deserve that. Instead, I alter my train of thought. "Everything I've said these last few days, I've meant it. Every word, Callie. I want you in my life."

A tear escapes down her cheek and I can't stop myself from reaching out to her. I pull her into my arms and she melts against me, my shoulder catches her tears. "Please, please, don't hate me," I whisper, unable to bear the thought that she'll never forgive me.

"I just don't understand, I feel safe with you. I don't want to leave," she speaks into my chest, not looking at me.

"I know, baby, I'm sorry." I hold her tighter. "If you don't want to come back, I understand. I know there isn't much here for you. But, I'm always a phone call away, whenever you need me." I tip her chin up to make her look at me. "Whatever you want from me, Callie. I'm here."

"What if I need you now?" She asks, her voice a whisper. I don't have a good response, so I just crush my lips to hers, needing to taste her one last time, in case this is the last time. She responds immediately, pressing her lips to mine, and opening her mouth so my tongue can slip in. We stay like that for seconds, minutes, an hour, I don't know, but I don't want to stop.

Once we stop, I'll lose her smile, her laugh. I'll lose the sweet way she talks in the morning, her voice still filled with sleep. It only took a few days to learn these intimate details about her, and I know I would miss it the rest of my life. No matter what it takes, I have to get her back, there's no option, my life is nothing without her. She's become everything to me.

"Come on, we gotta go, I'll follow you to the state line," I mutter against her lips, not wanting the words to come out.

She stiffens in my arms before letting go. "I never knew emotional whiplash could hurt so bad." Her words gut me, but I don't say anything, I'm not strong enough to. The misery I feel as she climbs in her car has to be punishment. Punishment for past crimes or for a life I never deserved, I'm not sure. I get in my truck as she puts her car in drive, driving away from me without even a glance in her rearview mirror. I easily catch up, following her as we descend the mountain, then to the interstate. The lump in my throat has not eased, and I'm sure there is a permanent scowl on my face, but I can't stop trying to get a look at her in her mirrors. Not once, the entire drive to the Tennessee border did she look back, not once.

I pull over on the side of the road and watch as her car gets further and further away. My hands slam against the steering wheel, and I roar a scream. Fuck! This is not fair, it's not fucking fair. I am going to kill those bastards, fuck them for doing this to Callie, to me. I pull out my phone, finding Callie's contact and the heart she put next to her name, I wince at how drastically the day changed from just this morning. Sending her a text, I ask her to call me when she gets home safely. Hoping that she'll do it, because not knowing will drive me crazy with worry.

I think for a second about following her all the way home, but decide against it, not wanting to waste time. I plan on taking care of our little problem as soon as I can and as fast as I can without leaving any evidence behind. Dammit, I wish I still would have given her a gun and made sure she knew how to use it. My brain is so scattered I forgot. Fuck.

I pull back onto the interstate, heading back towards Whitewater, and make a call to the local tow company. A nice old lady answers, so I turn on the charm, asking her to pull up a tow record from yesterday. I told her that I needed to know who called in to have my wife's car towed, because I was worried she was cheating on me, and her boyfriend was probably the one who called since they were together. The lies roll easily off my tongue, and she eats up every word, giving me a "bless your heart" and an "Oh you poor thing" before putting me on hold to search the records.

As I'm waiting, I ponder the idea of Callie as my wife. Something I never thought too much about before her. All my past relationships weren't even close to serious, let alone marriage-worthy, I was always too committed to the job. Callie, though, I would have given it all up in a heartbeat if she was a choice.

The lady from the tow company clicks back into the call, interrupting my thoughts. "Okay, sweetie, I don't have a name for you, but the caller did leave their number behind on our caller ID. Would you like it?" Not a name, but something to go on, hopefully, a piece of the puzzle that will lead me right where I need to go. I get the number from her and thank her for her time, disconnecting the call.

Scrolling through my contacts, I know exactly who I need to talk to next. "Hey, Jesse, I need your help."

Chapter Thirty-Seven

Callie

My life has turned upside down in a matter of days. Three days ago I was driving home from Georgia, listening to break up songs, cursing my ex's name. Now, I couldn't care any less about him. Yet, I'm on the same interstate back to Tennessee, crying my eyes out, heartbroken over another man. I'm not sure how it's possible that I fell head over heels in love with Nathan in three days, but the feelings I have right now confirm that I'm undeniably in love with him. I feel broken. The rational part of my brain knows that he didn't want to send me away, he just wants me to be safe and out of harm's way. The irrational part is devastated that it ended like this. It started as a shitty situation, but meeting him was fate. Deep down, I feel like we were meant to find each other.

My phone pings a message from an unknown number. My heart leaps, hoping it's Nathan telling me to turn around and come back to him. It is Nathan, but that's not what it says.

Call me when you get home. Be safe, baby.

Fresh tears spring to life in my eyes, blurring my vision. I quickly wipe them away so I can see the road clearly. Why is this so hard? He said I could come back, he said he wanted me. Why does it still feel like this goodbye is final?

Those few minutes after he told me he wanted me to go back home felt like my heart had been stomped on. He had just fucked me ruthlessly, then told me I needed to leave, no discussion. That fucking hurt. Then I walked outside and saw that he was in just as much pain as I was. He didn't want me to leave, but once again my shitty circumstance is ruining everything. I'm the one in danger, and Nathan is doing what he can to keep me safe, just as he has since the moment I met him.

The rest of my drive home is on autopilot, so lost in thought that my GPS startles me every time she speaks to give me new directions. After a couple of hours, I pull into the driveway at my parent's house and turn my car off, but I can't make myself get out. How am I going to explain all of this to my parents? Hey, I have a couple of guys trying to kill me and I'm totally obsessed with the guy who saved me from them. It sounds stupid to me and I'm the one in this situation.

He told me to come back if I wanted to, but I just got done living with a boyfriend and that definitely didn't work out. I can't move to North Carolina to pursue a relationship that is barely even a relationship, that's crazy. I am crazy. I need a drink. And sleep.

I take my time getting out of the car with my bags, not looking forward to the conversation ahead with my mom and dad. As soon as I see my dad in the doorway, the dam breaks and I start sobbing all over again. He holds me, my mom crashing into us from the side, joining in. I didn't realize how much I needed them until now. All the sadness, anger, and fear caught up to me, making me weak on my feet.

They usher me up the steps and into the home I am familiar with, the one I grew up in. The family pictures on the wall and the scent that I'd know anywhere, a mix of fresh laundry and coffee, calms me as I enter. I missed this home, I missed my parents. I hadn't seen them in a few months, and even though I was living in an apartment on my own before I moved to Georgia, I was still home for dinner at least once a week.

My mom asks if I want to talk about what happened, but I shake my head, afraid any words I speak will lead to more hysterics. She brings me a glass of wine and my dad covers me with a throw blanket, urging me to get some rest.

"We'll figure everything out, tomorrow," my dad assures me, tugging my mom towards the kitchen, forcing her to give me some space. For the first time in months, I feel like I can relax. There is no question whether or not I belong here, no question if I'm loved or not. There is peace in belonging somewhere. No matter where life takes me, I know I'll always be safe here.

After two sips of wine, I fall asleep right where I'm at, not waking until after midnight.

I rub the kink in my neck, grab my bag, and walk toward my old room turned guest room. I know my mom will have it set up for me because that's how she is. I remove clothes from my bag needing to change for bed, but when I pull out my phone charger it hits me that I never told Nathan I was home. I dig through the front pockets of my bookbag, looking for my phone. It lights up, three unread texts, and one missed call. Shoot.

Nathan: Callie, you home yet?

Nathan: Let me know that you're safe baby.

Nathan: Call me, please. Even if you don't want to

speak to me. I need to know you're okay.

Nathan: MISSED CALL

Oh no, I never meant for him to worry, I just fell asleep and forgot. It's so late I'm afraid to call him and wake him up, so I send him a text.

I'm home! I'm sorry I fell asleep as soon as I got here. Don't worry, I'm okay.

My phone pings as soon as I set it down on the nightstand, another text.

Nathan: Call me.

I hit the call button right away, surprised he's still awake, but eager to hear his voice even if he's pissed about me not calling him earlier.

"Hey," he answers immediately, the low timber of his voice giving me butterflies despite all of the ups and downs today.

"Hi," I respond quietly, hoping my parents won't hear me talking through the walls. I decide to go outside on the front porch while we talk, needing some fresh air anyway. The darkness of night isn't so intimidating here with all of the street lights illuminating the neighborhood.

"I miss you," his admission does nothing to calm the swarm of flutters in my stomach.

"I miss you, too," I tell him honestly. I want to tell him so badly how crazy I am about him, but I still don't know how I feel about it yet either. I feel crazy, that's for sure, but I'm afraid I'm jumping in too soon, and too fast.

"What are you doing right now?" He asks. The question seems odd since it's the middle of the night, surely he assumes I'm in bed.

"I'm outside on the front steps, I didn't want to wake my parents." Saying it out loud makes me feel like a teenager again, sneaking out to make a call to my boyfriend. I giggle at the thought.

"What's so funny?" His voice seems lighter, happier. I tell him my thoughts, that coming home to my parents makes me feel inherently adolescent.

"I'm afraid my dad will come out at any moment and confiscate my phone. Then scold me for talking to a boy." I laugh at the thought.

"Do you think he would like me?" His question catches me off guard, I hadn't even thought of that. In my head, it was always me going back to Nathan, our world still revolving around just us. Meeting each other's family makes this real, and it makes me happy that he might want that.

"I think he'd like you. My mom will *lovvee* you," I emphasize the word suggestively, knowing how my mother is. I imagine them meeting, and how it would go. My dad would give him a firm handshake, acting tough, and my mom would fawn over him, ever the hostess. At the end of the day though, they'd both approve, because they'd see Nathan for the good man he is, just like I have. They aren't ones to hold back punches, both of them told me not to make things serious with my last boyfriend. They asked me not to move, but I didn't listen. I never felt super serious about him, but I did move, and look where that has gotten me. Back home, and with a price on my head.

He hasn't said anything yet, but I can hear noise in the background, like wind or white noise. "Are you in bed?" I ask him out of curiosity.

"No," giving no further context.

"Thenn, where are you?" My interest is piqued.

"In my truck," he responds, plainly, still not giving me any information.

"It's so late. Why aren't you in bed?" My concern is growing, afraid that he's out doing something reckless. Like hunting someone, namely a certain Sheriff.

"I had to check on something. Why aren't you in bed?" He throws the question back to me.

"I slept on the couch for hours and now I'm not tired. Plus, I'm glad I'm getting to talk to you," I say sheepishly, feeling shy even though I've already had sex with the man. Being vulnerable this way is harder, putting my heart on my sleeve in hopes that it's not crushed.

"I'm glad you're awake," he responds. Suddenly, headlights light up the street as a truck pulls down the road toward my parent's house. A twinge of fear passes through me, constantly unsure of my surroundings and realizing it might not be safe to be outside all alone. I exhale, blowing out the breath I was holding when I recognize the truck.

"No fucking way," I exclaim. The truck parks on the curb, and Nathan jumps out immediately walking towards me, a big grin on his face. I jump up, my phone long forgotten in the grass, and cross the yard towards him in a run. I don't care that we've only been apart for half a day, I don't care that I've only known him for three days, I'm so happy to see him. I crash into his arms, clinging to him with relief. "Why are you here?" I ask him in disbelief.

"I told you, I needed to check on something." He cradles my face in his hands. "I got worried when I didn't hear from you, I needed to know you were safe." His lips meet mine, kissing me long and hard, his worry pouring out of him.

"I didn't mean to make you worry," I say, breathless from his kiss. "But, I'm really happy to see you," I wrap my arms

241

around his neck, holding him tight.

Chapter Thirty-Eight

Nathan

Six hours. That's how long I went without hearing from her before I said *fuck it* and jumped in my truck, driving the two-and-a-half hours here to Tennessee. Jesse was able to give me Callie's parent's address pretty easily since I didn't technically know where she lived.

After I left the service, Jesse joined a special unit doing more classified work. He can't tell me much about it, but he joked that he's a lone wolf like me now and that he'd only ever be a part of another team if I were on it. I joked back that it was because I was the only one who always saved his ass. We have less to talk about these days, but he's the only one I keep in contact with from my old unit.

Without risking getting in too much trouble, he was also able to tell me who the number belonged to that called the tow company. I owe him big time for helping me, a debt he'll refuse to let me pay. But, I'll find a way.

I was getting off the interstate when Callie finally texted me, telling me she was safe. The anxiety riddling my body eased, but I still needed this moment. I needed to hold her in my arms. It was probably overzealous of me to make the drive here, but I don't care. When it comes to her, I'd do anything.

The happiness on her face at seeing me wasn't half fuckin' bad either. Her presence radiates through me, making me feel like the luckiest bastard on the planet. There's still an ache in my gut, of words unspoken, feelings unshared. It's almost painful holding back, and not telling her how fucking sorry I am for sending her home without telling her how I really feel. "Callie, I-" I start to say, but can't finish my sentence, my mouth not letting the words come out.

"It's okay Nathan, I know."

Does she know? The way she looks at me, I swear I see the same love burning in her eyes, a reflection of mine. It's enough, for now, my thoughts and my words will catch up to one another eventually. My actions will speak for themselves until then. I kiss her again, hard, feeling her soft lips against mine is like ecstasy. Like I can see the future, and everything only makes sense if she's in it. I just hope she thinks so too.

"Come inside with me," she whispers against my lips. My body reacts instantly to her voice, her sultry tone making blood rush straight to my cock.

"I can't come into your parent's house in the middle of the night, baby. That'd give off a bad impression," I groan, wanting to be the voice of reason, but desperately needing to bury myself in her.

"Nathan Wolfe, I am a grown woman, and I don't need permission to bring a boy over," she says sternly, like she's scolding me, it's kind of hot. "I want you to come inside and fuck me… quietly." She pauses, losing some traction with her argument knowing that our sexual encounters up to this point have been nowhere near silent. She continues anyway.

"Are you really going to leave me, after I've had such a bad afternoon? I cried all the way home," she pouts. I'm sure it's mostly for dramatic effect to persuade me to come inside, but the thought of her crying in her car does me in. The thought of being the reason for her tears kills me.

"Fine, sneak me into your room, you vixen." I smooth the pout from her lips with my thumb. "I'm sorry if I made you cry," I tell her honestly.

She kisses the pad of my thumb as it swipes across her lips. "I didn't expect that leaving you would be *that* hard. I didn't like it."

"I didn't like it either, especially how we left things. I meant it Callie, I'm all yours if you'll have me. Once you're out of danger, I plan on doing whatever it takes to keep you in my life. I'll move here, take you on a date every night, dance with you in the moonlight," I show her exactly what I mean, taking her hand and spinning her in a circle, and then pulling her close again. I sway us back and forth where we're standing, in the middle of her parent's front yard, behaving like an absolute fool.

"But, what about your cabin?" She asks with disbelief in her voice.

"It'll be a permanent vacation spot, whenever you want to get away." I had already thought about this on the drive here. I built the cabin for me, there's no way I'd sell it, but it's not worth staying in if Callie's not there with me.

"You're insane," she says with a kiss, confirming what I already know. "Come on," she takes my hand, dragging me inside. We tiptoe up the stairs and she leads me to the first door in the hallway, quietly shutting us inside the room. Without any trinkets indicating it would have been her childhood room, I'm slightly disappointed. I wanted to see chubby, gap-toothed childhood pictures on the wall.

My disappointment is long forgotten though when I see Callie stripping her clothes off right in front of me. Her eagerness lights a fire in me. I toe my shoes off, following her lead, needing her as badly as she needs me.

Our naked bodies clash, a fight of hands and lips, I pick her up and carry her over to the bed, laying her down, gently. She's so beautiful, her soft curves beckoning to be touched. I descend on her, careful not to make the bed squeak, kissing a trail from her belly button to her neck. I whisper in her ear, "I told you I planned on taking you nice and slow tonight, baby."

She smiles the sweetest smile at me, making my heart skip a beat. "Make love to me, Nathan," she whispers back. Every fucking day, I want to tell her. I would promise it if I could because it's all I want, but the reality is that she's still in danger. They are still in Whitewater, and I still need to eliminate the threat. So instead, I have to respond the best way I can for now.

"Your wish is my command," I whisper, making her giggle. My fingers find her wet folds, making her gasp. I give her a look, urging her to remain silent. She nods in understanding as I push two fingers into her tight pussy, making sure she's ready for me. Her back arches off the bed when I hit the spot deep inside her. The position thrusts her perfect tits in my face, so I bury my mouth between them, lightly biting her soft skin. I suck one nipple into my mouth, while my fingers fuck her, eliciting a small squeak from her. Her noises always sound so good to me, and it's hard to encourage her to be quiet. I switch to her other needy peak, flicking the point with my tongue. This time when she moans, I take my fingers from her warmth and stick them in her mouth, forcing her to be quiet. She sucks her juices from my fingers, making my already hard cock turn to steel.

Her eyes are hooded, filled with lust, begging for more. I sit up, preparing to move between her legs, but she puts a hand on my chest, silently urging me to lie down. Eager to see where this will go, I let her move me to my back, propping my head up on the pillows so I can watch her. She crawls between my legs, and kneels, hands already reaching for me. She wraps her fingers around my cock, working it slowly up and down. I watch as her breasts bounce with her movements, giving me the urge to fuck them. I make a mental note to add it to my list of ways I plan to fuck her.

She lowers her mouth to my cock, her tongue swirling around the head before sucking it into her mouth. My eyes roll back in my head at the sensation, my hands bury themselves in her hair, keeping it out of her face. Squeezing the base with one hand, and cupping my sack with the other, she swallows me down as far she can go. My fingers are probably clawing her scalp, but I can't help it, her mouth feels too damn good. Her head bobs erratically up and down, deep-throating me over and over. My hips buck into her mouth uncontrollably, our love-making session quickly turning into the best blowjob of my life. I so badly want to shoot my cum down her throat, watch it drip down her lips, but not tonight, I'll add it to my list.

I pull her head from me, holding it still while I catch my breath. I want to tell her how fucking amazing she is but I'm too out of my mind to whisper. She licks her lips, and I almost cum at the sight, her bright eyes burning into mine.

She crawls up my body before I can make a move, still wrecked from her sucking the soul out of me.

Straddling my hips, she grinds her hot center on me, the wetness from her pussy mixing with my slick cock. Her hands are planted on my chest, using me for leverage, pushing her tits out. This time they're close enough to grab and I don't hesitate, palming them, massaging her soft flesh.

I feel the heat from her tight opening against the head of my cock right before she impales herself fully, taking every inch. I have to bite back my groan at how fucking good she feels. Her head is thrown back in ecstasy as she rides me, taking me exactly how she wants. Watching her use me like this is the sexiest thing I've ever seen, and I don't mind at all that she's the one in control right now, but I need more.

I wrap my fingers around her throat, using my other hand to spur her hips forward and back, meeting her thrust for thrust. The place where our bodies are connected slams together violently, over and over, neither of us satisfied yet, our aggressive need for each other is too great.

The momentum is too much though, and as much as I want to keep fucking her like this, and harder, the bed starts to squeak. She hears it too, slowing down with a small whimper of need. I sit up so our chests are pressed together, crushing her lips in a kiss.

Chapter Thirty-Nine

Callie

His lips, his hands, his hardness inside me, I'm consumed by him. I can feel the back of my eyelids burning with tears while he kisses me, overwhelmed with my feelings for him. It's more than desire, more than the heat in his eyes when he looks at me, more than the passion in every kiss. I am undeniably in love with him. I'll never get enough of this. I don't care about how odd our situation is, or how fast it happened, I don't care what people think, all I care about is Nathan. Nothing has ever felt more right than this.

A salty tear escapes from the corner of my eye, rolling down my cheek until it's caught by our mouths. Nathan pulls back, noticing the moisture. "What's wrong?" He asks with so much concern in his voice it makes me smile, always in awe of his sweet nature towards me. His hands cradle my face, searching my eyes for the cause of my tears.

I shake my head, wiping the wetness from my face. "They're happy tears, I promise." I lean my forehead to his, closing my eyes and enjoying this moment, soaking in this connection with him.

"Do you believe in soulmates?" I whisper after a few seconds, nuzzling my nose along his cheek.

Nathan flips me over suddenly, but silently, still mindful of my parents down the hall. "I thought it was all bullshit, until now." Still inside me, he starts moving slowly, making me moan. My arms and legs are wrapped around him, holding him to me so closely that I can feel his heart beating. He cradles my head in his arms, kissing me tenderly.

"I think I was put on this Earth to find you Callie," he whispers against my lips. My heart almost can't take the emotions those words conjured. I truly believe that despite everything crazy going on, Nathan is mine. We'll do what it takes to be together.

"You're mine, Nathan," my admission encourages him and his thrusts become more demanding, holding me in place so he can fuck me harder, deeper. His length is causing a build-up of pressure deep within me, making my entire core start to tense, and my walls clench around his cock, like my pussy wants to trap him inside me.

"Fuck, baby, you're gonna make me cum," he moans in my ear, his voice making my pussy clench again. My breathing is erratic, and my body begging for the orgasm that I'm on the brink of. He pounds into me once, twice more, and it sends me over the edge, my hips thrusting forward into his with my climax. He catches my screams in his mouth, his release following shortly after mine. Like, the slut I am for him, I savor the warmth of his cum inside me, feeling completely owned by this man and loving it. Our breathing is the only noise in the room, both of us exhausted, our bodies slick with sweat.

Nathan turns to the side, taking me with him so we're still

face to face, my legs still wrapped tight around his waist hugging him to me. He makes no move to separate our bodies, a picture of serenity on his face. His eyes are closed and his face relaxed, perfectly at peace. I could easily spend the rest of my life sharing these moments with him, being the one to make him happy. Heck, I think my heart is going to combust from happiness, and how proud I am to be the one he's chosen. He keeps to himself, he doesn't enjoy being around people, but he wants me. He's proven that more to me today than any other guy has ever. I thought moving to Georgia with my ex would make me feel like I belonged with him, but it never did. The ex before that convinced me he loved me, but refused to say the words because they were "overused". I tried to accept that, pretending like I was the cool girl who didn't like romantic gestures, but it was never true.

Even though Nathan hasn't said the words either, I know his feelings for me are greater than anything I've ever experienced before. I feel it in the way he holds me, I see it in his eyes when he looks at me, I sense it when he worries. Every selfless act proves he'd rather put my needs over his own.

I drag the tip of my nose along his, getting his attention. "I don't want you to move here," I whisper. His eyes snap open, looking at me puzzled. "I'll come to North Carolina. We can still date, I don't have to move in right away, I know this has all happened so fast. But, it's your home, and you shouldn't have to leave it," I finish, kissing him softly on the tip of his nose.

He studies me for a couple of seconds like he's gauging if I'm serious or not. "Callie, it's only my home if you're there. Are you sure?" He asks. Our faces are so close I can feel his soft breath on my lips.

"I'm sure," not hesitating with my answer, my mind was already made up. "It's your dream home, and... I like the fireplace," I say, teasing him. He kisses me hard, claiming my mouth with his, I gasp when I feel his hardness grow again, still inside of me.

"If you come to North Carolina," he slowly starts moving in me, making me groan. "You're going to be in my bed," his fingers find my clit, drawing circles across it, "every night."

His thrusts aren't extreme, just enough that I can feel the ridge around the head of his cock rubbing my g-spot, my clit receiving the majority of the stimulation. I'm still sensitive from our earlier lovemaking, making me fidget from the tremors coursing through me. His lips stay on mine, keeping me silent, allowing me solely to focus on how good he's making me feel and nothing else.

"Move in with me, Callie." My brain is so focused on his movements, that I hardly process his words, not able to answer him. My thoughts are swimming on the edge of another orgasm, I'm so close to tipping over I can't concentrate on anything else.

"Nathan... It's too much, I can't..." I'm babbling, not able to form a clear sentence. My mouth bites down on the closest thing to me to silence my cries. My tongue tastes his salty skin, lapping at it, kissing it.

I had bitten him right between his shoulder and neck, too overwhelmed with pleasure to be concerned if I hurt him or not. His fingers work my clit faster, not acting at all affected by the teeth print I left on his skin.

"Cum again, for me, baby. I need it," his words make me whimper with need. My body trembles with my impending release. He grips my hair with his empty hand, pulling it firmly, forcing me to tilt my head up, making eye contact with him. "Move in with me, baby," I swear my eyes are seeing stars, it's all too much, and even though I think he knows my answer, he wants to hear me say it. But, my lips are having a hard time forming any words.

"Yes," I choke out.

"Yes, what?" His fingers work me faster, and his cock pumps in and out of me harder while he taunts me. It's too intense, my orgasm rips through me, stealing my breath. "You're such a good girl, I love making you cum," he whispers to me as I come back down to earth. I realize he's stopped moving, his length still rests inside me, primed for his release, waiting for my answer.

"Yes," I say between breaths, "I'll move in with you." Finally, after answering his question, he smiles, kissing me softly.

"I love you, Callie." My eyes widen, not expecting him to say it, yet, with everything between us happening so suddenly, but his eyes are a direct window to his soul, gazing at me with such sincerity, I feel my own eyes filling with tears.

"I know." I kiss him, unable to resist, "I love you, too." His eyes squeeze shut at my admission, processing what I said before crushing his lips to mine with vigor, rolling me to my back again. He starts pumping in and out of me again, claiming my mouth with his tongue.

"Say it again," he says against my lips, I can hear the emotions pouring out through his voice.

"I love you," I tell him without hesitation. This carnal bond between us is amplified now that we're not holding any feelings back. Our souls aflame together like they were meant to be. "I love you so much, Nathan," I tell him again, needing him to hear it, to believe it.

"You're mine, Callie," he says through gritted teeth, his release close.

"I'm yours," I promise, "all yours." My vow unleashes him, and his cock drives into me a final time, filling me completely.

"I love you, baby," he breathes, still catching his breath.

"I know," I repeat my earlier statement, without a doubt in my mind about it.

Chapter Forty

Reluctantly, I pull out of Callie, not wanting to separate, but aware of the mess we've created. Or, rather, I've created. I don't think I've ever cum twice in such a short period, and not expecting to after I had made Callie orgasm again. But, hearing her tell me she loves me made me crazed, I needed her again more than I've ever needed anything. I still can't believe it, she loves me. I don't know how it's possible for this perfect woman to love me, but damn I'm grateful. I've got to be the luckiest son of a bitch alive.

"Think you can use your secret Boy Scout skills to sneak us into the bathroom across the hall without getting caught?" She teases me, both of us grinning at each other like love sick teenagers.

"I'll do my best," I joke, pulling her up from the bed. I don't let go of her hand until we cross the hall, and shut ourselves in the bathroom. She turns the shower on after getting us two towels from the closet. It's a modest bathroom, a white acrylic tub with a shower curtain, like in most homes. We have to take turns washing, trying to be quick because we both can't be under the hot water at the same time. We're both giddy, our moods through the roof, making it difficult to stay quiet. We swap back and forth under the water, hardly enough room to maneuver around each other, which is no problem, just one more reason to have her body pressed up against mine. I even attempt to help her wash her hair, but my hands wander, mostly caressing her firm ass and cupping the fullness of her chest, her skin feeling like silk, slick from the shampoo.

I stifle a yawn, but it doesn't escape Callie's notice. "Oh no, I forgot you haven't even gotten to sleep yet. I'm so sorry." She hurriedly rings her hair out after rinsing off a final time, turning the shower off.

"Don't apologize. I've had the best night of my life," I tell her truthfully, squeezing her ass as she steps out of the tub, making her squeak. Throwing a towel at me playfully, she giggles when it smacks me in the face, my eyes still transfixed on her nakedness. I'll never get tired of hearing her sweet laughter or seeing her incredible body.

"I've had the best night, too." She smiles sweetly, leaning against the sink with her towel wrapped around her, too beautiful to resist. I wrap my towel around my waist, stepping towards her. I brush my thumb across her cheek, remembering how a few days ago I craved to do just that. How far we've come that I get to kiss her soft lips, hold her body in my arms, and love her, uncontrollably.

"This doesn't seem real yet," I admit to her, our voices still nothing but a whisper.

"Come on, I'll let you get some sleep and prove it all over to you again in the morning," she says with a mischievous, sultry, smile, making me fall even deeper in love with her if possible. She tugs my hand, and we sneak back into her room, not bothering to get dressed before sliding under the sheets. I pull her body into mine, holding her close.

"I love you, Callie," I whisper into the darkness of the room, kissing her forehead.

"I love you, too," she whispers, kissing my neck in return. We drift to sleep, content to be a hundred miles away from any of our problems.

* * *

The next time I open my eyelids daylight is streaming in through the blinds, along with whispering coming from outside the bedroom door. I know it's locked so I don't move, glancing down to Callie, still curled into my side with her head on my chest. There's a light knock, making her eyelids spring open, and a female voice sounds through the door. "Callie, we're making breakfast. It'll be done in about twenty minutes."

Callie sits up, rubbing the sleep from her eyes. "Okay, thanks Mom," her voice still gravely, not sounding fully awake. She turns to me, smiling when she sees that I'm watching her. "Good morning," she whispers, leaning down to kiss me, her wild hair falling across my chest.

Her gentle kiss isn't enough, I pull her on top of me, trapping her in my arms so I can really kiss her. "Good morning," I finally responded after getting my fill. "Do you want me to sneak out?" I ask her, understanding if she doesn't want her parents to know I spent the night in their home, uninvited.

"Absolutely not. Just let me go out there and warn them that you're here," she crinkles her brow, "and probably clarify that you aren't a Bed and Breakfast owner. Or married." She rubs her forehead, clearly not eager to have the conversation.

"Tell them the basics, then come get me. I'll help you explain everything." She smiles at my words, sitting up so she's straddling me. "Callie…" I warn.

"What? We have twenty minutes." She tilts her head, her smile turned devious. Her bare pussy is hovering above my cock, hard as a rock since I woke up next to her. I'm dying to bury myself in her, feel her warmth wrapped around me, but I'm hesitant now that I know her parents are awake. What kind of jackass does it make me to fuck their daughter while they're in the other room, unaware of my presence in their home? It feels disrespectful, and I don't want to start things off that way.

"I want you so fucking bad. But, I can't. I don't want your parents to find out I'm here and realize what I was in here doing to their daughter," I cringe at the thought, her dad wanting to kick my ass two seconds after meeting me. I'm in this for the long haul, and that wouldn't boast well for the longevity of our relationship. I normally don't care if people like me or not, but I respect Callie enough to want to be on good terms with her mom and dad.

She pouts but gets off the bed. "Such honor…" She rolls her eyes at me, but I catch her smiling before she turns to grab some clothes. I admire her curves as she tugs her running shorts up over her ass, pairing them with a matching sports bra.

"Have you ever taken any self-defense classes?" I ask her,

hoping she has since I never taught her how to use a gun.

"No, I've always wanted to. My gym doesn't offer stuff like that, and I never wanted to pay for a class if it didn't seem reputable." She pulls a big t-shirt over her head, only leaving her toned legs on display.

"I want to show you some things. It'd make me feel better," I regret the words as I say them. Her face drops, reality sinking back in. No longer in our blissful bubble from last night.

"I'd like that," she whispers, her mood completely shifted from moments ago. She walks over to the door, pausing before opening it. "Here goes nothin'."

I wink at her, hoping to get a smile. Instead, she rolls her eyes, only giving me half of a grin. Good enough.

I lay there for a moment after she leaves the room, wondering if I'll be able to hear them talking, but after a couple of minutes of silence, I peel myself off the bed.

Finding my discarded clothes takes a minute, each piece scattered throughout the room in our haste last night. The last thing I find is my shirt, crumpled up in a heap by the dresser. I hold it out, examining the damage. It looks rough so I tug at the cotton, trying to straighten some of the wrinkles. The door creaks open making my head jerk up at the same time I hear the same woman's voice from earlier.

"Oh my... no wonder." I'm looking at an older version of Callie. Identical if it weren't for the faded auburn hair that's pulled back behind her head, and the soft lines of age in her skin.

Standing here shirtless, I should apologize or introduce myself or something, but I hardly react. I can't even utter a word, too busy picking my jaw off the floor from being caught off guard. Thank God I pulled my jeans on already.

"Mom, oh my god." Callie shuts the door quickly, saving me from saying anything. "We'll be out in a minute." She slumps against the door, covering her face. "I'm sorry, I didn't know she was beelining to the room or I would have stopped her."

I laugh, "She seems nice." The incredulous look she gives me makes me laugh harder. Making her cross her arms over her chest, glaring at me.

"Not funny. She's nosey. What are you doing?" She asks when she notices I'm still tugging at the wrinkles in my shirt.

"I didn't plan ahead when I came here last night This is my only shirt and it's seen better days," I shrug.

"Well, here." She digs through her bag and pulls out a familiar t-shirt, handing it to me. It's one of mine, perfectly folded still from my closet. I look at her for a second, surprised she has it. "I might have wanted something of yours before I left… I'm sorry I should've asked," she admits sheepishly.

"You never have to ask, baby, I'm glad you wanted it." I take the clean shirt, tossing the dirty one on the dresser.

"In that case, I guess I can tell you that I also took this…" She bends over and pulls out the flannel she wore two nights ago. I hadn't even realized it was gone. I laugh, amused that she felt like she had to sneak them out, but glad that she wanted a token of me, even after how we had left things yesterday afternoon. I pull her into me, feeling grateful that I can, having no more barriers between us. Callie could have walked away from me yesterday and never looked back. I could have driven all the way out here and she could have closed the door in my face. I don't want to imagine how hard it would be to get over her. Hopefully, I never have to. I plan to do everything in my power to make her happy, to keep her.

"Ready to do this?" I ask her, holding her tightly in my arms.

"I'm glad you're here," she whispers into my neck, sighing softly.

"Me too," I admit, honestly.

Chapter Forty-One

Callie

We walk into the kitchen, and I'm expecting an ambush, but both of my parents are seated at the dining room table waiting. My mom's eyes bulge out when she sees Nathan again. Even though this time he has his shirt on, he's still an impressive specimen. My dad's face doesn't give much away, he's just calmly waiting for answers. I haven't gotten to tell him directly what has happened the last few days, only speaking to my mom those few times on the phone. I'm sure he's worried, but I don't think this conversation is going to lessen any of it, unfortunately.

"Mom, Dad, this is Nathan," they exchange niceties, my dad standing to shake Nathan's hand. The interaction makes me grin, almost seeming normal. We sit down across from them at the kitchen table, but I fidget in my chair, suddenly feeling awkward. It's hard to know where to start. My mom speaks up, saving me.

"Go ahead, get some food before it gets cold, then just start from the beginning, sweetie. Your father needs to hear it all from you. I've been terrible at relaying our conversations, it's been a lot to process." She starts pushing plates and bowls around, encouraging everyone to fill their plates. It only takes a few minutes for us all to have pancakes, eggs, and bacon on our plates. Not putting off the conversation long enough, unfortunately.

I take a drink of my orange juice and start from the beginning. I feel strong, my voice hardly wavering as I explain my attack. Only struggling a little when I explain almost being raped. Nathan moves his hand to my knee, grounding me, and helping me move forward with my story. When I get to the part involving Nathan, I can't help but look at him while I talk. Still, so in awe of him, and how lucky I was to have him as a guardian angel that day. A tear escapes my eye, relaying to my parents how scared I was, and how I really thought I was going to die in those woods. The thought of never seeing them again, or that they'd never know what had happened to me.

Nathan brushes the tear off my cheek, jumping in on the conversation. Explaining to them what he saw and how he decided to help me. I watch him as he talks, admiring the way he speaks, so strong and in control of himself. My mom is also captivated by him, I can tell, and I don't blame her. My dad looks like stone though, hardly removing his eyes from the table top, he looks grim hearing my story unfold. Nathan explains everything until we arrive back at his cabin, looking to me to continue from there. I know he is wondering how to handle explaining our relationship, effectively putting it on my shoulders now. I squint my eyes at him, mockingly. *Coward.*

"Nathan rescued me, kept me safe. He took care of me when I was utterly broken that night after everything finally caught up to me. I won't ever be able to thank him enough for what he did for me." I look him in the eyes deeply, meaning every word. "Then he continued to take care of me. He helped me with my car and took me to the Sheriff's department. Then got me the hell out of there when I realized the Sheriff might be one of the bad guys." I clear my throat, gearing up for the next part. "The Sheriff knows the guys who attacked me, and we think they're going to try to kill me to keep me from exposing them."

The silence in the room is heavy, waiting for my parents' reaction. My mom is speechless, which is not like her. My dad stands up so abruptly that his chair almost topples over. He starts pacing back and forth behind the table. "What the hell type of hell hole did you end up in? The Sheriff of the town you wandered into wants to kill my daughter?" He yells, surprising me, making me and my mom startle. I've hardly ever heard him raise his voice in anger.

"I know, I have the worst luck in the world," I whisper, my earlier bravado all but gone. "That's why I came home yesterday. Nathan was trying to help get everything sorted, he even called the State Police, but the Sheriff made his threat clear, so I left right away even though I didn't want to."

"So, what did the State say?" My dad asks me, but Nathan answers instead, not at all affected by my dad's distressed state.

"When they talked to the Sheriff, he denied all involvement. Denied knowing who attacked Callie. The State police won't get involved unless they have evidence that he threatened her, or evidence that he knows the culprits," Nathan looks at me as he finishes speaking, but I'm stunned. He hadn't updated me on his latest conversation with them, and now I'm realizing just how screwed I am. He continues, "I hadn't heard from

Callie after she left yesterday, and I was pretty worried after talking to Trooper Malec. That's why I came here so late last night, I needed to make sure she was alright."

"You drove all the way here in the middle of the night because you were worried about Callie?" My mom asks Nathan, a softness in her voice, blanketing the room in calmness. My dad sits back down in his seat, affected by the shift in the room.

"Yes ma'am," Nathan responds, leaving no room for doubt.

"So, what are we going to do? Do I need to contact a lawyer or the FBI?" My dad asks, I see his mind reeling, his focus solely on trying to solve my problems. My mom's focus is directed right at me and Nathan, her eyes pinging back and forth between us.

"The FBI won't get involved unless the crime crosses state lines. I don't think they're brave enough to do that. That's why I wanted Callie to come home, I think she'll be safe here." The way he avoided the first part of my dad's question has my mind wandering. He's not one to sidestep a question, but it's exactly what he did. *What are you going to do, Nathan?*

"But there are still men out there that want to kill my baby?" My mom finally rejoins the conversation, realization sinking in for her.

"That won't happen," Nathan states boldly.

"How do you know that?" My dad asks, anger lacing his voice, again. I know he's angry about the situation, but he shouldn't take it out on Nathan. Luckily, Nathan doesn't seem fazed at all by my dad's tone.

"I'm going to find the proof I need to get the State involved. Taking down the Sheriff will lead to the other two," Nathan states simply, his thumb lightly tapping on my knee is the only indication I have that he's unsettled by the conversation. His face is still a cool mask of certainty.

It's also the first time I've ever heard him say something and know for a fact that he's lying. I don't know how I know for sure, but my gut is telling me that he's not being honest. There is something he isn't saying, and I know it. My parents believe him though, both of them visibly relaxing at his response. I stay quiet, not wanting to question him in front of them. I look at him though, making sure he realizes I know he's full of shit… He's focused on his plate, taking a bite of his food, fully ignoring me. Mhm definitely hiding something.

"What makes you qualified to handle this?" My dad asks rudely. My fork clanks on the table from my surprise at his tone. Nathan subtly nods his head, stopping my retort.

"I spent the better part of a decade in Army Special Forces, sir. I've done reconnaissance in more than fifteen countries," he answers plainly, still completely unphased by the tense atmosphere.

My dad gets up again, mumbling something about needing air before going out on the back patio. We sit in silence for a few minutes, my mom still bouncing looks off of me and Nathan. Eventually, she starts clearing the table, shooing me off when I try to help. She's halfway into the kitchen when she turns around, catching our attention.

"So… Was it love at first sight, then?" She asks, making my jaw drop. "What? I figured you were sleeping together, but I'm not blind."

"MOM!" I cover my face with my hand, embarrassed to be called out so blatantly. Thank God my dad's outside. Nathan interjects, answering for me without any hesitation.

"I knew the moment I saw her that I was willing to die for

her," he pauses, looking at me before continuing. "It wasn't long after that I realized I didn't want to live without her." My breath catches in my throat, hearing him tell my mom that, so easily. I never doubted his feelings, but it's still hard to imagine he feels that way, that he could love me that much. I'll probably never feel like I deserve it.

My mom presses a hand to her chest, feeling the impact of his words just as I am. "Thank you for saving my baby girl, Nathan," she says with trembling lips before disappearing into the kitchen, not giving him a chance to respond. Probably needing a minute to collect herself. I don't join her right away, giving her space.

Instead, I take advantage of our moment of privacy, kissing Nathan softly. "I love you," I whisper against his lips, meaning it so deeply from within my soul.

"I love you, too," he smiles, cupping my cheek lightly, bringing his head close so he can whisper in my ear. "I think your mom might be falling in love with me too," he can't contain his laughter after I pull back and slap him lightly on his chest. He holds the spot as if I wounded him.

"Not funny," I try to say seriously, but his laugh is contagious, making me hide my smile by shoveling a pancake in my mouth.

"I'm gonna go talk to your dad," he says as he stands up from the table.

"What? Why?" I ask, glancing towards the patio where my dad is leaning against the porch railing, staring into the yard.

"He's worried about you, Callie, and I know what that feels like. I can't imagine how it is as a father, but I want him to trust me. I want him to know how serious I am about keeping you safe." He drops a kiss on my head as he walks towards the back door, sliding the glass door open and giving me a wink as he closes it. He's so hot, I can't help but grin like an idiot at him.

My mom comes back in the room, and both of us watch my dad and Nathan talk. We can't hear what they're saying, but it looks serious. I'm afraid that it's not going well, my dad hardly seems to be able to look at Nathan. So, it surprises me a couple of minutes later when Nathan holds his hand out, intending to shake my dad's hand, but instead, my dad pulls him into an embrace. A quick pat on the back then he releases him, but it looked like a hug nonetheless. My mom and I scatter before they turn around, pretending to be busy in the kitchen.

Chapter Forty-Two

Nathan

My head's reeling a little bit when I walk back into the house. Not expecting how the conversation with Callie's dad went. I'm still processing what he said when I see Callie eyeing me from the kitchen, probably wondering what went down. I clear my throat, not sure what to tell her yet, so I change tactics. "I need to get going. There's a couple of things I need to take care of back home." It's not completely forthcoming, but it's enough of the truth for now. Callie squints her eyes slightly but doesn't acknowledge my half truth.

"I'll walk you out." There's a formality to her tone that puts me on edge, but I follow her out after telling her mom goodbye. We get to my truck before she says anything, climbing into my passenger side.

"What aren't you telling me?" She asks, keeping her eyes pointed toward the floorboard like she's afraid to look at me.

"What do you mean?" I can't stop the words from coming out, my natural instinct to evade being caught.

"Please, don't lie to me." Her voice is so small and it kills me. I'm caught between lying to protect her or telling her the truth, and reaping the consequences that will bring.

"What do you want to know?"

She looks at me, skeptically, and I'm impressed she's so astute to my bullshitting but uneasy about what's to come.

"What are you really planning to do once you get home?" She's looking at me directly now, waiting to see how I respond, reading me for deception. Smart.

"I'm going to keep an eye on the Sheriff, see if he leads me to Tony and Bub," I deliver my response as simply as I can, hoping she'll accept it and move on.

"And then?" She prompts, not letting it slide. I grit my teeth, not wanting to answer her question. Fuck. I don't want to lie to her, but I'm not ready to draw back the curtain and ruin her opinion of me. I've enjoyed being the hero in her eyes, someone who only does good. But, it's far from the truth and I've only been lying to myself. I rub my jaw, avoiding answering her question. "Nathan. What are you going to do once you find them?" She asks again, forcing my hand.

Might as well rip the bandaid off now, so she can run inside to the safety of her own home once she learns the truth. It's inevitable. "I'm going to kill them," I say clearly, so there's no question whether she heard it correctly or not. I keep my voice low and even, void of emotion. She needs to realize this isn't a rash decision, it's been well thought out, and there will be no changing my mind. Even if it means losing her.

She doesn't say anything right away, and I don't know which is more concerning, her silence or the fact she didn't go running from the truck trying to get away from the killer she's sitting next to. I wait, giving her the time she needs to process what I said, but wishing I could hear her thoughts. I don't regret my choice to go kill those bastards, because I know she'll finally be safe once and for all. But, it will kill me if she can't stomach being with me after I do it, a constant reminder of the worst event in her life.

"All three of them?" Her voice is calm, without a hint of the fear I expected.

"Yes," answering simply.

"Are you out of your mind?" She lashes out, the anger is evident on her face, not exactly the reaction I was expecting either. "You're crazy," she adds, shaking her head.

"I'm no stranger to killing people, Callie. I won't be able to live with myself knowing they're still breathing. Knowing they hurt you already, and would do worse if they got to you again." I shake my head to rid myself of those thoughts. I watch her, waiting for her reaction.

"And what am I supposed to do when you're arrested for murder and I lose you forever?" Her voice cracks. The anger is one thing, but the tears in her eyes are like a sledgehammer to my chest, knocking all the wind out of me. I didn't consider that perspective, because I don't plan on getting caught, but I understand her pain. The idea of ever losing her kills me too.

"I won't get caught. I'm too stubborn to live my life without you." I reach out to capture her jaw, afraid she'll flinch away from me, but she doesn't. She lets her face rest in my hand, my thumb traces her soft cheek. "I'm going to do whatever it takes to make sure you're safe," I vow. "I understand if…" I pause, the words getting caught in my throat, "I understand if you aren't happy about it. I just hope like hell you'll forgive me."

"Forgive you for what?" She asks, confused.

"Forgive me for being a murderer," I don't mince my words, needing to get my point across. I've killed before, this is just the first one unsanctioned by the United States government. We sit in silence, she mindlessly plays with my fingers resting on the center console. Lost in her thoughts.

"I don't think you're a murderer. Not when they deserve to die for what they did to me. I would have killed them if I had the chance, I just wasn't strong enough," she says so softly that I have to watch her lips to catch every word.

"You survived, Callie. That's strength. Killing is just about opportunity. They had you outnumbered and restrained, you're lucky to be alive with those odds," I tell her, sincerely.

"I was lucky because of you. Not because of what I did... If I had been able to kill them when they attacked me, you wouldn't be in this situation." She shakes her head as if scolding herself.

"I wasn't there the whole time, baby. You made it to me all on your own, and you made it out of that clearing on your own two feet. You survived. And, I'm damn proud of you for it." Pulling her into me by the back of her neck, I press our foreheads together. Forcing her to listen to me. "So damn, proud of you."

She sniffles back her tears. "If you remember correctly, you had to carry me out of those woods." She looks at me incredulously, but I can tell her mood's lighter.

"You're a beautiful woman, I was more than happy to carry you." I give her a cheeky grin, making her laugh. That sweet sound makes it impossible not to kiss her senseless. I take my time, savoring her soft lips against mine, exploring her mouth. I don't know how long we'll be apart, but I know it'll be too long. Any amount of time will be. She takes her time kissing me back, neither of us wanting to pull away first.

"Promise me you'll be careful, Nathan. I want to come

home to you," she whispers the plea against my lips, kissing me again.

"I promise, baby. I'll bring you home as fast as I can." I leave a final kiss on her forehead, reluctant to leave her. She climbs out of my truck, blowing me a kiss with tears in her eyes. I don't pray, but I pull away from the curb, thanking God for giving me, Callie. The next time I come to Tennessee, it's going to be to move her back home with me to North Carolina. We're going to leave all the bad behind us and build a life together. I'll spend every day of my life proving to her how much I love her.

The further I drive the darker my thoughts get. The light Callie emits has been distracting me, and now that I'm away from her, the anger is seeping back in. I spend the rest of my drive devising my plan. It's going to be a lot of recon, I'm going to have to watch Sheriff Donahue until he leads me to the other two. Hopefully, it doesn't take long. I'm eager to get my girl back, and these scumbags are keeping her from me. I think about how I'm going to do it. If I have my choice, I'll strangle the Sheriff with my bare hands, forcing him to gasp for breath as he dies. Once I get a hold of Tony and Bub, it's hard to say what will feel right. I thought about burying them alive, torturing them in their final moments. Giving them exactly what they deserve.

It's too unpredictable though, not knowing how long it will take them to die. I need to kill them with my own hands, see the life drain from their eyes.

Maybe, I should drag them back out to the clearing I first saw Callie in, the one they chased her into, and line them up side by side, public execution style. Put a bullet in them and leave them there to be picked off by scavengers.

As much as I want to make them suffer, I have to play it smart. Callie was right, I can't get caught, there's no chance in hell I'm missing out on a life with her when I just found her. I'll take my time, watch where the Sheriff leads me, then I'll eliminate them once and for all.

Chapter Forty-Three

Callie

Two weeks later

Every morning I wake up to an empty bed and go to sleep the same way. Each day passes by slower than the last. I've hardly heard anything from Nathan, but it doesn't stop me from checking my phone a hundred times a day. I've received a handful of texts, all a quick *I love you* from him, while my responses are left undelivered. The one and only phone call was from two days after he left, warning me he'd be going off the grid and keeping his phone turned off. He didn't want to risk any evidence pointing to him if an investigation ever occurred, something about his phone pinging towers and giving away his movements. The way he talked so casually about his plans was alarming, but I trust him. I have to, or my heart wouldn't be able to handle the worry.

"I'm asking you to put all your faith in me, baby. I know it isn't fair, but I'm asking you to trust me. Just hang with me until all this is over, and I'll never leave you in the dark again. I promise."

That phone call was full of promises and *I love you's*, but it still feels like a boulder weighing on my chest. It's hard not to let my concerns creep in, especially as more time passes. Every night I lay awake in bed hoping that he's safe. Four nights ago I cried for hours when I realized if he got hurt, or died, I wouldn't know. We aren't married. I doubt his family even knows about me. If something were to happen to him, who knows how long it would take for me to find out?

Since that night I have felt sick every morning when I wake up, with little relief throughout the day when my anxiety is causing knots in my stomach. I've hardly eaten a meal because of it, not able to stomach feeding myself when Nathan could be lying dead somewhere. All because of me.

One day ago, I bought a pregnancy test. My constant overthinking is making my emotions rage out of control. I'm on birth control, there is no reason I should be pregnant, but my insistent nausea is concerning. Rationally, I know it's probably just stress, but with my luck lately, I need to be sure. Not having enough courage to pee on the stick until this morning, I sit on my bed, staring at the small white test sitting on the dresser. I have two minutes to ponder my life choices. The thought of being pregnant seems ridiculous, my brain doesn't even want to consider it. Luckily, I know it could only be Nathan's since I wouldn't go near my ex when I knew our relationship was spiraling.

Am I ready to have Nathan's baby?

I'm not ready to be a mom, and I definitely haven't had enough time with Nathan to even have the family talk with him, but... Having his baby? I think one day I would like that. Just, not today. Please, not today.

With thirty seconds remaining on my timer, I get choked up imagining Nathan as a dad. He'd be a wonderful father, I have no doubts. I think he'd be a good husband too. My eyes sting with tears even thinking about getting an entire life with him. My timer goes off, signaling that the test should be complete, but I'm glued to the bed. My feet aren't moving even though my brain is telling me to get up.

I take a couple of deep breaths, preparing myself. It's going to be okay, I chant in my head, over and over. I stand over the test, picking it up with trembling fingers, immediately seeing the negative line. My breath wooshes out of me, relief washing over me. Thank God, a baby is not something I was ready to add to the mix of this fucked up time in my life.

So, why am I crying?

Tears pour down my face, I stare at my reflection in the mirror that hangs above the dresser, and I feel like I'm looking at a stranger. All of the ups and downs in the last few weeks have changed me in a way that I look unrecognizable.

I feel like I've aged five years, but I guess being kidnapped, assaulted, and almost killed could do that to a person. Not to mention the impending doom hanging over my head that the love of my life could die trying to avenge me. What the hell has happened to me? I'm living in the plot of a movie instead of real life. Now I'm mourning a child that never existed. I need to get a grip. I spend the rest of the day trying to get some work done, still not caught up from taking so many days off. The monotony of data spreadsheets and emails is always consistent, boring even, which is much needed with all the excitement in my personal life.

I work until the sun starts setting, and the days are getting shorter as it draws closer to Thanksgiving. My birthday is in a couple weeks and all I want is for all of this to be behind us. I want to sit by the fireplace at the cabin, watch a movie with Nathan, and never have to worry about either of us being killed. Seems reasonable enough.

I shake my head, clearing any hope that my life will be normal anytime soon. My phone starts vibrating, an unknown number appears on the screen. Assuming it's a telemarketer I ignore it, letting it go to voicemail. When the same number calls back right away, I get an uneasy feeling in my gut. I answer it hesitantly, afraid of what is waiting for me on the other side of the line.

"Hello?"

"Hi, I'm calling for Callie Richards." It's a woman's voice, her words are soft spoken.

"This is her." I'm trying not to hold my breath, but my nerves are getting the better of me, I'm immediately fearing the worst.

"Hi, Callie. I'm calling from St. John's Hospital regarding a patient that's been admitted." My heart sinks. I'm not familiar with the name of that hospital, so I can only assume it's not one around here but one in North Carolina. I don't respond but she keeps talking. "Nathan Wolfe was in an accident, he was brought in unresponsive. The doctors were able to work on him, but he's currently in a medically induced coma.

"What? Oh my God!" I feel like I can't breathe, my whole body is trembling uncontrollably.

"Family is being notified, it's probably best for you to make arrangements to visit the patient as soon as you can. The doctor isn't sure how his condition will be by morning," she continues, giving me an address for the hospital and directions to the parking lot that will lead me to the right door. I don't know how I managed, but I wrote what I needed on a scrap piece of paper, ending the call with the hospital worker.

I jump from my chair and immediately throw together an overnight bag, hardly paying attention to what I'm grabbing. I left a note on the kitchen counter for my parents telling them Nathan was in an accident and I needed to go back to North Carolina, I'd call them when I could.

They had gone out to run errands, but I'm worried if I tried to call them now I'd break down as soon as I heard their voices. I'm trying my best to keep my tears at bay, needing to keep myself together enough to drive the two hours to the hospital.

As I'm pulling out of the driveway, the clock on the dash tells me it's only been fifteen minutes since I ended my phone call with the hospital. I type in the address I need as I head for the highway, hoping like hell there's no traffic on the way there.

It's dark, my headlights illuminating the roadway in front of me. The majority of the evening commuters are home by now, leaving me plenty of room to weave around the few cars and trucks also heading southbound. I try not to imagine Nathan lying in a hospital bed, tubes and wires littering his body, the tears already burning the backs of my eyes. The blurriness from my wet eyes makes it hard to see, so I try focusing on anything and everything else, but my thoughts are solely on Nathan laying alone in a hospital bed dying.

I crank my music up, drowning out my inner turmoil. It works enough to dry my tears for now, but it doesn't keep the guilt away. This is all my fault. I should have fought harder to make Nathan stay out of it. I shouldn't have let him go two weeks ago. All the caller said was that he was in an accident... Maybe it was random and didn't have anything to do with my attackers. The chances of that seem slim, but I don't have any answers yet, making it hard not to think the worst.

I make the drive in less than two hours, having pushed the speed limit the whole way and pull into the south lot of the hospital like I was instructed. It must be a special entrance for the ICU because there seems to be less hustle and bustle than in the parking lot next to the emergency department. I pull into the first spot I see and take a deep breath. I'm afraid. My body is a bundle of nerves, preparing for what I'm about to walk into.

The parking lot is dark, only lit by a few street lamps, but the doors of the entrance nearest to me are lit up, beckoning me to get out of my car. I take my backpack with me, not wanting to return to my car for anything if I'm stuck waiting a while.

As I make my way through a couple of rows of cars toward the entrance, my phone starts ringing. I think about ignoring it, but it could be my parents and I don't want them to worry. I stop on the sidewalk to take the call, not wanting to disturb anyone inside since it's late in the evening. It takes me a moment to fish my phone out of the deep pocket of my bag, but I finally grab it before the last ring.

My heart stills when I see Nathan's name on the screen. What the hell? My hands suddenly feel clammy. Why would I be getting a call from him if he's in intensive care? The sweat trickling down my spine tells me what my brain hasn't come to terms with yet... I fucked up.

Chapter Forty-Four

Nathan

I rub my eyes, tired of straining to keep them open. I've been at this for too damn long. For two weeks I've been following Sheriff Donahue around, I've been in my truck more than my house. My ass hurts, my back aches, I'm pissed though, more than anything. I've been all over this town, stalking the Sheriff, waiting for him to slip up, but he hasn't. He goes to work, goes on calls, goes to the bar, and goes home. Almost every day it's been the same thing. A few times he's slipped me, getting too far ahead of me while I'm trying to stay under the radar. He's either really lucky, or he's not as dumb as he looks. Either way, I'm sure he'll let his guard down soon. One mistake, that's all I need.

I'm sitting in the diner now, just down the street from the Sheriff's department. I sip on a cup of coffee, keeping an eye on the cruiser parked right out front. It hasn't moved in nearly two hours, even though it's late and the Sheriff usually has gone home by now. The lights in the lobby have been turned off, but a couple of windows are still aglow, indicating the offices inside are still occupied.

The town of Whitewater is small, and the rest of Rollins

County is dispersed across the mountains. If the Sheriff is corrupt, it doesn't surprise me that he's gotten away with it for this long. There's no one around to check him. I wonder if more women have disappeared from the highway, their cars later towed because of an anonymous call. The number of a caller leads right back to this very police station. Jesse told me as much when I asked him to dig into it. The number was registered to the Sheriff's Department, but not a specific person. I can only assume it was Sheriff Donahue, although I haven't met any of the other deputies. They might be just as bad as he is, they are on his payroll, and they could very well be under his thumb in all of this.

I sigh, finishing my cup of coffee, debating on whether or not I should call it a night and crash in my bed tonight. Sleeping in my bed reminds me of Callie though, my chest gets tight just thinking about her. I miss her, but I know it's for the best. She is safe where she is, at home in Tennessee. If she was here with me it might cause the Sheriff to do something reckless.

I wonder what she's doing? Is she thinking about me as much as I am about her? I can only hope the physical distance hasn't changed her mind about us, and that the novelty of our relationship hasn't worn off.

Those thoughts are enough to make me pull my phone out and power it on. I'm in a neutral location in town, a public space. If someone were to question my whereabouts, I'm here to eat, not to be a stalker. Obviously.

The waitress brings me my change as I pull up Callie's name to call her, I leave my tip on the table and return to my truck parked out front while it rings. It rings so long I think it's going to voicemail, but it suddenly clicks over, like someone answered it but I don't hear anything.

Finally, after a few seconds, I hear her. "Hello?" Her voice is so quiet, almost shallow.

"Callie?" I know it's her, but it doesn't necessarily sound like her either.

"Nathan," she breathes my name out like she's on the verge of tears.

"Callie, what's wrong?" My heart is beating fast, but I'm holding my breath, waiting for her to tell me she's okay.

"I think I messed up," her voice trembles, but I can hear her moving, the wind making the sound crackle. A car door slams shut before I have a chance to respond.

"What happened? Where are you?" I ask her, the panic clear in my voice. I'm too on edge to remain calm, hearing the fear in her voice.

"St. John's Hospital. I thought you were hurt," her voice is still shaky.

"What made you think that?" My brain registers that St. John's is only 30 minutes from here, so I hit the gas, heading in that direction. She hasn't responded yet, making me pull the phone from my ear to make sure the phone is still connected. "Callie?" I yell, probably harsher than I should have, but I'm too worried to care.

"Someone is watching me," she whispers, even though she's inside her car like she's afraid they'll hear her.

"Callie, what the fuck is going on? Get out of there!" I yell into the phone again. I hear her start her car, the engine coming to life.

"I'm sorry, someone called me and said you were here and you were hurt. I sped here without even thinking. I thought you were dying." She's fully crying now, her tears evident even through the phone.

"It's okay, baby. I'm okay. Just get the hell out of there and get back on the highway, I'll meet you halfway." I try to calm my tone, so I don't upset her more, even though I'm terrified. There is no reason someone would call her, not unless it was a setup. As I drive by the Sheriff's Department, I glance in the windows. With the lights on and it being nighttime, I can see right inside. No one's there. It's empty. Fuck. He must've slipped out the back. I slam my hand against the steering wheel. Fucking bastard.

I hear tires squealing through the speaker, and Callie's breath catches. "No, no, no..." She's mumbling, her fear projecting through the phone.

"What is it? Callie?" I floor it, I know it's not possible to get there any faster but I'm not thinking rationally. "Callie?" I yell again, needing to know what's happening. Glass shatters, and I hear her scream. I feel the blood drain from my face, the air is knocked from my lungs at the sound.

I hear another door slam, and then silence. This can't be happening. I fucked up, I should have never left her by herself. I should have known they'd try to lure her back. FUCK! I don't want to disconnect the call but I need to call the police.

My thumb hovers over the end button, hesitating before I finally hit it. All I can think as I punch in 911, is that I hope that wasn't the last time I get to hear her voice. Full of fear and hopelessness.

The call clicks over, but before the dispatcher can finish their initial greeting or take charge of the call, I'm quickly relaying what happened. She asks to stay on the line with me until I arrive but I decline, telling her I'll talk to the officers once I arrive.

Next, I call the only other person I can think of. Jesse answers on the first ring.

"What's up, buddy?" He answers, but I can't even respond right away, my anger has taken my voice away.

"They took her. They fucking took her," I manage to finally grunt out. I don't need to explain who I'm talking about, I filled him in on Callie. He told me he'd help if I needed him, and now I fucking need him. I should have taken him up on his offer earlier, but I thought I had it handled. My stupid fucking ego is going to get my girl killed.

"What do you need?" His voice is all business, not an ounce of hesitation. My fucking, brother. I ask him to do something that I hope I won't regret because it's incredibly illegal, and if he gets caught, his job is on the line. Unlike me, he plans to have a full military career and retire when he's halfway in a grave. He has access to databases, and information technology that I have no right to ask him for, but I'm desperate.

"I need a location. I need to know where they took her. Cameras, phones, something. I need to find her before they kill her," my voice breaks on the last sentence, my agony is tearing me apart.

"You got it. I'll call you as soon as I have something."

"Jesse. I..." I can't finish my sentence, not sure what to say, but I feel a singular trail of wetness roll down my cheek. I can't lose her.

"We'll get her back. Be careful, brother." He ends the call, leaving the cab of my truck eerily silent. He knows what I'm asking is illegal. He didn't even hesitate to help. If I make it through this alive, I'll gladly be indebted to him for the rest of my life. I just need Callie back.

The dark roadway stretches out in front of me as I race toward the hospital. The streetlights flashing over me as I speed past them put me in a trance, forcing me to remember the horrible shit that I've locked away. Memories, like still shots from that one singular night in South America assault me.

Darkness.

Blood.

Screaming. Crying.

Bugs swarming around an exposed porch light.

Sweat trickling down my forehead.

Death.

Despair.

A slaughter.

Chapter Forty-Five

Nathan

I pull into the hospital parking lot, knowing exactly where to go because of the cacophony of blue and red lights lighting up the southern side of the building. My pulse thunders in my ears while anxiety claws at my chest. I need to see where it happened, where they took her. A deep pit in my gut is reminding me that she might not be alive already. For all I know, they could have off'd her right here in the parking lot. It would be suicidal since the hospital has cameras, but these guys don't strike me as the brightest individuals. I just hope they snatched her and took her to another location, it'll give me time to find her. I just need a little time.

I pull as close as I can to the cruisers already on scene, multiple officers are pointing their flashlights in and around her car. Glass is shattered all over the pavement, and the driver-side window has been busted out.

I don't see a body. I breathe a little easier, knowing she's not in a body bag already, but it's not enough. I need to know where she is, I need to know she's okay. I get out of my truck, as casually as I can, I walk up to the officer that's taping off the crime scene.

"Man, what happened?" I ask, trying to seem like a nosey onlooker, hoping this guy will give me a crumb of information to go on. The officer looks at me, he's a young guy, probably a rookie. I can see in his eyes he's taken aback by me like he wasn't expecting anyone to try to speak to him. I don't want to intimidate him, but I need something to go on, it's killing me to know she's in trouble. I maintain eye contact with him, standing my ground so he doesn't blow me off.

"We're not sure. It was reported as a kidnapping, but we haven't been able to review the security tapes yet. It's an active crime scene though, I need you to keep moving along," he finishes, adjusting his spine to show his full height. I get it, he's trying to be an authority figure, I can respect it. I just don't give a shit right now.

"Any blood?" I ask, not taking his cue for me to leave.

"Excuse me?"

"Is there any blood in the car? Any signs that the victim was injured?" I ask through gritted teeth, losing my patience. It's not this guy's fault, I'm just losing my mind not knowing what happened to her for sure. He eyes me wearily, suspicious now of my line of questions.

"I can't discuss that. What's your name, pal?" He reaches for his radio, clearly ready to alert everyone else of my odd behavior.

"Doesn't matter. Have a good night." I turn to go back to my truck, leaving the officer behind me. He calls out, wanting me to wait, but I don't. As soon as I reach my truck, I get in and take off, back towards Whitewater.

My mind's reeling. What have they done with her? Are they torturing her? Have they already killed her? What's their plan? The questions are making me crazy. My teeth might crack from how hard I'm clenching my jaw. I spent the entire drive back beating myself up. How could I let this happen? If I get her back -no, when I get her back, she's never going to forgive me. I was supposed to protect her, I promised I would.

I beat my hand against the steering wheel over and over, feeling so out of control. I wipe my palm across my face, the tension making my head ache. I can guess they probably took her to whatever place in the woods they were aiming for the last time they had her… I just need a location. Hopefully, Jesse can find something, because if not, it'll be like trying to find a needle in a haystack. A haystack that I'll burn to the ground trying to find her.

I turn left off the interstate, going to the only place I can think of that makes sense. It only takes a few minutes to pull up in front of Sheriff Donahue's house. A small double-wide trailer, with white siding that's more yellow now with age. I've been here multiple times in the past two weeks, and I've memorized every detail of the outside. The mailbox is slightly askew and weeds are growing up the siding that are almost as tall as the trailer. It's not well kept, I can only imagine what the inside looks like.

There aren't any cars out front, aside from an old Ford Ranger sitting under a tarp, but it's missing an engine, a project not touched in years by the looks of it.

I pull my gun from my holster and get out of my truck, jogging to the back of the house. I peek through the back windows as I go. It's dark inside, the lights from the appliances are the only thing glowing. Without thinking twice about it, I kick the back door in. Even with it locked, it easily pops open, the latch old and cheap. Seems like minimal security for a member of law enforcement, but this guy strikes me as someone who thinks he is untouchable.

Clearing the trailer doesn't take more than a minute, it's mostly open, only a few doors to check behind. Satisfied that I'm alone, I start searching through papers that are strewn across the kitchen table. Mostly bills, "past due" written on a lot of them. Of course, he doesn't pay his bills, what a low life. Surely, he gets paid well as the Sheriff. Where does his money go? I know he's a drunk, but even alcohol isn't that expensive, not in these parts.

I sift through the papers some more, giving up after a couple of minutes. Fuck. There has to be something here. I see a landline telephone on the kitchen counter, a blinking light indicating there is a voicemail. I click it, listening to it on speaker, hoping I'll get lucky and it's dumb or dumber giving away their whereabouts. Unfortunately, it's a 30-second message from the Sheriff's mom, scolding him for not calling her. Damn.

I stand there in the middle of the kitchen, staring at the ceiling. What the hell am I supposed to do? I can't go get her if I have no clue where she is. My chest is still aching, the thought of losing Callie is like a knife to my fucking heart.

Thinking of her lifeless, killed by these fuckers... I feel like I could puke. I've seen terrible things in my life, I held Chester's dead body in my arms after he was shot, and I felt his blood soak into my clothes. That was the only thing close to how I feel right now. When it's someone you care about, it hurts so much worse. War zones, torture camps, all things I could turn my emotions off, and get the job done.

There is no turning my emotions off now. I love her too damn much. The cotton of my shirt is lined with sweat, my body struggling to hold it together. This can't be it, this can't be all the time that I get with her, it's not fucking fair. I take a few deep breaths, needing to reign in my agonizing thoughts. I look at the landline again, thinking how odd it is to even have one in this day and age.

Something the lady from the tow company had said clicks in my brain, *the caller left their number on the caller ID*. What if he's been communicating with Tony and Bub on the landline? Not wanting to trace it back to his office... I snatch the phone up, clicking the buttons I need to show me the call log. One number at a time appears on the small screen, I have to arrow over for each new number it lists.

They're mostly random, with a few names attached to local area codes, none that I recognize. After going back a few days, I notice one number appearing over and over, but it's not local, maybe a prepaid cell phone. However, one of the dates a call was received was the morning Callie was first attacked. Could it be?...

I write the number down and stuff it in my pocket. It's all I got and I have to hope it will lead me somewhere. I exit the trailer through the back again, not caring to fix the door. I get in my truck and pull away from the house, hoping no one paid too much attention to how long I was parked there. It's late, hopefully, all of the neighbors are in bed.

I call Jesse as I head back towards my cabin, praying he can trace the number back to a location, and I need to be prepared when he does.

Chapter Forty-Six

Callie

My head is going to explode, I can hear my blood pumping, a rhythmic thumping in my ear. Where am I?

I don't open my eyes, afraid to see what's waiting for me. This sensation is eerily similar to the day I was attacked by Tony and Bub on the highway, except this time, I remember everything that happened instantly. Maybe, because this time I was expecting it, the initial stage of disbelief is unnecessary.

As soon as I had reversed out of my parking spot and put it in drive, a van pulled out in front of me, blocking me in. I immediately recognized it as the work van Tony and Bub drove. Before I could react properly, one of them busted out my window and knocked me out with something. A fist? A rock? I can't quite recall that detail.

My stomach is rolling, like I might throw up, meaning I probably have a concussion. Ugh! Why am I so stupid? I should have known it was a setup, and now I let Nathan down... All I had to do was stay away and stay safe, but I fucked it up.

A shuffling sound from somewhere near me makes me

squeeze my eyes shut. Too afraid to be caught looking, I focus on my other senses instead. The smell of burning wood has assaulted my nasal cavities since I woke up like there is fire nearby, but there's also a mustiness in the air that reminds me of mildew. My fingers twitch slightly against the hard surface I'm lying on. It's not cold metal like the van was, it feels hard, like wood, but dirty. The grittiness of it scrapes against my fingertips. More noise from nearby, makes my breath catch in my throat... A grunting sound comes from behind me making it obvious that I'm not alone.

This is it, this is when I'm going to die. My parents will be devastated... I want to scream imagining how brokenhearted they'll be. And, Nathan... I'll never get to see him again. The tears fall through the cracks of eyelids, not able to be contained. I try to steady my breathing but it's no use, I feel like I'm starting to hyperventilate, my body is trembling from the effort to stay still.

When I can't squeeze them together any longer, I finally creep my eyes open, slowly taking in the room bit by bit through my lashes. The low light is making it hard to focus on anything, and my tears already making my vision blurry.

Through the crack in my eyelids, I make out a pair of shoes a small distance in front of me. They move slightly, making me jump, the sudden movement startling me. After my very noticeable reaction, I hold my breath, waiting to be hit, kicked, or anything, but nothing happens.

Relieved that they haven't noticed I'm awake, or that they don't care, I continue focusing on the shoes. It takes me a moment to gather enough courage to direct my line of sight upwards, but when I do, I'm caught off guard. In front of me, about 10 feet away, is a woman. She's sitting with her knees pulled up, leaning against a wall, her wrists and ankles tied, a cloth stuffed in her mouth.

I don't recognize her, but a part deep in my brain is telling me that I know her. Everything is still kind of foggy though and I can't access the information from my memory. My eyes trail across her form, desperate for a clue. When my focus lands on her eyes, I freeze. It's pure terror looking back at me. Her eyes are open wide, blinking wildly. I can see where trails of tears have fallen down her cheeks, and her graying hair is sticking out all over her head like someone tried to pull it from her scalp.

Her nostrils flare with every breath, the darkest parts of her eyes ping back and forth between us, her toes bounce making my attention draw to her where her hands are resting on her knees. Her silent plea is loud and clear... She wants me to untie her. I'm still frozen in place, too afraid to move. I know I don't have time to be scared, if I want to live I have to get out of here. I just wish I knew where "here" is. I also wish I knew where Tony and Bub are.

I pull in a lungful of air, exhaling shakily, trying to convince myself to be brave. It hardly works, but the thought in my mind that I'll never see Nathan again, that I'll die before I can live my life with him, has me raising myself onto my hands and knees. Another deep breath, and I swivel my head left and right, taking in my surroundings. It looks like an abandoned hunting cabin. I was right about the floors being covered in dirt, as well as almost every other surface. There is a small wood-burning stove in the corner of the room closest to the unknown woman. Behind me are an old card table and two mismatched chairs, sitting next to a poor excuse for a kitchen. Trash litters the surface of the tiny counter, dishes are piled in the single-tub sink, and the oven looks ancient and out of commission.

My gaze lands on the front door to my right, and the hallway to my left. I don't know where our captors are, but for now, it's just me and this woman alone in what I guess is the living room, except there's no furniture to suggest that. No couch, no chairs, just empty space aside from the flaming heat source in the corner.

On my hands and knees, I slowly drag myself across the floor. I don't know why they didn't tie me up, but I'm thankful for their mishap. The floorboards creak as my weight shifts over them, making me cringe with every sound. Coming closer to her now, her face is so familiar, but I still can't place how I know her. She looks like she's been through hell, the tears she shed are still stuck in her lashes, and her nose is running from the excess moisture. She's older, dirt is caked across her cheeks, built up in the creases of her skin, defining her wrinkles.

My fingers shake as I try to undo the knot at her wrists. Her mouth is gagged, and the fabric wraps around the back of her head. If I can get her hands free, she can work on that knot while I work on her ankles. My nerves are too out of control and I can hardly function, my dexterity is almost nonexistent, making me fumble with the ties. It looks like they used a torn bed sheet, the material is too smooth and I can't get a grip on it with how tight it is.

"I'm sorry, I'm sorry," I mumble under my breath, knowing I'm our only hope and I'm failing miserably. I'm not making any progress, I'm not going to be able to loosen any of these knots. I probably need a knife, but I try the ties at her ankles anyway. If I can at least get her feet loose then we can make a run for it, and worry about her wrists later.

Her ankle ties are easier, the space between her legs giving me more room to work at the fabric. I pull the knot loose, finally releasing the breath I was holding. Thank God, one thing is going right. I hear her muffling something through her gag, trying to grab my attention, making me glance up into her frightened face. Simultaneously, as I see the panic widening her eyes, the hair at the back of my head is grabbed in a vice grip.

"What the hell do you think you're doing?" The slimy voice skates down my spine, racking my stomach with a wave of nausea. *Tony.*

He drags me backward by my hair, the pain hardly registering because of my shock. That's when I see his face, the man from my nightmares. He's so close, his face inches from mine. "Did you miss me, you little bitch?" He sneers at me. His breath would knock me on my ass if he weren't holding me upright. His teeth are crooked and gray, the ones that are left anyway, reminding me of every meth addiction advertisement I've ever seen.

I don't respond, I can't, and I think it pisses him off because next thing I know I'm being tossed across the room, and slamming into the wall. The impact rattles my teeth, making me see strobe lights behind my eyes, my head pounding in succession. The nausea finally takes over and I heave the contents of my stomach right onto the floor. Trembling, I pull myself up to my hands and knees so I don't faceplant in my vomit.

"You dumb, bitch!" Tony yells, making me cower against the wall. It doesn't matter, he stomps over to me and I catch his boot to my stomach. His kick knocks the wind out of me, making me slump to the floor again, barely missing my puke. I stay down this time, not daring to move, not wanting to entice him further. He starts pacing the floor, each step making me flinch. He shouts suddenly, making me jump. "Bub! Come on out here. It's time to play."

I look at him and regret it immediately. The expression on his face terrifies me, a mixture of rage and perversion making him look so twisted and ugly, that it disturbs me to my core. I think I might prefer the demonic version from my nightmares.

Chapter Forty-Seven

Nathan

Three hours.

I've been out of my mind for three hours. Not knowing what horrible things Callie could be going through. My mind has gone to its darkest depths, imagining the hell they might be putting her through. The hell that I know depraved men are capable of inflicting. My thoughts keep drifting back to that night at the farm in South America, to the girl I couldn't save. She could have been someone's Callie.

* * *

Six years ago...
Classified location, South America

"Brandt, get these kids out of here, take them back through the cornfield, and wait for us. Let's move." The response to my command is instant, and the remaining five members of my team head in the direction of the old farmhouse. Using the darkness of the night to cover our movement, we draw closer to the old two-story building and hunker down. Jesse kneels behind me, both of us assessing our surroundings.

Much like the shed our hostages were in, the house is deteriorating. Broken windows, holes in the roof, and garbage littering the outside. The occupants don't give a shit. They'd probably make a home out of any abandoned slum if there were drugs inside.

Music is playing loudly from indoors somewhere, a few of the windows are dully lit with the unmistakable yellow light from an old lamp. The back porch is cloaked in shadows, the singular bulb acting as a porch light hardly illuminates anything. Nothing is visible from our location, we'll have to get closer to know if the girl is there or not.

Best case scenario, she's on the porch and we can snatch her up and get the hell out of here. Worst case scenario, she's in the house and we'll end up in a firefight. Leaving the other guys to cover us, me and Jesse move silently towards the broken-down steps of the porch. With agonizingly slow steps, we ascend the steps making as little noise as we can, each board threatening to break below our boots.

My gaze sweeps across the porch, my night vision goggles casting everything in a green glow when my eyes catch on a pair of bare legs jutting out from behind a ratty floral couch.

"I see her, no visual on well-being yet, standby," I whisper into the intercom, relaying the information to the rest of the team. I creep towards the couch, careful to avoid the crumpled beer cans scattered across the floorboards. Jesse hangs back, keeping his gun trained on the back door, ready for any unwelcome interruptions.

The bare legs, clearly belonging to a young woman, are covered in cigarette burns. The round wounds are marring her flesh from her toes to her inner thighs. It takes some maneuvering, my large frame struggling to squeeze into the space she's tucked into beside the couch, but when I do I get a chill down my spine despite the humidity in the air.

The visual is something from a horror film. The young woman lays before me, completely nude, covered in burns and blood. Knife marks across her torso form a crude version of the drug cartel's insignia. Her vacant eyes stare up into the sky, even in the distorted coloring of my night vision, I know they're milky blue. Not an ounce of life remains in this poor girl's body.

For some reason, even after all these years, her lifeless eyes make me think of Chester. Death is common in this line of work, so I don't know why this girl is forcing me to remember the one thing that haunts me. Maybe, it's her innocence or the fact that her sister is out there waiting, unknowingly about to receive the worst news imaginable. The unavoidable grief she's about to experience makes my limbs feel heavy, my movements stagnant.

What if it was my sister? The thought makes me dry heave, needing more than a few seconds to collect myself.

Not wanting to deliver this news, but not wanting to linger near this house, I pull a worn blanket off the old couch and wrap her body up with care. I treat her with the tenderness I would want to be afforded for my own family. Brushing hair off her forehead, I take one last look at her achingly youthful face, feeling my blood boil.

So young, her entire life over before it even began. All because she chose to spread the word of God in a country she was unfamiliar with. It's hard to believe there is a God when things like this happen, and entirely too often.

When Chester died I was so angry, cursing "the man above" for taking away my friend's life. Eventually, I stopped blaming God, realizing I couldn't blame something that didn't exist. My reality of the world is too bleak, people aren't deserving of forgiveness, and there is no saving of your soul.

My thoughts are reinforced as I fold the edge of the blanket over the girl's face, hiding the dried blood dripping from her nose and the edges of her mouth, hiding the busted blood vessels around her eyes, and the bruising around her neck and across her cheeks. A sight her sister should never have to see, it'll just haunt her like a ghost from her past. Like mine do.

I grit my teeth, forcing myself to get it together, to forget Chester, to forget how much this young girl reminds me of my sister, to forget that underneath all of this, I'm still human. I plaster on my impenetrable shield, ready to finish the job, "Target is deceased."

* * *

My phone rings, pulling me out of the deep hole of the past my mind has entered. Seeing Jesse's name on the screen, I answer immediately.

"I got a location," Jesse states as soon as I connect the call. At his words, my phone dings, a message showing coordinates to a property deep in the woods.

"I owe you one," I reply, gathering my things to leave,

"How'd you get the information?"

"Don't worry about it, the less you know the better." I can imagine him smirking as he says it. "It's an old hunting cabin, owned by the Sheriff's in-laws. I think they belonged to some sort of militia group back in the day. All types of shady shit in that family tree," he scoffs. "It's the only thing that made sense, the only place secluded enough for holding someone against their will." Jesse's words sink in, reminding me of my reality right now. Callie's deep in the woods with these bastards, the knowledge alone is enough to make me insane.

An image flashes in front of my eyes of Callie lying on the cold ground with pale, milky blue eyes staring up at me. Every ounce of warmth drained from her body. The visual is enough to make me want to scream, hardly containing myself enough to not fall to my knees, I have to take a deep breath before I can speak.

"What if it's a dead end?" I say through gritted teeth, more to myself than to him.

"That's a possibility, but I think this is it. The Sheriff is married to Vanessa Porter, she has two brothers -Anthony and Benjamin. They have no known address, I think they're living in Mommy and Daddy's cabin. It's got to be the two guys that took your girl. Or, it's a hell of a coincidence, but we don't have anything else to go on."

I sigh. The information is good, it has to be. Anthony and Benjamin have to be Tony and Bub, I won't accept any other possibility. I have no room for error, and no time for false leads.

Before I can second guess anything else, I'm running and jumping into my truck, speeding down my driveway towards the road. "Jesse…" I pause, not sure what to say. I don't know how to express the gratitude I have for him right now, he's the only thing giving me a chance at saving Callie. He's saved my life so many times in the years I've known him, but this... He's saving Callie's life, and that means more to me than my own.

"Go get her, bring her home, marry her, whatever," he laughs, easing some of my tension, "but, please, don't make this a suicide mission, man." His words are suddenly serious again, "I'm giving you time to get a head start, drop some bodies, whatever you need to do, but, I need to know you aren't leaving that cabin in a body bag. I need to know you have a plan or I'll call in an anonymous tip to your Trooper pal, Malec. Make him come after your dumb ass since I'm too far away to help."

I don't even know how he knows about my communication with Trooper Malec, I don't remember ever telling him about that. I'll just file it away with the other information I don't want to know how he knows.

"Do you remember what we did after we found that girl in South America? How little I cared about my own self-preservation? All I cared about was vengeance. For her. For that girl and her sister," I ask, not needing a response because I know he remembers.

"I remember," he answers immediately, confirming it for me anyway. We went from friends to brothers that night. He followed me into what could have been a suicide mission, not leaving my side for a second. I probably wouldn't have made it out alive if it weren't for him having my back.

"This is different. I don't plan on dying tonight, Jesse. I still have a whole life to live," I reassure him, knowing he understands. Out of anyone, Jesse knows my outlook on life, at least what it looked like before Callie. I hardly had anything to live for, not even myself, constantly throwing myself into the most dangerous missions, not caring if I lived or died. Not now though, I have everything to live for now, Callie is worth living multiple lifetimes for.

It doesn't stop the fear though, Callie might already be dead, or I might be walking into an ambush. I know the risks, and I have no choice but to take them. I don't want this to be a suicide mission, but if giving my life means Callie will be safe, then I've already accepted that fate.

"If something does go wrong, take care of her for me, Jess. Make sure she's okay. That's all I ask." I swallow back my emotions, not used to feeling this way. Vulnerable. My heart feels like it's flayed open, an inch away from being stomped on.

"Nothing is happening to you, Nathan," Jesse fires back.

"Jesse," I prompt, needing him to reassure me this time.

"I'll make sure she's okay." His response is barely above a whisper like he struggled to say the words out loud.

"Thanks, buddy." I take a deep breath, trying to collect myself.

"Anytime. Be safe, brother." He ends the call, leaving me with the silence of my truck as I fly down these mountain roads. Preparing myself for the most important fight of my life.

Chapter Forty-Eight

Callie

All I see are stars. Over and over, Tony throws me down, kicking me across the dirty floorboards. Picking me up to sneer some filthy, degrading words in my face, then dropping me again. I feel so helpless, my brain won't cooperate, and my thoughts are too scattered from the beating I'm taking. Every time I open my eyes, I have to squeeze them shut again to ward off the dizziness from being thrown around like a rag doll. I need to run, I need to escape, but my body is so rattled I don't think I could make it ten feet without falling.

I choke as Tony's boot knocks the wind out of me again, the tears coming from me are silent from the lack of oxygen in my lungs. I don't know how much longer I can take this. I don't know how long I've been here, but it feels like these are going to be my last moments. In pain and crying, being left for dead on the cold dirty floor.

"What do you want from me?" I scream, the words coming from somewhere deep within my soul. My will to live is crumbling, I might as well use my last bits of energy to yell at the man doing this to me.

"Let's start with an apology! Me and my brother were shot at! Because of you!" Tony yells back at me. Gesturing to his shoulder, wrapped in a white bandage. "And look at his face!" He points to Bub, who I just noticed standing in the opening of the hallway, watching the entire ordeal. His cheek has a red, puckered scar running the length of it.

"You kidnapped me! You fucking psycho!" I cry, not understanding how someone can be so deranged. I know I have no hope of surviving, not with people who aren't right in the head, there's no reasoning with someone like that.

Suddenly, the front door opens, and a gust of cold air fills the space drawing my attention. Any hope that it could be someone here to save me diminishes as soon as I see that it's Sheriff Donahue standing in the entry, simply gawking at the scene before him. His eyes linger on the woman still tied up against the wall, and if I'm not mistaken, he looks sorry for her. Why? Why her? Why not me?

That's when it hits me, my brain fog clears just enough to remember why this lady looked so familiar. She's the Sheriff's secretary, the one who was at the station the day I went to report my incident. Why is she mixed up in this?

"Tony, you no good son of a bitch. I told you to use Doris, not to fucking tie her up. She did what you wanted, didn't she? Now you've dragged me even deeper into your shit than I ever wanted to be!" He yells at Tony, slamming the front door closed behind him as he walks further into the cabin.

Tony grabs me under the arm, hauling me up so I'm closer to his face. "Ah, yes, ol' Doris had the pleasure of setting our trap. Should we give her a round of applause for her incredible performance? You know, making you believe your beloved mountain man was taking his last breath in the hospital." He laughs exuberantly, making spit fly at my face. I cower away, trying to avoid it.

I glance in Doris' direction, feeling betrayed by this woman I don't even know. Even though I know it's unfair, she's obviously a victim in this as well. I try to give her an ounce of empathy, knowing this is probably the last night for both of us to be alive. Two women whose lives are ruined by these selfish, cruel men.

She's crying, her eyes pleading with mine, I think apologetically. It doesn't matter, I've already forgiven her. Nothing she did outweighs the hatred I feel for the man beside me, and the other two standing in the room not doing a damn thing to help.

"It's okay, Doris, it's okay," I tell her, needing to relieve her conscience, giving her the only bit of relief I can in our situation.

Tony scoffs, dropping my arm, and in turn, letting my body slam to the floor again. "Bub, take the old lady to the back. Do what you want with her." He dismisses them with a wave of his arm. Bub excitedly takes Doris by the arm, dragging her across the floor and down the hallway. The eagerness is wrong, his pleasure in the situation is so incredibly disturbing, I have to squeeze my eyes shut to avoid thinking about what he's going to do to her. As if not seeing him drag her away will change her outcome.

"Now, me and you. We're gonna have some fun." Tony's face twists into a smile, as sinister as he is. "My brother-in-law here," he points to Sheriff Donahue, finally connecting the dots for me. "He's gonna wait outside until we're done."

"Tony, I don't want to be involved in this shit," Sheriff Donahue huffs.

"Too damn, bad. Unless you want me to tell my dear sister where you've been spending your nights, you do as I say," Tony lashes at him, making the Sheriff hang his head in defeat.

"You're going to let him kill me because of a little blackmail? Are you fucking kidding me?" I'm too exhausted to care that my outburst is risky. I can't believe what I'm hearing. The selfishness and lack of remorse for our lives continues to baffle me. Where is their humanity?

"Kill you? Girl, I'm not going to kill you. I'm fixin' to sell you," Tony whispers in my ear, making my blood run cold. Sell me? I didn't think this could get any worse.

"To who?" My voice squeaks, not able to contain the fear I feel.

"That's no concern of yours. The next stop for you is the back of a semi heading North." His laughter cackles in my ear, making my whole body shake.

What the hell did I get mixed up in? Human trafficking? I thought that stuff only happened on TV. This doesn't feel like real life at all. I can't catch my breath, short bursts keep escaping my lips, the impending panic attack finally catching up to me. My whole body is trembling now, I curl into myself on the floor, not able to move. I can faintly hear Tony and the Sheriff arguing by the door, but I can't make out what they're saying. It doesn't matter, my life's over anyway, not by death but by captivity.

I just wish I could see Nathan one last time, and tell him I love him. I picture his face in my mind, the way his eyes crinkle when I finally coax a laugh out of him, his soft lips against mine. I imagine touching him again, being wrapped up in his strong body as he holds me in his arms. I hope he doesn't regret meeting me and sharing the time we had together. Even though it's only going to bring him more pain in the end. Something I never wanted to do to him. He's been through so much, and now he's going to lock this away as another nightmare that plagues him.

The tears escape my eyes, the saltiness burning the raw skin around my eyes from crying so much. I never meant to cause him more grief in his life, but I'll never regret meeting him or loving him. I just hope he believes I died, it'll be better than knowing the alternative. The harshness of what faces me will probably be worse than death, something I don't want him to live with. That burden can stay with me.

The exhaustion is too much, my panic attack has depleted my last energy reserves, and I feel the blanket of sleep closing in on me. My eyes refuse to open anymore, so I let my conscious mind fade, welcoming the escape from reality and this nightmare.

Chapter Forty-Nine

Nathan

It's a cold night, I can see my breath in the dim light of the full moon. It's just enough light to illuminate the hunting cabin, the darkened windows sharply reflecting the moonlight. From my spot in the tree line, I'm blanketed in darkness, assessing my surroundings. Part of me wants to rush the front door, go in guns blazing, and put a bullet in anyone who stands in my way, but I know that it's not the smart move. If I act irrationally, letting my emotions cloud my judgment, I could get Callie killed. She doesn't need the erratic version of me that would burn the world down for her, she needs the cold and calculated Special Forces veteran. The years of training and experience that's been ingrained in my blood.

So here I sit, giving myself five more seconds to pull my head out of my ass and breathe. Clearing away my fear for Callie, and my hatred for the men I'm about to face, and putting on my impervious mask to get the job done.

I stalk quietly towards the lit windows of the cabin, hoping to get a visual inside, assess, and make my plan. The window has a film of grime over it, weathered from years of neglect, making the glass foggy. I use the heel of my hand to swipe at the corner of the window sill, clearing a smudge to see through.

I take in a blurry view of the living room. Even though it's dimly lit, I can make out the bottom half of a body lying in the center of the floor. It's a bad angle and I can't see the top half, but my gut is telling me it's Callie. My Callie. My stomach twists violently, and flashbacks of the girl in South America torment my brain. The first thing I saw then was her legs, before being met with the gruesomeness that still haunts me.

What if that's the case now? Am I already too late?

I squeeze my eyes shut, refusing to see the girl from my nightmares, refusing to let that become the reality right now. I don't open my eyes again until I'm back in the present, back in control of myself. Taking another deep breath, I look back in the window, looking for any sign of life from her. A toe twitch, anything.

She still doesn't move, the sweat rolls down my neck making me achingly aware of how terrified I am to lose her. My muscles are tense, and my body is ready to spring into action, but I know I need to refrain. Assess. Plan. Engage. Anything out of that order can cause chaos and casualties, something I can't risk. Not with her.

I scan the rest of the space, looking for her captors. I can't see anyone, but I can faintly make out voices coming from the inside by the front door. Two voices. And it sounds like they're arguing. With my gun ready, I edge closer to the front door, losing the visual inside but picking up their words through the gaps in the siding.

"I'm done. I want out. Don't call me for help anymore, because I'm not doing it!" The voice that sounds like Sheriff

311

Donahue booms.

"You're done when I say you're done. I haven't been keeping all your dirty little secrets from my sister for nothin'. You're mine until I decide I don't need you anymore." Tony, I assume, spits back at him.

"Tell her, I don't care. She's planning on going through with the divorce anyway! Get rid of the girl, then lay low. I'm not bailing you out if you get arrested!" The door flings open, and I hardly have enough time to dive back behind the side of the house before the Sheriff storms outside.

I hold my breath, staying completely still so I don't make a noise and blow my cover. I hear him mumbling and cursing under his breath, then kicking rocks across the gravel driveway.

"DAMMIT!" He yells into the black night, before getting in his car, whipping it into reverse, then accelerating towards the road.

As much as I wanted to confront him tonight, his being gone means there is one less threat to Callie inside. I know Tony's in there, and I can only assume Benjamin, *Bub*, is somewhere in there too.

I tense when loud music starts playing from inside, the noise is out of place in the dead quiet of night. Slinking back over to the front window, I curse when I don't see Callie on the floor anymore. Fuck.

Using the volume from the grunge metal playing to cover the sound of my entry, I slip inside with my gun raised, sweeping the living room. I confirm that she's no longer in this part of the cabin. Tony must've taken her down the hall, the only other direction he could've gone while I was watching the front.

I don't hesitate, if he's taking her back there for nefarious reasons, or to escape out the back, I'm not going to give him a chance. I keep my gun trained ahead of me as I creep down the hallway. Another curse falls silently from my lips as I approach three closed doors, the music from the living room is still drowning out any noises coming from inside. I'll have to clear each room until I find her. Fuck, I don't have time for this, he could be doing anything to her right now.

I slowly turn the handle to the first door on my right, throwing the door open. A closet. Just dusty shelves and old mason jars filled with spent bullet casings. None of it looks fresh like it's all been sitting here for a while. Hopefully, it's not an indicator of how much firepower they have on them. One door down, two to go.

Next is the middle door on the left. A small stream of light is coming from the crack at the bottom, I take a deep breath, hoping Callie's behind this door. I want to get a hold of her and get her the hell out of here. Then I'm never letting her go.

A shadow passes through the light, someone's definitely in here. I twist the handle, pushing the door open simultaneously, not giving whoever is inside any type of warning that I'm coming.

The sight in front of me is unexpected. Benjamin is standing in front of the bathroom sink naked, aside from some ratty boxers, scraping lines of coke onto the countertop. He's wide-eyed upon seeing me, his skin so white you'd think he was seeing a ghost. Unfortunately for him, he'd be better off if I was a phantom, and not a man hell-bent on retribution.

I grab him by the neck, smashing his face into the sink bowl. His clammy skin is disgusting and I don't want to touch him

313

any longer than necessary. "You thought you could take my girl? And I wouldn't come for you?" I whisper next to his head, his large body is trembling but he doesn't dare fight me.

He whimpers like a little kid, "I'm sorry, I'm sorry, it was Tony's idea."

I grit my teeth, annoyed by him and his cowardice. I push him off the sink so he flops onto the toilet, his busted nose from the sink is pouring blood into his mouth, and cocaine residue is smeared across his face.

Two more good thwacks against the sink and he would have had a cracked cranium and brain matter oozing out, but I want him to see it coming when I shoot him between the eyes.

To enunciate my plan, I push the barrel of my gun right between his eyebrows, "Any last words?" I ask, pressing harder into his skull after each word.

Before he can respond, I hear another whimper coming from behind the shower curtain. What the fuck?

Keeping my gun on Benjamin, I use my free hand to peel back the curtain. I should've checked behind it in the first place, but I'm not thinking clearly, my emotions are clouding my judgment.

I'm startled when I find an older woman, lying naked and bound in the tub. Her eyes are big and round, she's terrified. She whimpers again when she sees the gun in my hand. Understandably, she doesn't know I have no intentions of hurting her as they have. I tilt my head, taking in her features, and then I finally recognize her. Miss, looks more like a librarian than a secretary, from the Sheriff's department.

I slowly closed the curtain back, restoring the small screen of privacy she had.

"Where are her clothes, Benjamin?" He doesn't respond, he simply squeezes his eyes shut, as if he can ignore me.

"Did you rape her? Like you tried to rape Callie?" Like a light switch, the consequences of his actions register, regret evident on his face. Except, I suspect his regret is due to being caught, not remorse for his perversions.

I shouldn't shoot him right now, it'll blow my cover, but I hate rapists. I can't stand the thought of them walking this earth, lying in wait, ready to force themselves on unsuspecting victims. A man like that deserves to be put down like a dog.

Callie's tearful words sweep through my brain, Bub tackling her to the ground, trying to take what wasn't his. I imagine his grimy hands pawing at her, the crude words he spoke to her.

The repulsion I feel for her sake, for what he and his brother put her through, is enough to make my hands shake. A thought flashes through my brain. What if it was Callie lying bound and gagged in the tub, with no clothes, at the mercy of this man in front of me? The thought of it is too much, and all I see is red.

I press my gun even harder into Bub's forehead. "You're a sick mother fucker."

POW!

* * *

Callie

I feel myself being dragged. My shoes must've fallen off at

315

some point because my bare heels are taking a beating. My thoughts are still jumbled, and the fog in my brain is starting to clear, but I realize I'm having trouble focusing because of the loud music playing. It's so noisy, the words don't sound like words and the base is too strong. Why can't someone just turn the music down?

My feet thump over a threshold, and I realize I'm being dragged into another room. Instantly, the music is the least of my concerns. I open my eyes, my dizziness finally starting to cease, and take in the room around me. I'm in a bedroom, same dirty floors and wooden walls as before. This room is colder, and I immediately feel the chills across my skin. Or, maybe it's from the terror coursing through me.

I don't dare look behind me as I'm hauled up onto a bed and dumped. I can only imagine it's Tony, the stench of body odor and stale beer clings to the air. Tears sting the backs of my eyes. I don't know if a person can eventually run out of tears to cry, but I have to be getting close. It feels like this entire situation is draining all of the life out of me.

Maybe it's better that way... The less liveliness I feel, the less it will hurt when I'm shipped off to the next psychopath. I think that I've accepted what I'm about to succumb to physically. Tony will rape me. Then he will probably let Bub rape me. Then who knows who will violate me after that? It makes me sick to think about, but maybe accepting that it's going to happen will prepare me to get through it, mentally.

I'll never be the same after tonight, and my life as I know it is over. The tears slip from my eyes as I mourn the version of me that had a normal life, with loving parents, and Nathan. My heart bleeds for him and the life we never got to have together. The life that this man has taken from us. My sadness quickly turns to rage.

My body lurches as a hand grabs my shoulder, pulling me to the side of the bed where I'm forced to finally look Tony in the face.

"Ah, so she is awake. I was worried I'd be stuck fuckin' ya while you were passed out. It'd be too much like fuckin' a corpse," he laughs. "It's no fun like that, trust me," he leers at me, his eyes traveling up and down my body. The body that's covered in bruises that he inflicted.

"You're disgusting." I spit in his face, the burning hatred I feel is spurring me on. If my life is over tonight, then I'm going to go down fighting.

He slaps me across the face, and even though I expected it, my jaw cracks from the sudden force. The taste of copper quickly fills my mouth as my ears ring from the impact.

"I'll show you *disgusting*." He slides his belt off and loops it around my neck before I can lunge out of the way. My reflexes are still too slow after passing out. He has it pulled through the buckle, tightening the leather against the flesh of my neck before I can get a chest full of air.

The belt tightens around his fist at the back of my head, forcing me to crane my neck to look up at him. "If you wanna keep breathin' girl, you're gonna behave." He pulls the belt tighter again for added effect, making the leather bite into my skin painfully.

I claw at it, but it's no use, it's too tight already and he's right. If I fight him too much he'll just strangle me to death, or at least until I pass out again.

A loud noise from the hallway makes him loosen his grip on the belt slightly, giving me enough room to suck in some air. After a couple of seconds, he stops paying attention to the door, satisfied we won't be disturbed, and resumes his attention on me, tightening my noose.

"On your knees," he demands, but I refuse to move. I think I'd rather die than get on my knees in front of him. I don't think I can suffer through any more degradation at his hands. I refuse to give him the satisfaction of my compliance.

"FUCK-" I suck in a ragged breath through the tightness of the belt, "YOU!" The hoarseness of my voice is hardly audible through the screamo music still being blasted from somewhere in the cabin, but it doesn't matter. Tony sees my defiance and his anger is evident. He raises his hand to strike me again, and I squeeze my eyes shut, bracing for the blow, instead, I hear -*POW!*

A gunshot rings out, so close there's no mistaking the sound. I scream as loud as I can. "HELP ME, PLEASE!" Though the sound comes out no louder than a whisper, the air is hardly able to escape through my closed windpipe.

"Shut up, you bitch!" Tony hauls me up by the tail of the belt, squeezing my throat painfully. He forces me flush against him, my back to his front, making me a barrier to whoever he suspects is about to come through the bedroom door.

The door is kicked open, and bits of wood and metal splint off the door frame from the force of it. A sob tears from my throat as Nathan enters the room, his gun pointed directly at us. If I could breathe, I'd feel relieved, but the slow suffocation I'm experiencing leaves no room for celebration.

The belt tightens around my neck, making it impossible to inhale, all I can do is gasp for small breaths. My eyes find Nathans, and even though on the exterior he seems cool as ice, his eyes are burning with rage. His jaw clenches, clearly seeing the fear in my own eyes. I know he's on the verge of losing all control, I can see the frustration from not having a clear shot, Tony is effectively using me as a human shield. Part of me wants him to shoot anyway, become a martyr simply to rid the world of the evil that's standing behind me, slowly strangling me to death.

"Let her go, Anthony," Nathan says through gritted teeth. *Anthony*. That must be Tony's real name. How does he know that? How did he know where to find me?

It doesn't matter, I'll tuck those questions away for later if I even make it through the night. My throat burns from struggling to breathe, and the skin around my neck feels like it's being ripped in half by the belt.

"NO! You'll just kill me," Tony cries from behind me, pulling the belt even tighter, making it impossible for me to get any breath at all. All I can do is claw at the leather, and plead with my eyes, plead for Nathan to help me. I know at this point I'm panicking, my fight or flight is begging me to escape, but I'm powerless.

The room is closing in, and darkness from losing so much oxygen starts clouding my vision just as I see someone else come through the doorway. *Sheriff Donahue*.

He has a gun too, and it's pointed at the back of Nathan's head. He doesn't even know he's there, his eyes are still locked on me and Tony. All I can manage to do is reach out my hand toward Nathan, attempting to warn him.

I barely register Nathan's back stiffening as he feels the barrel of the Sheriff's gun press against the back of his head before everything goes completely black, and I'm gone.

Chapter Fifty

Nathan

I feel the hard barrel of a gun almost in the same instance as Callie slumps to the ground and passes out. FUCK!

"Lower the gun." I recognize the Sheriff's voice instantly. The music drowned out his approach, just like it did mine. I point my gun to the ground, mentally preparing for what's about to happen next. I fucked up, I let someone sneak up on me because I was too focused on what was in front of me. I fucking failed her. Again.

"Now, drop it to the ground, and kick it across the room." I reluctantly do as he says, feeling the pressure of his gun against my skull the entire time. He would have done it by now if he intended to kill me, but he still has plenty of time and opportunity to change his mind, so I don't risk it.

For the first time in my life, I'm not ready to accept that I might die. If I die, then Callie is left to the mercy of these bastards, and I can't let that happen. And, if there is any chance we survive this, I want to live for *her*, for a life together.

"Fucking shoot him, Donny!!" Tony screeches from across the room, Callie still lying at his feet.

"Shut up, Tony!" The sheriff yells back, clearly frustrated

with him.

"Donny Donahue?" I can't help myself. "That's a dumb name." I'm rewarded with a whack to the back of the head so hard I drop to my knees.

"Donny is because of my last name, you dimwit," the Sheriff sneers at me, his ego too fragile to take the jab. My head is throbbing, but I'm fine. I've taken worse hits, but they don't know that. I keep my face down, holding my head in my hands, giving them the false assurance they need to continue their conversation as if I'm not here.

"Why don't you just kill him? Then we can take the girl and get the cash for her, and deal with his body later tonight." Tony suggests to the Sheriff, stepping over Callie's slumped body on the floor. His foot bumps her leg, making her stir. Her eyes flutter open but they quickly close again.

My chest constricts, seeing her lying there and not being able to go to her yet. All I want is for her to be safe in my arms, but I'm still racking my brain trying to figure out the best way to get out of here without either of us catching a bullet. Then, what Tony said finally clicked in my brain -Get cash for her?

My stomach drops, realizing what he means. He intends to sell Callie. That's the missing piece all this time. I never understood how they could be so brazen, why they were being so persistent. I thought they were just perverts, freaks trying to lure women off the side of the road. They still are, but really, they're in it for money.

My hands fall from my face, no longer in the mood to hold up my façade. I've always heard that human trafficking is a huge issue in the United States, never seeing it for myself on American soil. For it to be happening in my own backyard makes me sick.

"How does an officer of the law get involved in human trafficking?" I can't help but ask, too angry to care if there are consequences.

"I'm not!" The Sheriff yells, pushing his gun harder into the back of my head.

"You are too involved, Donny! Don't act like this is all on me." Tony puffs up his chest, trying to convey toughness, when he is anything but.

"I get the cars towed, that's it! I don't ever lay eyes on anyone involved. You promised you wouldn't leave any mess behind for me to clean up, Tony. This is all on you!" His shouts rival the volume of the screamo music blasting through the cabin, and I recognize his words to be a guilt-laden confession. He regrets his involvement, but it's too late, he's in too deep.

Tony doesn't respond, he simply paces the room, shaking his head. He's obviously in over his head and he doesn't know what to do, giving room for the Sheriff to speak up again.

"I'm not interested in killing people in cold blood, I only came back to get Doris. I'll convince her to keep her mouth shut. Just let me take her home, then you can do whatever the hell you want with these two," the Sheriff explains, "but Doris, she doesn't deserve any of this."

"And Callie does?" I ask, my voice sounding cold. Deadly. Even to my own ears.

"Shut up," Tony grits in my direction.

"You should ask your brother if he deserved what he got…" I tilt my face up, looking at them directly, so there's no misinterpreting my words. Their faces are priceless, the Sheriff looks sick, and Tony looks like he can't believe someone else could dare to be as cruel as he is.

"What did you do?" Tony spits out, running out of the room. A second later, "NOOO!"

The Sheriff looks torn between going to see what Tony is seeing and staying put. The gun's still pointed in my direction but he's looking out into the hallway.

I use the distraction, launching up off the ground and easily snatching the Sheriff's gun from his hand. It happens so quickly that he only has a second to look dumbfounded before I slam the butt of the gun against his temple, hard enough to render him unconscious instantly. His body buckles, crashing against the door as he falls.

"Nathan?" The sweetest sound comes from across the room, making my body go completely still. Callie is sitting up, pulling the belt from around her throat, her movements are sluggish, like she has no strength. She looks like my beautiful Callie, but utterly broken. The deep red marks around her neck are almost purple, her eyes are bloodshot. I want to go to her, but this isn't over, so I use every last bit of control I have to stay where I'm at. I place my pointer finger over my lips, signaling her to stay quiet for me, hating the confusion that sweeps over her face. She gives me a small nod, trusting me like she always has.

I walk down the hallway to the bathroom, finding Tony exactly where I thought he'd be. Sitting on the floor, cradling his dead brother. Despite the blood, and the brain matter from being shot point blank, Tony is stroking Bub's cold cheek. It seems as if he does have a heart after all.

"Just kill me. My brother is all I had. Just get it over with," Tony speaks solemnly.

"You'll die tonight, but not by my hand. Get up," I demand, because my plan is already in motion. Tony looks at me

323

puzzled, but for the first time, it seems he has nothing to say.

* * *

Callie

I sit in silence as Nathan comes back into the room and then out again, dragging the Sheriff's body out toward the living room. It's all I can do to keep my body propped up against the side of the bed. I ache everywhere and my throat is on fire. Through the pain, I'm trying to wrap my brain around what happened. Nathan found me, somehow he found me and saved me once again. It's hard to comprehend how it's even possible, so I save my energy and just accept the fact that I survived.

The loud music is finally turned off, and after five, maybe ten more minutes, he returns. He hesitates though, standing in the doorway, raking his eyes over my form. His hard features are devastatingly handsome, even with faint speckles of blood scattered across his face. His eyes are different from when he first found me, they're softer now, and the coldness he directed toward the other men has dissipated.

"Are you okay, baby?" He asks so softly, I hardly hear him. Am I okay? In general, no, not really. But, I am alive, and he's here. He seems like he has everything under control, which is no surprise considering what I know about him. He's always in control.

"Yeah, I think I'm okay," I tell him, truthfully. My voice is hoarse, my throat burns as I speak. I'm in pain everywhere, but the bruises will heal, and I'll definitely need therapy after tonight, but at least I'm alive.

He finally comes over to where I'm slumped on the floor, slowly, like he's afraid he's going to spook me, and drops to his knees beside me. "I'm so fucking sorry. I never should have left you. I…" He pauses, raking his fingers through his hair, making it stand up and look messy. "I understand if you blame me. I told you I'd keep you safe and I fucked up. I fucked up, baby. I'm so sorry."

He's undoubtedly distraught, and it almost makes me want to laugh. Not at him, just at this insane situation. I'm the one who fucked up, I knew better than to be lured back here and I fell for it anyway, yet he's the one apologizing. I can't find the words to explain any of that though, or how grateful I am to see him again. I'm afraid even if I tried, I'd lose my voice, each breath feels like sandpaper against my throat.

I do the only thing that feels right, I wrap my arms around his neck and squeeze him as hard as I can manage. I need him to feel how much I love him and need him. He doesn't waste a second, wrapping me in his arms like I've been dreaming about for weeks, and mourning since I was kidnapped again. I had accepted that I might not ever see him again.

He holds me like his life depends on it, and despite how badly it's hurting my brittle body, I hold on just as tightly. I didn't know if I'd ever get to do this again, I thought the life as I knew it was over. I weep into his neck, somehow still managing to produce tears after crying all night. He strokes my hair, murmuring how much he loves me, how much he missed me, how scared he was for me.

"Can we go home yet?" I manage to whisper, sniffling against his shoulder. His home, *our* home.

"Almost, just gotta tie up a few loose ends." He holds my face up, wiping away the tears with his thumbs, and I notice a few of his own tears moistening his cheeks. I wipe them away gently, my heart aching, knowing how terrified he must've been when I was taken.

"Do you want to stay in here? Or, go out there with me?" He asks, nodding his head in the direction of the living room. The direction he dragged the Sheriff in.

Part of me wants to stay curled up in a ball on the floor, never having to see their faces again, but the bigger part of me doesn't want to leave Nathan's side again. Not even for a second, no matter what he's about to do. I'm not brave enough to be alone yet.

"Let's go," I say roughly, holding my throat like it will help, then immediately regretting it when the tender skin stings at my touch. He looks distressed by my pain but doesn't say anything, his face says it all. Sadness. Regret. Rage.

Nathan leans in, kissing me softly. "I love you. You are everything to me, I hope you know that." I open my mouth to speak, but he shakes his head. "Don't speak, I know it hurts," he kisses me again, sealing my lips.

I lean into it, savoring the way his mouth feels against mine. I truly don't think I'd be alive if it weren't for this man. He has become everything to me too, and I know whatever comes next, we'll get through it. Together.

He nods towards the front of the cabin. "Come on, the police will probably be here soon." I don't ask how the police knew to come, or how he knows they're on their way, I simply follow him as he takes me by the hand, walking us to the living room.

I'm greeted by the sight of Sheriff Donahue and Tony tied to chairs, facing each other. Their torsos are bound so tightly that they look as if they're struggling to breathe. Good.

Quickly glancing around the room, I realize Bub and Doris are nowhere to be found. The thought that he might still be somewhere hurting her makes my stomach clench in disgust.

"Where's Bub? He has the Sheriff's secretary," I push the words out my throat even though it feels like my tonsils have been put through a meat grinder.

Nathan turns to me, cradling my face in his large hands so he can speak directly to me without the other two overhearing. "I already took care of him, don't worry. I sent the secretary away." He shrugs, making it seem like we just had a conversation about moves in a chess game and not human lives.

I nod my head "Okay," because it's all I can muster. I'm too exhausted to think any more about it. He searches my eyes for something, I'm not sure what, but after a moment he seems to have found it, turning back to the men in the room.

"Alright, boys. Time for a fun little game." Nathan takes a gun from his waistband, a revolver. "Sheriff, you seemed to have misplaced your gun. Good thing I found it for you."

This side of Nathan should scare me. He seems so detached, so void of emotion, but he's also calm, and confident. This is the cold, killer he warned me about, yet I feel absolutely safe in his presence, and a hint of excitement. These men have made my life hell, and he intends to punish them. A normal person should be worried, but I must not be normal, because my heart swells at the sentiment.

The version of me three weeks ago would have been

terrified to be here right now, surrounded by violence, by the prospect of death, but now I'm eager to see the conclusion of all of this. To finally put this chapter of my life to rest.

I watch as he discards four of the six bullets from the chamber, tossing three of them to the ground, one at a time. Cold. Calculated. Making both of the men flinch each time a round clammers onto the wood floor. The fourth he puts into his pocket.

He spins the cylinder, aligning it with the barrel so it's ready to be fired. I don't know what he has planned, but I'm watching with curious fascination. He walks up to the Sheriff, placing the gun in his hand, and holding onto it so it stays aimed right at Tony's chest. The Sheriff, flinches at Nathan's nearness, visibly trembling.

"Go ahead, pull the trigger," Nathan commands, his tone full of ice. The Sheriff whimpers at his words, not moving at all, other than his uncontrollable shaking.

"I was afraid you'd get cold feet," he *tsks* at the Sheriff, forcing him to angle the gun upward towards himself, the barrel resting just below his dirty mustache.

"You either get to pull the trigger at yourself or your brother-in-law, which is it?" He asks, not letting the Sheriff move the gun an inch. Maintaining total control over him. I stay silent behind them, taking everything in.

I watch him as he taps the gun against the Sheriff's mouth as if he's waiting for an answer, *tick, tock, tick, tock*. His head tilts to the side as if he's studying his prey, his body language eerily calm.

If this is how he operates as a civilian, I can't imagine seeing him in action when he was active duty. He was probably even more menacing.

He must see something in his expression that I don't because he nods his head and finally lets the Sheriff point the gun back at Tony. It only takes two seconds before he moves his finger over the trigger, and pulls it back.

Click.

Chapter Fifty-One

Nathan

"Y ou no good, sorry son of a bitch!" Tony yells after the blank shot. Clearly, he doesn't like it when he's the one being shot at.

"Again," I tell Sheriff Donahue. I feel his arm flinch at my command, but he doesn't shoot, his body frozen in fear.

"Again," I say even deadlier. Getting my point across this time, I watch him as he pulls the trigger back, slowly.

Click.

I'm enjoying this. The fear I'm invoking in these mother fuckers is sweet revenge for what they put my girl through. And the secretary, who is hopefully halfway down the mountain by now.

After I had told her to get dressed, she fell to her knees apologizing for the part she played in luring Callie here. She seemed miserable enough already, and what she went through with Bub was probably punishment enough. So I told her to get the hell out of here. She was so frightened, she didn't question me at all, just took off outside.

Tony's still throwing around curses like it will do anything to save him. If only he knew his fate was sealed the first time he took Callie. He never should have chased her into my arms, because once he did, he was on my hit list.

Then, he had the balls to take her again. I won't be making the mistake of letting him live this time, the bullet he catches tonight is going to be a kill shot. God forbid he would be able to keep roaming the Earth with his depravity.

"Again." The demand makes Tony squirm as if he can move out of the way. As if I'd let that happen. The hammer moves as the trigger is pulled back, releasing with a *click.*

Another blank.

I probably only have about fifteen minutes until the State Police make it here. After I had gotten both of them tied up, I texted Jesse telling him we were safe, and then called 911, knowing it would take them some time to rally a couple of cars and make it this deep into the mountains.

I look at Callie, my strong, beautiful Callie. She's leaning against the wall, watching the display in front of her. She looks exhausted, but there isn't an ounce of fear in her eyes. She's braver than most people, even if she doesn't realize it. She's amazing. I give her a small wink, before turning my attention back to the Sheriff.

"Again." His whole body is shaking, making his arm vibrate against the chair he's tied to. I hold the gun steady in his hand, not letting the barrel point anywhere but right at Tony's chest.

"You can't do this!" Tony whines, not accepting that his death is inevitable. "You can't just kill us like this!" He continues to fight against his restraints.

"You're right." I pull back slightly, giving Tony a false sense of hope. "I should do much worse. You deserve worse for everything you put Callie through. I should have slaughtered you in cold blood."

331

"Instead you're making me do it," the sheriff whimpers, "because you don't have the balls." His snot runs down his face as he cries.

I lean in close to say the words I want him to hear directly into his ear, but loud enough so Tony can hear. "I slaughtered thirteen men in four minutes for killing a teenage girl who was nothing but a stranger to me. What do you think I'd do for her?" I nod my head in Callie's direction. "Lucky for you, she wants me to stay out of prison. So, I'm giving you the easy way out instead of torturing you to death. But, don't push me. I know more ways to kill a man than you could ever dream of."

The Sheriff whimpers again, while Tony mumbles incoherent words of disbelief. "Shoot him, or I'll make you regret ever being born." I feel his finger flex as he pulls the trigger back achingly slow.

"I'm sorry, Tony," he expresses right before he reaches the trigger break.

POW!

Finally, a bullet. Tony grunts at the impact, his chin dropping as the redness blooms across his dirty t-shirt. Blood gurgles up his throat, pouring out his mouth. Just like that, he's gone.

The relief I feel that he's dead is instantaneous. If that makes me a monster then so be it. At least Callie can live happily knowing Tony's dead.

The Sheriff whimpers and cries beside me, almost making me feel sorry for him. Almost. Unfortunately for him, his fate was also sealed when he decided to side with Tony and Bub, and then threaten Callie's life. Poor guy should have just stayed in a bar somewhere drowning his liver.

I look back behind me again to check on Callie. Her eyes are wide, but she still doesn't look scared. She is staring at Tony's dead body with such intensity, and what almost looks like satisfaction. Good girl.

"Okay, Sheriff. Your turn." I point the gun back in his direction, and only one bullet remains. Two shots. 50/50 chance. He knows it too. "Any last words?" I ask, more so to torment him than for anything else.

"Fuck you." He spits out at me. Pulling the trigger, more surely than he had the last four times.

POW!

50/50 chance and the Sheriff just lost. The bullet tears through his skull, killing him instantly. The vacant look in his eyes confirms it. This death is just as satisfying as Tony's. He might not have physically attacked Callie, but he threatened her life, and most likely aided his brothers-in-law in taking her the second time. His death was just as deserved.

I take my time untying the ropes, dropping both of their bodies to the floor. I wrap the gun securely in the Sheriff's hand, staging the scene like a murder-suicide, rearranging things as needed to sell it.

The missing three rounds go back into the gun. The fourth still housed in my pants pocket will stay with me. I retrieved my bullet casing from the bathroom where I shot Bub, making it look like he was shot by Sheriff Donahue too, just like Tony. The extensive damage to his head will make it impossible for them to tell what type of gun it came from.

I don't go to Callie until I'm finished, because I know once I go to her, my walls will crumble. The perfectly composed trained killer will evaporate as soon as I have her in my arms again.

She's turned me into more of a man since she's come into my life and less of a machine. Her being taken from me tore every bit of the steel coating from my heart, forcing me to feel every emotion I've ever suppressed. Now, she's safe. I've eliminated every threat to her, and I finally feel like I can breathe again.

One last look around, confirming I've covered our tracks, and I make my way to her. She looks exhausted, squatted down with her arms wrapped around her knees, leaning heavily on the wall for support. Her head rolls back to look at me as I approach, and her soft smile barely reaches her tired eyes.

"Let's go, baby," I tell her, softly. I know she's using every last bit of her energy to stay awake, especially after what she's just witnessed. Maintaining a brave face after everything she's been through and the emotional turmoil she's experienced in these last few hours is more than most can handle.

Leaning down, I scoop her up, cradling her against my chest. I breathe in her scent as she buries her head in my neck, her favorite spot. I feel her lips against my skin as I exit the cabin. "You saved me, again," she whispers.

"And, I always will," I respond, kissing her temple. "I'm never letting you go again."

"You promise?" She asks, sleepily. I can feel her body relaxing as she drifts closer to sleep, lulled by the motion of my arms as I carry her.

"On my life." I hold her tightly as I make my way through the woods back to my truck. Tiny flurries of snow swirl around us, making the night sky look too beautiful after what just transpired. The sirens wail in the distance, the cop cars approaching the cabin as we get farther away.

My call to 911 earlier was just another way to cover our tracks. I told them I had been tipped off to her location and was able to retrieve Callie without her abductors noticing. I explained to the dispatcher with my faux frightened tone that I was afraid for our lives and that I was getting her as far away as possible. I'd call back when we were safe.

Now I'm holding Callie, just as I did the first time I met her, wrapped in my arms as I carry her to safety. This time there are no reservations about running my lips across her temple, no unanswered questions about the future. She's mine to hold, mine to keep safe. My future.

Chapter Fifty-Two

Callie

I wake up, feeling overly warm, my whole body humming with contentment. I shift to snuggle closer to the heat source when my brain catches up and my memories come sweeping in, along with the throbbing pain. I open my eyes to the orange glow of the sunrise coming through the windows, basking the living room in the unmistakable light of morning. I'm in Nathan's living room. Thank God.

The fire crackles, making me tense, still feeling a little jumpy from the attack. The flames are dying down, only partly responsible for the heat I feel. The other source comes from the hard body I'm leaning on, the even rise and fall of Nathan's chest is calm against my cheek. The blanket I'm wrapped in falls from my shoulders as I look up at his face. His head is leaned back against the back of the couch, eyes closed. He looks peaceful, the worry and anger erased. My heart swells for my sweet, brave man. I'm still not sure how he found me last night, but I'm so grateful our story isn't over. The thought of losing him makes my chest ache. I hope that feeling becomes a distant memory now that those monsters are gone and I can have my normal life back. My life with him.

"I can feel you staring," the low timber of his voice startles me. I was so distracted swooning over him in my head that I didn't realize he was awake.

"I like looking at you," I respond, giving him a featherlight kiss against his jaw. I'm rewarded with a small sleepy smile, one that makes my stomach flutter.

He traces my face with his fingertips, barely touching me in the spots that I know are probably deeply bruised. His eyes are solemn, "I thought I'd lost you." His forehead rests against mine as if he can't stand to be any further apart.

"But, you didn't. You found me. I'm safe, because of you." My hands cradle his cheeks, bringing his mouth to mine, needing to kiss him. To feel him. His lips sealed over mine, not wavering. Connecting him to me, like we both so desperately needed.

"I'll make sure you're safe for the rest of your life. I won't ever screw up again," he vows, breaking my heart. He carries so much unwarranted guilt, a weight he doesn't deserve.

"None of this is your fault, Nathan. None of it. I'm only here because of you. My heart is still beating because of you, because of your risks. You're the hero in my story, don't blame yourself for anything. I screwed up. I let them trick me into being caught." I shake my head in disbelief at myself, feeling stupid for falling for it so easily.

"You thought I was hurt, and came back for me. It just shows how big your heart is. I don't deserve it." He kisses each of my cheeks lightly, then my nose.

"You deserve the world, Nathan," I say breathlessly as I kiss him again.

He shakes his head. "I don't want the world unless you're in it. I only see a future for myself now because of you. You are everything worth living for. I don't want anything else," he whispers against my lips, not daring to put distance between us. "I love you, Callie."

"I love you, too. So much." Even with how close we are, I can see the intensity in his eyes. I get what no one else does, the emotions written all over his face. His feelings, expressions, the good and bad, he allows me to see him. Every version. Every part.

* * *

We spend the next few hours lazily together on the couch, each movement I make is a reminder of the beating I endured last night. My stomach is bruised and so are my ribs, but I keep my breaths short, not letting myself inhale deeply enough for my lungs to inflate all the way. It's pretty miserable, and I'm sure it will be worse tomorrow, but I'm alive.

Luckily, my throat is only a little sore, completely manageable compared to the rest of my body. The skin around my neck is painfully sensitive, but I refuse to look, afraid the sight of it will send me spiraling.

Other than a few looks of regret from Nathan when he catches me wincing and hardly leaving my side for one second, he seems completely calm and collected. Even though the police are on their way to question us about what happened. He assured me that he took care of everything, and promised that there was nothing to worry about. But, I am worried. I watched two men die last night, technically by Sheriff Donahue's hand, but Nathan was pulling the strings. I was complicit in their murders, even though I was originally their victim. I'm also happy that they're dead. As fucked up as that might be, I think the world is safer now that they are gone.

He also filled me in on everything else that happened while I was being manhandled by Tony before I even knew he had come to rescue me. I just hope Doris is long gone and safe. I don't know how involved she was after luring me to them with her phone call, but she didn't deserve to be beaten and raped.

He explained how Jesse helped him find me, admitting that if it weren't for him, he'd probably still be running around in circles trying to figure out where they took me. I made a mental note to thank him for my life when I finally meet him.

The morning turns to the afternoon when finally the police arrive. To my surprise, Trooper Malec is the one taking our statements. He's younger than I thought he would be, and tall. Very tall. I imagined a similar version of Sheriff Donahue, old and washed out. Instead, he looks closer in age to Nathan, and almost as good looking. His reserved demeanor reminds me of Nathan's stoicism as well, almost making me wonder if he served in the military too. Or if they could be friends.

He explained that he requested to be put on the case when he found out we were involved. A few times his eyes linger on me, focusing on my bruises, a guilty look plaguing his face. He knew I was in trouble when Nathan originally contacted him, and he was powerless to help me, confined by the law and his higher-ups. I understand, and I don't blame him.

He goes over their findings at the hunting cabin and their

prediction of what went down -Sheriff Donahue panicked when he realized I had escaped, killing the brothers and then himself, knowing he would be persecuted once I went to the police.

Malec hesitates, his eyes boring into Nathan's. "As far as I'm concerned, this is a pretty cut-and-dry investigation. There isn't any reason for us to believe anything else went down after you set Callie free... Just do me a favor, and lay low for a while. Don't give anyone a reason to question your story."

Nathan doesn't humor him with a response, a silent under-standing passing between them, but he does shake his hand when the trooper turns to leave. Making me the only one in the room even slightly overwhelmed by his implication.

I breathe a sigh of relief when he's gone, exhausted from putting on the charade. I had to put on my best face, acting completely surprised to hear of their deaths, as if Nathan hadn't told me all of it already. As if he hadn't already told me exactly why he staged the scene as he did. I'm exhausted by how fast my mind has been racing with worry. Worry about being caught, worry that Nathan would get in trouble, that we would crack and accidentally tell Trooper Malec what really happened.

I asked Nathan before he arrived how he could pretend this was all normal, and why he wasn't freaking out like me. His cool demeanor was completely different from my anxiety-ridden state.

He explained, "I learned a long time ago how to be invisible. A lot of people don't realize that the United States Army doesn't want war heroes, they want ghosts."

The far away look in his eyes as he told me is something that will probably always be there. He hasn't told me everything he's done, and I'm sure a lot of things he never will, but I'll always be here to pull him back out of the past, to stay in the present. With me.

Chapter Fifty-Three

Callie

After a couple of days, my ribs were healing well enough that I felt like I could ride in the car without being in too much pain. Sudden movements and deep inhales still made me wince, but I felt like I could handle the slight jostle of a moving vehicle. Against Nathan's hesitancy, I insisted we make the trip back to Tennessee to retrieve my stuff from my parents' house. My car, which is still impounded as evidence, should be released sometime next week according to Trooper Malec.

I am ready to move on with my life. I don't want to feel like a victim. Without the threat of kidnapping or death looming over my head, I'm ready to start this next chapter with Nathan. I am ready to make the move official because he's already become home to me, there's nowhere else I want to be.

For the first time in my life, I know I'm exactly where I belong. The few days I spent healing after the incident were just that, healing. Nathan pampered me with hot baths and delicate touches. I wasn't stuck in my head, worried about my next plan, or afraid that I was doing the wrong thing. Despite everything, I was content and happy.

So, we spent the last two days at my parents, packing up all of my things into Nathan's truck. The only tears shed were when I was saying my goodbyes because this time I knew that when I left my parent's house, it was final. I know my days of using them as a safety net are over, and the next journey of my life is starting.

* * *

"How are you feeling?" Nathan asks for the hundredth time since we left my parents, his right hand squeezes my thigh, never not touching me at some point during this road trip. He's doted on me constantly, always worried that I'm in pain or uncomfortable in some way, very Mother Hen-like.

"I'm fine, I promise." I can't help the laugh that escapes, amused by his constant worry. He gets it honestly, the other day he finally called his mom to fill her in on everything that has gone down this month, and she spent the majority of the phone call worried sick about me, a perfect stranger. She didn't seem the slightest bit concerned with how unorthodox Nathan and I's first encounter was, or how quickly our relationship has flourished. She simply insisted on coming for Thanksgiving to cook for us. She promised that it would make me feel better to have a home-cooked meal made by her rather than Nathan. I didn't dare to disagree.

Though I am nervous to meet her, she seemed incredibly sweet over the phone. Nathan swears that I'll love her, but he still gives me plenty of opportunity to get out of it. He tried canceling on his mom twice, worried that it would be too overwhelming for me "in my condition," but I made sure he didn't. Despite my still-healing bruises and reddened neck, I can't wait to meet his family. They are a part of Nathan, and I want to know every part of him.

"Will your mom and Thea be there by the time we get home?" I ask since Thanksgiving is tomorrow already.

Nathan sighs, "Yes, they made sure to remind me that they still know the code to the door." He rolls his eyes, but I can tell how much of a soft spot he has for them. "I can still tell them to get lost, at any point, if they're too much. I don't want you to stress about anything, you need to heal."

"I'm fine. Everything will be great," I say, squeezing his hand. "I'm looking forward to meeting Jesse, too."

"Eh, I don't know if he'll come. He's met my mom before, but I'm not sure if he'll be into the family gathering thing or not. He said he'd see what he could do, but it's not likely he can get the time off. He doesn't have any family, so he usually lets the other guys get their requests approved first." Nathan shrugs, acting indifferent, but I know how much Jesse means to him. He was his best friend already, but after everything he did to help me, Nathan will never let it go.

"My parents really like you, you know. I hope your mom and sister like me," I admit.

"They'll love you. I promise." He lifts my hand to his mouth, kissing it, making me smile. Everything he does still gives me butterflies. I still can't believe this is all real sometimes, and that I get to spend my life with him. Hearing him whisper sweet words in my ear after making love to me every night, promising to love me forever, begging me to marry him, to let him put babies in my belly. I laugh at the latter two, knowing how soon all of that talk is. We've only known each other for a month, and even though we have planned on forever, we have plenty of time.

Which reminds me… "What were you and my dad talking about yesterday? You seemed pretty buddy-buddy."

"Uhh, I don't remember, probably just guy stuff. I don't know." Nathan's the worst liar when it comes to me, he can fool everyone else, but not me.

"You're so full of shit," I scoff. "You're both usually pretty reserved around people, I was just surprised to see that you've hugged him multiple times now. It's very sweet."

"Hey, I am a nice guy, but I'd hardly call a few pats on the back a hug." He shrugs, making me roll my eyes.

"Hmm. Can you at least tell me what you talked about the first day you met him? On our back porch? He 'hugged' you then, and I was floored." I ask, remembering back to that day. Nathan had just told me he loved me the night before, but I also had the weight of the world on my shoulders. Tony, Bub, and the Sheriff were looming over my head and I was a bundle of nerves.

I realize after a moment that Nathan still hasn't responded to my question, his silence usually meaning something bad. "What? What is it?" I ask.

He sighs, "I don't know, I wasn't planning on telling you this. I don't want it to change your perception of your dad…"

"What is it? Just tell me," I insist.

"He was distraught that day. He was terrified for his daughter. When I went to talk to him after breakfast, he needed something to hold onto. Anything to give him hope that you were going to be okay, that you were going to make it through everything alive. So… I told him that I planned to kill them. Plain and simple, I told him I didn't plan to come back for you until the threats were eliminated." He pauses, gauging my reaction.

I'm still absorbing everything he's said. On one hand, he told my dad his plan before he even told me... On the other, my dad knew Nathan was planning on killing people and he didn't try to stop him. He also didn't try to warn me away from him. Interesting.

"What did he say?" I barely manage to whisper the words, taken aback by this new information.

"He thanked me. Told me if I were to get in any trouble, he'd hire the best defense lawyer he could find. He'd put the house up as collateral if he couldn't afford it. I promised it wouldn't be necessary, but he still assured me he'd take care of me no matter what. He was glad that I was looking out for you." Nathan finishes, patiently waiting for my response.

To his surprise, I start laughing. The stomach-clenching type of laugh that is making my bruised ribs ache, but I can't help it. Nathan stares at me, barely glancing at the road. "What?" He asks.

"Apparently, I get my view on justice from my dad." I keep laughing, incredibly amused that I found someone so perfect that even homicide doesn't scare me or my parents off. What a catch.

"Yeah. I guess I shouldn't have been surprised when you were more worried about me going to jail than actually killing people," he jokes, but his smile doesn't quite reach his eyes.

"Because I know you. I chose you despite anything you planned on doing. Despite anything from your past," I add. "I heard everything you told the Sheriff and Tony that night. I've had every opportunity to run, and I haven't. You're stuck with me."

I know how heavily his military operations weigh on him, how he still worries that I'll judge him for what he sees in his head and in his nightmares. His wounds go deep, but I plan on helping him heal every single one if I can.

"You're crazy, woman." This time his smile does reach his eyes.

* * *

We arrive home to the cabin to a blue SUV parked out front, presumably his mom's car.

"Here goes nothin'," I say, trying to hype myself up.

"It'll be fine," he says, and I don't know if he's trying to convince me or himself. "Plus, they'll be gone after tomorrow, and we won't have to see them again for a while."

"Uh, I should've probably warned you, but I think Thea has every intention of spending Christmas here," I warn.

"How would you know that?" He asks, genuinely curious.

"She already has a stockpile of ugly Christmas Sweaters in your spare room. I found them the day I was looking for something to wear." I giggle at Nathan's expression. "She has enough for a week, minimum."

He groans, "Oh boy."

Epilogue

Nathan

I don't recall a time over the years when I truly felt like I was missing out on anything specific. The military was demanding, I traveled a lot, and I only made it home for a visit a couple of times a year if I was lucky. So that meant plenty of missed holidays, yet it never really bothered me that much. Now, standing here in my kitchen, watching my mom prepare food and my sister talking Callie's ear off, I don't think I could ever miss a holiday again. I don't ever want to miss out on any of these moments.

There was always something missing from my life, a void that I couldn't fill. I thought my career in the Army would be enough, but it wasn't. I thought starting over somewhere on my own would fix it, but it didn't. I've quickly come to realize that Callie was the missing piece all along. Since the moment she entered my life, she felt like the perfect fit, healing something in me that I thought was way past repair.

I know how serious PTSD can be for soldiers. I never thought it was an issue I had, blaming the nightmares or the flashbacks on anything other than the trauma that my brain refused to forget. A couple of times since I moved into my cabin, I woke at night worrying that I built this place as a tomb and not a home. Worried that the bleakest parts of my brain would overtake me and my family would find me here after losing my final battle to the darkness.

Since meeting Callie though, I realized why I really built this place. For the fresh start that I deserve. For the life that I get to create with her. I'm not running away from life anymore, I'm finally embracing it.

"Hey," Callie whispers in my ear, interrupting my thoughts. "You okay?"

I wrap my arms around her, careful not to squeeze her tender ribs. "I'm more than okay," I whisper against her lips before kissing her. She giggles, pulling away from me, acting shy with my mom and sister in the room.

"I want to show you something," I tell her, pulling her hand to follow me down the hall.

"If this is some lame attempt to get me into bed, you're not clever. Your mom and sister are here!" She whisper-shouts against my shoulder as I stop in the middle of the hallway.

"As much as I would like to, that's not what the surprise is." I gesture to the spare room door that is closed in front of us.

"Umm okay." She hesitantly opens the door, gasping when she sees inside. The nearly empty room has transformed into a fully furnished office space, a big desk centered right under the window with a bouquet of burgundy roses proudly displayed on top. Flower petals are scattered across the shag rug underneath it. Must've been my sister's dramatic touch. She and my mom helped set this up while we were at Callie's parents' house. I had already ordered the desk during my two-week-long recon mission, hoping to surprise her once she was ready to move in. However, things escalated and I never even had a chance to pick it up before she was taken.

Once she was safe and sound, I set the rest of my plan into hyperdrive, telling my sister exactly what I needed help with. I gave her some ideas and insight into Callie's personality, and she ran with my credit card, literally. Thea picked out shelves, decorations, and office supplies. Even adding an empty picture frame to the corner of the desk. She made sure to scold me over text when I told her I didn't have a photo with Callie yet.

"Oh my, what is all of this?" She asks, amazed by the transformation.

"I wanted this to be yours, this is your home now. You deserve an office, somewhere you can plug your laptop in to give your book bag a break. Or, if you want we can get a big monitor or two, make it legit." I'm blabbing but I can't stop, nervous about what she'll think of my surprise. I want her to feel like she has a home base, but I don't want to impose.

"If you don't like it, or if you don't want to work here, it's no big deal. I just wanted to give you the option. Hell, my sister works at a library not too far from here. You could always visit her and work there for the day if you get tired of it up here." I rub the back of my neck, still waiting for her response. I'm second-guessing everything once I notice tears in her eyes. "Callie?"

"I love it, I absolutely love it. Thank you!" She launches herself at me, wrapping her arms around my neck, finally letting me breathe easier. "No one has ever done anything like this for me. It's amazing, but it's too much. All of this stuff is too expensive, I can help pay you back-" I cut her off before she can finish.

"You're not paying me for shit. Call it an early birthday

present," I wink at her, remembering our conversation weeks ago. She clearly remembers too, busting out laughing.

"Okay, okay, you win. You've officially given me the best present ever." She uses her hands on my cheeks to pull me in for a kiss, and I greedily reciprocate, taking advantage of this moment of privacy since we have house guests. I pick her up by her thighs, and sit her on the desk, nestling my body right between her legs.

"I changed my mind. This. This is how you can pay me back. Let me fuck you on this desk." I thrust against her, showing her just how much I mean my statement.

"Nathan," she moans. "This isn't fair, your family is here."

I groan grumpily into her neck. "I know, you're right, but I do still plan on fucking you on every surface of this room, and the whole damn house."

She giggles, but she knows exactly how serious I am, my raging hard-on still pressed against the apex of her thighs. "I love you, Nathan. Thank you for my present, and for everything." She kisses me sweetly, dragging me back to the real reason I brought her in here.

"I actually have one more surprise," I admit, pulling away from her. I fumble through the drawers on the desk, pretending that I don't know exactly where I need to look.

"You've done enough, really." She laughs at my chaotic display, jumping down from the desk to finish inspecting the room.

"Here, I found it," I say to her back as she examines a picture on the wall. I hold my breath as she turns around, anticipating her reaction.

"Oh my gosh!" Her hand flies to her mouth before she doubles over laughing. A full-body laugh that I know is making her ribs ache. It makes me slightly regret this surprise.

"You got me a pink razr!!" She claps giddily, snatching the cell phone out of my hand. Immediately flipping it open and closed dramatically. "Where did you find this?"

"It's top secret. You'll have to power it on, but it should be charged," I prompt her, waiting for her to do it. I can tell the second she realizes what's happening. The light of the screen in her eyes shows me she can see the home screen, reading the four words I had typed there.

"Callie, I love you more than life itself." She looks at me, her tear-filled eyes tracking me to where I'm down in front of her on one knee, holding a velvet ring box with her mother's engagement ring. "I promise to show you every day, how much I value you and how grateful I am to have you in my life. You've made me a better man." Her head is already shaking, yes, but I continue with my final question anyway. "Will you marry me?"

The End

Thank you for reading! Catch a glimpse of Callie and Nathan's wedding in Book Two. Jesse and Thea's story is next!

About the Author

Amber Cassidy is a stay-at-home mother, utilizing this new chapter to explore her dream of writing. This author has a Bachelor of Science in Psychology and a Minor in Sociology. Previous work as a Mental Health Specialist has enabled her to observe the intricacies of the human mind and how it is affected by significant events in one's life.

You can connect with me on:
- https://www.tiktok.com/@ambercassidy_books
- https://www.instagram.com/@ambercassidy_books

Also by Amber Cassidy

This author is currently working on multiple stories to include in the Chance Encounters Series. Her hope is to complete five interconnected novels, each involving a different couple.

First Touch
Jesse and Thea's Chance Encounter comes next...